C000274590

POLYXENA

A STORY OF TROY

AuthorReputationPress®
Creativity & Branding

POLYXENA

A STORY OF TROY

H. ALLENGER

Copyright © 2019 by H. Allenger.

All rights reserved. No part of this publication may be reproduced, distributed, or transmitted in any form or by any means, including photocopying, recording, or other electronic or mechanical methods, without prior written permission of the publisher, except in the case of brief quotations embodied in critical reviews and certain other noncommercial uses permitted by copyright law. For permission requests, write to the publisher, addressed "Attention: Permissions Coordinator," at the address below.

Author Reputation Press LLC
45 Dan Road Suite 36
Canton MA 02021
www.authorreputationpress.com
Hotline: 1(800) 220-7660
Fax: 1(855) 752-6001

Ordering Information:
Quantity Sales. Special discounts are available on quantity purchases by corporations, associations, and others. For details, contact the publisher at the address above.

Printed in the United States of America.

ISBN-13   Softcover   978-1-95102-092-7
               eBook   978-1-95102-093-4

To Susan

Acknowledgments

I am indebted to the following sources: *The Meridian Handbook of Classical Mythology* by Edward Tripp, *The Iliad* by Homer (translated by Robert Fagles), *The Reader's Encyclopedia* by William Rose Benet, *Illustrated Encyclopedia of the Classical World* by Michael Avi Yonah and Israel Shatzman, and *The Aeneid* by Virgil (translated By Patric Dickinson), published by New American Library.

CHAPTER I

M Y NAME IS POLYXENA. I am the last of five daughters born to Hecuba, second wife of King Priam of Troy. My older sisters are Ilione, wife of the Thracian lord, Polymnestor; the chaste Cassandra; Creusa, wife of Aeneas of the Dardanians, allies of our city in our long war with the Greeks; and the lovely Laodice, married to the Greek Telephus of the Tegeans so he would not involve himself in this costly war. Were it not for Laodice, I would be regarded the most beautiful of King Priam's daughters.

I have many brothers: Hector, Paris, Helenus, Deiphobus, Polites, Troilus, and Polydorus being the more notable among them. Rather I should say I have but one brother, for the others were slain, three by none other than great Achilles himself. Troilus fell earlier in the war, slain by Achilles before his famed falling-out with Agamemnon. Polydorus, the youngest and most beloved of my parents, who was forbidden to participate in the fighting but inadvertently found himself caught up among our warriors during one of the many battles waged back and forth before the city, was struck down by a spear cast by that mighty Greek. And there was Hector, the hope of our city, whose prowess and strength endeared him to all, most especially to my father—oh, how we depended on him!—slain before the city walls in single combat with Achilles, in full view of us. Who can forget the sight of his body dragged behind the wheels of the victor's chariot? Then Paris fell, and later Deiphobus, when our city was taken on that horrible night after we dragged that wooden horse left by the Greeks within our gates, and so also Polites. As far as I know, only treacherous Helenus survives.

Troy has fallen. So many heroes, their daring feats now but memories, are gone, among them my loving father, King Priam, whom I adored more than anyone. Although he was a remote figure to me, as I saw him only infrequently in my early childhood, his glances at me warmed my heart, and his eyes shone whenever they beheld me. While at times I felt he doted too much on Laodice, this did not diminish his admiration for my own accomplishments, and he was not wanting in providing me with the gratitude and affection I eagerly sought from him. He was slain in the courtyard before the altar of Zeus, entreating the god's protection of his subjects, but to no avail. It was Neoptolemus—may he be forever cursed!—son of Achilles, who struck his sword into the defenseless old man, and I remain pitiless in my condemnation over what he has done to me.

We are captives of the Greeks now, confined to the makeshift tents set up for us. My mother is awarded to the cunning Odysseus, the man most responsible for our fall, and I do not know what the fates have in store for her. What hardships she has had to endure. To suffer the death of her beloved husband and nearly all her sons, how is it possible to live after such horrors? And poor Cassandra, always dogged by ill fortune, was raped within the temple of the very god she so devoutly served and is now in the hands of Agamemnon. My dear sister-in-law, Andromache, is claimed by the same Neoptolemus who had slain my father and so adversely touched my own life. Only Helen appears to have come out of all this fairly well, though I am sure she is heartsick over all that has happened.

My misfortune was to have Neoptolemus fall in love with me; for this I am to die at the commemoration rites to his father. A strange destiny has brought me to this point, circumstances contrived by displeased gods and goddesses; I am able, at least in part, to determine my own causality behind these, for it's true that I rejected Neoptolemus's advances, but I never once professed to love him. Somehow he had the expectation that I would willingly belong to him, because his father, Achilles, was attracted to me—as I was to him—and yet, for reasons only you, Divine Aphrodite, can know, this magnetism did not transfer to his son.

To you, Immortal Goddess, I reveal my thoughts. I entreat you to receive them and forgive my omissions of courtesy at the times I felt you neglected me. As I face death, lying awake in my cot, and try my best to compose myself, difficult as it is for me, for I must be honest in saying that I truly fear it, I will commit myself to recall how all this came about. Even as I recollect the events shaping my present condition, I am struck by the strangeness of it all, for rarely can it be said that happenstances so beyond my control were to affect my personal being in such a detrimental way. Indulge me my misapprehensions, for I realize my story represents a personalized view of this horrid war that came upon us. I must relate to you how it all appeared to me as I experienced it and as I understood it so that I might make sense of it all and learn why it has led me to this outcome. Grant me the solace I seek; spare me the horror that comes from the realization of having lived a futile life.

I do not have the time to convey my early childhood to you, which was not that different from the usual upbringing of children, nor do I choose to say much about the shock on everyone's face when Paris first brought vain Helen, the Spartan Queen, to Troy. Yes, I believed her to be vain, but then, who can really blame her? Truly she was a most beautiful woman with her golden hair and unblemished, pale skin, a face so radiant that, when she smiled, everyone's heart melted at the sight. I have heard that, throughout her entire life, men have craved her, that all the royal princes of Greece sought her hand in marriage. With all that attention endlessly heaped upon her, who can hold it against her that she should hold her own charms in such admiration? Even my father, who initially was bent on sending her back after arriving here, soon fell under her spell and became an advocate for her staying with us. And to be fair, Helen befriended me from the start, and I was somewhat gratified that she seemed to favor me above the other women in the palace. I suppose it is true that I actually liked her, in spite of the grief she brought us. Besides, what Hector once told me was true enough: Helen was but a pretext for the vile Agamemnon's true design—to control the cities and the trade of the Aegean. Our city stood as an obstacle to his greed and ambition.

Nor will I cover the time when the mighty Greek host—indeed appearing as a thousand ships, stretching as far as we could see into the western horizon—came upon our shores and the long war began. I will never forget the look of dismay on my father's face as he beheld the fearsome spectacle from the upper walls of the citadel, the inner fortress of our city encompassing the royal palace. Nobody believed that such a force would come here. All the Greek cities were represented there, led by famous names we had long heard about—the crafty Odysseus of Ithaca; recklessly bold Diomedes, the Argive leader; Ajax of awesome strength and size; the famed archer, Teucer—but none of them was more familiar than Achilles, commander of the Myrmidons. We knew that Agamemnon, king of Mycenae, assembled this massive army and was the driving force behind the invasion using his brother's, Menelaus's, aggrieved loss of Helen as his excuse. In spite of this initial shock, soon a general atmosphere of optimism prevailed among our people, and we were confident—our allied support and Troy's impregnable walls bolstering this—that, in the end, we would be triumphant and scatter the remnants of Agamemnon's fleet back across the sea.

But that was nine years ago. The war evolved into a protracted conflict that engaged nearly all the cities of the Hellespont and beyond who befriended us and were our allies. Agamemnon assigned his bold subordinate, Achilles, to subdue most of these centers, and he waged a relentless war against them. When he attacked the city of Lyrnessus, after having killed its ruler and his family, Achilles took Briseis, daughter of the slain king, as his concubine, a move that subsequently was to cause his notorious rift with Agamemnon. His mission thus accomplished, the war now centered primarily around Troy itself and was marked by repeated and bloody battles that ended in stalemates, with neither side gaining the upper hand. I am sad to say that it was during this time that I lost, first, my brother Troilus and, then, our much-beloved Polydorus, both slain by Achilles— how I hated him then! Still, my father retained his optimism and told me that the strain of the ceaseless combat was more telling on our enemy than our own forces.

Then it happened that we had cause to rejoice, an event that gave credence to my father's premonitions. As it was explained to me, when Agamemnon was forced to give up his own concubine because her capture was disfavored by the gods who sent a pestilence upon the Greeks, he took Briseis from Achilles as compensation for his loss; apparently this was the supreme commander's prerogative. The angry Achilles withdrew his Myrmidons from the conflict and sulked in his tent not far from our city. It was during this time that our soldiers, under the valiant leadership of my brother, Hector, nearly drove the enemy from our shores. But fate intervened, and the gods favored the Greeks.

When Hector killed young Patroclus, believing him to be Achilles, as he wore his armor, a youth much favored by Achilles, the pitiless Greek warlord reentered his army in the war. We all remember how he came toward our outer wall in his chariot and challenged Hector to single combat, adorned in magnificent new armor that glistened in the sun. Hector, after a sad farewell to his beloved Andromache and infant son, Astyanax, met his bold adversary before the main gate. Losing heart at first, or perhaps he meant to wear out the Greek, Hector was chased around the city three times before turning to face Achilles. In the ensuing combat, he was slain. To our horror, Achilles stripped him of his armor and tied his ankles with a rope that he then attached to his chariot and dragged him back to his ships. I shall never forget the pain in my father's eyes; he sank back into his royal chair and openly wept. All Troy was in tears. Helen and I held up Andromache to keep her from falling down in her extreme grief.

A few days later, my father sufficiently recovered from his despair and was emboldened to enter the Greek camp at night and personally appear to Achilles for the body of Hector so that it might receive a proper funeral. I do not know how he persuaded the seemingly coldhearted warlord to accede to his wishes, but Achilles relented and allowed my father to return with the body of his favorite son. The city held a funeral rite befitting so noble a warrior, burning his cleansed body upon a huge pyre adorned with precious belongings after numerous eulogies had been rendered. There was so much lamentation. Everyone in Troy was overcome with sorrow and openly wept. The sense of loss that permeated the scene filled us with dreadful forebodings over who would now be the bulwark of our defenses, a role that we could not conceive of anyone but Hector performing.

This, then, is what defined our present situation, which I have but briefly touched upon, when I was called upon to do my part in the war effort. Up to this point, I was merely an observer to the great conflict engulfing our lives and viewed the transpired events with a certain detachment that excluded me from those who are actually participants in these. It is here that my account truly starts, for now I have become actively involved in our deadlocked struggle and seek to assist in bringing it to a victorious conclusion for Troy. As I begin, I am in the seventeenth year of my life but am often told that my erudition extends far beyond these years and that I conduct myself in a manner bespeaking of greater maturity. Older women, and indeed men also, have confidence in my judgment, placing value in what I say, and confide in me things they would normally not relate to someone of my age. I believe this is why I was chosen by my father to carry out an assignment that was to make me a major contributor in the conduct of this war. Here is my story.

Chapter II

T HE DISMAL PALL CAST OVER Troy following the funeral of noble Hector was all pervasive. Few people spoke about it, but you could read the consternation in the worried look of their eyes and their grim countenance. My father was so grief stricken. He spent days in utter solitude, confining himself to a smaller chamber within the palace so he did not have to see anyone or speak to anyone. I only saw him one time during these days; he was such a pitiful sight, the strain of his loss edged in every furrow of his brow. He did acknowledge my presence, a twinkle coming to his eyes and a faint smile lasting for but a moment in his otherwise somber demeanor, perhaps somewhat embarrassed that he should reveal himself in such a fashion or wanting, in that brief instant, to spare me his own sorrow; it affected me so deeply that I could not hold back my own tears.

Helen and I tried our best to console the horribly bereaved Andromache, but she was so forlorn and downcast that we feared she might take her own life; I believe that only the presence of her baby, Astyanax, kept her from doing so. At times, she hurled abuses at Helen for having brought such misfortune to Troy, unfairly I thought, for she herself supported her husband's position that Helen was but a pawn in the greater schemes of Agamemnon. Then, after that, Andromache was torn with remorse over her earlier outbursts and begged for Helen to forgive her callousness. I do believe she was sincere in her apologies; it was such a hard time for her. Helen appeared to understand this and sought to comfort Andromache with gentle hugs and words of condolence, and her efforts seemed to have their effect after a while. She was much better at this than I; her deep concern touched us all. When Helen wept, her lovely face contorted in anguish with flowing tears, everyone seeing this was moved to pity.

During such a time that Helen and I were comforting Andromache, sitting on the couches abundantly placed in our main residential chamber, a courier from the council hall of the palace intruded upon the scene.

"Polyxena," he called out my name, "your father, Lord Priam, requests that you attend his meeting with his advisors."

I could not believe it. I had never even seen the inside of the council hall—I did not think women were allowed there—and now I was asked to be there. I felt my heartbeat pounding within me as I scampered across the inner courtyard separating our living quarters from Troy's power center.

I was amazed to see all the major commanders, ministers, and advisors of King Priam assembled before me as I entered the hall, bigger than any room I had ever seen, very cavernous, with tall, evenly and widely spaced columns holding the high ceiling in place above a broad rectangular floor. Everyone was standing, even though chairs were available along the walls, except for Priam who sat in the royal throne at the opposite end of the entrance door. The dignitaries were gathered in clusters that represented their affiliations, I assumed. They ceased their talking when I walked in and approached my father, and I knew that something of primary importance had been discussed. I sensed that somehow this was going to involve me.

"My daughter," Priam introduced me to his assembly. "She is Polyxena."

I already knew some of the persons in attendance. Of course, my brothers, Deiphobus, Paris, and Helenus, looking very distinguished in their ankle-length formal tunics, were there, standing next to Aeneas who was now the chief commander of Troy, having been appointed to succeed Hector at this position. This noble lord, broad shouldered and strong, with dark eyes and beard, was the son of Anchises, King of Dardania, and was said to be much favored by Apollo. I also recognized the elder, Antenor, another Dardanian and a highly respected advisor, as well as his son, Agenor, known for his bravery and now one of our major battlefield leaders. Next to them stood another elder, boisterous Antimachus, the most staunch advocate for our war, but known to be quite greedy, and the priest,

Laocoon, who, like my sister, Cassandra, had the gift of prophecy. Among the allied commanders, I remembered Glaucus of the Lycians, attired in a golden knee-length vest, and Memnon, from distant Assyria, with his long, curly beard and pleated robe. I walked past them, sensing an anticipation in their glances at me, as if scrutinizing my worthiness, until I stood next to my father.

"No doubt you are wondering why I called for your attendance here," my father continued behind a faint smile. "A distinguished calling is thrust upon you, one which could provide us with much-needed assistance in our present situation. We have already determined that your services will be required. I merely wanted everyone here to see you, to have them realize that my judgment in you is not misplaced."

So whatever I was going to be asked to do had been decided, I thought to myself, and it appeared to me that my only purpose here was to give my father the pleasure of consenting to his well-conceived idea. I nodded my agreement, unsure if I actually meant it.

"We have concluded," my father continued, "that you, as a woman, would serve us best in securing another ally for Troy. You will head a delegation to go to Themiscyra."

"Themiscyra?" I asked, not familiar with the place.

"The city of the Amazons, about a two week's journey from here by land—we no longer control the seas—beyond Phrygia, along the shores of the Great Northern Sea."

The Amazons. A nation of women warriors as ferocious as any army of men that ever took to the field. I had heard of them from our oral chroniclers but had never seen them and did not think they existed.

"You are to meet with their queen," my father went on. "Her name is Penthesileia. She once promised me her support, should I need it—I absolved her of a crime she committed, of which she was most grateful. You must persuade her to enter this war on our behalf and to threaten the enemy on its northern flank. Are you daunted by this?"

I did not immediately answer, for, while surprised that such an important assignment was being entrusted to me—certainly I had no idea how I was to go about accomplishing this task—an element of excitement surrounded this enterprise. I was not averse to embracing a venture that would take me away from here for a while, and the fact that it was of such great value to Troy made it very momentous for me.

"I don't think so," I finally replied in perhaps a more hesitating manner than I had intended. "I feel I should do my part in our city's defense," I then added and was gratified to see that this comment solicited a very favorable response from the assembly. I could see this in the smiles and pleasant gazes emitted by all present.

"You have pleased me," my father said, apparently quite happy over my performance, such as it was. "I knew I could depend on you. I shall brief you later on the full aspects of your mission, but for now, you may return to your quarters."

I left the hall amid words and gestures of approval, making me believe that I had done the right thing and had won everyone's confidence. Only my brother, Helenus, appeared to give me a disparaging look, and this alarmed to some degree, for he had the gift of being able to predict future events. But my initial worry was readily dispelled when I thought of the mission expected of me. At last I was to do something useful for our cause, something to help us win this prolonged war. The more I dwelled on this, the more thrilling its prospect became, and I eagerly anticipated its beginning.

When I returned to our palace residence hall, I found my mother, my sister, Cassandra, Helen, and Andromache anxiously waiting to hear what I had to say. After I told them what had been planned for me, I found my mother's reaction not at all pleasing.

"This is madness," she said. "You're a woman—and too young— for such a dangerous undertaking. I shall talk to Priam about this. Don't worry, my dear, I'll get him to change his mind."

"Please don't, Mother," I sharply opposed her offer.

"What's this you say?" she angrily denounced my resistance, her fierce glare slicing through me. "You object to my interceding for you? How ungrateful. War is not the business of women, and Priam has no right to place such a requirement on you."

"Don't involve yourself in this, Mother," I replied.

"What's the matter with you?" my mother nearly shouted. "You sound as though you *want* to do this."

"I do," I said forcefully.

"What? I don't believe it."

"Please, Mother," I pleaded. I wanted her to understand. "Yes, I want to do this. I'm happy Father has confidence in me. I have an opportunity to help Troy. It means a lot to me. Don't deter him from his purpose. I beg you."

My outburst quieted her, but I saw her eyes moistening and knew she was deeply upset over my resolve, or perhaps her inability to sway me from my wishes. She was truly worried about my safety, and I appreciated that. I gave her a reassuring hug in order to render her a degree of comfort. She openly wept and held on to me for the longest time before releasing herself from our embrace.

Helen and Andromache were more supportive to me. Both wished me success on my venture and fully recognized its value to us. For my sister-in-law, the mission seemed to have taken her out of her doldrums, at least temporarily, as she took an active interest in wanting to help me in my preparations. She seemed to grasp the strategic importance of my father's plan for me—no doubt an influence of Hector's discussions with her—and knew the impact this would have on the war.

As for Cassandra, she said little but had a troubled look in her eyes that did not sit well with me, grating at my resoluteness. My sister had the ability to see the future—for this she was made a priestess of Apollo and resided in his temple much of the time—a rare enough talent that probably required her presence here and made her unsuitable for the same mission I was asked to undertake. Yet her gift did nothing that actually helped us; she was so unconvincing in telling us of her insights, due to a pronounced lack of forcefulness in relating these to us, I believe, that nobody took her seriously or even acknowledged what she had to say. I once made a record of her prophecies regarding coming events and was astonished to learn that she had been correct in all her predictions. In spite of this, I am ashamed to admit that I regularly disputed her warnings and even ignored them. I most remember when she told me not to ride my pony, Pan, but I did anyway, and he broke his leg when he stepped into a hole, throwing me to the ground. I was only bruised, but Pan had to be killed. I mourned his loss for the longest time. And she warned Father that sending Paris to Sparta would bring war to Troy. So, clearly, she was not mad, as many here have suggested, and it may be a grave miscalculation to outright dismiss her words as nonsense. Aware of this, you can understand my discomfort as I perceived an intense glare coming from her.

"Will I fail in my mission?" I asked her, coming directly to the point of my consternation over her alarming looks.

"No," Cassandra answered after a brief pause. "You will succeed in getting the Amazons to fight for Troy."

Her answer did not offer comfort to my disquietude.

"If that is so," I replied, "why do you have this distressed look about you?"

"You misread me," Cassandra said.

"I do not," I hastily responded. "You have seen something that you're unwilling to confide in me. It's evident enough in your eyes. If you won't tell me, it must be something unfavorable to me. You mean to spare me this."

"I have not seen it," said Cassandra, and then she stopped, as if grappling with whether she should continue. After what seemed an interminable time to me, she proceeded. "I feel this coldness whenever I concentrate on what you are tasked to do. A chill encompasses me. I'm unable to ascertain what this means, but, oh, Polyxena, I do fear for you."

She did not succeed in making me feel any better.

"Am I going to be harmed on this expedition?" I wanted to know. "Will I die?"

Cassandra's fear-ridden eyes pierced me.

"Not on this expedition," she presently said, "but you will come to know people through it of whom you should beware. This is as much as I can tell you."

Her answer told me that she knew more than she was letting on, but I was comforted in some measure to hear that I was to complete my mission satisfactorily. Whatever ensuing consequences would arise from that, I would face as they arrived. As for her admonitions on meeting people I should be wary of, I can avert this by keeping any strangers at a distance and not getting involved with them. I felt better as I thought about this.

Later that same day, as I sat by myself on one of the benches in our inner courtyard, contemplating my future enterprise, both thrilled and, at the same time, somewhat afraid of it, I noticed my father approaching me, looking so regal in the maroon-colored royal cloak that draped his white frock. Tall and lean, with his whitened hair and beard, he appeared as the perfect embodiment of dignity and kingship, a truly majestic figure. He slowly walked up and took his seat next to me, and even though he did not say anything for some time, I felt a comfort in his presence; I would have sworn he was thinking what I was thinking. Finally, he looked at me and began to speak.

"Are you having misgivings about this?" he asked me.

I glanced into his eyes—they revealed his comprehension of my thoughts—but did not answer him. I did not feel a need to, for he knew my turmoil.

"Dear Polyxena," he then said, "I would never willingly expose you to unnecessary risks. Our dire circumstances force me into taking this measure. Without Hector to lead us, and with Achilles back in Agamemnon's camp, we must wage a defensive war that we cannot sustain for a prolonged period. Our provisions will be depleted eventually, and we will face deprivations that will seriously weaken us. If we ever get to this point, we would have to capitulate. You realize this, I'm sure."

"Yes," I told him as he paused for a moment, "I do."

He was pleased at hearing my assent before continuing, "If you can get Penthesileia to threaten the Greeks from the north by reclaiming the cities they took from us and through this restore our supply lines as well as potential reinforcements of soldiers, Agememnon will be forced to counter her moves. He will have to divide his army and, in so doing, reduce his strength at Troy. Our estimation is that we would then launch an all-out drive against his remaining force here and thereby gain a great advantage for us, one that would win us this war."

"I understand, Father," I said, his plan making a lot of sense to me, and I was struck by the gravity my own performance would have in all this.

"We concluded that a woman could better influence Penthesileia," my father went on. "She would be, let us say, more responsive to your entreaties, being naturally biased in your gender's favor and likely to regard you as one of her own. With a man, we run the risk of alienating her."

He then stopped talking, perhaps to assess whether what he had said impacted me, which meant he solicited a response from me that would confirm my willingness to carry out his assignment. We sat in silence for a while until I surrendered to his expectation.

"Is it true," I said, "what they say about the Amazons, that they have no breasts?"

My father gazed at me, then broke out in short but hearty laughter; this was the first time I heard him laugh since the death of Hector.

"Perhaps it may have been true once," he chuckled. "But certainly not for Penthesileia. She is very much a woman. It's quite obvious."

"What is she like?" I was curious to know.

My father now knew that he had my full support for his plan and that he no longer needed to apply any more effort toward persuasion in this regard. He was thus lightened in spirit and demonstrated this with his exuberance as he spoke on.

"She will be in her low forties now, a tall woman, equal in height to most men, and of a slim but solid build. She had very expressive eyes, greenish in color, and her hair was sandy brown. She wore a red and black tunic that reached halfway down her thighs and was usually covered with a bronze chest plate. She had charm and could even be charismatic if she chose, but make no mistake about it, she was definitely the one in charge. There was a commanding presence about her that only those born to lead seem to possess, an aura of confidence that reveals itself in a certainty of action. For all that, she was also cruel on the battlefield and seldom took captives, preferring to slay them instead. Perhaps she's changed. It's been many years since I last saw her."

I was intrigued by what my father said and craved to hear more, saying, "You mentioned that you absolved her of a crime. What was that all about?"

"We were in an alliance then, for which I sat on a council regulating its laws; that is how I came to know her. Penthesileia was accused of having killed her queen, Hippolyte, but the evidence indicated it was actually an accident. In the heat of battle, she fired an arrow at an enemy lord, but during its flight, Hippolyte rode into its path and was struck down. I found no blame on her part for the unfortunate incident. She thanked me profusely for my verdict and promised to assist me if I ever needed her help. You have this in your favor in your appeal to her."

"I will do what I can," I said.

"You must succeed in this," my father emphasized, looking directly into my eyes with a startling seriousness that made me tremble. "Do whatever you have to do—whatever it takes—to get her assistance. Use your womanly charms if you have to; you know what I mean by that."

Yes, I knew what he meant. He alluded to Penthesileia's preference of women to men when it came to her love interests, and if I had to resort to pleasing her in such a capacity, I would have to apply the effort if I believed it necessary to secure her support. I hoped it would not come to that I said to myself, but I was resolved to undergo whatever condition was tossed my way in order to accomplish my purpose.

"I understand," I told my father. "You can trust me in this."

My certainty imparted a noticeable relief for my father, and as he rose to make his departure, he seemed happier than I had seen him in weeks. Before making his turn, he gazed at me, a glow emanating from his eyes that warmed me, and he made it apparent to me that our conversation had pleased him.

"Be ready to leave in three days. We have no time to waste," he said. "You will be provided with a small escort unit, perhaps ten soldiers—all we can spare—and an advisor. You may take two personal handmaidens with you if you like. I shall see you again before then. Good night, Polyxena."

"Good night, Father," I said as I watched him depart. I now fully grasped the weight of my assignment and its utmost importance to Troy. I was suddenly thrust into being a vital component in our grand strategy to end this war and could no longer withhold any reservations that may have previously possessed me. While this prospect filled me with occasional bouts of apprehension, for I did have fears about leaving my family, my city, for the first time in my life, without actually knowing if I would ever return to them, at the same time, I was awakened to an inner side of me that longed for a change and the challenges this duty presented. I savored the element of excitement that surrounded this mission, an opportunity to be of true value to my father's objectives, to please him in a most meaningful way. The more I thought about it, the more I came to embrace the task entrusted to me, believing myself fortunate even to receive it. My confidence grew, and I eagerly looked forward to its implementation.

CHAPTER III

THE NEXT TWO DAYS PASSED with noticeable swiftness. We were busily preparing for our departure with all the annoyances and frustrations that it entailed, not being able to decide what to wear, what to pack, how much was needed, adding items of clothing only to later discard them as unnecessary, and so on. Helen and Andromache assisted me in these decisions and selections; both seemed as thrilled over my impending journey as I was, and this had an impelling effect, raising my own excitement to even greater levels. Cassandra also came by from time to time to check on our progress; even she appeared absorbed in my preoccupation and no longer demonstrated any reluctance or misgivings toward these, having, I believe, recognized its importance to Troy.

I learned that I was to be accompanied by Agenor, son of the wise Antenor, who would command the escort of mounted soldiers, only a squad of ten, accompanying us. As he had led an entire battalion before Troy, this may have been conceived as a significant demotion for him, but not so, rather this emphasized the extreme importance of our undertaking all the more. Perhaps my father meant, by this selection, to alleviate any anxieties that might beset me; he need not have let that worry him, for my disposition was now such that I was quite eager to face whatever may come. Still, this called for an amiable relationship along the way, for Agenor and I were friends, and he was quite agreeable to me.

My advisor was also Agenor, for he shared his father's reputation for wisdom and was familiar with the customs and protocol of the Amazons. Like Aeneas and his father, he was a Dardanian, the closest of our allies, and was as much a part of our inner circle as any noble Trojan would have been. He had once lived among the Amazons, having represented Dardania in an ambassadorship there, which may have also accounted for his being assigned to escort me, as he would be recognized as their friend and ally. It appeared my father overlooked nothing, again verifying to me how much value he placed on this mission.

My two servants were Menodice and Thalia, both of whom had cared for me for much of my life, and I knew them well. I was pleased to have them accompany me, as it would allow me the nicety of more personal and intimate conversations, a respite from the seriousness of the discussions relating to my duties, if you will, which would undoubtedly come as a welcome relief to my more pressing demands. We were to be transported in a two-wheeled royal cart, which meant that it was canopied and enclosed on all sides with curtains—the driver sat outside this enclosure—and held a double row of cushioned seats as well as a small built-in nook, in which our chamber pot was placed. Our baggage was carried in a second open cart. A third cart contained the folded-up tent, which would be set up each night along the way for our comfort, as well as our cots and blankets and a few benches and chairs. Everything was in readiness when the time came for me to leave Troy.

I saw my father one more time during the early hours of the day of our departure. The sun had not yet broken the horizon with its intention to rise; indeed, it was still very dark as we made our preparations before the Dardanian Gates, assembled under the fires of burning torches. After we had loaded our carts and horses with all our equipment, my father approached me, carrying a white banner with the black letters of our city engraved on it.

"The insignia of Troy," he told me as he attached it to my vehicle, "upon a flag, designating you as an official envoy. This will grant you free passage on your return. Even the Greeks will not desecrate this, for to do so is to invoke the anger of the gods. But on the way to Themiscyra, you must avoid them, taking roads not controlled by them—Agenor knows which ones they are—and use proper caution against detection. Do not relate the nature of your mission to anyone except Penthesileia herself."

My father placed his hands on my shoulders and drew me toward him in a loving embrace. "Dear Polyxena," he said in a quivering voice choked with heartfelt concern, "that it should come to this, that I should have to send my beloved daughter on such a perilous journey."

"Please, Father," I said to ease his burdens. "You have, in fact, honored me by allowing me this opportunity to help win the war. Your trust in me is not misplaced."

He then released me from his clasp and gave me that tender, loving gaze and smile that I so dearly longed for from him.

"The gods grant you a safe passage," he said, letting go of me.

As I proceeded to climb aboard my cart, Andromache came up to me to give me a shawl, saying, "Accomplish this not only for Troy, but for me personally. Succeed so that we may exact our vengeance upon cruel Achilles."

I gave Andromache a protracted stare, amazed over how deeply she had personalized her loss, trying to understand it. While I shared her grief over our honored Hector and was as repulsed as anyone over the mistreatment of his body, Achilles fought him fairly in single combat and won. He cannot be faulted for that; that is the nature of war.

"I will," I replied at length, "for our vengeance."

After having said our good-byes, tears flowing abundantly in the process, my father directed Agenor to proceed. We left through a smaller gate on the back side of the city, facing inland, still under the dimness of early twilight, and spent the next hour or so passing by the tent cities of our major allied encampments. The main road was in our possession and secure from enemy patrols at this point of our route, and I believe the only reason my father wanted us to pass here before sunrise was that he did not want a multitude of soldiers witnessing our departure in case there were spies among them. Agamemnon was known to offer substantial rewards and safety to soldiers who betrayed their loyalty and assisted him with information that had significance in the conduct of his battles. We kept our silence until we passed the last of the camps and no longer felt a threat of being overheard by anyone. By the time the sun had risen above the horizon to grace us with its warmth and glow, we had passed the outermost encampment and found ourselves alone among the green plains, interspersed with wooded patches of forest.

We basically advanced in a northeasterly direction through Troad, the region around Troy, then turned east as we entered Mysia, the land along the southern shores of the Propontis, the sea connecting the great northern sea with the Aegean, following an old, worn-out dirt road that seemed never to be used. Once we cleared Mysia, we would turn north again, moving parallel to the Sangarius River until it flowed into the great northern sea. Our escort soldiers performed as scouts to keep us out of sight of the population centers so that no intelligence on our whereabouts would come to the Greeks.

Our days were somewhat monotonous and rushed, for we tried to cover as much distance as daylight permitted, and I often found myself nodding with sleepiness, although I tried to resist against it. The hot, glaring sun penetrating our cart seemed to oppose my efforts to stay awake, accelerating my drowsiness, and while I engaged in some lighthearted conversations with my servants, this was not enough stimulation to relieve my boredom. Menodice and Thalia evidently felt as I did, for I noticed that they also fought bravely to avoid succumbing to their first inclination: sleep. I attempted to maintain some interest in the varied landscape and wildlife along our road, delighting in seeing a brightly colored bird and in hearing its melodic refrains, but this absorption came at lengthy intervals and did little to alleviate the overall dullness afflicting us. Could I endure two weeks of this? Such were our days, but how different were our evenings.

Once we settled into a campsite for the night, our escort soldiers, after seeing to their horses, quickly set about pitching our tents and installing the furnishings to make things comfortable for us. We then sat wrapped in our blankets on our benches and chairs around a fire, upon which was roasted the catch of the day—usually rabbit or quail—and thoroughly enjoyed our companionship as we ate. We laughed and entertained ourselves with jokes and stories; one of the soldiers had a lyre with him, and we even sang songs. This was the time when we came to know each other, in some cases, quite well. By this, I mean that, although I avoided becoming intimate with anyone, and certainly the temptation was there, for some of the soldiers rendered me ample amorous looks, I cannot make a similar claim for Menodice or Thalia. I permitted them to conduct their flirting and teasing, but only to a degree short of outright kissing and fondling, as we did not know what the fates had in store for us. It may have been suitable to relish the present moment to the fullest, yet I did not want to risk invoking jealousies among the soldiers that could lead to hard feelings and resentment between them, thereby jeopardizing my mission. I thought it important to emphasize, by placing such a demand on them, that this trip was not to be a joyride, but had serious overtones. Agenor shared my viewpoint on this; he did not want potential problems arising that might impede his control over their discipline, especially when he rotated their nightly guard duty. Whether I was successful at this, I cannot know, for they could have easily made connections during the night while I slept, but I made certain that when I was ready to retire for the night, my servants likewise took to their own cots, and when I awoke the next morning, I still saw them there. Regardless, our evenings were very pleasant, and I have rather fond recollections of them.

Agenor frequently sat beside me at these times in order to instruct me on the habits and customs of the Amazons, although I often felt his presence had more to do with being close to Menodice whom I think he favored. In truth, as I observed the silent communication— the prolonged glances and smiles—between the two, I recognized that they were quite enamored with each other. In spite of this, I insisted that she adhere to the sleeping schedule I imposed on her—that is, the same as mine—but I doubt if I would have censured her for any deviations to this. That being so, it presented no actual obstruction to Agenor's efforts at educating me on the things he knew, for he was not at the point where he allowed himself to be distracted in his exertions. His attention was totally focused on me.

"The Amazons hold occasional mating feasts," Agenor told me, "when they invite men from adjacent kingdoms to have sex with them, usually after heavy drinking so the men can't recall their activity with any clarity, thus preventing their boasting of these."

I thought this amusing and said, "They're practical."

"They are," said Agenor in a broad smile, happy that he had Menodice's full interest as well as mine and Thalia's. "Only a selected number of Amazons get to participate in any particular mating feast, and these are then barred from the next one to two. This is so they don't impair their fighting capability with too many pregnancies."

"And the men they choose?" I asked "Are they just rounded up from these kingdoms?"

"It's not random. Only distinguished warriors are invited, men of strength and stamina, for they believe these traits will be transferred to their descendents. These they usually pick out from a lineup they request. The feasts are held to perpetuate this process of regeneration. Like all martial societies, the Amazons place great value in sustaining a permanent class of warriors—women, in this case—so they are always powerful and in domination of the men around them."

"So they never live with men at other times?" I was curious to know.

"Not as far as I know," said Agenor. "Themiscyra has very few of them."

"Hardly any men?" I thought this amazing. "I can't see this as being very pleasurable, nothing to arouse the senses."

"You don't know the Amazons, princess. They are indoctrinated from the earliest age to loathe all men, to know they're greatly superior to them in every capacity. So should they associate with any male, this would amount to an extreme indignity for them."

"So what happens to the male babies born to them?" I asked. "I assume they keep the girls."

"Boys are not actually killed, as the chroniclers have reported," Agenor informed me. "Most are returned to the place of their fathers, not always to their benefit—often more as an encumbrance to an ability to feed and shelter them—for who can know who the actual fathers are? Some they keep, but these unfortunate boys are not given any manly duties or trained in the skills of war; instead, they do menial tasks for the women overlords. I have heard that some are even emasculated."

"Emasculated?"

"Gelded. So they are unable to engage in sex."

"What about the girls?" Menodice asked.

"At an early age, they are disciplined to endure the rigors of a warrior's life, given endless physical exercise and trained in combat skills, especially in horsemanship, in which they excel. They are forced to endure the cold and severe weather conditions. And they are taught to look upon men with great disdain. Not all the girls make the proper transition to warrior status. Some simply are not strong enough, being small in stature; they end up serving as advisors, administrators, and caretakers, often skilled in medical practices."

"Are there any joys in their lives?" I wondered out loud.

"Few that I can tell," Agenor went on. "They have a harsh existence. Discipline is strictly enforced. Even minor infractions are punished with severity. Usually the offender is publicly flogged, but in the most humiliating way: stripped completely naked for all to see. But the worst punishment is for those who, as they grow into maturity and chance to meet men and fall under love's spell—for only Aphrodite can contrive these matters—are alleged to bring shame and disgrace upon the group, especially if they have attained full warrior status. They are considered traitors and are either banished or, in some cases, actually executed." I winced as I heard this, but my initial reaction was somewhat mollified by what Agenor said next.

"For all that," Agenor continued, "they appear to be quite satisfied with their condition. The traitorous actions seldom occur; even the floggings are relatively rare. They strongly believe that they are better off than women in other societies and hold in contempt those women who are acquiescent to men. This appears to be the common bond holding their realm together: their singular loathing of a male-dominated social order, and of men in general. No Amazon will ever do a man's bidding."

Now this was not altogether received by me without some appeal. Certainly women had little power or influence in our world, especially in the political sphere, and to hear that there were places where such conditions did not exist—and were even reversed—was a revelation. Yet to say that we were without any power would be very much erroneous—just look at what Helen has managed to do—but our strength rests more in our ability to manipulate the men, whose love for us makes them slaves to our fancies, rather than by us openly controlling the situation.

I began to notice, as Agenor related his information to us, his eyes consistently set on Menodice, that Thalia appeared to be discomfited over this. This did not settle well with me, for it told me that the opposite of my concerns over their creating jealousies among our soldiers was taking place here, that the envy has in fact arisen between my servant women over our commander.

"Do you see how he swoons over her?" Thalia told me after we retired to our tent, having left Menodice to remain a while longer with Agenor. "It's as if you and I did not exist for him."

"Why should this trouble you?" I asked her while spreading a blanket over my cot to ready myself for sleep.

"It shouldn't," Thalia quickly replied, "but it does. I feel as though I'm an outsider in their presence. I'm made to feel alone."

"You wouldn't feel that way if you didn't care for Agenor," I said. "I believe you have taken a liking to him."

Thalia, who had already taken to her bed, did not respond immediately, perhaps out of her own realization that such was indeed the case and that she could do little to alter the situation.

"It's so frustrating," she then said. "I can't help myself. He has no right to ignore me like that."

"I must ask you to keep your emotions under control," I told her.

"Maintain your composure, however difficult that may be for you. We cannot let anything impair the work we have to do."

"I understand," Thalia said.

I saw in her eyes that my counsel was not much comfort to her.

"Often these initial enraptures fade over time," I then added. "You will serve yourself better by not letting it affect you in such an evident way. There's a certain dignity in enduring one's difficulties stoically. Over time, this may even render you more endearing to someone."

Thalia seemed to appreciate what I told her, but maybe for the wrong reasons, for I believe I fostered a hope in her that she might eventually acquire Agenor's affection; this, however, was not my intention. I was speaking in the general and did not have a specific individual in mind.

"Thank you, Polyxena," she said as she covered herself with her blankets.

Menodice then entered the tent, evidently perceiving that we were ready to retire for the night, and without saying anything, she took to her bed. I was pleased that she did not deviate from the conditions I imposed on her and dutifully ended her conversation with Agenor; or was it he who terminated it? As I lay there, I heard a suppressed sigh of relief coming from Thalia and recognized this situation was more serious than I first thought.

Agenor was a handsome man. Physically, he was the very embodiment of the perfectly composed male, powerfully built and very strong, his muscular frame enough to delight any woman's fancies. If you add to this the charm and wit he exhibited in his usual bearing, as well as the authority in which demonstrated his abilities, you then have the ingredients for a potentially volatile association among those envious of, or enthralled by, him, as I was now witnessing with my servant ladies. And I must even admit that I felt momentary pangs of jealousy, or perhaps annoyance is the better word, over the attention he accorded Menodice that evening. This distraction worked on my emotions, causing me to feel slighted by it, and it is somewhat embarrassing to account for this, for I view Agenor as a friend, nothing more. I resisted these impulses whenever they struck me by diverting my attention from them.

The fact that Agenor, although now thirty years old, was as yet unmarried did not help matters. Highly unusual for a man that age, I can only attribute this to our protracted war so disrupting the normality of our lives—indeed it explains my own single status for want of available suitors—but I am certain he has a concubine to satisfy his sexual needs as all men do. With so many soldiers slain over the years of battling, there certainly was no shortage of women in Troy. Though I'm surprised that he should favor Menodice, for she was his own age, and it is customary for men to marry women at least ten years younger; the chances for Thalia, at age thirty-two, clearly did not favor her. I pondered if I should confront Agenor in the morning over the detrimental effect his actions had on our amity. I decided to let the matter rest, anticipating that Agenor was aware of the situation and would avoid aggravating it, and not wishing to strain my own relationship with him in case he took my admonitions the wrong way. I would address the issue only if it arose again. Such were my thoughts that kept me from getting a good night's sleep.

On the sixth day of our journey, we arrived at the southern shores of the great northern sea, the halfway point, and turned east. Our progress was good, having gotten there a day earlier than expected, but my own uneasiness became more pronounced as we drew closer to our destination. I was increasingly anxious over how I would conduct myself once I was there—so much was at stake—and what kind of reception I would receive. Only Cassandra's words that I would fulfill my mission provided me with a degree of comfort and helped to alleviate my fears.

The landscape was very different there than around Troy, with its more level ground and drier look. We now traversed over rugged terrain, with the mountains coming right up to the seacoast and abruptly plunging into it at frequent intervals, interspersed with green, grassy plains, where the rivers entered it. A cold wind consistently blew in off the waters from the north, penetrating our wraps at times and chilling us to the bone, but when it did die down, the temperatures were quite comfortable. Forests abounded in the mountainous regions, covering them from base to summit except for the taller peaks whose rocks stood expose to the sky, appearing awesome in their loftiness. These forests were lush, with trees in close proximity to each other and underbrush everywhere. We moved along a road that ran through the wilderness adjacent to the seashore, but it often rose in elevation, zigzagging back and forth over the ridges, where the cliffs directly met the sea. Needless to say, our progression was considerably slowed along this part of our journey, and as we proceeded along, I dearly longed for the open and more spacious lands of home.

Fortunately our evenings remained pleasant occasions for us, making the ordeals of the day a thing of the past, and we eagerly looked forward to them. Agenor, to his credit, had evidently picked up on my concerns over doting too much on Menodice—perhaps he himself understood the ramifications of his previous conduct— and assumed a more impartial posture as he spoke with us by the campfire. His talks were now more directed toward informing me of the protocol existing among the hierarchy of the Amazons so I would recognize the signs that were favorable to me or, conversely, worked against me. By knowing of these, I could direct my approaches to them accordingly, making the necessary adjustments as appropriate.

"You must never initiate a conversation with Penthesileia," Agenor told me on that first night on the seashore while we huddled close to the fire to keep warm, "or any of the high-ranking officials, for that matter. Always allow them to speak to you first; typically, you will respond to a question they have asked you. Be humble and courteous in their presence, but not with a gushiness that they would consider flattery. These are battle-hardened warriors who have a preference for frankness and honesty in their dealings with others."

"How do I press my demands on them?" I asked.

"Be straightforward with them and logical. Persuade them that whatever you ask them to do is in their interest as well as ours."

"This is so intimidating for me," I said, feeling a strain over the expectations my father placed upon me. "What if I should offend Penthesileia?"

"I wouldn't worry too much about it," Agenor said as he smiled. "You already possess many of the attributes lending you favor for this. Just be yourself, I guess is what I'm trying to say, behave in your usual nice manner."

I must say that Agenor had his own tactful way of making me feel good about myself. His words gave me the encouragement I needed at a moment when I seriously doubted my ability to continue on this.

"When you speak to Penthesileia," he went on, "address her as 'my queen,' 'my lady,' or 'gracious lady.' She does not like terms such as 'your highness' or 'your excellency.' And never say 'your royal so and so.' Amazon queens achieve their power through battlefield accomplishments, based on merit, and their acceptance as leader by others. They do not see themselves as nobility or in a context established along bloodlines as we do. There is no such thing as a Royal House of Themiscyra."

I nodded my understanding without adding a word. Agenor took the cue, knowing he had my undivided attention, and continued.

"You will know you're in Penthesileia's good graces," Agenor said, "when she asks you to sit beside her in her council meetings. Consider that the highest honor being bestowed upon you— outsiders are rarely offered admission to these."

This conversation was typical of the ones we engaged in on the following nights as more and more information was imparted on me until I actually felt as though I knew the Amazons fairly well. And as my knowledge about them was thereby enhanced, I became increasingly fascinated with their worldview and ways of living, and not all of it seemed negative to me. A world dominated by women for women, while quite a novelty, entertained a certain appeal for me. Yet I still rebelled against the notion of an absence of men in their lives.

I was encouraged that Agenor did his part in alleviating the tensions between Menodice and Thalia so effortlessly. He simply gave each of them equal worthiness in his eyes, beaming as he glanced from one to the other and smiling in turn as he spoke with them. He did this without my having to say a word to him about it—truly he was the son of Antenor. Surprisingly, Menodice did not appear to be slighted by this, for often when such things occur, the person who earlier received the disproportionate amount of solicitation would now come to feel herself neglected. I was not beyond suspecting that the two of them may have actually come to a mutual agreement to conduct themselves in this manner. If this was indeed the case, then I must congratulate them both for their display of sensitivity on the subject. I was much relieved when we retired for our nights.

Midway into the twelfth day, after we had crossed another of the seemingly endless ridges, where the mountains converged on the sea, we came upon an expansive treeless plain, somewhat flat and ideal for raising horses. As we headed toward the river bisecting this vast valley, we saw a distant community coming into sight. At first, I thought it was a mere village, but as we came nearer, it was obvious that its size and number of dwellings qualified it as a city, yet unlike any I had ever seen before. For one thing, almost all the buildings were built of wood; I saw only two stone structures and later learned that these were temples, one to Ares, god of war, and the other to Artemis, virgin goddess of the hunt, whose height rose well above the surrounding buildings. The tallest of the wooden constructions were but two stories and were located near the city's center, adjacent to the temples. By far the majority of houses were single floored and somewhat spread out. No barricades or walls ringed the place, openness being its defining feature.

"We have arrived," Agenor said. "That's Themiscyra."

"It looks quite humble," I responded. "Not what I expected."

"You'll like it better when we enter it," said Agenor. "I found the city's central district to have some charm when I was last here."

We continued in our direction toward Themiscyra when we noticed a group of mounted riders—seven of them—thundering at us in full gallop. Agenor halted our advance to await their arrival. I climbed down from my cart, thinking my increased vulnerability on the ground could better serve to demonstrate our submissiveness, and, shading my eyes with my hand, watched the approaching riders in silence. In the briefest time, they came up to us, reining in their horses to stop directly in front of the royal cart, where I was standing. This was my first look at Amazons. All the riders were women and, except for their leader, rather homely in appearance; no ship would be launched for their sake. But dressed as they were, in their full battle gear—metallic breastplates covering red or white tunics, wide leather belts with attached swords, bows that hung diagonally across their upper body, with quivers of arrows strapped on their backs, conical helmets accented by an elevated center crest, and boots of animal hide rising halfway up to their knees, leaving the rest of their legs exposed—they cut an imposing, even frightening, image.

While the faces of the six apparently subordinate warriors seemed plain to me, I cannot say the same for their commander whose helmet was adorned with a tuft of horse's mane and who wore a short, red mantle that was clipped to her shoulders and ran down her backside to waist length. She was a strikingly beautiful woman— even Helen would have found serious competition in her—and had an aura of authoritativeness about her that made it obvious she was in charge.

"You are trespassers here," she spoke out in her assertive manner. "You cannot come any closer."

"We are from Troy," Agenor replied. "We seek an audience with Queen Penthesileia."

"You are a man," said the Amazon commander. "You have not been invited to be here."

"I've been here before," Agenor said. "Perhaps you remember."

"Even so, man, my queen has not told me of expecting visitors from Troy. You must leave."

"I am Agenor of Dardania, now in service of Troy, and I once sat beside your queen in her council meeting. She will want to see me."

The Amazon commander's dark eyes glared intensely at Agenor, and I sensed that she did not appreciate his demanding posture, undoubtedly because he was a man and she bore the hostility for that gender I now knew was so typical of her kind. I felt that I had to intercede at this point and stepped closer to her horse.

"I am Polyxena," I began, "daughter of King Priam of Troy, tasked to be his envoy. I carry a message of great importance from him for your queen."

The Amazon commander turned to me, and as her eyes met mine, a glint of sparkle shone from them, indicating to me that she preferred my presence to Agenor's.

"And I am Antiope," she said after a lengthy pause, "second-in-command here. You say you carry a message of importance?"

"I do."

"Then say what you must. I shall pass it on to my queen."

"I'm sorry, Antiope, but I cannot. My instructions are to impart my words only on Queen Penthesileia herself."

I expected to be severely reprimanded for my audaciousness, but to my surprise, Antiope rendered me a soft smile as she continued to gaze into my eyes—I truly thought her most attractive—enwrapping me with her pleasant glow.

"Very well," she finally said. "I shall take you to her." She then pulled on her reins to direct her mount toward Agenor. "You, Dardanian, will come with us. The rest of your party must stay outside our city until my queen decides if we should quarter them." Having thus completed our introductions, we proceeded under our newly benign escort. When we came to the city's edge, Antiope directed Agenor and me to follow her while her warriors remained on watch over my entourage beyond the main entrance, a mere street with a guardhouse on each side of it. As I was on foot, one of the Amazons gave up her horse so that I could use it. I think I astounded everyone that I could readily ride it; I was, after all, sister of Hector, tamer of horses, and grew up with the noble steeds. That is how I came to Themiscyra.

CHAPTER IV

ANTIOPE LED US ALONG THE main avenue leading to the city's center, and I saw that Agenor had accurately described it as having charm. The wooden buildings were adjoined to each other and had a hominess about them that made you feel comfortable and imbued with a sense of serenity. I noticed that Antiope frequently glanced my way. I think she liked me, or maybe she just wanted to see my reaction to the sights passing us as we moved ahead. I returned her gaze with a smile, resulting in her looking away from me, only to have her repeat the procedure a short while later.

We came to a large double-storied house located at the heart of the city directly in front of an open square, where the first of the two stone structures stood. I was impressed by its fine masonry work.

"The Temple of Artemis," Antiope told me as she noticed my transfixion on it. "We honor her, and Ares, above all the other deities."

"Women built this?" I asked in amazement.

"No," said Antiope. "We do employ the service of men in our construction projects—they have some use for us. They possess skills we lack in such crafts. We get them from our alliance cities under agreements that we assist them in their defense against enemies."

"So you do allow men to live here?" I wondered.

"Some. The menials who serve us live in the worker's section of Themiscyra. The ones we recruit from our allies stay outside the city in temporary lodgings and only for the duration of a project," Antiope told me. "Wait here," she directed, pointing to a wooden building next to the temple. "This is our meeting house, where my queen usually spends her day. I shall see if she wants to meet with you."

Antiope dismounted and walked into the building in front of us, a single-storied structure, but with a massive gabled roof that nearly tripled its height, leaving Agenor and me to ourselves amid the gawking women guarding the place or passing to and fro in the square. It was obvious that Agenor's presence did not agree with them, for their hostile glares readily demonstrated their derogatory feelings. I believe they were highly incensed that I should be with him.

"You were right about their loathing men," I said and then smiled as I continued, "Are you such a despicable beast?"

Agenor let out a short laugh, saying, "Certainly to Antiope. Lord Priam was correct in giving you this assignment. I don't think I would have made much headway with them."

Fortunately, Antiope's return was not long in coming. She came forth from the guarded doorway and motioned for one of her subordinates posted there to see to her horse as she approached us.

"My queen is in conference," she said, "but she wishes to see you. Please follow me."

Agenor and I looked at each other; both of us must have been struck by the same thought, that Antiope's demeanor had noticeably changed to a more amiable persuasion as a result of her meeting with the queen. For the first time, she actually displayed cordiality toward Agenor. We got off our horses and followed her into the council hall.

For being a wooden structure, the inner hall had a greater spaciousness than I would have guessed and could easily have accommodated a hundred, if not more, people with ample room to spare. A number of women, clothed in various regalia, stood on both sides of the aisle staring us down as we walked between them to the end of the hall, where Queen Penthesileia was seated. My curiosity over at last seeing her filled me with an anxiousness I had never felt before, and I could not take my eyes off her as we moved closer. When we came within ten paces of her, Antiope halted and, by this action, directed us to follow her example. We then stood silently before the great warrior queen. I was awestruck being in her presence.

Penthesileia sat in an oversized chair that had a backside reaching far above her head and was centered against the wall concluding the corridor. Two other figures sat on both sides of her, one of them a man, whom I presumed to be her advisors. She was impressive in her comportment and dress, definitely a leader born to rule, exhibiting an authoritativeness, even when seated, that manifested itself in serene dignity and strength. Her red tunic was covered with a protective outer leather vest studded with metallic buttons, accentuated by her ample breasts, as my father alluded to, and tapering to a narrow waist that was circled by a wide sash-like belt. Her position as queen was emphasized by the golden headband she wore, which was welded into a diamond-shaped medallion on her brow. She first looked at me, her eyes very expressive, exuding a warm glow, and after thoroughly scanning me turned her attention to Agenor.

"Agenor," Penthesileia began, smiling at him. "Has it been ten years? You look well for all that What have you been up to since I last saw you?"

"Fighting for Troy, my queen," Agenor replied, "against Agamemnon's Greeks."

"Ah yes. The Dardanians and Trojans have a long-standing alliance. We have kept our eyes on this war. A rather long conflict, wouldn't you say?"

"Yes, my queen," said Agenor, "long and difficult."

"So I've heard. But you appear to be holding your own against Agamemnon." Penthesileia next turned her eyes on me. "And you are?"

"Polyxena, my lady," I answered, "daughter of Priam, King of Troy."

Penthesileia appeared pleased to hear my voice.

"Come closer, dear," she said. "I wish to have a good look at you."

I stepped forward until I stood only about a body's length from her. "My, you are a pretty one," Penthesileia then said, her eyes looking me over but mainly concentrating on my face. "Priam has always excelled in that domain. I was so sorry to hear about the fate of Hector."

Hearing Hector's name mentioned in a place so far away from home overwhelmed me with a sudden burst of grief, and while I did not say anything, I felt my eyes moistening as I quietly endured my painful sorrow. My temporary anguish did not escape Penthesileia's observation.

"Such sensitivity," she remarked, apparently deeply touched by my inadvertent display of emotion. "And so, so feminine."

As she said this, I momentarily thought that I had sabotaged my chances for success on my mission, but I then realized that she spoke more in a regretful sort of tone than out of derision over my weakness. The notion came to me that Penthesileia, despite her rulership over the Amazons, deep down may have desired the softer, more womanly side of our gender.

"As I am in a conference at present," Penthesileia next said, "I must see to its conclusion before I address your matter. You must be tired after your long journey. Antiope will settle you in my own residence during your stay with us. Agenor and the others of your group will be housed in our guest quarters at the city's edge. I trust this is agreeable to you."

"Yes, my lady," I said, hesitating in my response.

"Yes, dear?" Penthesileia said, taking not of my diffidence.

"If it pleases my lady," I said, "I should like to have my two handmaidens accompany me. They would otherwise reside alone among my male escort soldiers." I glanced at Agenor to see how he regarded my suggestion, but he gave me no indication that he disapproved of it, nor, for that matter, that he agreed with it. He was quite expressionless in his reciprocating gaze at me.

"Oh, by all means," Penthesileia replied. "We certainly would not want that. There are ample chambers at my residence." She then nodded her assent that we should leave her to her business, again giving me a loving gaze, before her eyes set on Antiope, directing her in an unspoken, subtle endorsement to lead us from the hall.

Agenor and I both rendered the queen a small, respectful bow of our heads and turned about to begin our departure.

"Polyxena," Penthesileia said, bringing me to a halt as I faced her again.

"Yes, my lady?" I answered.

"I know why you're here," she told me. "We have much to talk about. You must tell me all you know about your father. I shall see you this evening." She then motioned that I go with a slight wave of her hand. I rendered her a small curtsy and proceeded to join Agenor and Antiope, and we exited the hall.

Once outside, Antiope directed the same woman who had stood watch over our horses to lead Agenor back to our waiting group and, after seeing our soldiers to their quarters, to fetch Menodice and Thalia along with my baggage. She then directed me to follow her.

We walked toward a large, single-floored wooden structure only a short distance from the council hall and on the same square that the Temple of Artemis stood.

"She likes you," Antiope informed me as we proceeded. "I think you noticed that."

"I did," I told Antiope. "And the feeling is mutual. I like your queen."

"We hold her in great esteem," said Antiope. "If you look favorably on her now, you should see her in battle. No man, not even your Agenor— muscular as he is—could stand against her."

"He's not *my* Agenor," I was quick to point out. "I'm his friend, not his lover."

Antiope's eyes lit up when she heard this. A wide smile illuminated her face. I think she very much appreciated that I, being an object of desire for her, I believe, was not possessed by what was to her a loathsome man.

By this time, we came to the palace, if it can be called that, and entered through its front door of plainly assembled planks with the pelt of a deer hanging from it as adornment. Again I thought the building had a much larger interior than it appeared to have from the outside. Essentially, it was a square-shaped structure with a central hallway and rooms on both sides at one end of the building and a more open area at the other end, where a meeting and dining room as well as the queen's bedchamber was situated under a vaulted roof. By the standards I was used to, these were indeed austere surroundings and would never have qualified as a palatial edifice in Troy.

"This is your room," Antiope said, coming to a halt in front of the last doorway before the corridor met the open section. "You're next to the queen's chamber, ahead of you. Your servants will be in a room at the beginning of the hall." Antiope opened the door, and I looked inside. The room was smaller than I was used to, but it had a coziness to it, accentuated all the more after all the nights we spent in our tent. And there was a bed—how much more comfortable that would be than the narrow cots we had slept on.

She then went on to show me the wash room. I was surprised to see that fresh, flowing water entered along an indented trench carved into its stone floor and filled a cistern bordered by stepped walls.

"You may want to take a bath," Antiope said. "Soap and towels are on the adjacent bench."

I knelt down and placed my hand in the water. "Ooh," I exclaimed. "It's cold."

My comment solicited a smile from Antiope, and she said, "It's the same water we bathe in by the river, only we have diverted it into this building so our queen can have her privacy. If this suffices for her, it ought to do for a Trojan princess."

"In Troy, we have servants fill our tubs with pots of boiling water. You might want to consider that, Antiope. A hot bath is a gratifying experience."

"How degenerate. Such indulgence would sap us of our powers, soften us."

I spoke easily with Antiope. In spite of our different views and upbringings, we somehow related well to each other. Perhaps it is true that I was drawn to her physical beauty as, I believed, she was to mine. I very much liked her, but not in a romantic way. My desire for men was not diminished by any extent, as far as I could tell. Yet I was both intrigued and mystified over my unreserved banter with her. Hearing her speak aroused a curious stimulation in me, a sort of hot and cold flush in my face, unfamiliar to me, causing me to ponder over its lingering effect. I was not that discomfited by this, thinking it as somewhat sensual, but it also left me bewildered that such was my response.

"I guess I have to take the plunge," I told her. "I really do need a bath."

"Let me show you the rest of the facilities first," said Antiope, "and I will leave you to your privacy."

We next examined the lavatory area, which was in the same washroom, only behind a wall dividing it from the bathing section, and was flushed clean by the same water whose flow was continuous in and out of the cistern. After that, we walked through the meeting room, which contained a few chairs for relaxation, and the dining room, which, according to Antiope, was seldom used, as Penthesileia and her courtly favorites typically ate their meals in a communal setting within the council hall. When my tour was over, Antiope and I returned to the washroom so she could show me where to put things, like the discarded towels, and find additional cloths should I need them.

"We have our menials to clean up after you are done," Antiope told me. "Men do this work for us. I shall send them over shortly so you need only call on them."

"They won't be coming in here, will they?" I asked her.

"No. They'll wait outside until they hear from you," Antiope answered as she gave me a warm, penetrating glance. "I must see to the others of your party. Had I the time, I would join you in your bath." I looked at her as the strangest emotion came over me as if I actually wished that she did. That I even thought such a thing startled me. She was such a beautiful woman, and the idea of seeing her in the nude struck me as being erotically provocative, but then I fought off these urges, telling myself this cannot be. I loved men; they are the ones I felt pangs of jealousy over when they ignored me, especially when I desired them, and that I wished to have touch me. In this befuddled state, I could not find the words to answer Antiope, so I merely nodded my head as an acknowledgment that I had heard her. She smiled and then left, closing the door after her.

I spent little time bathing—the water was too frigid—but scrubbed myself thoroughly to wash off the dirt accumulated on the trail and felt refreshingly clean when I emerged from the tub. After I wrapped myself in a large towel, I left the washroom and went into my bedchamber, taking my clothes with me, and looked out the window, where I saw two men standing near the main door. They were plainly attired, with but a simple white tunic covering each of them.

"Are you the queen's attendants?" I asked them as I leaned out the window.

"At your service, my lady," answered one of them.

"I'm done with my bath," I said, uncertain of how I should go about ordering them to clean the washroom, as I had never before placed such a menial demand on men. I had no cause for my reservation, for they readily knew what they must do and directly set about their duties. I overheard their fussiness and dainty manner of speech as they undertook the work. They were more finicky than the women servants we had at Troy, which made me seriously question their manliness. Were they the gelded ones Agenor told me about?

I laid down upon my bed to await the arrival of Menodice and Thalia so they could dress me in a new set of clothes and was suddenly overcome with extreme tiredness, the fatigue of our arduous, fast- paced journey now hitting me, and without even realizing when, I fell asleep. Not until I was awakened by the sound of Menodice and Thalia talking as they hovered around me was

I aware that I had dozed off. My arousal did not ease the drained energy I felt within me, and only reluctantly did I come out of my wooziness.

"You must get up," Menodice said. "Queen Penthesileia requests your presence."

"Oh, no," I cried out in alarm "I'm not ready. I don't know what to wear."

"We have this chiton prepared for you," said Thalia as she held the white linen garment before me. "It will look lovely on you."

I got off the bed and had Thalia fling the ankle-length tunic over me, and as I tightened it with my waist cord, I noticed that my chamber was quite dark, lit only under candlelight.

"Oh, no," I repeated myself. "How long have I been asleep?"

"Since we've been here," Menodice informed me, "perhaps four hours."

"Why didn't you wake me?" I snapped at Menodice.

"We wanted to," she said, "but the Amazon queen told us not to until she was ready to receive you. She told us just a moment ago that she now wishes to see you."

"Where is she?" I asked.

"Here, in the dining room. She has some food for you. Thalia and I have already had our meal."

I hastily adjusted the fit of my chiton so that it hung properly from my shoulders and stroked back my hair as Thalia handed me a clasp to hold it in place. When I felt myself presentable, as much as I could under the short time available to me, I left my chamber and proceeded to the dining room. There I saw Penthesileia sitting by herself at the table while gingerly partaking of the meal placed before her.

"My lady?" I said as I waited for her permission to enter. Penthesileia turned her eyes to me—they emitted the same warm glow as when I saw her earlier—and she began to smile.

"My dear Polyxena," she began. "Come sit at my table. Have something to eat while we speak. You must be hungry."

"Thank you, my lady," I said as I took my seat.

So began my long conversation with Penthesileia that evening.

We talked about many subjects. In particular, she was very interested in the welfare of my father, and she expressed how grateful she remained over his adjudication at her tribunal when he cleared her of the charges that she had slain Hippolyte, her queen. She showed a keen interest in learning about our war with the Greeks, wanting to hear all there was to know, everything from the tactics applied and the leaders involved to their fighting skill and even the weapons they used. I told her of the events leading to Hector's death, of the rift between Agamemnon and his chief subordinate, Achilles, and how my brother's slaying of Patroclus caused the Myrmidon to rejoin the battle. I updated her on what the present situation was, my father's view of this and why he felt it necessary to send me on this mission. In saying this, I informed her of the grand strategy my father had in mind, how he hoped that, by her threatening Agamemnon's northern flank, the Greeks would have to divide their army to counter her moves and thereby clear the way for him to decisively destroy them at Troy. She was engrossed in all I had to say and, as I spoke of my father's estimation of Agamemnon's evil intentions, was often overcome with an extremely sober comportment as she reflected over these, apparently understanding their significance as it pertained to her own realm.

"We have long recognized," she told me, "that Troy stands as a major barrier against Agamemnon's expansionary visions. The man's greed is insatiable. Dominating all the Greek states is not enough for him; he must now control all the waters and lands around it as well. But we are a long way from Troy, so our distance assures us some security."

"If it pleases my lady," I spoke out, knowing I was not solicited to do so. I paused to see if I would be corrected for my transgression.

"Go on, my dear," Penthesileia said, permitting my indiscretion.

"I wanted to say, what if Troy should fall? Who would then oppose Agamemnon and stop him from enhancing his powers and claims over others?"

"The situation is problematic," said Penthesileia somberly, "embarking on a course of war, especially one that, once begun, offers us no other alternative but victory or defeat. I doubt if we could compromise on our involvement as a contingency dependent on whether our allies win or lose. Once we are in it, our destiny is inevitably bound to them."

"I must believe," I continued my impropriety, though now thinking of it as appreciated rather than disfavored by Penthesileia, "as my father does, that we will be victorious in this war. Otherwise, my being here is without purpose, as are my father's hopes in sending me here."

"For one so young, you have remarkable insight," Penthesileia replied after a moment of reflection. "I do hate the Greeks. We've not had good relations with them. They are very patriarchal and look upon women who show any kind of strong will or independent spirit with utmost scorn."

While I was heartened in my estimation that I was making headway, I found her latest words somewhat peculiar, for in truth, it occurred to me as she stated this, the Trojans held a view of women common with their enemy. Surely Penthesileia must have been aware of this.

"Agamemnon is the worst of the lot," I said. "He must be dealt a setback so he knows he's not invincible."

Penthesileia appeared amused at my response. She rendered me an ingratiating smile that seemed to suggest my commitment to my assignment was too obvious.

"It's getting late," she then said. "I must think about this. I shall discuss it with Antiope and the others in the morning." She then rose from her chair, stretched herself, and walked toward the door. "Have a good night, Polyxena," she said. "We will meet again tomorrow."

"Good night, my lady," I answered as she left. Now I was not as sure as earlier if I had progressed any. I was relieved that she had asked nothing more of me this night, for I again felt a weariness come over me and could barely keep my eyes open; my afternoon sleep could not alleviate the overall exhaustion resulting from our journey here. At this point, I wanted nothing more than to just sleep. I think I was gone the moment I slipped into bed.

By the time I woke up the next day, the morning was already half spent—such was my state of enervation—but then, we did stay up very late, well past midnight, yesterday, so it probably was not that far off from my normal schedule. Menodice and Thalia, as usual, saw to my needs and had everything prepared for me, including what I was to wear for the day. After washing and dressing, Thalia told me to go to the dining room, where breakfast would be served by the palace cook. Upon arriving there, I was pleasantly surprised to be greeted by Antiope. On seeing her, my heartbeat quickened and a tingling sensation came over me, accentuated all the more by her shining eyes.

"You must have been really tired," Antiope said, "to sleep this long. Come, sit down, and eat."

"Your queen and I stayed up very late last night," I said, taking my seat by the table.

Antiope gave me a strange look that suggested to me she felt some distraction over my statement. Was she feeling jealous?

"We talked, nothing more," I informed her, taking a pear from the fruit plate in front of me and munching on it. At hearing me, she reflected a noticeably happier disposition, which was very much evidenced by the widened smile enveloping her beautiful face. "Where is Queen Penthesileia?" I then asked.

"In the council hall. She does all her daily business there. We sat in conference most of the morning, discussing the situation at Troy, until she directed me to come here and wait on you. I'm to guide you around our city and show you how we live here."

I was more interested in knowing what the queen had resolved at their meeting, so I asked, "Was anything decided?"

"No," answered Antiope. "She said she needed more time and wished to be by herself."

While this was not the answer I sought, I could understand Penthesileia's hesitation in committing her Amazons to the war. She must have legitimately believed that Themiscyra rested safe enough beyond Agamemnon's reach or that, even if he should take Troy, his force would be sufficiently expended in the process, so it would be unable to continue on further excursions. I did not share this viewpoint, believing strongly that his ambitions placed no constraints on him, and was resolved to stress this point when I next saw her. I must make her realize that Troy's fall posed a direct and imminent danger to her.

"Antiope?" I said, pausing to drink from my cup. "May I ask what *you* recommended?"

"I can't tell you," she replied. "My queen has requested that nothing be said to anyone about this, not until she has come to a decision. She will meet with us again tonight to inform us on her intentions."

I nodded my acceptance of this, perceiving that to press the issue would not serve my intentions—I did not want anything to work against what I had set out to achieve—and reconciled myself to the expectation that I had to allow for whatever amount of time it was going to take.

After I finished breakfast, Antiope and I spent much of the day riding to the various sections of Themiscyra, where she introduced me to the many facilities and labors in progress that comprised its daily routine. We visited the training grounds, where the Amazon warriors engaged in their military exercises and practiced their proficiency in battlefield skills. I was astonished at the physical demands of their workouts—as strenuous as any I had observed in Troy—with the women having to lift and toss heavy rocks, always running to and fro from one work station to another, dueling with an assortment of weapons, and throwing spears on specified targets. But mainly they concentrated on archery, firing their bows from fixed positions as well as from horseback and always stressing the accuracy of their missiles upon an objective, either stationary or in motion. Truly they excelled in the art, rarely missing what they aimed at, and they measured their success by the speed at which their horses galloped across the field and the number of arrows they released as they rode by. What mastery they had over their horses. No other warriors so thoroughly existed as one with their noble animals so that rider and horse functioned as a single and inseparable entity.

I talked Antiope into taking me to the guest quarters, where Agenor and my escort troop were located. Although reluctant at first, for her loathing of men remained an all-consuming obsession for her, she eventually acceded to my wishes, and we soon arrived at the facility. There I was met by Agenor who came out of the building just as we rode up to it.

"Welcome to Themiscyra's bastion of masculinity," he grinned as he spoke, obviously elated over seeing me. "And you, Antiope," he said, looking at my partner. "It's always a pleasure to see your smiling face."

"Don't press your luck, man," replied Antiope. "My queen may favor your presence here, but I do not." She always applied the term "man" in an utterly derogatory tone.

"I wanted to see how you and the boys were doing," I said, lightly laughing.

"Well enough, princess," said Agenor. "We're serviced by those docile creatures that pass for men around here. They wash our clothes, provide our meals, keep our quarters clean, the sort of things women do for us in Troy." Agenor glanced at Antiope to assure himself that she had heard him. She did. Her gaze was most contemptuous. "It would be nice," he went on, "to have Menodice and Thalia visit us at times, to serve my men their drinks and bring the joys of feminine companionship to them, not sexual you understand."

"I can arrange that," I told him.

Agenor then lowered his voice so only I would hear him, saying, "I realize this is somewhat early, but are we getting anywhere?"

"I'll know by evening," I said. "Penthesileia plans to see me again, hopefully to declare her intentions."

With that, I felt my visit prodded to a close by Antiope, having lost her patience with being gawked at by Agenor's men who seemed to drool over her good looks. I waved my farewell to Agenor as I turned my horse around, and together, Antiope and I rode off.

"What is it you don't like about him?" I asked her.

"He's a man," she answered. "That's enough for me. Their preoccupation is to assert their superiority over us, to enslave us to their fancies. They want us to do their bidding and submit to their base instincts, to be ever under their control. I am my own person. No man will ever possess me."

I wanted to ask Antiope if she ever had any physical urges to be consumed by them but decided this to be imprudent. I strongly sensed that she desired me—a woman—and to imply through such a question that I myself held such notions may have dampened her enthusiasm for me. I thought it best, in order to secure my success on this mission, to be regarded in the most favorable light by everyone whom I felt could influence the outcome I sought. And to be truthful, I was now bewildered by inclinations that previously had never surfaced for me. I found myself enticed by the conception of her full beauty before me and of me savoring the amatory pleasure the tenderness of her touch would give me. This troubled me to a significant extent, and I tried to sway my mind from it, but every time I looked at her and she at me, the images returned to torment me further.

We next rode to the working area of the city, where, to my surprise, most of its occupants were men, not the effeminate, weak-bodied ones who served us at the palace, but big, burly, strong-muscled men who manned the forges of the fire pits, hacked and sawed the wood for timber beams, welded into shape the spear points, swords, and shields of the armaments, and framed the wheels of the carts they built to carry supplies required for sustained military operations, among numerous other labor-intensive tasks.

"Some are permanent residents," Antiope told me after noticing my puzzlement over this seemingly contradictory situation, "kept from the time they were born to us, but stronger in body than others and desirable for the heavy work. But most are on loan from neighboring kingdoms—the ones I told you about—and reside here, where they work. We consider this area as being outside the city proper."

"Are the resident ones slaves?" I asked, nudging my horse forward.

Antiope mused over my question for a time before answering, "I suppose they are, but not in the typical sense. They are free to go about their way and may even mingle with our women—if they can find one who is interested in them—but must live in this quarter and have no promise of rising above their station. Yet occasionally, one of them does. One of my queen's most trusted advisors is Lycus—you saw him yesterday—but then, he's a brilliant thinker."

"Are they the gelded ones I've heard about?"

My question struck Antiope as humorous, which she announced in a mild laughter behind her flashing grin.

"Goodness, no," she declared. "The reports are grossly exaggerated. We only do that to the incorrigible ones, those who rebel against all disciplinary measures and simply cannot be tamed. If they submit to our authority, nothing happens to them."

"Then what makes your palace servants so meek?"

"That's how we rear them. They are indoctrinated from childhood to behave that way."

I learned much from Antiope that afternoon, and by the time we finished visiting the working facilities, the day was sufficiently spent to make our return to the palace coincide with serving the evening meal. As usual, one of Antiope's warriors tended to our horses. All I was required to do was dismount and wash myself before entering the dining room. I had grown very fond of my stallion—his name was Zephyrus, after the west wind, a handsome animal and easily managed by me—and I felt a momentary loss at seeing him led away.

Soon after Antiope and I had taken our seats in the dining room, we were joined by the great queen herself. Penthesileia greeted me with her familiar soft smile and warm eyes, a welcome leaving me with an impression both encouraging and comforting. I could not help but respond in kind to the regard offered me. As we dined on the tasty dishes furnished by palace servants, we spoke of how we had spent the day and what I thought of it all, small, introductory talk, a prelude to the more ponderous words I wished to hear.

"I consulted with Lycus, my chief advisor, over this matter," Penthesileia said next, "as well as my leading commanders. We are all in agreement that it is in our best interest that Troy hold out against Agamemnon. We prefer that his forces be destroyed; only this will stop him from continuing on his quest to subjugate all the kingdoms he views as his rivals. If, by our intervention, Priam succeeds in accomplishing this, then this is the prudent action for us to take."

I was overcome with feelings of both joy and relief as Penthesileia spoke these words. Cassandra was correct again when she told me this would be the outcome of my visit here.

"I have called upon a war council to convene here in four days. That should allow its members enough time to get here," Penthesileia continued.

"But," I could not hide my disappointment, "but I thought my queen had already made her decision."

"I did," said Penthesileia, "for Themiscyra. But we are a nation with five other cities. I must have a consensus of their rulers if we are to go to war. Our laws demand it. Also, we need to have the kings of Paphlagonia and Pelasgia agree to this."

"Kings?" I was even more confused now. "I always thought the Amazons did their own fighting."

"You have much to learn, Polyxena," Penthesileia replied, pausing to take another sip of wine from her goblet. "Tell her, Antiope."

"We are horse warriors," Antiope informed me. "We can fight our own battles in spacious fields, facing an enemy there, because we are mounted and our horses can maneuver without obstacles on open grounds. But if we are to recapture cities that the Greeks have taken and acquire these for Troy, we will need a large infantry component. Only foot soldiers can take and hold enemy strongholds. We need men for this; the Paphlagonians and Pelasgians have traditionally served us in this capacity. We cannot wield the heavy shields and arms that foot soldiers carry with the same ease that men can."

"But I saw your women on the training grounds," I said. "They bore their heavy burdens capably enough."

"True," said Penthesileia. "And they could overcome an average man in combat. But to go against an equally well-trained man, as most infantry soldiers are, is another matter. Our strength lies in our use of horses, our mobility."

I reconciled myself to the delay facing me, recognizing the naïveté of my previously held estimation of this enterprise. In fact, I now realized that, even if the war council decided to take up arms, the assembling of the armies, the logistics, and coordination entailed in all this, to say nothing about the slower-moving infantry units, undoubtedly would amount to even greater deferments. I failed to grasp the sheer scope and complexity of this operation and, in my ignorance and impatience, minimized its requirements.

"I understand," I said, resolved to accepting the realities facing me.

"You need not worry about Troy, my dear," Penthesileia then said, lightening my burdens. "Agamemnon will remain in his stalemate. Priam will not launch his assault against the Greeks until they have divided their forces to counter us. We control the situation now."

"My queen sounds certain that she will get the approval necessary," I said.

"Believe me when I say the issue is decided," she answered with a confidence that left me feeling quite elated. I wanted to hug her in my joy but refrained from it in deference to the protocol governing my standing with her. There was no need to exhibit my delight, as both the queen and Antiope readily perceived it, their wide smiling at each other denoting this to me. I had succeeded.

CHAPTER V

A RECOGNIZABLE ROUTINE ESTABLISHED ITSELF FOR me in the days
that I waited for the war council to assemble. I arose in the mornings
to dine with Menodice and Thalia—Penthesileia was never there at
breakfast, always getting up before me, even when I thought I got up earlier
than was usual for me—after which I was met by Antiope, and we rode out
together to see the various sights. She always brought Zephyrus to me, and
I grew increasingly fond of him, wanting even to own him. I participated
in doing physical exercises at the training grounds, where we spend all our
mornings, and became quite skillful at the bow and arrow, although firing my
missiles from a standing position rather than on Zephyrus. Under Antiope's
tutelage, I began to significantly improve my aim, and soon I was hitting the
targets with great accuracy, relishing the exhilaration that accompanies such
accomplishments. We typically partook of a meal while still there, where I
came to know many of the Amazons by name and enjoyed my raillery with
them, and then went on to visit Agenor and my escort soldiers, still frowned
upon by Antiope. I allowed Menodice and Thalia to spent their afternoons
with them, as I had no particular need for their services, the palace men
sufficing for our household tasks. My own afternoons remained usually in
the accompaniment of Antiope. She took me to a variety of artistry shops,
where I learned to make my own clothes—something never taught to me at
Troy—mostly of leather material and very durable.

As I think of clothes, I will mention that I now dressed as the Amazons, at least during the day, still preferring my lighter linen and woolen chitons for the evenings. Antiope gave me some of their wear, and admittedly, the shorter tunics worn by them, which only reached halfway down the thighs and were made of sturdy cotton, stood better suited for riding horses, as were the calf-high leather boots. I had two sets of tunics, one white, the other red, and a squared, brown woolen cloak with a hole in it for slipping over my head so I could cover my upper body when colder winds came upon us. At first, I shunned the leather vests and skirts worn over the tunics, not being able to conceive myself as a warrior, until Antiope told me that they protected my body not only against weapons, but also from falls, especially if my horse took a spill. I thought of Pan when she said this.

I should perhaps also add that Antiope and I became intimate during this time. I suppose it had to be expected, for we were very fond of each other and soon realized this was leading us to a longing for more. It all came about one hot afternoon while we were hunting for deer in some distant woods, and we came across a small stream that had an inviting deeper end along one section of its run. Antiope suggested that we plunge into the water to cool off as well as wash the dust from our bodies. I cannot forget the sensations I felt as she removed her clothes and stood naked next to me. She was so lovely to behold, and I felt goose bumps all over me. My heartbeat accelerated to an incredibly fast pace, and a hot-and-cold tingling enveloped me. She then took hold of my garment and slipped it over my body, leaving me in full exposure before her—the intensity of my anticipation rose to a feverish pitch—and it was at this point, with our proximity to each other, that our lips met. We then pursued this initial contact with gentle caresses and tender fondling. And so we spent the rest of the day in blissful, impassioned embraces, relishing the sheer pleasure of our time together to its fullest extent. We did not return until near nightfall and never did get our deer.

Once we had taken that first step, there appeared to be no adequate justification for further reservations about our urges, and we saw no merit in withholding what we so much desired. Consequently, our intimacy soon occupied the following night. I will not mention what we did, except to say that I found the overall experience most enjoyable and was gratified for having undergone it. I do not think I could have done this with anyone except Antiope. She enflamed in me an unbelievable excitement, combined with an intense longing, over her touching me, and I simply melted into total submission under her spell. I had no control of my emotions in her presence.

I sometimes had the feeling that Penthesileia also very much desired me, for she never lost that warm glow in her eyes when looking upon me and seemed particularly to enjoy my companionship in the evenings. Yet she placed no other demands on me except that I keep her company when we ate our late meals. Perhaps she knew what was happening between Antiope and me and, in her wisdom, meant to spare her leading commander the pain any such request might have on her. I think I also loved Penthesileia, but in a different sort of way. She was very much like a mother to me—tolerant of my erroneous conceptions, nurturing me in my proper etiquette and mannerism, assuring my understanding of the things she related to me, and ever concerned about my general well-being. As the time for her war council neared, I began to have troubling thoughts about how much I was going to miss her when all this was completed.

Finally, the day of the scheduled conference had arrived. It's coming was heralded by an influx of numerous dignitaries, identified to me by Antiope as we observed them from the palace. Kings and their generals, Amazon chieftains, priests and priestesses, all coming into Themiscyra under the banners signifying their realms.

"Come, Polyxena," Penthesileia told me as she was headed for the council hall. "You will sit beside me during the proceedings. I have already requested that Agenor also be there."

The honored position, I thought to myself, reminded of what Agenor had told me.

"Yes, my queen," I replied as I hurriedly ran up to her.

We entered the hall, where everyone was standing waiting on the queen's arrival, and moved to its far end, passing the throng on both sides of us, until we took to our chairs located there. I saw Agenor at the front of the group only a few paces from me. I was seated to the left of the queen while Antiope sat on her opposite side. Lycus, a somewhat portly, short man with snow white hair and beard, stood directly in front of us.

After the introductory formalities were dispensed, Penthesileia announced to the group the nature of my father's request for assistance, the reasoning and necessity behind it, and the ramifications it held for them, and it became clear that her explanation left them in sobering contemplation. For the longest time, nobody said anything at all, all being absorbed in their deliberations, until Penthesileia, grim in countenance, again spoke out.

"I do not believe," she said, "that Agamemnon will stop his policy of expansionism. Priam is correct in asserting that our own kingdoms will be next on his list of regions to conquer if he succeeds in taking Troy."

"Not if Agamemnon expends his army in the effort as it so appears to us," one of the kings declared. "Let his weakened force come. If we stand united against him, he will not conquer us."

"Perhaps, but the point is, if we confront him now, while he is committed to the siege of Troy, we enhance our chance to defeat him, more than if we later face him by ourselves, even if we are united. This is the time to strike."

"The risks are great, my queen," said another king.

"So is the opportunity. If we miss it, we shall never have it again. We will never forgive ourselves."

There ensued a considerable debate among the assembly's members, separate groups squabbling among themselves at length, until finally one of the kings again spoke out.

"We realize the potential gains, great queen," he boomed forth loudly, clearly trying to dominate the floor. "But we believe its uncertainty is of greater concern than our assurance that we can later face Agamemnon if united."

"What is there to lose?" Penthesileia then said. "If we attack now, we can inflict severe damage to his forces, thereby assuring ourselves that he will no longer be able to threaten us. Were Troy to fall, we would spend much of our lives worrying about the future threat he poses for us. Believe me, that threat will always be there."

This again sparked a lively debate among everyone. This time I felt that Penthesileia's argument had significant weight, as it was eminently logical and could hardly be denied. I sensed things were going our way.

"You bring out a good point," the other king said. "But how do we even know that he means to dominate us?"

"Let us be realistic," answered Penthesileia. "He came to Troy. How far is that from Mycenae?"

"He had provocation. The Trojan, Paris, violated the accords existing among nations by abusing the hospitality of King Menelaus, his brother, when he took the Spartan's wife."

I winced as I heard this, yet I could not claim that such was not the case.

"What are you telling me?" Penthesileia asked. "That you would wage a war over the loss of a woman?"

"No ordinary woman, my queen. They say the Spartan queen is the most beautiful woman that ever lived."

"My question to you remains the same," said Penthesileia, unimpressed. "Would any of us wage a war over her? Of course not. This just confirms what we already know: the war is being fought to fulfill Agamemnon's aims at aggrandizement. He wants power, the power to rule over all the kingdoms within his grasp. As my Trojan princess, here, told me a few days ago, he must be taught that he is not invincible." She then looked at me and added, "I like that."

"We are asked to go to war over a condition that does not presently exist," the same king said, "for the sake of one that may exist in the future. I prefer to act upon the facts facing us today than on your conjectures about what happens tomorrow."

"So you may," Penthesileia told him. "But it does not resolve the question of our security, for you now place your future safety in the hands of others rather than in the measures we ourselves can take to guarantee this for us. I prefer to be the master of my own house."

This quieted the king. I was amazed at Penthesileia's ability to counter the arguments thrown her way. She was a sight to behold, calmly gazing over the assembly as she shifted her eyes from person to person, exuding confidence, very much in charge. I saw that Agenor was likewise impressed by her performance.

"We have all benefited from Troy's hegemony over our regions," she went on. "Our trades have flourished, unimpeded by levies that could have been imposed, and we have had no infringements on our autonomy, being essentially free to do what we want. My personal view is that I owe some measure of gratitude to King Priam for this. I would indeed be ungracious if I turned my back on him in his hour of need."

"My queen, your sentiment is of no concern to us," the king declared, reasserting a position of authority that he must have felt he had momentarily lost. "Our participation in this war must be based on the advantages such actions will obtain for us."

"Then it is your self-interest we speak of," said Penthesileia. "Maintaining our alliance is of benefit to you, for we have both profited from this. So if we now decide to counter the threat facing it and see it in our favor to meet the challenge immediately while our enemy is engaged with another adversary, thereby minimizing our own risks in the venture, the advantage this offers us should be obvious to you. Clearly, it is in your interest."

She is brilliant, I thought to myself. How thoroughly and completely she dominated the proceedings, indisputably trouncing her opposition and leaving them sulking in their defeat. Agenor and I looked upon each other in our sheer admiration of her.

"You all know," Penthesileia continued, "I do not like the Greeks. My dealings with them have never been to my satisfaction. They flaunt their alleged superiority over us, declaring us to be barbarians and thinking it beneath their dignity to conduct proper relations with us. I say to you, it is time to put them in their place. Let them feel the stings of the arrows we barbarians will inflict upon them."

This brought forth a resounding cheer from the audience, especially from her Amazon compatriots who evidently read more into her message than mere derision, I believe, and saw it rather as a denunciation of the enemy's assault on their womanhood. I glanced at Antiope. She returned my gaze with a glint of joy reflected in her eyes that told me she was highly inspirited by Penthesileia's declarations. No more doubt remained with me that my mission had been accomplished.

At this juncture, Penthesileia informed Lycus to receive the vote on her proposed actions. All the Amazon commanders heartily shouted out their approval, as did the allied kings, but in a more subdued tone. Enthusiasm ran high, very much as if an eagerness for battle had taken hold of them— no, intoxicated them—and filled them with so much fervor toward its implementation that no sober reflection or deliberation on the seriousness of its nature could constrain them.

Penthesileia leaned toward me, beaming in her smile and saying, "You must have greater faith in what I tell you. Did I not say the issue was decided?"

I simply looked at her, quite awestruck not only over how magnificently she had managed the assembly, but also over her perception of my earlier qualms about her abilities to do so. I did not think my reservations were apparent, for I thought I had repressed these sufficiently enough as to be undetected. But she saw through this and was correct in saying that I lacked the trust in her that I should have had. Truly Penthesileia was a remarkable woman, a queen in every respect.

The resolution to take up an offensive against the Greeks transformed Themiscyra into a hub of ceaseless activity. Weaponry had to be forged and amassed, armor had to be fitted and tested, both physical and unit training were accelerated and refined, and warriors drilled in their formations and exercised battlefield maneuvers, stressing their responsiveness to commands. Provisions of food, primarily sun-dried strips of meat and hard-baked bread, were accumulated, as well as water containers, either of clay or pouches made from animal parts, which were loaded aboard the carts—there must have been over a hundred of them parked along every street and square of the city—accompanying the army on its move. They were packed with tent and all the associated equipment that went with this—the ropes, stakes, cots, benches, chairs, and tables—nothing was omitted, not even tableware. All the preparation was directed toward the conduct of a long, sustained military operation.

Interestingly enough, Penthesileia directed Agenor and the escort soldiers with him to train some of her Amazon units in infantry combat skills, a task they took up with expedient relish, for the boredom of their nonproductive existence at the outskirts of the city surely had gotten the best of them, and they craved to do something more useful. Agenor was the perfect individual to lead such training, as his skill and courage at Troy was known to many, and as a consequence, the women under his tutelage, in spite of their indoctrination that led them to regard men with scorn, were impressed enough to readily submit to his lessons. As it chanced, Antiope and I rode up to the area where this training was taking place. I was on Zephyrus—what a horse! He so easily responded to my commands that I could have led him without uttering a single word, just by small motions of my hand or body. We saw Agenor, shield and weapon in hand, demonstrating to a rather hefty woman the maneuverings in dodging the thrusts and blows from a sword. Upon seeing us near him, he stopped his work to cheerfully welcome us.

"Give my thanks to your queen, Antiope," he said. "This is a better use of my time than anything else I've done since coming here."

"I wouldn't have granted you this favor, man," said Antiope. "There is nothing that we can learn from you."

"Oh, no?" answered Agenor. "Would you care to test that?"

Antiope, her lovely face contorted in a sneer, eyed Agenor with obvious contempt and then dismounted.

"We shall see, man," she said as she took the shield and sword from one of the students and moved forward to face him. "Teach me something."

"Make your move," Agenor said. We all were watching with anticipated anxiousness, not knowing how this would play out. Who should I favor? I liked them both.

Instantly, Antiope lunged at him, the full force and weight of her body behind the stroke of the sword she carried. Agenor neatly parried her thrust with his own blade and next slammed his shield into Antiope's body as she tried to recover from her attack and sent her reeling under the impact. Somehow she managed to stay on her feet and again pounced on Agenor. Every blow she meant to strike him with was deftly blocked by either Agenor's own sword or shield. No matter how often Antiope tried to drive her weapon home, he evaded her swipes. Then he went on the offensive. Skillfully countering her every move to strike him, he bashed her shield with such powerful velocity that she was continuously forced backward under the hammering.

I became aware, as I was observing the spectacle, that, in spite of the appearance that this was an evenly matched contest, such was not the case. I had seen Agenor fight before the walls of Troy and had some knowledge of his moves in battle. There were clear instances in this duel where he could have rendered the decisive thrust, ending it. Instead, he permitted Antiope to regain her aggression, thwarting her counterstrokes blow for blow. It made for a spectacular presentation, without doubt enthralling the Amazons bearing witness to it, their enthusiasm clearly favoring their commander as they beamed, even cheered, when it appeared she made a significant blow, but it was wholly directed by him. In the end, it became obvious to everyone that Agenor was going to win the contest, but he secured his victory in such a benevolent style that he could not help but gain the admiration of his audience. He simply allowed the weight of the heavy shield and sword Antiope wielded to wear her out in exhaustion. While he still stood calmly by, Antiope fell to her knees, no longer able to lift either.

Casting aside his own shield and sword, Agenor stepped up to the spent Amazon and extended his right hand to her. She clasped it, and in one smooth pull, he lifted her back on her feet.

"You're quite a woman," he told her, grinning from ear to ear. "Did you learn anything?"

"I did," Antiope replied under her heavy breathing and then added, "Thank you, Agenor." For the first time, she addressed him by his name.

As Antiope and I rode off I was debating whether to inform her of my estimation of the contest they had just waged. I did not want to disillusion her about any conceptions she held over her effectiveness. To my great surprise, Antiope had come to the same conclusions I had arrived at earlier.

"Agenor spared me from humiliation," she told me. "I am grateful for that."

"So you know?" I asked.

"Yes. I saw it as I was fighting him. He avoided, or willingly did not carry through, the strikes that would have flattened me. He could have made me look extremely bad, and he chose not to."

"Agenor is the son of Antenor, wisest of my father's counselors, and demonstrates the same wisdom." I said. "He's a good man."

Antiope said nothing more on this, but I could see in her eyes that she was profoundly affected by today's event, as it seemingly turned her long-held ideas about men topsy-turvy. Her demeanor was one of someone wrestling with her deepest convictions and troubled over her discoveries. But perhaps I was misreading her. She may have been simply upset over having lost her confrontation with Agenor. At any rate, we rode the rest of the way back to the palace in silence, as I thought it best to leave her to her tribulations.

Upon arriving at our residence, I was told by Thalia that Penthesileia wished to see me in the council hall. I hurriedly proceeded there, and when I entered the building, I saw the queen seated by herself—no one else was present—in her regal chair.

"Come, sit by me, my dear," she greeted me.

I took my place beside her, warmly eyeing her and eager to hear what she had to say.

"It will take another week before we can begin our campaign," Penthesileia told me. "The delay is in large part due to our allied kings approaching this undertaking halfheartedly. I suspected such would be the case during our war council. They were noticeably reserved over our decision. I sincerely hope this does not create a problem for us."

"What can go wrong, my queen?"

"I am worried that, if we face adversities, they may lose their resolve in backing us. At worst, they may abandon the operation altogether. Let's hope not."

"But the day is set. It will proceed."

"Oh, yes. You need not doubt that."

With the commencement of the operation determined, I now felt it prudent to approach the matter of my continued stay at Themiscyra. I was most anxious to inform my father of what I had accomplished, that his faith in me was justified.

"Then I suppose," I began, "I should, by your leave, my lady, consider my departure. My father must know of this."

"That is what I wanted to talk to you about, Polyxena," Penthesileia said. "I desire that you accompany me on this campaign."

I was stunned, not only over the notion of endangering myself in the exposure to battle, but also because I could not conceive my company as having any further value to Penthesileia or for her Amazons. Indeed, I would have considered my continued presence more hindrance than help to them. And yet, there also was an alluring aspect to her request. But I could not determine why. Had I developed an affinity for their way of life? Was it the prospect of being with Antiope that much longer?

"Don't worry," Penthesileia said, evidently sensing my apprehensions. "You will be safe enough. We will place your tent well behind the lines, next to my headquarters, where my own advisor, Lycus, stays."

"But what would I do? I know nothing about warfare."

"Do not discredit your talents. You know more than you think. You are very precocious for one so young. I strongly believe that, in the course of this campaign, your observations will be of use to me."

She gave me that assured look, as if she knew what my answer would be.

Penthesileia had more faith in my abilities than I did. I could not see myself advising anyone when it came to battlefield tactics, being largely ignorant of these, and I questioned I there was another purpose behind her request.

"You have told me of your familiarity with some of the Greek commanders fighting before Troy," she said. "Do not underestimate the importance of this. These may be the same ones we will face."

While I would not have disputed this, it still seemed an insufficient reason for my being asked to accompany her expedition. I was now more concerned about how I would get word to Troy on our impending move.

"My father must be told, my lady," I said. "His own battle plan is contingent upon knowing this."

"I wouldn't worry much about Priam not finding out," Penthesileia told me. "He has his intelligence network to alert him. News of our success will certainly reach him. But if it will ease your conscience, Agenor can carry this message to him."

The thought of dividing up the small group I had with me never occurred to me, but now that it was presented to me, I believed it to have some merit. Without being encumbered by our equipment-laden carts, they could cover the distance on horseback in a considerably shorter period of time than it took us to get here. Even though I recognized that my father would not launch his counterstroke against Agamemnon until the Greek had divided his army to move against Penthesileia, which afforded us ample time, for it depended upon her triumphs, I still thought it best that he be apprised of the situation as early as possible. Who knows what other plans that would lead him to consider?

As the problem of notifying my father was no longer the paramount issue in my mind, I found myself brimming with excitement over the venture proposed to me. I had no adequate explanation for the sense of euphoria that came over me. It seemed to me that, if I had any sense at all, I should have feared the prospect, but I felt the exact opposite, avidly embracing its uncertainty and even looking forward to it. I think this may have been, in large measure, due to an inner wish that I might continue the companionship of Antiope and Penthesileia, women I have come to admire deeply, and share a major undertaking with them. Such are the events that impart everlasting imprints in our minds and are never forgotten.

"Will you consent to this?" Penthesileia asked me, snapping me out of my absorptions.

"Yes, my lady," I answered without any hesitation.

"Well then," Penthesileia said, smiling "you have made me very happy, my dear. It's quite late. Perhaps you should wait until tomorrow before informing Agenor of your decision. We don't want to ruin his sleep."

I laughed as I heard this, thinking that he would indeed be disappointed, especially as I intended to keep Menodice and Thalia with me. I did not want anything slowing him down on his return to Troy. But then, he was very wise and would readily understand my purpose in doing this. I wondered if I would miss him.

Penthesileia then excused me so she could continue her contemplations in solitude. She still refrained from asking me to accede to more personal matters, which somewhat puzzled me, for she made it obvious that she really liked me. I believed she knew what was going on between Antiope and I and chose to forego her own desires for the sake of maintaining her amity with her chief commander, but perhaps I am having flights of fancy here; she probably had no need for intimate relation. Can this be?

Regarding Antiope, we continued to spend more nights together in blissful repose, always in my chamber by mutual agreement, contented to be in each other's presence and savoring the sweetness of our intimacy. She was so alluring, her body exquisitely shaped— even you, Divine Goddess, might have stood in envy of her—and I readily concede that I possessed no compunctions in my admiration of her beauty. That was when I was with her, intoxicated by her sensuousness and overwhelmed by the attraction this held for me, yet at other times, when I was by myself and soberly reflected over this, I severely censured myself for what I considered my aberrant behavior, casting disparagement upon my abuses and feeling a sense of shame over this. Then I would see her again, and all my self-doubting and aspersions would vanish as I once more fell under her charm. Such was the emotional turmoil in which I endured my relationship with Antiope, and yet, were I to have a choice over its continuance, I unquestionably would have preferred that this be so. That was the influence she exerted over me, the sheer appeal of it, pleasurable and insatiable, so that I was utterly seduced by it and in her captivity.

The morning after Penthesileia spoke with me, I rode out on Zephyrus to the guest quarters to meet with Agenor, my intention being to inform him that he must return as quickly as possible to Troy and of my continued stay with the Amazons. I met him there just as he was preparing to go to the training grounds for his daily drills.

"No Antiope?" he asked as I dismounted and approached him. "I've come to see you two as inseparable."

"The queen has her occupied this morning. I need to speak to you about a change of plans. Penthesileia has told me that she means to begin her operation six days. You must get word of this to King Priam."

"Just me? What about you?"

"She has requested that I accompany her on the campaign. She says I will be safe enough, and I believe her, but I won't be able to return to Troy in the foreseeable future. I can't go with you."

Agenor received the news with collected soberness.

"In six days," he said in his reflection. "Well, yes. I'd best prepare for the journey. I should probably leave this very day."

"That's what I was thinking," I told him.

"I expect Priam will be pleased over what you've done here, Polyxena, but I don't think he'll appreciate that you didn't return with me."

"I've little choice," I said, not exactly being honest. "When a queen wants something of you, you're obliged to obey her. Isn't that so?"

"I suppose," he answered, giving me an odd look. "What purpose can you possibly serve in doing this?"

"I'm not quite sure. She seems to think that my having seen some of the Greek leaders in action at Troy will have some importance to her."

"It could, but why would she prefer your company over mine? I actually fought with them and can better advise her on this."

Agenor brought up an interesting point. I pondered over this momentarily and concluded that Penthesileia must have deemed that, as an Amazon queen, she had to project the image of not being beholden to any man for counsel. But that did not make sense, as she was going to have Lycus there.

"I don't know," I told him, "but I thought it inappropriate to question her. I don't think my father will be offended as you do."

"Maybe not *offended* but certainly not happy."

"He'll understand."

"As you say. Who do I take with me?"

"Your mounted soldiers. On horseback, you should make good time. Leave the carts and their drivers behind, and take only the equipment you need with you. I'm sorry, but Menodice and Thalia will stay with me. Penthesileia's own servants will see to us."

Agenor briefly studied the situation and must have come to the same conclusion as I did earlier, for he seemed to understand the necessity of expeditiously delivering our message to Troy, and made no protestations over the urgency placed on him.

"I'll be ready to move out by noon," he said.

"Then I shall leave you to your preparations, but we'll want to see you off. Don't go before I return with Menodice and Thalia."

Agenor nodded his approval and assisted me in mounting Zephyrus. I rode back to the palace to inform my servant ladies of the condition I had imposed on them, not feeling altogether at ease over my determination without having at least warned them of it. But then, they were here to attend to me, so their continued presence, whether on the campaign or at home, fell within their duty requirements and was not open to discussion. As it turned out, my concerns were unnecessary, for both of them accepted their consignment without objections, their only disappointment being that they had to give up the friendships they had developed with the men. Menodice appeared particularly distraught over Agenor leaving, but she bore her sorrow in silence and consoled herself with expectations that she would again see him once we returned to Troy. *Oh Aphrodite. Your afflictions can be so painful.*

After I had informed Penthesileia and Antiope of Agenor's decision to depart this very day, both of them expressed their desire to see him off and joined me and my ladies as we walked to the quest quarters. By the time we got there, everything appeared in readiness for the journey. The morale among our escort soldiers seemed exceptionally high, with demonstrated expressions of eagerness and enthusiasm. They longed to get back to their own surroundings, to consort with fellow warriors, and to participate in the more meaningful missions they had been trained for and that better defined their existence. Agenor, on seeing us near him, stepped forward to directly face Penthesileia.

"My queen," he addressed her. "I am pleased you came by."

"I was honored by your visit, Agenor," replied Penthesileia. "Our duties have prevented us from getting closer, as it now requires you to leave us. Antiope and I want to thank you for the training you gave my warriors."

Agenor looked at Antiope, and she returned his glance with a faint smile and a nod of her head, an acknowledgment of her indebtedness to his previous discretion, a display that amply reflected the loveliness of her face so that he was quite transfixed in viewing it, delaying his attention toward the queen.

"If it helps our cause, my lady," he finally said, "then my efforts were well worth it."

"Ever the diplomat," Penthesileia said. "You may inform King Priam that we have targeted Ascania—in Phrygia—as our first objective. From there, we will proceed westward to reclaim the cities along the way, until we reach the Hellespont. This ought to agitate Agamemnon enough to initiate the move we expect. I shall return his Polyxena after our operation is completed."

Agenor bowed his head, saying nothing more, but expressively demonstrating his courtesy toward Penthesileia with this gesture. Following this exchange with the queen, Menodice, Thalia, and I mingled with our soldiers to give them their farewells and well wishes. There ensued an abundance of hugs and kisses, not to mention tears, as we said our good-byes. Agenor clearly revealed his sorrow over leaving Menodice, and the two of them clung tightly to each other while they whispered their parting words. I felt as an intruder when I came upon them to bid him a good journey.

"The gods grant us victory," I said to Agenor. "The matter is in their hands now. We have done all we could."

"Not we, *you*, Polyxena," he said. "King Priam will be so proud."

"I could not have done it without you. Give my regards to my mother and sisters and to Helen and Andromache. Tell them that I look forward to the day when I shall again see them."

"I will, princess," Agenor replied, and then he embraced me and gave me a gentle kiss on my lips. I was deeply affected by his action, being suddenly overwhelmed by the sense of loss his absence would hold for me, and felt my eyes moistening as he released himself from me. And with that, our farewell meeting came to a conclusion, leaving me feeling deeply saddened in its passing.

Agenor then directed his soldiers to mount up, and after having climbed onto their steed, they spurred them into a steady trot along the road leading west from Themiscyra. I stood there, silently watching them fade into the distance. Both Menodice and Thalia openly cried, while I tried to keep my own emotions in check by refraining from such an outburst. I could not help but wonder what Penthesileia and Antiope thought over our conduct and present grief. They had quietly observed our obvious sentimentality patently demonstrated, an exhibition so unfamiliar with their upbringing and indoctrination—perhaps even offensive to their taste—that their reaction to this either left them dumbfounded or feeling sorry for us, because, being weak and fragile, we succumbed so easily to the cheap emotionalism they inured themselves against. The thought crossed me that I may have diminished myself in their eyes, but when I looked at Antiope, she appeared to be quite sympathetic to my distress; her loving glance told me that perhaps she understood.

"Well, that's that," Penthesileia remarked, indicating her intention to return to the palace. "Agenor has his task to do, and we have ours." And so we began our walk back. I had recovered from the deep sorrow that previously afflicted me and was ready to greet the new realities facing me. Agenor was gone, and I missed him—and would continue to do so—but a larger phase of my mission lay ahead, and I was resolved to confront it.

CHAPTER VI

HE SIX DAYS FOLLOWING AGENOR's departure elapsed quickly for me, thanks to the mounting stimulation offered by the arrival and massing of the many elements constituting the Amazon army, now ready to move out. Everything stood in readiness, all preparations and provisioning having been completed, and exactly three weeks from the time the war council had approved this course of action, we initiated its onset. Joined by the infantry components of our allied kingdoms, the Paphlagonians and Pelasgians, each nearly an army in themselves, with the Amazons comprising the cavalry wing of the force, a formidable juggernaut was to descend upon the Greeks ruling over Ascania. We numbered twenty thousand strong, divided equally between the Amazon horse soldiers and their male counterparts, the alliance foot soldiers, and including a huge logistics element that supported both. Our spirits soared in our confidence that we would destroy the enemy and drive him from our lands.

I was in my royal cart, waiting for my place in the procession, when Penthesileia took her post at the head of the army, on horse and magnificently arrayed in her battlefield attire, with Antiope riding next to her, equally impressive in dress, as we departed Themiscyra. They wore their metallic breastplates, gray in hue, over their leather vests and red tunics, upon which was clipped a small, waist-length cloak, designating their command position, with their bronze helmets fastened to their saddles—they did not wear these at present—and their lower legs covered by greaves. All the Amazons were mounted—an enthralling spectacle—their quivers strapped to their backs and bows extending diagonally across their chests. Many of them also carried shields, which they presently attached to their saddles, as well as swords and axes that hung from waist belts. Some were also armed with spears, which they fastened to their horses as they marched, a novelty for them resulting from Agenor's training, Antiope told me.

Penthesileia's army was divided into squadron and division levels, each under its own identifiable banner and commanded by an officer who was responsible for the discipline and welfare of the warriors under her. Great prestige was attached to these positions, and only the most courageous and dedicated women, their skills and attributes proven in combat, could aspire to achieve them, or hold on to them. A common trait among these commanders, aside from their physical and mental toughness, was their contempt and loathing for the male gender, which, if recklessly exhibited, often alienated their allied soldiers. Restraint had to be exercised by them whenever the Amazons marched with, as they now did, an alliance contingent.

As for the infantry arm of our force, this was filled by the male warriors provided by the allied kings and led by their appointed generals, Borales of the Paphlagonians and Lethus of the Pelasgians. Contrary to what the chroniclers had told us, Penthesileia maintained an amiable relationship with the kingdoms surrounding her. Always practical, she knew that the security of her own domain rested in large part on the strength of her neighboring monarchs, and she accordingly bolstered them through various compacts, arranging for alliances to promote each other's defenses as well as improving trade. She well understood that her horse soldiers were ill suited for certain tasks and, to succeed in such operations, a powerful infantry was necessary. These warriors were armed with heavy weaponry— massive shields covering most of their body, long spears, clubs, and swords—and when clad in their own armor and helmets, they bore a load nearly equal to their own weight. Such a burden placed the Amazons at a disadvantage, which, in spite of all their intensive training, worked against their effectiveness.

At first, I proceeded on the march in my royal cart, accompanied by Menodice and Thalia, which trailed the fighting units, moving with the wagons of the supporting elements, carrying the provisions and materials necessary for conducting a sustained campaign. But shortly into the expedition, Penthesileia requested that I ride alongside her and Antiope from then on. I was never more happy to see Zephyrus than when Antiope brought him to me, and I felt absolutely certain that the stallion regarded me in the same way, for he truly responded wonderfully to my control of his reins, its familiarity being received with utmost contentment. Few moments in my life can compare with the sheer elation that swept over me as I rode with Penthesileia and Antiope at the head of our column. I felt I was one of the commanders of that mighty host, a thrill unmatched in all my worldly experiences, pride and satisfaction all in one, a sublime sense of power and strength.

As on the journey to Themiscyra, which seemed ages ago, I found the most pleasurable of our times to be those evening hours after we had settled into our encampment, following a long day's march, when we all sat around the fires to eat and talk and enjoy the company we kept. My tent was pitched adjacent to Penthesileia's headquarters, which also served as her and Antiope's sleeping quarters, where I and both Menodice and Thalia stayed. I could feel a burning sensation on my face after my long exposure to the sun—something I avoided earlier when I spent most of the day in the shade of my cart—but I was quite happy despite this and very much enjoyed the merriment we engaged in.

I finally got to know Lycus during our evening chats, and he and I took an immediate liking to each other. He reminded me very much of Antenor, not quite as old, but exhibiting the same sort of mannerisms that characterize those possessed of great intellect—the deliberations over what was heard, as if digesting things word for word, pointing out the options available on every issue, and rarely fixed on a single interpretation. When he told me on the first night into our march that he was married to an Amazon, my confusion was evident to everyone in the company seated around me.

"You have an Amazon wife?" I said in my astonishment. "Are you a masochist? How does that contribute to any domestic tranquility?"

My comment drew laughter out of Penthesileia and Antiope who seemed to get pleasure out of observing my obvious perplexity.

"No, no, my dear," Lycus replied. "We are quite in love. I've now been married to her for nearly twenty years."

"She was smitten by Aphrodite's spell," Penthesileia added. "We meant to banish her, but Lycus interceded on her behalf, and so we permitted their marriage. Even we cannot deny the workings of the goddess."

"And they reside in Themiscyra?" I asked.

"Oh, yes," Lycus answered. "We are both happy in our circumstance."

"Doesn't your presence there stand out as an exposition for the other Amazons that an alternative way of living exists for them?"

Lycus deferred answering this to Penthesileia who said, "Ordinarily, you would think that, but these occurrences are so rare that we can afford to abide them. In general, we don't see it as a failure of our teachings. Our women are very much Amazons."

So another myth about the Amazons was shattered for me, but it also confirmed what else Agenor had said about them: they were very content with their lot and unlikely to give up their lifestyle. That their top leadership tolerated the occasional abandonment of their lifelong indoctrination surely stood as proof of that.

This was typical of the conversations we held during successive nights in that I gained an increasing knowledge of things I knew little or nothing about and found myself absorbed in the illuminations presented. I do admit that the Amazon way of life was not without its appeal. They were very much in charge of their own affairs and did not depend on a man to lead them. Could this be why Penthesileia wanted me to accompany her? Did she see in me a potential member of her horde?

My nights with Antiope became restrictive as a result of our lack of privacy due to having to share our tents with others, me with Menodice and Thalia and she with her queen and two other generals. In fact, we had only one occasion to engage in loving intimacy when she stole into my tent late at night after everyone had fallen asleep. Our difficulty was that the rigors of the day placed such a demand on the necessity for sleep that we found ourselves beleaguered with extreme weariness when we failed to get it. Despite this, we enjoyed our companionship, even if not sexual, and remained quite content with our situation.

On the fourth day after leaving Themiscyra, we arrived at Ascania, a city by a nearby lake bearing the same name, lying amid the expansive, treeless plains that comprised much of Phrygia, and we were amazed that the gates to the city were thrown open for us without as much as even token resistance being offered. When Penthesileia entered the city, she was greeted by the local lord and his entourage.

"Where are the Greeks?" she asked them. "We were told they occupied your city."

"There was a small regiment of them here," answered the lord. "When they saw your army coming, they fled."

"You allowed a small number of them to dominate you?"

"We did what we thought prudent, my lady. They presided over us under the threat of massive retaliation if we did not submit to them."

Penthesileia regarded the lord's answer as without having much credence, and I could detect the contempt she held for what appeared to be an obvious display of cowardice on the part of the city's leadership.

"You call yourselves allies of Troy?" she berated him. "King Priam deserves better than this. You allowed mere words to intimidate you. What sort of support will you give him now that we have you back under his sphere?"

She had shamed him. He stood red faced before her, momentarily at a loss for words, until at last they came to him, and he profusely apologized for his remissions.

"We will do our part in driving out the invader, my queen," he said among other things. "If Priam requests our assistance, we will provide it. We have soldiers to send him."

However unimpressed she may have been by the lord's answer, Penthesileia thought it best to let the issue rest and made no more allusions to it. Instead, she assumed a much friendlier posture as she declared certain requests of her own upon Ascania's officials.

"We will camp outside your city before marching on. Perhaps you could provide us with hot food and drink in the time we are here."

"Willingly, my queen," their lord said, pleased that no more signs of derision were sent his way.

We stayed at Ascania for two days, recuperating from the aches and pains inflicted upon our bodies from riding day after day, resting up our horses, and visiting the sights the city had to offer under the escort of our hosts. On the second evening, we received an invitation to dine at the royal palace. Eight of us attended, including Penthesileia, Antiope, Lycus, and I, along with the generals of the allied armies. The meal, served to us as we were entertained by musicians and dancers, was a wonderful respite to the hardships the rigors of the march imposed on us and was highly appreciated. By the time it was concluded, I am sure the local ruler felt himself purged of his earlier indignation and back in Penthesileia's good graces. The comforts of civilized life had its attraction. I think I missed Troy more that night than at any other time I was with the Amazons.

We resumed our march on the following morning, the open meadows now more hilly but still stretching before us as far as the eye could see, and two days later, we came upon Otrea, another Phrygian city that was taken by the Greeks earlier in the war and that now stood as a major defensive site for them in the region. We knew when we saw it, with its large number of stationed troops in evidence, both on its walls and on patrols outside, that this city was not going to simply bow down to our coming as Ascania did and that we faced a serious battle in taking it.

We set up our camp some distance from the city and waited through the rest of the day until all our units were merged. No engagement would commence on this day, but we expected that, in the morning, both our own and the enemy's army would be assembled across the field facing the city's northern wall. Penthesileia called for a meeting of the chief commanders that night, and they formulated the battle plan. I sat in on the conference and again found myself awed by her authority over the matters at hand, unflinching in her exercise of power over her cohorts and in total control. The upshot of her plan was that she would use a feigned retreat by the allied infantry to lure the enemy force forward, and after they did so, she was going to use her cavalry to hammer it from both flanks. To make the bait more enticing, she would hide the bulk of her Amazons behind the low-lying hills around Otrea, leading the Greeks to underestimate her strength. Her tactics invoked considerable praise from those present, and when the meeting finally ended, everyone was brimming with confidence over tomorrow's outcome.

That morning, just as we had anticipated, the Greek force, enhanced by its local auxiliaries, moved forth from behind Otrea's walls and took up its battle formation in a long line of warriors with a depth of six to eight rows. We countered their deployment by assembling our infantry along a solid line, facing them, although only three rows deep. Penthesileia positioned herself at the head of the Amazon cavalry on the right, while Antiope led the one on the left, each with only a fraction of their force under them— too few to be viewed as a threat to the enemy commanders—while the remainder waited some distance away, out of sight. With all in readiness and both armies facing each other, the captains of each side rode forward to the middle of the field for the traditional conferring that preceded any battle. I do not know what was said between them, as I watched from some way off—I was at the headquarters tent with Lycus—but the meeting was of short duration, and its participants soon returned to their own lines.

"What do they talk about " I asked Lycus.

"Oh, just basic introductions, to see the leaders they're facing," Lycus said. "Mostly they make assessments of each other, as if that gives them insight into their fighting abilities."

Penthesileia would shine if that was the case, I thought. She excelled in exuding confidence, and her self-possession often was intimidating. The enemy commander ought to be shaking in his boots.

No sooner had the leaders returned to their own ranks when the air was pierced by blares of trumpets, the signal that spurred the lines into their advance. Our infantry stepped out in a solid front, each soldier's shield touching another's shield, with spears protruding between them, appearing as an impenetrable moving wall. The Greeks likewise moved ahead, but when they came within a hundred or so paces of our line, they began to run at full speed toward it, and in so doing, they disrupted the cohesion of their formations. In a horrific clash of arms, the two sides collided, the impact startling even us who viewed it from a distance.

Like a battering ram, the Greeks rushed upon our wall of warriors, shield crashing into shield, hurling their spears and swinging their swords, slashing at exposed limbs and hacking at opponents who countered them stroke for stroke. Blood gushed forth from horrid wounds, spear points penetrated flesh, skulls were smashed, and the cries of agony amid cheers of triumph rose throughout the carnage. Men collapsed in pools of their own blood, shrieking out in their death throes, writhing in pain as they were trampled by their cohorts advancing over them. I saw a spear protruding from the mouth of a soldier as he fell, another had his head severed from a sword that slashed him in the neck. Some, as they were dying, clung to their opponent's shield, dragging it down so their compatriots could slay him. The scene was horrifying to behold and yet incredibly engrossing in its intensity.

Under the severe hammering, our infantry, while able to keep their line intact, regressed steadily, stepping farther and farther backward toward our own positions. Then, one and all, as if on cue, they turned about and began running from the field. The Greeks, believing victory in their grasp, hastily pursued them, their formations now in complete disarray. I was actually witnessing our battle plan reveal itself in front of me, yet the situation seemed confusing, and I was not entirely certain if such was the case.

"Are we losing the battle?" I asked Lycus.

"No," he answered without hesitation. "Watch what happens next."

At that moment, I heard the hoofbeats of thousands of horses as Penthesileia's Amazons from the right and Antiope's from the left, now fully merged, entered the fray, a sight that had me holding my breath. At breakneck speed, they thundered across the field toward their opposition, now scattered into small groups, catching them off guard, and cut them down wherever they stood. Soldiers on foot had little chance against mounted warriors, and our Amazons made short work of them as they rode into the masses, firing arrows at first and then hacking them with swords and clubs.

Penthesileia led her horse to crash into one of the enemy generals. He used his body and shield to trip the animal, and both horse and rider plummeted to the earth. The queen got up, shield in hand, and rushed upon the commander, still reeling under the impact of their collision, and they met in deadly combat, thrusting and parrying their swords, deflecting blow after blow with their shields. Just when it appeared he was getting the best of her—my heart pounded at triple pace—Antiope rode up and struck the general in the leg with her lance. As he staggered under the pain, Penthesileia thrust her sword into his neck with an upward stroke. He fell heavily to the earth, dead before striking it.

While my eyes focused on the action between Penthesileia and her assailant, similar scenes echoed all across the battlefield as horses and riders collided with soldiers on the ground and cut them down where they stood. In most cases, the Amazons merely galloped past them, firing their arrows with lethal accuracy, usually striking them in the face or neck, but often enough, a soldier managed to throw off a rider or cause a horse to stumble, and in the ensuing encounter, if the rider was not disabled in the fall, the soldier killed her or was killed himself. And while the Amazons were inflicting their damage, our infantry did an about-face and rejoined the slaughter, leading to a total breakdown of discipline among the Greeks. Now faced with destruction, many of the enemy soldiers dropped their weapons and shields and ran from the field. Those who chose to continue fighting met certain death, as they were hastily dispatched from assailants attacking them both from their front and from their rear. With all hope of victory gone, some of the defenders gave up the fight and surrendered to us.

Before the morning was half spent, the battle at Otrea was over. We had triumphed, but I did not feel the sense of exhilaration over this as I had believed I might. For one thing, we had incurred considerable losses, especially in our infantry component, which took the brunt of the fighting, and that is always dispiriting. But there occurred another event in the aftermath of the battle that shocked me to the core. I am loath to relate it, but it happened and needs to be told.

After the fighting had ended, both sides went about the gruesome work of amassing the dead, human and animal, tending to the wounded who were brought to the medical stations now abundantly placed about the field, and collecting the weapons scattered all over. As this was going on, perhaps as many as two hundred Greek prisoners, stripped of their armor and hands tied behind their backs, were lined up in several rows before Penthesileia and her commanders, including Antiope. Lycus and I came upon the scene just as the Greeks were ordered to get on their knees while an Amazon, knife in hand, stood directly behind each one of them. I looked with alarm upon the captives, fearing what was about to ensue. Some of them were but boys, handsome to behold, with a frightened look in their eyes.

"No," I cried out as I neared Penthesileia. "You can't do this!"

She gave me a harsh look, as if I had severely infringed upon a sacred ritual, a breach of protocol, an undermining of her authority.

Then she turned her eyes away and, with the wave of her hand, directed the women to slit the throats of the prisoners in front of them. I heard the gurgling sounds of their blood entering their windpipes, their coughing and gagging, and saw their eyes roll back into their sockets before they slumped to the ground. I stood aghast at what I had seen. Tears came to me, and I confronted Penthesileia weeping uncontrollably.

"How could you do this?" I wept. "I don't believe this!"

"They were Greeks!" she nearly shouted at me. "Our enemies! We do not mourn over our enemies."

"They surrendered to you!" I lashed out. "They placed their lives in your keeping. You owed them your protection!"

"Do not try to lecture me, foolish woman," Penthesileia stormed, startling me with her bitterness. "What would you have me do, release them so they can fight us again? Yes, I could have crippled them or blinded them, rendered them incapable of fighting, but what kind of life would that be for them? It is better that they died here. I asked you to accompany us because I believed you had what it takes to be one of us. I was wrong. You will never be an Amazon."

Her reproach silenced me, but I was still not able stop my weeping, and all I could think of doing at the moment was to run away from it all, wishing I had never seen what I had, but before leaving, I had to say more.

"If this is what it means to be an Amazon," I said through my tears, "then yes, I could never be one of you." And with that, I walked away, but not without first glancing at Antiope who stood silently by and lowered her head upon seeing me, as if embarrassed over all that had transpired.

I continued to sulk in my tent throughout the rest of the day and even late into the evening, resolved to forego my meal. I did not know how to face Penthesileia after my emotional outburst and tried to rationalize my conduct as appropriate although now beset with much doubt over it. The reason for the queen being here was to assist Troy in winning the war— what she was doing favored us—and I was out of line to condemn her actions and possibly jeopardize her helping us. I was so appalled over the killings, the sheer cruelty of it, that I could not erase the image from my mind. The fear-ridden look in the eyes of the victims before the slaughter commenced will hound me for the rest of my life.

In my duress, I failed to notice that someone had entered my tent and walked up to where I was sitting, staring blankly at the tent wall but seeing nothing. When I suddenly realized I was not alone, I turned my head and saw Penthesileia standing there. Our eyes met, and I became overwhelmed with deep remorse over what I had done earlier that day.

"I'm so sorry, my lady," I said, fighting my resurgent tears again. "I had no right to speak to you like that."

Penthesileia sat down beside me on my cot.

"You are still so young, Polyxena," she said, her warm glow returning to her eyes. "But in your innocence, you have given us a lesson that deeply touched us."

"What does my lady mean?"

"You are a Trojan princess, and yet you wept over the fate of the Greeks. You did not see them as your enemy?"

I paused before answering, not having perceived my actions in that context.

"No," I then said, "not as they were, bound up and helpless. All I saw were frightened boys, someone's sons. They were all so young."

I think I detected moistness coming to Penthesileia's eyes, for she seemed sadly affected by my words.

"Such empathy," she said. "You are very much a woman."

"I regret my weakness, my lady."

"Weakness?" Penthesileia pondered, then continued. "No, I see wisdom, and kindness, in you. You have shown us something today. You placed the humane side of us above our baser instincts. Perhaps it is better to temper war's brutality with some mercy."

I fell into her embrace, and we both wept while comforting each other. I think I loved her more at that time than ever before. Penthesileia longed for the gentler feminine touch, which, I believe, she equated with the possession of a deeper sensitivity, a sentimentality that was missing, or at the least suppressed, among her warrior women by the method of their upbringing and training. She appeared to have found that in me, and I felt gratified that my presence should bring out this quality in her.

"Come, my dear," she said. "Let us join our campfire. You must have something to eat."

Together we left the tent and walked over to the fire, where the rest of our group sat by, partaking of their meals. A silence hung about as we took our place among them, sitting next to Lycus. I saw all eyes riveted on me. At first, I felt embarrassment. I thought they were still angry over my condemnation of the queen's actions. But as I looked at each of them in turn, and especially Antiope, I sensed in their gazes that they held an admiration for me. Everyone smiled at me, and when Penthesileia handed me a wine cup, they all exuberantly commenced their chatter, many expressing their pleasure at having me back in attendance. Their welcome made me feel as one of them again, and I had no further reservations in abstaining from relishing the food placed in front of me.

"We're delighted to see you," Lycus said, gleaming in his grin. "Your absence put us in a depressive mood. Nobody felt like talking. But see? Everyone's happy now."

I stroked Lycus on his bearded chin, smiling at him, and, by this simple gesture, evoked an unspoken approval from all who saw me. I believed myself back in everyone's good graces, and this left me feeling secure and comfortable as the rest of the evening enfolded us.

We stayed at Otrea for an entire week, requiring that length of time to consolidate the fruits of our victory. As the local kingship had, in great measure, been replaced by the Greeks who meant to acquire a permanent hold over the region in order to prevent its allegiance from reverting to Troy, no hierarchy existed to maintain control over the populace. Penthesileia called for numerous meetings to resolve the matter of leadership, to arrive at a consensus over who should be the next ruler, and, once one was selected, to assure his commitment to our effort in support of Troy. For the people, the issue was much simpler. They had been under Troy's dominion before, remembering it as a prosperous time for them, and to learn that they were back under it posed no difficulties for them. Most still retained their loyalty to Priam. We also replenished our depleted food supplies, although less was needed now because of the more frequent cities in closer proximity to each other. The strength of our force was not yet a critical concern, in spite of the casualties we sustained in taking Otrea, but could become one as the campaign continued, so we recruited a volunteer complement of warriors to augment our infantry, which we kept on call for future use. Thus preoccupied, the time at Otrea passed quickly for us.

During at least three of the nights we spent there, Antiope and I resumed our intimate companionship. The matter was still a delicate one, for we stayed in our tents rather than at the palace, not knowing from day to day if we would move on, and I had to assure myself that Menodice and Thalia were asleep, even though a curtain separated my space from theirs, before letting Antiope share my bed with me. They probably knew, and I often berated myself for taking precautions that may have been unnecessary, but I thought it best that our affair remain discreet, in perception if not in fact, so that a deniability could be claimed if an issue arose out of it. I was certain that Penthesileia knew, even though Antiope never alluded to it. At any rate, we conducted our affair in silence, to the extent this was possible, savoring the sweetness of our contact for much of the night, until she slipped back to her own tent while still dark.

I also spent much of my days with her as we rode from area to area, checking on the progress of things, namely, overlooking the various tasks Penthesileia allocated to her warriors each morning, such as refurbishing weapons, caring for the horses, loading the supply wagons with new provisions, and so on. We were such perfect friends, not only in that we could talk about everything and everyone, but it was as if we were also able to read each other's minds and often knew ahead of time what the other was going to say. Only once did we talk about my behavior after the battle.

"She was very upset with you," Antiope said of her queen. "I have rarely, if ever, seen her so angry."

"Yes," I said. "It frightened me."

"We did what we had to do."

"I suppose so, but don't lie to me, Antiope; you didn't feel good about it. I looked at you and saw that you were very much shaken up by it."

"No," Antiope said, lowering her eyes as if ashamed. "I don't know. You have caused me to question it. Had I not met you, I doubt I ever would have. I was more certain of things before I met you, or Agenor."

"So you disapproved of what I did."

Antiope appeared lost in her deliberation, hesitating in answering me, and her uncertainty discernable in the teariness that came to her eyes.

"No," she finally said. "I loved you all the more for it."

I looked at Antiope, deeply moved by her divulgence, but I saw that the confession came awkwardly for her, as she was wrestling with her internal demons and knew she did not favor prolonging the discussion. Instead, I nudged Zephyrus into a gallop, and we rode off to our next work site.

CHAPTER VII

O
N THE EIGHTH DAY AFTER the battle fought at Otrea, we resumed our march and proceeded for Pedasus, a city in Mysia, very formidable in appearance, as it was atop a cliff side adjacent to a river, with its main gate and walls actually below it. It had been conquered by Achilles a few years ago and was now garrisoned by a sizeable Greek detachment in order to keep it under the enemy's dominion. We arrived there two days later and set up our encampment within sight of the city's citadel, making no pretensions about our purpose for being there and announcing our presence in this preponderant way in order to induce fear and consternation among its inhabitants. Whether we accomplished this was not known to us at the time; however, as it happened, one of the Penthesileia's advance squadrons intercepted a Greek patrol coming from the neighboring city of Zelea, bearing a message that it would lend support to Pedasus if an attack was imminent. This told us that Pedasus's worries were very real and that, if we could prevent its forces from uniting with Zelea's, the battlefield advantage was ours.

Consequently, Penthesileia sent her cavalry units out to patrol the area separating the two cities, greatly reducing her strength of those around Pedasus, and relied on her infantry component to confront the Greek forces there. Her dilemma was how to coax the Greeks to come forth from behind the city's walls, for she could not afford to besiege it, having neither the time nor the machinery for such an operation. Then, during one of her planning sessions with her commanders, she hit upon the solution.

"Let them get word to Zelea," she told us. "We shall release their patrol and allow it to complete its mission."

"This is madness," Boralis, the Paphlagonian and more outspoken of the two infantry generals, angrily responded. "You would have us fight both armies at once?"

"Hear me out, Boralis," Penthesileia said. "Even if they are united, we still have a numerical superiority over them, not that much, I admit, but yet an advantage. We face a different problem here: to get them out from behind their walls and challenge us. They will never merge, because my Amazons will attack the Zeleans while on their march. We can catch them in the open, an ideal situation for my mounted warriors."

"So you leave us to attack Pedasus's walls? That's a bloody business."

"My expectation is that, when the Greeks see my army depart they will come out to engage you."

"Why should they do this when we still outnumber them?"

"Because they will know we are moving on Zelea's army that is coming to their assistance. This imposes an obligation on them to do their part in defeating us."

"And if they don't?"

"Don't worry," Penthesileia confidently asserted. "I know how they think. You shall have your battle."

"Even so, if they can escape back to their walls, we have no advantage over them."

"That is why they will confront you, knowing this option exists for them. My hope is that, once we have defeated the Zeleans, or at least forced them into a retreat, we can return in time to assist you. It shall be as in Otrea. How else are we going to get Pedasus to commit to battle?"

"We can simply bypass them," suggested Boralis. "One city is as good as another. Why undergo the difficulty in taking this particular one?"

Penthesileia gave the notion some thought, deliberating over its worthiness as it related to our overall strategy, and concluded that it countered our main purpose in prosecuting this campaign.

"Not so, Boralis," she finally said. "If we are to draw Agamemnon's divisions from Troy, our threat to him must be significant enough to warrant such action. We can only accomplish this by taking all the cities he holds here."

This silenced Boralis, and the meeting ended with a general agreement by all who were there. As usual, I was impressed by Penthesileia's authoritative presence and still swooned over this when Antiope and I left her headquarters.

"She's so convincing," I told Antiope. "To have such a grasp over every aspect of the subject."

"You must thank Lycus for that," Antiope said. "He's the brains behind her proposals."

Hearing this did not diminish my admiration for the queen. I understood well enough that strong leadership entailed an ability to appoint the right people for counsel, and in Lycus she had obviously made the proper selection.

"That may be," I said. "But, oh, her presentation. You can't deny she is fully in control of these meetings."

Antiope nodded her concurrence to my observations but seemed strangely subdued over my adulations, not demonstrating a similar enthusiasm of her queen as I would have thought. I was left with some pensiveness over this as we parted for our own tents. Had I overdone it? Was she fraught with insecurities over my favoring Penthesileia over her now? She need not have such worries. I did admire and love the queen, but as a caring mother. She did not arouse the intensity of feeling, the physical and emotional attraction, that drew me, often unwillingly, to Antiope.

Penthesileia contrived an interesting means by which the Greek patrol was released to send their message to Pedasus. She simply instructed the guards to get careless on their watch, to huddle about their campfire as an entire group, thereby failing to maintain their vigilance, which allowed the captives to escape, undoubtedly commenting among themselves how stupid the Amazons were. She next issued directives preventing her own patrols from capturing any messengers leaving Pedasus for Zelea. The sheer simplicity of the scheme rendered it such credence that it was guaranteed success, and that is, in fact, exactly what happened. No sooner had the escaped patrol reached Pedasus, than, only an hour or so later, several riders were seen exiting the city's main gate and heading down the road leading to Zelea. We watched them galloping off, smiling at each other.

Nothing happened the next day, as neither side initiated any action. We were awaiting word from our scouts that Zelea's relief force had departed the city, while Pedasus's generals were holding out for their arrival. Nor did anything happen the following day. However, on the third day, the expected news reached us: Zelea's army was on the move. Penthesileia assembled nearly the whole of her cavalry, leaving only a handful of her warriors behind, and prepared to intercept it.

"If fortune favors us," she told Boralis as she was getting ready to ride out, "I shall see you later today."

"Strike them hard," Boralis shouted. "Both there and here."

Amid the rumbling sound of thousands of horses spurred into action, the Amazon army galloped across the broad, hilly plain in two major columns, one led by Penthesileia the other by Antiope, an exhilarating spectacle. Lycus and I stood next to Boralis as we viewed them riding past us and into the distance. How I wished I could have joined them.

Boralis then left us and directed his officers to call his army and that of the Pelasgians into their battle configuration. Trumpets blared, and shouted commands echoed and reechoed across the campground as unit after unit formed up and, once assembled, began marching toward the field lying in front of Pedasus. The prelude of any battle was a time of intense activity and great anticipation, and I admit that I got caught up in the excitement of the moment, thrilled at seeing the procession pass by, my heartbeat pounding inside me. I could understand why soldiers eagerly flocked to the calls of their banners and assumed their duties with relish and gusto; its effect was intoxicating. Once the units arrived at the field of combat, the army stood in a long line, several ranks deep, and silently waited for the enemy to make its move.

Just as Penthesileia had predicted, within an hour after our battalions had taken up their battle stations, we heard the blare of repeated trumpet calls emanating from within the city's walls, soon followed by the creaking sound of its massive gate opening up. Then poured forth legions of armored warriors, numbering at least five thousand in my estimation, more than we had been led to believe, hurriedly assembling themselves into a similar extended line opposite ours. This completed, the two armies stood in place amid an eerie quietness, separated from each other by a distance of about three hundred paces, and delayed their impending assault only for the consummation of the traditional meeting of their generals.

I saw Boralis and the Pelasgian general walk forward to speak to their counterparts from the opposing side. For a considerably longer period of time than at Otrea, they conversed among themselves, leaving me to wonder about its protraction, until they returned at last to their own ranks.

"Why did they talk so long?" I asked Lycus.

"I don't know," he answered, the concern etched in his face, "but I don't like it."

"What do you mean?"

"More was discussed than merely the usual prebattle harangues. My suspicion is that they talked about their reason for being here, the politics of it."

"You look worried about it."

"I distrust it," Lycus replied in his sober demeanor. "I'm questioning their commitment to our cause."

Just then, another trumpet call burst forth, and we saw the two lines charging at each other. In an instant, they collided with a sickening crunch that reverberated across the entire field.

Soldier fell upon soldier, jabbing with spears, thrusting swords at their assailants, parrying the lethal blows with their shields. They slammed into each other, smashing shields into bodies, each trying to cut down the opponent he confronted, with the whole of the lines deadlocked in combat. I saw certain warriors, from both sides, whose aggressiveness clearly set them apart from their comrades so that they dominated the scene and directed my eyes toward them. One of them, fortunately a Paphlagonian, struck down one opponent after another, slashing and hacking his way deep into the enemy ranks until he found himself in isolation from his unit around them. The Greeks surrounded him, and I saw him go under, but not before inflicting severe damage upon his attackers. Then I saw nearly the identical scene repeated, only this time a Greek warrior exacted a horrible toll on our soldiers. From my standpoint, for the longest time, neither side appeared to gain the advantage, and the battle was a stalemate.

The fighting was ferocious. In spite of the repeated attempts by the Greeks to split our lines, assaulting the sections of it perceived as being weakest, only to have their penetrations countered by reinforcement units sent there, they made no headway. The dead and dying piled up in these areas, their blood flowing everywhere, and throughout the chaotic clashes rose agonizing screams as weapons tore into flesh. I was horror stricken over seeing this carnage, much more gruesome than what I saw at Otrea, and could not believe that anyone could endure such a slaughter. And yet the armies fought on, neither side willing to concede to the other.

But eventually, our numerical superiority began to assert itself, and gradually, our incessant pounding against the Greeks started driving them back. Hundreds, if not thousands, of the combatants lay where they fell, causing their comrades to stumble over them and to step on them as they fought to regain ground previously lost, ground now strewn with bodies, a pitiful sight. Weariness was presently much in evidence, with soldiers faltering under the strain of wielding their heavy arms, some even dropping their shields and weapons, a situation that favored us, for we were able to rotate our units in the fighting, permitting them to get a respite in their arduous grind as we possessed the greater numbers.

Then a most amazing thing happened. We were astonished to see Pedasus's main gate being closed while its army was still embattled against our forces, leaving it outside without a means for retreat. I glanced at Lycus. Neither of us could believe it. At the time, it seemed like such an improbable event, but as we found out later, it made perfect sense under the circumstances leading to it. The Greeks had amassed every one of their units in their attack on us, so none were left in the city, leaving the monarch without a sufficient number of his palace guards. The people, still loyal to Troy, saw their opportunity and rose in rebellion against him, storming his residence armed with makeshift weapons, farming tools, whatever they had available. After disposing of him—I did not know if they killed him—they disarmed the few soldiers still within the city and closed its gate.

Now the Greeks were in a dire circumstance. Unable to retreat, they were doomed, their only option left being a dash to the nearby woods, about a league's distance from the bloody field. Surrender was not considered—I was later told—for they knew what happened to those who capitulated at Otrea and were not about to incur certain death when a possibility of survival existed in reaching the forest. The Greek commander ordered his remaining squadrons to take up a wedge formation, and no sooner was this accomplished when they launched a drive against our left flank in an effort to escape the trap. Our thinner line there could not stand up against such a concentration of warriors and fell apart under the assault. Once the Greeks had made their breakthrough, with no other obstacle standing between them and their presumed sanctuary, many of them discarded their more cumbersome armory, helmets and shields, and ran at full speed toward the tree line.

At the very moment the Greeks chose to make their run, a column of Amazons, led by Antiope, came galloping out of the distant hills and charged headlong in the direction of their flight. What happened next was nearly as horrible to watch as the slaughter of the captives at Otrea. The situation represented the best that any horse-mounted archer could hope for, and Antiope's warriors made the most of it, riding alongside the fleeing soldiers and firing their arrows, one after another, until one found its mark and toppled its prey. Many of the runners were struck with several of the missiles and yet tried to hobble forward, even when no more safety existed for them, eventually falling to the ground. Some turned to face the riders bearing down on them, and in one case, a soldier cast his spear and struck an Amazon in the neck, hurdling her off her horse still in full trot. An instant later, a missile struck him in the eye, and he also tumbled forward, screaming out in agony. Another somehow managed to bring down horse and rider, and he swung his sword across the Amazon's neck as she tried to get up, slicing it wide open so he nearly severed her head from her body. Then he climbed on the horse that had gotten back on its feet and rode from the field; I know he escaped the slaughter, for although a few of the Amazons chased him for some distance, they soon gave up on this and rode back, letting him get away. Some of the Greeks did manage to reach the forest, their pursuers being effectively stopped by the undergrowth, and no effort was exerted in hunting them down, but these were very few. For the most part, the Greek force at Pedasus was totally destroyed.

Antiope rode up to Boralis who had returned to the headquarters tent, a shocked look on her face as she surveyed the field littered with the dead and dying.

"I came as soon as I could," she told him as she dismounted.

"Between Otrea and Pedasus, I've lost a third of my army," moaned Boralis bitterly. "That is incapacitating! Where is your queen?"

"At Zelea, negotiating the surrender terms. She will be here later today."

"So you had success."

"We caught their army in the open and annihilated them."

Hearing this appeared to soothe the commander's troubled soul to some degree, the color returning to his ashen face, although he remained visibly upset over the enormity of casualties the battle had cost him, nearly in tears as he scanned the field. He then walked back to the battlefield to accurately assess its aftermath, checking on the work going on, the collecting of the dead, both ours and the enemy's, treating the wounded to the extent this was possible, for many lost their limbs and would no longer serve any useful function, and generally clearing the ground of weapons, clothing, armor, and other material discarded during the fighting.

"He's angry," Antiope said to me. "And he'll be angrier when our queen returns."

"Why?" I asked.

"Our losses were very few compared to his. He will find this out tonight when we burn our dead. I can't believe how many fell here."

"It was intense," Lycus said. "For much of the time, we didn't think we would prevail."

Antiope was clearly disturbed over what she saw, speaking in a slower, trembling voice, perhaps because she too understood that our infantry, in taking the major impact of both recent battles, had been dealt a staggering blow, one that could hamper its future operational capability, and this did not bode well for us. I sensed her concern, her demeanor being one of sober introspection, which she readily revealed in her concentrated look.

"I shall return in a while," she said after some time. "Boralis and I must ride into Pedasus and speak to its ruler, whoever he is. Let me borrow Zephyrus; Boralis will need him."

With that, she got back on her mount, grabbed the reins of Zephyrus and, leading him by her grasp, headed to where Boralis was standing, where I saw the two of them talking for a few moments before he got on the horse. Together they entered Pedasus's gate, opened again after the battle was over.

Penthesileia returned to our camp just before the sun sank over the horizon, riding at the head of her complement of warriors, and I realized the gravity of Antiope's earlier uneasiness, for nearly the entirety of the Amazon army returned intact. They had lost, in total, perhaps no more than one hundred warriors. Compare this with the nine hundred forty-seven dead and over two thousand wounded— many of whom would yet die—among the Paphlagonians and Pelasgians, the numbers now having been verified. Needless to say, these figures did not settle well with our infantry generals, and they let their discontent be known in that evening's conference.

"You say you annihilated the Zelean army," Boralis bellowed forth. "And yet your losses are but a fraction of ours. How can this be? How large an army did they have?"

"Approximately two thousand," answered Penthesileia. "They were on foot and in the open. They had no chance against my mounted warriors."

"Two thousand? That's what we were told would be at Pedasus, but they fielded over five thousand."

"Our intelligence was faulty," Penthesileia quickly replied, her lips tightening. "We relied on reports we received at Otrea. Obviously, that was a mistake."

"And *we* paid the price for it, as we did at Otrea. We're bearing the heaviest burden of this campaign by far. The disparity in our losses today leads me to believe that our strategy unfairly punishes the infantry arm of our force. We need to make changes." Boralis was livid and emphatically slammed his fist upon the palm of his hand.

"You had the choice of augmenting your army with local units from Otrea," Penthesileia reminded Boralis uncharacteristically, for she rarely dwelled on matters that were concluded. I sensed she was under heavy pressures and found herself squirming for the first time. "You rejected them."

"Untrained and undisciplined volunteers, my queen. We're not well served by them."

"I grieve for your losses, Boralis, but we both agreed on the tactics we would apply today. I should not be made to suffer any castigation over this. However, to ease your mind, I do consent to making changes that will mutually benefit us. I will no longer leave your infantry entirely without cavalry support. This is fair enough, don't you agree?"

Boralis appeared to appreciate that. Once again, Penthesileia had deftly directed the issue for her adversary to decide. By soliciting an answer from him, rather than dictating a solution to him, she made him a party to an agreement from which he could not escape any future responsibility, under our present situation, a necessary approach.

"I do, my queen," Boralis said.

"Think about this, Boralis," Penthesileia added. "We destroyed two enemy armies today, no small achievement. True, it came at an expense, but we have ended all Greek influence in this region. We can terminate our operations here."

Both allied generals responded favorably to Penthesileia's words. Boralis, in particular, was satisfied.

"Does this mean," he said, "that we'll march north? Back to our kingdoms?"

"No. It means we march west, according to our original plan."

"We still go to the sea?" Boralis asked, revealing disappointment in his inflection.

"Yes," Penthesileia asserted. "By doing this, we pose the greatest threat to Agamemnon. If we recapture the cities controlling the Hellespont, we cut off his sea passages, directly affecting his ability to reinforce and supply his army at Troy."

Boralis nodded his assent, although he did not appear altogether pleased over the prospect, even if he did concur with its overall strategy at the outset of the campaign. As I watched him, I became increasingly uncertain of his continued commitment to our cause, and I was reminded of what Lycus told me earlier: that he distrusted the Paphlagonian's motivations. A mutual accord seemed obtained by the time the conference was concluded, but I did not think anyone was comfortable over it.

"He can be such a pain in the ass," Penthesileia told me afterward. "He knew all along what our plan was. To feign surprise that we would still go to the sea was outrageous."

"He wanted you to change it, my queen," I said.

"No doubt, my dear," said Penthesileia, warmly meeting my eyes. "We must be cautious of him. I fear he may have his own agenda."

Later that evening, after all the dead had been stacked upon two massive pyres—one for our fallen, the other for the enemy's—we gathered around these and rendered our eulogies, delivered by the allied generals and Penthesileia, before setting them ablaze. Pedasus's citizens were tasked to emplace the slain Greeks on their stack, considerably larger than ours and requiring an enormous amount of wood. Soon the fires roared into the night sky, crackling and sizzling, brightening up the vicinity and crowd that stood solemnly about amid the surrounding darkness. The occasion was somber, few of us spoke as we watched the remains of the day's action consumed in the hot flames, and by the time it was over, the gloominess that hung over us did nothing to alleviate the depression we felt.

We spent another week at Pedasus, again much of our time taken up in strengthening the bonds of its allegiance to Troy, which remained actually quite solid, considering the years it had been under Greek occupancy. We used the city as our base in securing the area, with much of our attention devoted to nearby Zelea whose commitment to Troy was not as forthcoming as Pedasus's and who had to be forged through greater persuasion and exertion of effort.

It seemed Zelea's loyalty had shifted toward the Greeks during its long occupation, and Penthesileia had to apply coercive pressures, even threatening to displace its leadership, in order to secure its compliance. Also, we required sufficient time to recuperate from the effects of the battle we had fought. The wounded had to be treated. While a number of them still died, many more recovered, at least enough to be of some practical use, if not in wielding arms, then at maintaining and distributing supplies, refurbishing weapons, guarding the camp, and such functions.

I also learned during this time that my outburst at Otrea over the fate of captives was not as clear an issue as I then thought. We were an army on the move and had no means by which we could hold prisoners, that is, without encumbering ourselves with burdens we could hardly afford. We had no way of feeding them or even guarding them if we were to go into battle; I suppose we could have disarmed them and then let them go, but that guaranteed no security for us that they would not fight us again. Penthesileia was right in censuring me; the matter was problematic at best. In my ignorance, I failed to comprehend all that it entailed or even if my position was feasible. I hated war, for it imposed exceptions on us that contravened our better moral judgments, sacrificing these for the sake of the expediency that featured paramount under battlefield conditions. I say this because, to solve this dilemma, Penthesileia turned the few captives we had over to the local officials so we did not have to deal with the problem; I think she did this for my sake, not hers. Pedasus's ruler had them slain outright, while Zelea kept them in captivity for possible ransom. War is cruelty. In its harshness, it reduces us to compassionless participants, stealing from us our benign tendencies and hardening our nature to the savagery that defines it.

Chapter VIII

T HE FALL OF PEDASUS, AS I was to learn later when I returned
to Troy, sent shockwaves through Agamemnon's camp. Losing
Otrea and Zelea, while undesirable, was tolerable for him, but to
lose Pedasus, that impacted severely upon him. Then to discover that we
were marching for the coast greatly compounded his fury, for he readily
perceived that his years of warfare waged to isolate this area from Troy, the
compacts he had arranged with the cities there, the network of defenses
he had established, all was unraveling before him. I was told that he raged
day after day, shouting out the most profane abuses against us, and swore
he would exact his revenge on Penthesileia and her Amazons. Oh, how I
would have relished the sight of Agamemnon fretting and fuming over the
work we did here.

We proceeded west in Mysia, its treeless plains now replaced by greener,
more wooded and hillier terrain as we drew closer to the Hellespont,
targeting two more of its major cities, Practios and Pityea, for conquest.
Both had been one-time allies to Troy before Achilles made his famous
foray through this area, when he cut a wide swath from the Hellespont to
Troad's southern shores, the same operation in which he sacked Lyrnessus
and took Briseis from there. With the capture of these cities, we would
once again control access to the great northern sea as well as the Hellespont

connecting it to the Aegean. They were of strategic importance and could shift the balance of the war decidedly in favor of Troy.

We had been underway for nearly a week when one of our advance scouts came riding up to the head of our column, where Penthesileia, Antiope, and I were stationed.

"A Greek army stands between us and the waters, my queen," the rider barked out, breathing heavily.

"How many?" asked Penthesileia, her eyes narrowing.

"Not that large, perhaps one-third as many as ours, maybe even less."

"Mounted or on foot?"

"On foot, my queen. I think they arrived on ships."

"Well then," Penthesileia grinned, "we shall have to teach them another hard lesson. It seems Greeks are slow learners. How far?"

"Half a day's ride, my queen."

Penthesileia waved the rider on and turned to Antiope and I.

"We'll continue advancing until we're within sight of them," she said. "Then we'll set up our camp."

"I don't understand," I said, more to myself than those present. "Understand what, my dear?" Penthesileia asked.

"Why so small a force? We've accomplished getting Agamemnon to divide his forces at Troy, but with this size army, he's not weakened himself much by it."

Penthesileia and Antiope looked at each other. I could tell what each was thinking, that their effort here did not produce the anticipated result and may have been for minimal gains. I saw the soberness in which they regarded the situation and momentarily worried if they might not have felt as though I had led them astray.

"No matter," Penthesileia then said, easing my anxieties somewhat. "Once we take care of them, Agamemnon's predicament remains unchanged. He will have to send another army or lose all he has gained here."

Much puzzled over the halfhearted measure taken by Agamemnon, we continued our advancement until late afternoon, when we arrived within sight of the Greek encampment, noticing their clustered tents along a distant hillside. As our army was of considerably greater numbers, we had no concerns about being seen nearing the enemy position and settled for a camping spot only about two leagues from it. After our tents had been erected, as it was still daylight, Antiope and I rode closer to the Greek camp to see if any more information could be deduced from our observing it.

"What can you see?" Antiope asked me.

"Their standards. I can make out Boeotians and Thessalians and—oh, no," I paused.

"What is it, Polyxena? Don't keep me in suspense like this."

"Myrmidons," I said, much alarmed over what I discerned.

Antiope did not grasp the significance of what I had just said but was herself startled over my apparent trepidation, glaring wide-eyed at me.

"Who are the Myrmidons?" she asked tensely. "Why are you frightened?"

"They're the Greeks led by Achilles," I said.

"Achilles? I've heard of him. Was he not the man who killed your brother, Hector?"

"By reputation, the greatest of all Greek warriors. Yes, he killed Hector in single combat before our walls."

"A reputation evidently deserved. We've heard of the greatness of Hector."

"My fear is justified, Antiope. Agamemnon had no need to send a larger army, because he has Achilles leading this one."

"That's ridiculous, Polyxena," Antiope scoffed. "He is a man, not a god. We know how to deal with a man."

"Among the Greeks, it is said that he's the son of Peleus by the sea goddess, Thetis. They say the gods claimed that a son born to Zeus and Thetys would one day rule in Olympus, so he arranged for her to mate with the mortal, Peleus, to avert this threat to his powers. Thetis then bathed her son in sacred fires to make him immortal. When Peleus saw this, he stopped her and severely scolded her, causing her to abandon them and return to the sea, but her work was accomplished; she succeeded in making him immortal. I've seen Achilles fight; never has there been as much as a scratch inflicted upon him."

Antiope gave me the strangest look, suggesting I might have lost it.

"It's true," I said. "He comes out of every battle unscathed, even when he's in the thick of the fighting. Men all about him are dead and wounded, but he's completely free of injury."

"That's good fortune, nothing more," Antiope declared. "Let's get back and inform our queen of your concerns. Achilles is better known to her than to me. I'm sure she'll want to know about this."

When we returned to the headquarters tent to relate our discoveries to Penthesileia, her reaction was more introspective, yet in her inquisitive nature, she wanted to learn all she could of her would-be opponent.

"Perhaps Thetis still watches over him," she concluded. "Certainly he's formidable in battle, clearly demonstrated when he plundered this region years ago. But he had a much larger army with him then. He's obviously a powerful man to have killed great Hector as he did. Extraordinary. Still, it's foolish to allow this to intimidate us."

"My intent was to alert you to the dangers we may face, my lady," I said.

"So you have, my dear. And I do not mean to idly dismiss your warnings, but let us be realistic. Look at his numbers, no more than—what?—five, perhaps six thousand warriors, while we are nearly sixteen thousand, most of these my Amazons on horses. Even mighty Achilles cannot stand up to mounted warriors. He has no walls to hide behind, no horses of his own, no mobility such as we have. Clearly, we have a major advantage here. Battles are won by having a numerical and material superiority over an enemy."

While I could not dispute what Penthesileia had said, for the actuality of the situation made it evident that logic was on her side, an uneasiness gripped me, besetting with the gravest apprehensions over what I thought was a misplaced confidence in her assessments. This was Achilles we were up against! Favored by the gods! Agamemnon had justification for believing his army here would suffice, something we should not lightly disregard. But I knew that any further attempts to dissuade her from her determined course would not be considered, and so I nodded my agreement to all she had said.

That evening, Penthesileia held her typical conference within her headquarters tent before the day of anticipated battle, where she formulated its tactical plan while in discussion with her principle commanders. As usual, the meeting evolved into two clashing sides, pitting our allied infantry generals against the Amazon leadership, but I no longer viewed this in an antagonistic context as before, for our battle plans arose out of such confrontations, deriving from the points and counterpoints brought forth in the arguments, and we benefited from it.

The plan that evolved out of this conference was that our infantry would hold its position before our campsite, preventing the Greeks from reaching it and seizing our supporting supply units, while two of the mounted columns, under Antiope, would divide and attack from both sides. Penthesileia was going to lead a third column in a wide circle, unseen from the Greek position, and strike from behind. The idea was to crush the enemy force between our solid standing infantry line and the lateral and rear attacks of our cavalry.

"You will not have to take the initiative," Penthesileia told Boralis, "but simply hold your ground when the Greeks advance. We will harass them with our arrows, firing at them from both flanks in repeated charges. My rear attack is meant to demoralize them to the extent that they will want to escape from the trap. Their disunity will make them easy targets for my archers "

"The plan hinges on the Greek advancing upon us," Boralis scowled, appearing scornful of her design. "How do we know they mean to do this?"

"They did not come here to wage a defensive war, that serves no usefulness for them, for it permits us to ignore their presence altogether and continue our march to the coast. No. They have to take the offensive in order to stop us."

"As you say, my queen," he conceded, still frowning. "We will have our units in place."

With that, Penthesileia adjourned the meeting, and everyone quickly left, leaving only her, Antiope, and me there to recollect our thoughts and comfort ourselves in the decisions that had been made.

"He's so confrontational," Penthesileia confided. "This entire campaign could have been so much easier without him."

"He's a man," Antiope replied, rendering her typical derogatory slur upon the gender, her lifelong prejudices reasserting themselves. "What can you expect from that lot? Boralis is so representative of everything I hate about them. The obnoxiousness, the boisterous mannerisms, and they're burly and repulsive to look at, with the body hair and all. And he smells bad."

Penthesileia laughed, thinking Antiope's last statement quite humorous. "None of us have bathed since we left Pedasus, Antiope. Your comment applies to everyone."

"We're cleaner in habits than they are, my queen. No, I don't think I smell anywhere near as bad as Boralis."

"Take a whiff of her, Polyxena. Tell me what you think."

My face flushed, an involuntary reaction that had both of them laughing. To be honest, I did not detect much of an odor from Antiope, not one that I regarded as offensive anyway, but that may have been because my own less-than-desirable aroma prevailed for me. But that could not be, as I took daily sponge baths. I played along with the request asked of me and leaned my body up to Antiope, sniffing her repeatedly, which now reddened her face a bit.

"Infinitely better," I said. "I'll take Antiope every time."

We all heartily laughed over this and continued our hilarity for some time, until finally, Penthesileia assumed a more serious comportment.

"Tomorrow, Polyxena," she said soberly, "I want you to display your envoy flag before your tent. You still have it, don't you?"

"Yes, my lady," I responded, an uneasiness coming to me. "It's inside my royal cart. I can fetch it."

"Also, I recommend that you wear your Trojan dress," she added, now heightening my apprehension. "Just a precaution," Penthesileia said when she saw my worry. "Sometimes, in spite of all our planning and expectations, things do not go the way we want. This is particularly true in battle. We want to have all ends covered."

I nodded my concurrence but had a distinct feeling that something troubled Penthesileia. Even though she chose not to divulge anything further to me, the disquietude she implanted was very real to me. The distraction this gave me was enough to disturb the harmony I felt earlier, and it arose repeatedly from then on to spoil my efforts at enjoying our company. She gave me one more grave look before I left her tent that evening, a look that lingered for the longest time in my mind, one I was unable to dismiss. Before retiring, I directed Menodice and Thalia to retrieve Troy's embassy standard from the cart.

In my restlessness, I could not sleep for most of the night, as I rehashed over and over the features of Penthesileia's face in its obvious consternation. She had never previously asked that I display Troy's standard, and that she did so now meant there had to be something to it. *I should not torture myself so*, I said to myself endlessly. I needed to be rested for tomorrow, and my mental activeness at present did not help my situation at all. As I tormented myself in this fashion, I heard a whisper in the dark.

"Polyxena?" The voice was Antiope's.

"I'm awake," I whispered back.

Antiope slunk next to me under my sheets, rubbing me with her sensuous body—she was nude—and we began kissing and fondling each other, our exploring hands touching upon our most private features while keeping our heavy breathing to a minimum under the pleasurable contact. I so relished the sweetness of it all. After an indefinite period of time—it elapsed all too quickly for me—we mutually terminated our intimacy, and Antiope rolled over on her back next to me.

"I do need a bath," she said in a whispered laugh.

"It's been a week. We all need one," I whispered back.

"I found it distracting."

"Apparently not enough to keep us from doing what we did."

Antiope nearly broke into a full laughter, trying her utmost to keep her outburst muffled, and I listened to her chuckling as she refrained from sounding off.

"Shhhh," I said. "You'll waken Menodice and Thalia."

We continued at length, just lying beside each other, whispering insignificant phrases and words, giving our oohs and aahs, until the seriousness of tomorrow's requirements took hold of us, prompting us to make our separation. As quietly as she had entered my tent, Antiope crept out of it, granting me one more brief glimpse of her lovely nakedness before she flung the tunic, earlier cast off, over herself. Her appearance was what I needed to take my mind off my earlier tribulations, for now I was thinking more about our encounter than of Penthesileia's troubled demeanor. While I still could not sleep, my present thoughts were more enjoyable in passing the time.

At early dawn, before the sun cracked the horizon, Penthesileia had assembled the riders who would accompany her on her circuitous approach against the Greeks. We had all arisen to see her off, for she meant to make a wide sweep of the area that kept her out of sight from enemy observation and required enough time so that her assault corresponded with our other coordinated attacks. Before departing, she glanced into the adjacent campground, where our infantry had located itself, its soldiers only now coming out of their tents.

"Begin your attack after the Greeks advance to within a few hundred paces of you," she told Antiope. "By then, Boralis should have his units in position."

"Ares grant us victory," Antiope replied.

Penthesileia glanced my way, a faint smile came to her, and she nodded her head once, as if to say all was well. The she ordered her column into a walking gait so the thunder of galloping horses would not reveal her intentions to the enemy. In quietness, we watched them fade into the distant hills.

More than two hours later, the Greek camp was stirring with activity in its preparation for battle. Anxiety mounted for us, because Boralis had yet to move his battalions into their prescribed location. His warriors had been assembled but did not advance, while other soldiers were taking down their tents and loading them into wagons.

Something was wrong. Then, to our great astonishment, his army began to march away from us.

"What's going on?" Antiope grew agitated.

"They're leaving," I said in my alarm. I was very much frightened by what I saw. All Penthesileia's worries suddenly had meaning for me.

"Here comes Boralis. He'd best have an answer for this."

Boralis, accompanied by Lethus, his Pelasgian counterpart, walked up to where we stood before the headquarters tent.

"I am here to tell you that we have had enough," he said. "We are returning home."

"Have you gone crazy?" shouted Antiope. "Get your army in position. Now!"

"The gods be damned if I will," Boralis scowled. "We've taken our last order from your haughty queen, so high and mighty, always thinking she knows it all. Did she ever take advice from us? No. Not once."

"Who can blame her?" Lycus interjected. "Your advice has been anything but wise."

"Be careful who you insult, old man. We're sick of being led by women. We are men. We decide for ourselves who we fight and when we fight."

"Traitor," Lycus yelled out. "Treacherous swine!"

"Do not tempt me, old man. I strongly suggest you keep your insolence in check."

Their heated exchange very much frightened me. I silently wished Lycus would desist in his inflammatory instigation, expecting the worst to happen.

"Swine!" Lycus screamed at him, stepping directly in front of his nose to emphasize his contempt.

In an instant, Boralis unsheathed his sword and thrust it deep into our chief advisor's chest. Lycus, a stunned look in his eyes, clutched the gaping wound left after the sword was withdrawn from his body. He fell forward, striking the ground at my feet. I knelt down and cradled his head in my arm. He gazed at me, declaring his pain and shock with his eyes. Blood was oozing from his mouth. I was horror-struck and in anguish, and as I held him close to me, his eyes never left mine until the sparkle within them went out. He died in my arms. I clung to him and gently laid his head on the ground, never before having seen death that close to me, and gradually rose to my feet, still dazed, while everyone else around me—Antiope, Lethus, several subordinate Amazon commanders—looked upon the scene in stunned silence.

"Idiot," Boralis denounced Lycus even in death. "I warned him. You all saw it. He invited it. I was provoked."

"Swine!" Antiope repeated, having overcome her initial astonishment. She fitted an arrow to the strings of her bow and directed her aim at Boralis.

"Shoot me, and my warriors will attack you," shouted out Boralis.

We all held our breath as Antiope continued holding her firing stance, poised to unleash the arrow meant for Boralis, until, at last, she lowered her arms, eliminating the threat.

"You shall live," Antiope told him, "so that someday I may wreak my vengeance upon you."

At first, Boralis seemed unnerved by Antiope's words, but after some rationalization, he must have viewed the possibility as somewhat unlikely, judging from what he next said.

"Get by the Greeks first," he snarled as he walked away.

"Cowards! Recreants! Swine!" Antiope shouted after him, calling him anything she believed would rile him.

His declaration before departing focused Antiope back on the grim situation facing her. She called on one of her warriors.

"Ride as fast as you can. Tell Penthesileia what has happened. Hopefully, she can make it back here before the battle starts."

The woman rode off at full gallop to the cheers of the companions who had been with her. Their spirits remained high despite the desertion of Boralis.

Now facing an enemy without ground troops, Antiope knew that, with about seven thousand mounted warriors at her disposal, she still possessed a battlefield superiority over her opponent, and while it may no longer have been possible to crush the foe, she could nevertheless inflict serious injury upon him. She could accomplish this without Penthesileia's column but with it, the Amazons could yet decisively defeat the Greeks. Her decision was to play a stalling game with them, keeping them from advancing, first by a show of force with all her soldiers lined up on their horses and then by harassing them with aggressive and repeated charges, until she was reunited with her queen's detachments.

Accordingly, Antiope ordered her army to take up a wide formation, horse abutting horse, covering the entirety of the field, facing the enemy's position on the hillside opposite our own across the valley. I could not know what the Greeks may have thought when they viewed the spectacle, but for me, it was very intimidating indeed, a formidable wall of horse soldiers ready to spring into action. The maneuver resulted in the desired effect, for we saw that the Greeks, who had already formed their own attack line, remained in their stance.

"We've kept them in place," Antiope said. "For a while, anyway."

"Why only temporarily?" I asked.

"Because when they see us merely holding our positions, will become suspicious and start to believe we are afraid to do battle with them. This will embolden them into initiating the action."

"Do we wait for this to happen?"

"No. I must keep them on edge. I can accomplish this with maneuverings of my own, until they wise up to these." With that, Antiope ordered certain units on the left of the line to amass in an assault grouping, as if preparing for a charge. The execution of these moves used up a considerable amount of time, assisting our stalling ruse, while, in the process, keeping the enemy at bay. Once Antiope had successfully clustered her forces on the left, she waited for another hour or so, then repeated a likewise deployment on her right flank, again designed to consume as much time as possible and again managing to keep the Greeks from moving against us.

She continued playing this cat and mouse game through most of the morning, always suggesting she was about to make her attack and then refraining from it. And all the while, the Greeks, evidently baffled by these shifts of units, stood their ground. I was truly amazed that it seemed to work for this long.

But eventually, as Antiope mentioned, the Greeks appeared to have finally wised up to her stalling and near noon, we heard the trumpet calls that signaled their advance. Slowly and in rhythmic cadence, a line of shields, with long spears protruding forward between them, was coming toward us. My heart was pounding. *Why isn't Penthesileia here? What's keeping her?* Antiope was more composed than I as she observed the enemy approaching; I wanted to run away, and she sat seemingly serene upon her horse, awaiting the impending collision of arms. Two other riders were with her, one on each side of her, and I saw her direct one of them to proceed to her left wing's commander, where a heavier concentration of warriors were now massed. When Antiope saw that her message had been delivered, she raised her hand, holding a sword, and waved it forward. Responding immediately, in a thunderous roar, the whole left side of our army galloped straight for the advancing Greeks.

The Greek line stopped and hastily shifted about so it would face our attacking force, which was about to strike them. But again, after firing volleys of arrows from horseback, the Amazons avoided direct contact, skirting the Greeks as they rode by them, unleashing more missiles upon them. Some of the arrows found their mark, and I saw a number of the enemy fall, but for the most part, the Greeks used their large shields to cover themselves and avoided being hit. But I saw the purpose of Antiope's feigned assault—more time used up—and the enemy again stood its ground, expecting another attack. She kept our numbers intact, without sustaining casualties, while simultaneously holding the enemy at its distance. What splendid generalship!

Shortly past noon, we heard a rumbling coming from the distant hills and saw the clouds of dust rising into the air.

"It's Penthesileia," Antiope rode up to tell me. "She's back."

Penthesileia! I was never more relieved. The mention of her name filled me with utmost allayment. My deepest fears were suddenly abated. Her arrival appeared to cause consternation among the Greeks, for they now backtracked from their previous gains, clustering themselves about halfway between their farthest advance and their camp.

Penthesileia soon arrived at our headquarters and dismounted from her weary horse after a long, hard ride. Antiope was there to meet her, having left her station in front of her army when it looked as though the enemy was retreating. Once we entered the tent, the queen's countenance became grim, and she paced back and forth as she was updated on the events of this morning.

"I can't say I'm surprised," she said. "I never did trust Boralis. From the start, he let his dissatisfaction be known. But to kill Lycus? What a contemptible beast."

I could see the hurt Penthesileia felt over her advisor's death. Her voice trembled, and her eyes were teary, but she bore her loss in silence, rendering her suffering all the more acute. There is greater dignity in subdued grief than in the undisguised exhibition of it.

"I shall hunt him down and kill him when this is over," promised Antiope.

"Do that. But to the matter at hand, what is your assessment? Can we defeat them?"

"Absolutely—now that you're here. And the sooner, the better."

"Not for at least an hour. The horses must rest."

I did not share Antiope's confidence, primarily because of the Myrmidons present among the Greeks. I had seen them battle at Troy and knew them to be ferocious fighters, unlikely to be intimidated even by our remerged force or by the fact that we were mounted.

"We shall have to attack them with our axes and swords," said Penthesileia. "Arrows will not penetrate their shielded ranks or win the battle for us."

"Axes?" I said, distressed over what I was hearing. "But—but that means charging into their formation, fighting up close."

Both Penthesileia and Antiope looked hard at me, not altogether pleased over my demonstrated reluctance, deeming it naïve, I think.

"Why, yes, dear," Penthesileia replied, "it does. And your objection is plain to see."

"There are Myrmidons among them, my queen," I said. "Their fighting skills are known to me. I would not want to face them in hand-to-hand battle. I've seen them overcome odds greatly against them. And Achilles leads them."

Penthesileia did not appear that attentive to my warning. Quite the opposite, I think she may have regarded my opinion as intrusive upon a conclusion already arrived at or, at best, based on unwarranted fears.

"You worry too much, Polyxena," she said. "Quite natural when considering your inexperience in these matters. In many ways, you are still much the child; I do love you for that. It's not as if we will confront them feet to the ground. We plan to ride into their ranks, disrupting and scattering them so they end up standing individually against us. What can a soldier on foot do against horse and rider?"

"Myrmidons do not fight as individuals, my queen. They fight as a team."

"That's enough, Polyxena," Penthesileia rebuked me, harshness in her tone. "One day you will learn that success in battle depends largely upon the spirit in which you engage it. You cannot allow your morale to be undermined by negativity. Your concerns, even if well intentioned, can be disheartening. But you are new at this, so it's understandable."

Just then, we heard another distant trumpet call, and almost immediately thereafter, one of the Amazons rushed into our tent.

"What is it?" Penthesileia asked.

"The Greeks, my queen. They're advancing on us."

I saw a momentary shocked expression on Penthesileia's face, but she quickly regained her composure, although a perturbed look remained in her.

"Advancing," she muttered, "on us, with all our mounted warriors?"

Antiope was no less alarmed over the news.

"What unmitigated audacity," she declared. "Have they lost their wits? This is suicidal."

"So the issue is decided. Come, Antiope; resume your command. They mean to have their battle. Let's give it to them."

Penthesileia glanced at me before leaving the tent, an uncertainty edged in her face. My own comportment could not have helped her any, for I was beset with anxiousness, fearing not only for my safety, but for hers and Antiope's as well.

I followed them outside as their horses were brought to them.

"We have accomplished our mission," I told Penthesileia. "We forced part of Agamemnon's army to come here. Do we have to fight this battle? I'm so afraid."

At first, Penthesileia glared at me, making me tremble at the coldness of her stare, but then she must have detected the deep concerns I held for her, or perhaps I overly paraded the duress in which I found myself and it moved her to pity; whatever it was, her eyes soon emitted that familiar warm glow so endearing to me. I swooned under its spell, responding in kind and yielding her a faint smile. She smiled back, melting my heart—her message to me that all was forgiven—and then ascended upon her mount.

A cacophony of shouts, the hastily and repeated issue of orders upon orders, reverberated across the camp, directing the Amazons to take up their attack formations. Antiope, looking quite elegant in her conical helmet, assumed her post in front of the column she always led into battle on our left flank. Penthesileia rode forward and stationed herself at the head of the division extending from the center to the right. For a moment, horse and rider simply waited, each of the Amazons now with a shield strapped to their back, along with their bow and quiver, and a weapon in hand. Their shields were crescent shaped and, when on their backs, leaned more to one side than the other, but the concave side always pointed up. Antiope once told me this was so their quivers remained exposed and so there would be no interference when reaching for arrows, the bow still their weapon of choice in warfare. I did not know how the shields were carried when they fought on foot.

By now, the Greeks had passed their previously obtained forward position before doing their backtracking and came at us in a solid line stretching for half a league and several ranks deep, at least four, from what I could tell. They advanced in unison, shield meeting shield, in step to the count of cadence, a fearsome spectacle. We looked at death, cloaked in a metallic sheen of reflected sunlight, approaching us.

I next saw the Amazons grasping their shields—the concave side faced forward—and brandishing their swords or axes in readiness for the assault, only waiting for the signal to spur them ahead. My apprehension intensified, my palpitating heart pounding within me. I cursed myself for my lack of conviction that we would prevail. I did not question whether a superbly trained Amazon, physically and mentally strong, would overcome an ordinary man in a one-on-one encounter; my reservations were over her matchup with an equally superbly trained man. I remembered the duel between Agenor and Antiope, a battle of such equals, and the outcome was never in doubt. The Myrmidons were tough, highly disciplined, trained to endure the rigors and stress of combat. My fear was valid.

Now less than five hundred paces from us, close enough that I could distinguish the features and movements of particular individuals, the Greeks maintained their ordered ranks as they steadily proceeded on. The tension tore at me. How much closer would they be allowed to come? In a heartbeat, I had my answer.

"Attack!" shouted Penthesileia.

On the left, Antiope shouted out her "Attack!" Exploding forth, the deafening thunder of thousands of horses split the air, charging full speed upon the enemy. I stood breathless. Closer they came.

The line did not budge. How could they just stand fast against the horde descending upon them? Suddenly, the Greeks hurled their javelins, all the ranks simultaneously, darkening the sky, aiming not for the riders, but for their horses. They fell in the hundreds, if not thousands, their horrible neighs piercing ears, spears sticking out of their bodies, and throwing their riders to the ground. In the fury of the charge, the fallen mounts caused the ones coming up behind them to tumble over them, likewise hurling rider and horse into the dirt. If the rider was not killed or injured in the spill, she was momentarily dazed, recuperating from her disorientation, and then, having recovered her senses, dashed upon the enemy on foot.

Those riders who did not fall under that initial volley of spears continued their assault and were met by another surprise. The Greeks lunged forward long lances, twice the length of a normal spear, holding these rigidly in place as the attacking force collided into them. A horrid crunch arose under the impact, the screams of the horses, the clash of weapons, the shrieks of tossed riders. In what no one could have ever imagined, nearly half the Amazon force was neutralized in the opening phase of the battle, wiping out their previous field advantage. The many Amazon warriors now on foot resumed their attack, crashing into the Greeks who, against all odds, held fast in their positions in spite of the hammering they took from the mounted assault.

I could see the right side of the Greek line steadily advancing, fighting its way onward as it cut down the opposition it met. Using their shields as an impregnable defensive barrier, one interconnecting with the other, the first rank covering the front, the succeeding ones providing cover against arrows from above, they pressed ahead, looking very much like a gigantic turtle crawling forward. *These must be the Myrmidons*, I thought; no one else functioned with such precision or in such unison Then I saw the golden-crested helmet and gleaming shield of one of its members. I had seen that armor before: this was Achilles.

In the meantime, as the Myrmidons kept up their drive, on the Greek right, at our left, Antiope had made a penetration against her opposition, leading her riders through the wall of defenders that confronted them. Even at this distance, being mounted, I could see them hacking and slashing away, cutting down the enemy soldiers that seemed to have completely surrounded them now. I feared for her. *She has to get out of there*, I thought. She had no means of escape if the Greeks engulfed her. As if sensing what I was thinking, I saw her reverse direction and ride back to the outer edge of the enemy line.

The Myrmidons were now within two hundred paces of my location. No longer in their turtle shell, they spread themselves along a wider front but still fought in groups of three to four warriors in order to stand up against the mounted warriors that still assailed them along with those on foot. I could see the soldier I believed to be Achilles deftly sidestepping and parrying the weapons thrust against him, wielding his counterblows, and bringing down any Amazon springing at him. He clearly stood out above anyone else on the field, and my attention was riveted on him. Then, suddenly, he started running in my direction. I was petrified.

Out of nowhere, a rider—Penthesileia—galloped toward the golden-crested soldier. He measured her approach, stooped down to pick up part a broken lance, and, just as she was about to run over him, jumped aside and thrust the point of the spear deep into the horse's belly. In a loud snort, the horse staggered, then plummeted, first to its knees and finally body and all, striking the earth in its full weight. The broken fall enabled Penthesileia to jump off without herself falling to the ground, and she stood face-to-face with her foe. They moved in circles, cautious, making their assessments, holding shield and sword, ready to pounce upon each other at the right moment. I felt my pulse in my neck.

Suddenly, the Greek rushed forward, swinging his sword. She thwarted his blow with her shield and lunged at him, but he deflected her thrust with his weapon. He struck back, the full force of his strength behind his stroke, and she again blocked it with her shield, but the impact sent her reeling backward. He leaped at her, and she stepped aside and swung at him, but he averted her counterstroke, using his shield to stop it. He next slammed his shield hard into hers, at the same time swinging his sword. She checked him with her sword but once again staggered under the collision. Then— No! The gods have pity!—as she raised her sword to strike him again, he imbedded his blade deep into her body, his thrust entering just under her armpit. She tottered, her arm dropping under the weight of her shield and her weapon falling out of her hand, and fell forward. My heart stopped.

"Penthesileia is dead!" shouted an Amazon from near the scene, a call repeated over and over that almost instantaneously swept across the length of the battlefield. "Our queen is dead!"

I glanced back to where she had died and received another shock as I saw the soldier who had killed her remove her helmet and the armor from her body along with the tunic she wore, until she lay naked before him.

Even from my vantage point, her white body had a sensuous quality about it. I could see that the soldier appeared wholly transfixed by it. He just stood there for the longest time, gazing at it, his head seemingly bowed in sorrow. I was heartsick. Penthesileia deserved better than this.

News of Penthesileia's death had an instant and severe demoralizing effect on the Amazons still immersed in the fighting, and their resolve suffered as a consequence. No longer disposed toward any aspirations of victory, depressed over their loss, seeing no more purpose behind their efforts, they shed all motivation to continue the battle. They broke ranks, disengaging themselves from the enemy, and started riding away from the field, picking up some of their comrades on foot and riding double, but leaving many behind to fend for themselves.

Antiope rode up, dismounted from her horse, and rushed to me, tears flowing from her.

"You must come with us," she said in a broken voice. "Please join us, but we must go immediately! This very moment!"

I looked into her teary eyes, her beautiful face vividly revealing her despair, appearing lovelier than I ever remembered despite this. "I'm so sorry, Antiope," I said through my own weeping. "I cannot abandon Menodice or Thalia or my cart drivers."

"But the Greeks."

"I'll be safe enough. My envoy standard will protect me. They won't infringe on what the gods sanction."

"Please, Polyxena, I beg you. Come with me."

I fell into her arms, moved to great pity over her sorrow, knowing how much I would miss her.

"I must return to Troy," I said. "I'm so sorry about all that has happened."

"The Greeks are coming, my lady," one of Antiope's companions said. "We must go."

Antiope released me from her embrace, then holding me at arm's length with both her hands on my shoulders, she longingly gazed into my eyes.

"I shall never forget you," she said to me. She then drew me to her face and kissed my lips. I swooned in its sweetness.

Then she let go of me and mounted her horse, her unhappiness very visible to me. She rendered me another of her evocative glances.

"I left you a present so you might remember me," she said. "He's hitched to your royal cart."

"Zephyrus?"

"He's yours. Good-bye, Polyxena. Have a safe journey home."

And with that, Antiope rode off without again looking back at me. I watched her moving away, feeling more alone than ever before in my life and with a terrible emptiness that hurt beyond belief.

"I love you," I said, my tears flowing.

What a day! Event outpaced event, driving away the emotions of one moment with those entailed in the next. The grief of Pentheliseia's death was replaced by the sorrow of Antiope's departure, which was now replaced by dread. My fears mounted as the Myrmidons came rushing up to the headquarters tent, where my servant women and I had taken refuge, as if mere curtains could protect us. We held on to each other, afraid of what might happen next, when suddenly, our flimsy barrier was torn down by the soldier who had killed Penthesileia, his golden-crested helmet and polished breastplate distinguishing him from anyone else. He was standing there, looking us over, and when his eyes met mine, they fixed themselves on their object for an extended duration. I thought his bluish eyes very expressive and could not turn mine away from his, as if captivated by his gaze.

"By your banner, Trojans," he said in an assertive voice.

We said nothing, being too frightened at the moment.

"Speak. What are your names?" he asked.

I overcame my initial jitters enough to end my hesitation.

"I am Polyxena, daughter of King Priam of Troy," I said. "These are my servants, Menodice and Thalia."

"Priam's daughter," he remarked, genuinely surprised. "A royal princess." He removed his helmet and let his fair hair wave freely from its confines, shaking his head. He was, by any measure, a most handsome man with an almost beautiful face, if such a description might be applied toward that gender. He again looked me in the eye, revealing no particular emotion.

"I am Achilles," he said.

CHAPTER IX

I COULD NOT BELIEVE IT. I was standing face-to-face with the man most responsible for the pain and suffering inflicted upon our family, the cruel monster, the heartless beast who had slain noble Hector and Troilus and Polydorus, a mere child, and so many of Troy's defenders. And now Penthesileia. I glared at him, my eyes piercing him in my stunned amazement. He did not seem affected by it, reacting by momentarily averting his gaze from my stares but then resuming his glances.

"A princess—of Troy," he slowly repeated next. "How much do you suppose Priam would pay in ransom for you?"

"You cannot ransom me," I told him, annoyed that he would even think this.

"Oh? And why not?"

"I carry the official insignia of envoys. Zeus himself grants us our sanctity. I am under his protection. Even you—great as you are—cannot oppose what he has ordained."

Achilles thought about this for a moment, looking rather dignified in his deliberation, and then a faint smile came to him, and his eyes glowed.

"So you think I'm great," he said.

He surprised me. That he should hone in on my ill-chosen words—ill chosen because I certainly had no intention of feeding his vanity—instead of the issue in discussion. *How do I get out of this?*

"Everyone has heard of your deeds," I said. "I would be remiss not to acknowledge them. I use the word 'great' in that context."

His smile widened, and he replied, "Well said, princess. You display the diplomatic skills of an envoy, so you must truly be. I shall grant you the sanctity you demand, but know this, I do it because I choose to, not because Zeus imposes the requirement on me."

"You lie to me. What is wrong with recognizing the gods, most especially Great Zeus, as our masters? Our powers are nothing compared to theirs."

Achilles gave me a sober look.

"You saw through that," he said. "Quite discerning of you. How old are you, princess?"

"I am seventeen."

"Close to my son's age. Neoptolemus is fifteen."

Until then, I did not know Achilles had a son. He looked younger than his actual age, which I now guessed to be about thirty. It fit together, placing him in his midteens when he sired Neoptolemus, very much the norm for both our people, Trojans and Greeks. *An odd name for a son*, I thought.

"How many are in your party?" Achilles asked, changing direction. "I assume your immunity extends to them as well."

"Yes, it does. I have Menodice and Thalia here and three drivers for my carts. I also have a noble stallion for my personal use, a gift from the Amazons."

"He belonged to you?"

"Do not tell me you took Zephyrus from me," I said, alarmed.

"Zephyrus. The west wind. Fitting for such a noble horse. I shall return him to you. So, princess, what will you do now? Do you know your way back to Troy?"

I did not—perhaps my drivers did—but I was not about to implore for his deliverance or entreat him to provide for our rescue. Better to figure this out later than to suffer the indignity of being indebted to such a man, a sworn enemy.

"I do," I lied but may have paused too long to be convincing. I am sure he did not believe me, his protracted stare hinting at this.

He spoke tersely but with carefully pegged words that were exact in meaning and precisely defined his intent.

"We will remain here—with you—for a while," he said. "We have work to do: see to our dead and wounded, clean up the field, retrieve weapons we can still use. Also, to give the Amazon queen a proper funeral."

I was astounded that Achilles would suggest that when his earlier conduct so blatantly flaunted a contempt for her.

"What a hypocrite you are," I angrily snapped at him. "I saw how you stripped her and gawked at her body. Do you now pretend you suddenly venerate her? Respect her? Your actions demonstrated the opposite."

He was highly embarrassed. His face flushed, and he turned his eyes away from me, as if ashamed to look at me, and he did not respond for the longest time.

"It is not as you think," he said eventually. "You do not understand."

"She was dishonored!" I yelled at him, the grief I withheld returning to me, the pain of her loss tearing at me. "She was a queen! She did not deserve such debasement!"

"No! She did not." Achilles countered, raising his voice in obvious agitation. "I know this. It's hard to explain. I had an admiration for her. When I saw her lying there, as beautiful in death as she must have been in life, so ... so fragile, all her vulnerability exposed to me. I felt compassion. True compassion. Emotions I've never before experienced. I had to—" He stopped.

"Had to what? Take your perverse pleasure in seeing her exposed?"

He glowered at me, the intensity of his gaze unnerving me.

"I had to absorb it," he said, "the sensations, the sorrow, the shame, all. You would not understand; no one can!"

I think I did. The hardened beast had, for the first time in his life— what a terrible thing to contemplate!—come to face his innermost feelings and had to reflect over this, struggling to accept it, perhaps even denying it to himself. To be only now introduced to these emotions, what a callous upbringing he must have had. My ponderings led me to silence. I merely nodded to indicate that I believed I knew what he meant.

He appeared gratified over my hushed reaction, or perhaps he was appreciative that my anger toward him had subsided, as it had, and he proceeded for the tent's opening, all the while looking into my eyes and keeping mine affixed to his.

"I shall see you later, princess," he said. Then he was gone.

I breathed easier, as did Menodice and Thalia, knowing no harm would come to us. I had faced the monster and escaped unharmed by the encounter. What a relief. Monster? Actually, no; this was too harsh an appellation, and I should refrain from regarding him so. In fact, I was troubled that I could not release myself from images of him still possessing my mind. The look in his eyes clung to me, even as I tried to dispel it, trying to concentrate my thoughts on other things. It disturbed me that the vision kept coming back.

"Can you believe it?" Thalia gasped. "Achilles. He was here, right in front of us."

"I thought I would die," replied an equally breathless Menodice.

I said nothing, although both women expressed my sentiment to perfection, our released tension overwhelming us. There is no greater feeling of elation than the one that comes from having surmounted a perceived life-threatening crisis without injury.

"How you spoke to him," Thalia said to me, "even *yelling* at him. I was so amazed that he took it. You had us worried that he might hurt you."

Thalia's words made me realize that I could have easily provoked the rage he was known to possess. That he checked himself from retaliating against me revealed to me something of his nature. Achilles, for all his reputed callousness and cruelty, was human after all, and he could be reasonable. He demonstrated this one other time, when he released the body of Hector to my father.

This terrible day still imparted one more assault upon my senses when the Greeks carried the body of Penthesileia to the front of the headquarters tent and left it lying there upon a stretcher while resuming the work of collecting the wood for burning the corpses of the combatants who had fallen. Afraid to go there at first, not knowing how I would react, I hesitated within my own tent until I finally overcame my reluctance and stepped forth to see her one more time. One of the soldiers had casually thrown a blanket over her, covering only half her body, leaving her exposed from waist up. I cannot adequately describe the pain that tore at me when I saw her. My immediate response was an outburst of sobs, being unable to suppress these, but then I soon stiffened my resolve and refrained from further weeping. I took the blanket and fitted it to cover her to her neck, averting my eyes from the gaping wound, and wiped off the trickle of blood still oozing from the side of her mouth. With the blood gone, her face was so serene, appearing as if she had gone to sleep, with eyes and lips closed. A warmth came over me, as I was comforted in seeing her so peacefully reposed. I sat on the ground beside her, not thinking anything.

Before long, Achilles came up to me, leading Zephyrus by a rope. He halted at seeing what I had done, touched by the sight, his countenance somber. Then he handed me the rope.

"Your horse," he said.

I rose, taking hold of the cord, and stroked Zephyrus's head; he was happy at receiving my touch. As we were standing there, four other Greeks approached us, coming from the battlefield strewn with casualties, one of them a misshapen, somewhat grotesque figure who limped in his walk.

"It is Eumenus and Prothous, commanders of the Thessalians, and Clonius, commander of the Boeotians," Achilles said. "I asked them to come here to see you, to let them know you are under my protection."

"And the—that strange looking man?"

"He is Thersites. I don't know why Agamemnon asked me to bring him, No doubt to be rid of him. The man is useless. His only talent is to criticize and offend, at which he excels."

I was introduced to each of them, and when I stood before Thersites, I found myself both fascinated and mystified, not to mention somewhat repulsed, over his hideous appearance and crooked stance, curious why he was a participant in a struggle reserved only for the fittest.

"Did your infirmity result from this war?" I asked him.

"You mean Agamemnon's war," he declared in a booming voice. "No, if you must know. I came along so that I might inform everyone about its true purpose."

"And what is that?"

"To make rich Agamemnon even richer," he replied, smug in his delivery.

Indeed, he had an acerbic mannerism, but I thought his answer accurately based and took a liking to him, his ugliness vanishing for me. I gave him a faint smile, and his eyes glinted upon seeing this. He then walked up to the stretcher and looked at Penthesileia's body.

"So that's her," he commented.

"Did you know her?"

"Only as a corpse," he said, startling me with his stark absoluteness. "A corpse Achilles has fallen in love with."

I saw the rage in Achilles, fire in his eyes and veins bulging from his temples. In an explosion of sudden fury, he unsheathed his sword and slashed it across the neck of Thersites, slicing it wide open, blood gushing from the deep cut. We stood in shock, the commanders as well as I, an abject look of horror on our faces. My legs quivered involuntary, responding to having witnessed violent death before my very eyes. Thersites slumped to the ground, clutching his throat, and was dead by the time he struck the earth.

"He has insulted us for the last time," Achilles said, wiping his sword clean on the dead man's tunic.

I was in a daze, stunned over what I had just seen, my senses numbed, unable to come to grips with the utter savagery of the act, the final, ultimate shock in a day filled with shocks. Was it even possible to endure any more of them? I placed my hands over my face, peering straight ahead through my spread fingers but seeing nothing in an attempt to alleviate the horrid scene from my mind. By the time I recollected my thoughts, all I could think of was what a brutal beast this man Achilles was.

"I'm sorry," he said, his face reddening. "You shouldn't have seen that."

I said nothing, still shaken by the incident.

The commanders with him, having more easily overcome their initial jolt than I, called on some subordinate soldiers to carry the dead Thersites to a nearby stack of accumulated bodies, where they dumped him ingloriously upon the heap.

"I'm not saying he didn't ask for it," one of them told Achilles, "but for all his insults, Agamemnon tolerated him. I don't think he'll be pleased over what you've done."

"Thersites has undermined our morale from the start," said Achilles. "I did Agamemnon a favor."

"He'll not see it that way. Thersites had a following."

"So what? What can Agamemnon do without me? If he chooses to make an issue out of this, I will withdraw my support for him as I did before."

"We don't have to tell him. We can say Thersites died in battle."

"No. Let him know."

Once again, Achilles apologized to me for his foul deed and then walked away in the company of the other commanders. I remained in a state of turmoil but gradually overcame my earlier revulsion— was I hardening to the grim realities around me?—and obtained comfort in stroking Zephyrus. I led him back to my royal cart, tied him to it, and returned to my own tent, where Menodice and Thalia waited on me, desiring my presence as a comfort to their own badly shaken dispositions.

Amassing kindling for the pyres was an undertaking of immense proportions, for more than a thousand Amazons and nearly that many Greeks lay dead in several stacks, where they had been collected, and when it became apparent that the work could not be completed by nightfall, Achilles ordered the work halted until morning. Penthesileia was to lie before her headquarters tent for another day. When I retired for the night, the entirety of the day's events unfolded in my mind. It was so incomprehensible, so unreal. My life had been totally altered from its dawn to its setting. Everything was turned upside down. A long day; so long that it seemed almost a lifetime in itself. Its telling exhaustion then overcame me, and I felt myself doze off, drained of the energy to struggle against it.

When I woke up the next morning, the first thought that came to me, after having to remind myself of my new realities, was to check on Penthesileia. I walked from my tent over to where she lay. She remained in her reposed slumber of death, a serenity in her face as the night before, but now I was resigned to the acceptance of her death and no longer afflicted with the horrible anguish that struck me yesterday. A sadness encompassed me, but I was free from the agony brought on by extreme grief, and I knew I would surmount my depression.

The work begun yesterday was resumed, and almost the whole day was spent in ridding the field of the remnants of the battle. More wood—much more—had to be collected for the pyres, and gradually the bodies of the fallen were covered with it. The carcasses of the horses were amassed but, apparently, would not be burned, for no kindling was dispersed about them; there must have also been over a thousand of them.

I was surprised to discover that a good number of Amazons had survived the carnage, and although most of these were wounded, some were able to move about and give assistance to the others. Free to carry on their activity, without the restrictions usually imposed on captives, such as they were, having lost the battle, no Greeks offered them help, but neither did they interfere with their own efforts to aid one another. I was informed by one of the soldiers that Achilles permitted them this privilege, not regarding them as captives, a revelation leaving me perplexed over the contradictory nature of this man. Again he showed a humane side, not the brutality of a beast. But then I thought that perhaps he did not consider them prisoners because they were women. Was it due to their gender or that he respected them as warriors?

Achilles came by my tent later that day. I was in the back, adjacent to my royal cart, caressing Zephyrus, my one joy during this sorrowful time. He approached me, and I found myself again unwillingly captivated in the aura emanating from his eyes.

"Zephyrus adores me," I began. "It's such a comfort."

At first, Achilles said nothing, but he seemed to take some delight in seeing me petting my horse, something that, I believe, other women he had known never did.

"A sign that you're a Trojan," he then said.

"Yes, we love our horses. I was raised with them."

"I've spoken with some of the Amazons. I'm willing to let them go and have them take their queen with them."

"What did they say?"

"Of course, they agree. But when I told them that I should like to honor Penthesileia in our way, upon a funeral pyre, they agreed to that too. What do you think?"

It flattered me, in a strange sort of way, that Achilles was asking me for advice. A man reputed to do things his own way, known for being difficult to control, even among the Greeks, was asking me—a Trojan! A woman!— what I thought. It had to be condescending for him, or did he actually care?

"Their custom is to bury their queens in secret places. I don't know what kind of rites they perform, whether they render them honors or simply inter them."

"They would not be belittled if we honored her?"

That Achilles should even trouble himself over this struck me as remarkable. Again, the beast in him demonstrated a benign side. I fluctuated in my regard for him, in one instance seeing him as the cruel fiend, in the next as possessing some sensitivity and warranting my consideration, if not my sympathy.

"I don't think so," I said. "They will accurately see it for what it is: a high honor."

He nodded his head to denote that my answer was agreeable to him, our gazes remaining locked. He had expressive eyes, and at this moment, they told me that he valued my viewpoint, very unexpected for a man of his reputation and renown, not known to defer his judgments to anyone, let alone women. But perhaps I was misreading them, as was so easy to do with him.

"I have made a decision about your status," he said.

"Oh?"

"I will escort you back to Troy myself."

The prospect was not very appetizing to me, for I much preferred being on my own, with my entourage, rather than bound to the whims of an enemy known for his volatile nature, being unpredictable at best.

"That's really not necessary," I resisted the suggestion. "I'm sure you have more important things to do."

"Not anymore. Now that you have failed in your mission."

How presumptuous of him, I thought.

"I did not fail," I said.

"You did. We stopped your allies."

"My objective was to draw part of Agamemnon's force from Troy. And here you are. So I did, in fact, achieve what I set out to do."

He glared at me momentarily, quieted by my statement, as if suddenly comprehending the true design of my father's strategy, but then readily snapped out of his introspection.

"Your mission failed," he repeated.

I was alarmed, for he clearly implied he knew something I did not. Can it be that all we had done here was for nothing? The notion was unthinkable.

"So will you agree to my escort?" he again asked.

"I think not," I hastily answered, not thinking what my rejection entailed.

"Reconsider," Achilles said. "The sanctity of envoys may be upheld by kings and armies but not by murderous outlaws. You need to be guarded if you mean to return to Troy."

Obviously, he was correct, and I remonstrated against my attempts to deny myself an offered service I was very much in need of. Agenor's squadron provided my security when we went to Themiscyra; I had no such protection now. Yet I remained uneasy about having our enemy performing an official duty for me. To surrender myself into the hands of the cruel Achilles, the very personification of Troy's nemesis, destroyer of so much I held dear, carried frightening ramifications for me. Worse, I had no assurances that, while presently composed and calm enough, his erratic temperament would not dominate him and lead him into negating his pledged commitment to me. Look what he did to Thersites, so sudden, without warning. But I could not risk unnecessarily endangering myself or my servants. *Why can't things ever be simple for me?*

"I will suffer no harm from you or your men?" I asked.

"I guarantee it," Achilles answered.

"And the same for Menodice and Thalia? And my drivers?"

"They will be safe."

"How will it look to my father, to everyone in Troy, if I make my appearance there under your escort?"

Achilles laughed, appreciating the irony of my predicament and thinking it quite amusing, the first time he displayed genuine cheerfulness to me, and I have to say, I was not untouched by it; his smile was charming to behold.

"It's not as if I have to walk you up to the Scaean Gates. We can part before then."

"Very well," I said, a bit nervous, even though I knew it was the only logical course for me to take. "I place myself under your protection."

He smiled in his satisfaction over hearing my decision, evidently considering it prudent. Or did he know all along I would arrive at that conclusion, that it never was a choice for me? Before turning to make his departure, he presented me once more with the radiance emitted from his penetrating eyes. I was beguiled—no, ensnared—by that glow. Then he walked off, leaving me to reflect over our encounter, his aura lingering in my mind.

Shortly thereafter, I left Zephyrus to return to my tent. I walked by the headquarters tent first to look upon Penthesileia for what I resolved would be the last time, but she had been removed. Instinctively, I looked over to the mound that been erected about a hundred paces away and saw that her body had been set at its top, about twice a man's height above the ground. I was to see her face no more. Just as well, I thought, disappointed and resigned to my situation, for it would have only accentuated a wish for things that could no longer be. In sadness, I entered my tent.

Later that evening, as the sun was setting, casting its red glow through the open flaps of my tent, I saw Achilles arrive and call out to me.

"Come," he said. "Bring your servants. We go to honor Penthesileia."

A hesitation tugged at me, but I shrugged it off and steeled myself toward seeing the concluding act of the drama that had unfolded in my life. I walked, with Achilles, Menodice, and Thalia behind me, in the direction of the stack, passing by the rows of warriors who had assembled there, among them several Amazons who had survived the battle but failed to escape due to injuries or being captured. I could feel their staring penetrate me, as if reminding me that I had been the cause of all that has happened. I sincerely hoped that they, because I was walking alongside their conqueror, did not think I had betrayed them or changed my allegiance for their cause. What did it matter? New realities had to be faced, and it was unlikely I would see any of them again.

After taking our place, standing near the front edge of the mound, Achilles, torch in hand, stepped up the ladder leading to a platform upon which the body of Penthesileia rested. He looked upon her at length, appearing deeply affected by the sight, his demeanor melancholy and grim. Then he addressed the throng.

"Our honors to the Amazon queen, Penthesileia. She was a warrior, a worthy adversary. And as a warrior, she shared a sacred bond with us all, for we as warriors value what this means. Loyalty. Honor. Courage. Fortitude. These are virtues of a warrior, what we admire and respect in ourselves, and what we can admire and respect in her. We mourn her and honor her, because she was as one of us."

With that, Achilles descended and set the flame of his torch onto various points along the pyre. Soon, the stack was ablaze, sizzling and crackling and shooting into the darkening sky. The other pyres were then also set afire, and as we stood silently around, not wanting to mar the solemnity of the occasion with spoken words, the whole field was brightened in reddish-yellow hues cast upon it by the roaring inferno. We remained there, not saying a thing, fully absorbing the spectacle, until at last the flames were reduced to glowing embers, blanketing us in the blackness of night. Overall, I thought the ceremony moving and dignified, fitting for a queen.

Penthesileia would have liked it.

CHAPTER X

WE SPENT FOUR MORE DAYS at the one-time battle site, the time it took to adequately prepare for our return journey. I was set to leave much earlier, but the Greeks took their time, most of it dedicated to loading their ships with all their equipment, the seashore being several leagues from our location, and repeated trips made from one to the other. Time was also needed to patch up the casualties, dressing their wounds, seeing to their comfort, permitting ample rest for those in fever and in much pain. Menodice, Thalia, and I offered our help in treating them and spent much of our days with the physicians, doing what we could to alleviate the suffering that prevailed among them. We also aided some of the Amazons still remaining, although by now most of them had left us to make the trek back to Themiscyra, not easy when hobbling on one foot or moving on crutches, as many did. They left in large enough groups, taking their bows and arrows with them, that I felt they could fend for themselves if met with danger. I could only hope the best for them.

I also spent an hour or so each day exercising Zephyrus, wearing my Amazon garb, and I became a common sight for the soldiers who saw me riding from one place to another. I think they enjoyed watching me on my horse, smiling widely and waving, sometimes even cheering, as I galloped by. Perhaps it was Zephyrus that aroused their interest, such a noble steed. We gave them some entertainment from their otherwise dull routine. I needed the drills to take my mind off the turbulence that marked the passage of these last few days; I had difficulty reconciling their transition, how so much can happen, turning everything topsy-turvy, like it all was a dream and never actually occurred. Zephyrus was my proof that I had lived the dream. Nothing Antiope could have done had more meaning for me now. How I love her.

My evenings, in the past always more enjoyable, at present left me with a sense of deep loneliness. The late hours afforded me too much time for reflection, something I did not need, as it heightened my depressive mood. My dark comportment did little to improve the morale of Menodice and Thalia whose familiarity with my mannerisms made them believe that they should leave me alone—the opposite of what I required—and they clung to themselves for most of the time. I must have been awful to be with. We were provided food by the soldiers, sharing their roasted game as well as the horsemeat that was so plentiful, but stayed inside our tent while we ate, which did nothing to mitigate our morose dispositions. Interestingly enough, and quite unexpectedly, it was Achilles, checking in to see me, who succeeded best at alleviating my desolation. He visited me regularly, wanting to cheer me up I think, and before long, we engaged in lengthy conversations. He brought me back into the present and away from my moping over what might have been, or should have been, and I soon began to see the value of this, even if I did not tell him.

He came by one afternoon as Menodice, Thalia, and I were busily finishing our packing, entering our tent after acknowledging his presence.

"I've noticed you've gone native," Achilles said on seeing me.

"You mean my clothes?" I replied. "I find the Amazon wear more suitable for my present situation, more durable, better for riding Zephyrus."

"You look good in them," he said. It pleased me to hear this. "I've come to tell you that my ships will leave in the morning."

"We won't be going with them?" I asked.

"No. We'll take the land route. I've selected twelve of my Myrmidons to accompany me. We are your enemy escort," he faintly laughed.

"Why are you doing this for me?"

"Because, as I once said, you need protection."

"So a Trojan woman's well-being matters to you?"

He thought about how he should answer me, glancing obliquely into my eyes, coming across to me as almost appealing in his circumspection.

"In this case, yes," he said.

"Then you like me?" I teased.

He beamed in his smile but would not directly answer me.

"Regardless of what you have heard about me and my alleged cold-heartedness, it would have greatly troubled me if I had let you embark on your journey by yourself to later learn that something awful happened to you."

He had neatly avoided my question and, in so doing, infused in me a fascination over his apparent shyness. I believed he truly liked me yet could not bring himself to come out and say it in his bashfulness. I had the unthinkable notion that I could use this to my advantage and exercise a degree of control over him. He seemed like an overgrown boy to me, and I rather liked that quality in him. For the first time, I returned his smile with one of my own; he appeared wholly enraptured by it, his dazzled look vividly imparting this notion in me.

"How can I ever repay you for your kindness?" I next asked, my words carefully selected to be intentionally suggestive and further arouse his inclinations.

He stumbled over his attempts to search for the appropriate response, amusing me in the process even though I kept a stoic face, and his face actually reddened a bit.

"Your safe arrival at Troy will be reward enough for me," he said.

He then turned to make his departure, perhaps finding the direction of our conversation too evocative for the moment, pausing to render me one more entrancing gaze that left me transfixed in its spell.

"I shall see you tomorrow," he said before walking out.

A myriad of emotions swept over me, not all of them well received, for I could not accept that I was finding myself attracted to him. No. This cannot be. He was the one most accountable for the misery and pain that had been cast upon my life; from my childhood to the very present, my first recollection of the suffering dealt my mother and father, my grief over the deaths of my brothers, my anguish over losing Penthesileia, all my life's misfortunes and heartaches were connected to the name of Achilles. That is my dilemma. The ogre in my life had only a name: Achilles. He was never an actual person. But now he existed for me in his true human form, as handsome as a man can ever be, strong, masculine, pleasant if he chose to be so. Unpredictable. Temperamental. Volatile. Cruel. Callous. Yes, he demonstrated all this to me. But then he also revealed sensitivity, passion, care, even tenderness. Who was the real Achilles? One thing was certain, he was no longer just a name.

Neither Menodice nor Thalia appeared pleased over my introspection— my long silence leading to their conclusions— which they accurately determined centered around my conflicting absorptions over Achilles.

"Never forget that he is Troy's greatest enemy," Menodice sternly counseled me. "I'm not liking what I see."

"What is that?" I asked.

"You seem to be having a change in attitude toward him. And don't think you can manipulate him with your guiles and change of heart. He is the brute he has always been."

So Menodice saw that too. Of course she was right, I told myself, and was proper in her admonitions, and my immediate impulse was to deny her observations, but upon reflection, I saw the futility in that. Instead, I chose to mask my inner conflicts with assertions that I was in control of these and fully understood what I was doing—a lie, but required at this time.

"We need his protection," I told her. "It's obvious we can't get back to Troy on our own. I'll thank you to keep this mind, Menodice. Don't erroneously judge me. I'm doing what I think necessary to secure our safe return. If this means displaying an affection for him, so be it."

"Don't pretend it's an act, Polyxena," Menodice replied. "I can see through that. What I saw was a naïve young woman falling under his influence, charmed by him. Don't let him sway you from our true purpose: to destroy our enemies. Achilles *is* our enemy."

Was she right? Was what I felt in his presence the result of calculated moves on his part? I did not think such was the case, for my drawn conclusions and cognitions were of my own making and were not formulated by anything he did or said. Or was it? Menodice was more astute than I had previously believed, but she was wrong on one count: I did indeed have a conviction that I could work Achilles's seeming fondness for me toward my favor. So in that sense, I was to manipulate him. I seized upon this point to press my case.

"You're wrong," I said. "I am very much in charge of the situation. I know better than to allow an enemy to use me."

The assertive manner in which I said this evidently convinced Menodice that she was wrong in her earlier assessment, for she apologized to me for her incorrect deductions.

"Forgive me, my princess," she said. "I misread you."

"I know what I'm doing."

"I'm sorry for doubting it."

When we retired that evening, conciliatory in our estimations, I noticed that our conversing had suitably extracted us from our doleful circumstance, and for the first time since the day of battle, I felt sufficiently at ease so I might get a good night's sleep. I was wrong. I could not shake the image of Achilles from my mind. The glow from his eyes, the aura they emitted, warm and drawing me into them, lingered in my head to once again prevent me from obtaining a comfortable rest.

A hubbub of activity greeted us on that final morning at the battle site. All the tents were taken down and loaded on carts bound either for the ships or our road trip. The Greeks took the headquarters tent, vacated and left behind when the Amazons hastily fled from the field, with them. By midmorning, the grounds had been cleared of everything, except at the far end, where the remains of the many dead horses were piled up and covered by clusters of carrion-eating birds who swooped and pranced about, relishing the windfall that had come their way, a repulsive yet fascinating sight. Enough uninjured Amazon horses had been left behind so that the Myrmidons accompanying us could ride.

With nothing but terrible memories existing for me at this place, I was eager to have us get under way. Menodice and Thalia rode in my royal cart, but I wanted to stay on Zephyrus, at least during the overcast days when I would not get sunburned, such as we had this day. After issuing his departing orders to the men returning by boat, Achilles climbed up on his horse, a somewhat scraggly looking creature that appeared having been lucky to survive the battle it had come out of, and joined our group.

"Anytime you're ready," he said to me.

"This is your horse?" I said when I saw the sorry beast, unable to keep from laughing.

My snickering elicited a grin from him, followed by a hearty outburst, and we both chuckled for some time before he halted the merriment by looking at me as if dazzled by what he saw. The thought hit me just then: I had not laughed in his presence before.

Obviously, he was delighted that I did. I became alarmed that, in this brief instance, I found pleasure in his company, relishing a joyful interval with him. What was happening to me ? We both appeared to be grappling with our innermost feelings attempting to surface themselves, shying away from their possibilities by denying them to ourselves. I was reminded of what I had told Menodice last night and involuntarily glanced back to the cart, its curtains up, to see if she had noticed what had gone on between us. She had. The frown on her face said it all.

"I'm ready," I told Achilles.

With a wave of his hand, he ordered us to advance, and we were underway. And so, in what had to be the irony of ironies, my Trojan companions and I were returning to Troy, under the benign escort of our Greek foes. Truly the gods have a sense of humor.

We moved without the sense of urgency that marked my previous passage through Troad, stopping often for resting the horses, despite stepping them and not proceeding in a gallop or even a steady trot, and therefore did not cover that much ground, perhaps only twenty leagues at most. By day's end, we settled into a camp, the soldiers setting up my tent, preparing the adjoining facilities and fires, and roasting the game they had caught. In an odd reversal of situations, we once again found ourselves amid a congenial atmosphere, enjoying jokes and stories, only now with the Greeks as our colleagues, fortunate that no language barrier, other than a noticeable accent, existed between us. Achilles took his place around the campfire, sitting next to me, and we frequently exchanged smiles and leering glances, suggestive of more than a casual interest in each other, even if we both knew that nothing would come of it. Or would it?

Spending an entire day and then a long evening up close with Achilles had an allure of its own, a subliminal seduction in progress, and I often sensed myself unwillingly drawn to him, as if unable to resist powerful urges dominating me. His prevailing masculinity, vigorous and strong, inescapable and almost addictive, left me with a longing to be squeezed in his muscular arms, an embrace that would shield me from whatever threat. He was a beautiful being, a paragon of manhood, the image of a living Apollo. I lashed at myself for possessing such thoughts, trying as best as I could to dispel these from my mind, rationalizing that he was an enemy—the worst of our enemies!—and nothing fruitful or even desirable could possibly come out of this, only to have the same notions resurging to dominate me once more. *Oh, Aphrodite, help me. This cannot be happening.*

Adding to my discomfiture, I strongly believed that he was possessed of similar feelings about me and suppressed his own battles against wanting to have me, for all his actions, his behavior and the aura from his shining eyes, led me to this conclusion. We shared an affinity for each other, while knowing that this could only result in unhappiness and heartbreak for us both if we succumbed to our baser instincts. So we resisted our impulses, the strain of our exertions very much evidenced in our glances. I wished at times that he would just seize me, take his pleasures on me, ending all my hesitations over this, and, through this, release me from my obsessive cravings. The question paramount in my mind, and I think also in his, was whether to submit to our impellent inclinations or continue resisting these, thereby depriving us of what we most desired.

This night we defied our temptations, and after the fires were reduced to glowing embers, we retired to our tents. I gave Zephyrus, tied to a peg outside my shelter, a long hug before joining Menodice and Thalia in our usual chat before bedding down.

"He loves you," Menodice said in a disapproving tone.

"What?" I feigned surprise. "Are you sure?"

"It's plain to see. The way he sits there, gawking at you with his lecherous look, drooling at the mouth. The signs are unmistakable."

I remained silent but took satisfaction in having his love for me affirmed by others, as it verified for me that my views on this were not mere delusions but had a basis. I felt my inner being elevated by her observation.

"You like that, don't you?" Menodice said scornfully, bringing me back to reality.

I looked at Thalia who seemed to be more sympathetic toward me, as if seeking an ally in support of my propensity, but she sent me no such message.

"Do I?" I replied.

"Oh, I can see it in you. Don't try to deny it."

"Well, it is flattering, don't you think?"

"How dare you! Flattered by our worst enemy taking a fancy to you? You derive pleasure from that? That is sick. Never forget who he is or what he represents. He is Troy's doom. I strongly suggest you think about that."

"I *do* think about that," I lashed back at Menodice. "All the time. But we're not at Troy now, nor are we likely to get there if I don't play my games with him. Keep that in mind ."

"Are you sure it's a game to you? I don't believe it."

"Believe what you like, Menodice. My efforts along this entire trip have kept us safe from the very beginning. I weary of your endless criticism over what I do. And so what if I admit to liking him? As long as it is but for the duration of our time together and does not reach beyond that, we are none the worse off for it. We have his protection, he feeds us, his soldiers put up our shelter—there is nothing wrong with showing my gratitude for that."

"You are a princess, not a whore."

"Enough," I shouted at her. "Never call me that again! I have done nothing to merit such a name nor the contempt you exhibit toward me."

That shut her up. She was a bothersome woman indeed. Her intransigence and lack of sympathy over my dilemma compounded my tribulations, leaving me beset with the gravest uncertainty and even self-loathing.

I had apparently upset Menodice enough that she decided to step outside the tent, to seek solace away from my presence, I think.

"Menodice means well, Polyxena," Thalia reminded me. "She has your interest at heart, as do I. It's because we fear for you that we're upset by what we see."

"I will not be addressed as a whore. Why do you fear for me?"

"A love that can never be—so it would be between you and Achilles—will result only in grief and sorrow, especially for you, burdened with a responsibility for Troy's survival. Isn't that what our mission has been all about?"

Now Thalia silenced me. I was particularly alarmed over her defining my situation as an unattainable love. She was correct in her assessment—I knew this—yet I rebelled against its acceptance. But hearing it mentioned made me ponder on its feasibility, its hopelessness, the nonexistent odds in bringing such a relationship to fruition. Without saying another word, I took to my cot, feeling awful, downcast, and sad, unable to see any solution to my predicament.

Menodice soon crept back into the tent and slunk into her cot. I heard her muffled sobbing, which did nothing to ease my tribulations, for I now felt even more horrible that I had inflicted such duress upon her. My first impulse was to go over and hug her and ask forgiveness for my callousness, but I could not bring myself to do so; the congeniality between us had been severely strained and needed time to heal. There are no easy pathways in life.

The next morning was glorious in its sunshine and cloudless sky, energizing me out of the doldrums still with me when I first woke up.

Menodice and Thalia, moved to pity over my earlier despondency, strove to cheer me up as they attended to my needs, washing me with sponges and dressing me, but their effort paled compared to the effect of the gorgeous sun on my disposition. A beautiful day. Let yesterday's worries be forgotten and relish the warmth and loveliness of today.

When I saw Achilles seated with his comrades about the relit campfire, cooking breakfast for us, all my earlier ruminations melted away, and I only thought about my present situation, enjoying being with him, seeing his smile, hearing him talk. The realization struck me that I was considerably happier when with him than anyone else, his presence affecting me that way, another indication to me of how my regard for him had changed. I was determined not to let anything spoil this for me.

After breakfast, the tents were taken down and loaded into the carts, and soon we were back on the move. While the sun remained close to the horizon, casting long shadows on us, I rode on Zephyrus, thinking I would not need protection from its rays until later in the day. I was riding across the fields adjacent to the roadway some distance away from our group, absorbing the freshness of the morning by myself, when Achilles trotted up beside me, and together we quietly proceeded along.

"I heard the commotion coming from your tent last night," he said at length.

"Did you hear what was said?" I asked.

"No. Only that some argument was taking place."

"It was over you."

"Was it?" he asked, his interest seemingly rising.

"Yes," I hesitated on whether I should tell him about it and decided I would. "Menodice thinks I have fallen in love with you and strongly objects to this."

"Have you?"

How should I answer? Truthfully, I believed that I had, but I still was not ready to make that concession, neither to myself nor to him, afraid of the consequences such an admission entailed.

"I don't know," I said, seeking the ambiguity that answer provided, and then added, "She also believes you are in love with me."

He halted his horse, thereupon causing me to bring Zephyrus to a stop as well, and gazed directly into my eyes, his countenance turning solemn.

"Menodice is right," he said. "I am very much in love with you."

He said it. No more speculations about whether he did or not, no more anticipation that he might, no more wishing, wanting, and hoping. It was true. He did. Conflicting sensations preyed on me, an initial joy in hearing his words, leaving me glowing in my elation, brimming with excitement, next followed by sadness, because under our circumstances, such a love could never be consummated. The grim reality of our situation posed an insurmountable obstacle to his adoration, leaving me speechless in its contemplation. My reaction was to stare blankly in stunned silence for the longest time, unable to find the words to express myself.

"I have fought it," he continued, "and denied it, telling myself over and over this cannot be, but no more. I must be true to myself."

He echoed my sentiments to exactness, repeating all the dissonance I was afflicted with, but took the step I was reluctant to take: admitting it. I had to wonder if having taken that step solved the problem remaining for him: overcoming the stark realities confronting us.

"You're not saying anything?" he remarked. "Are you upset?"

"No," I replied almost immediately, not wanting him to think this, then I paused in my search for an answer.

"But you're not happy about it," he said.

"No, I am," I said.

"You have a subdued way of showing it."

"This is so difficult for me. I am too absorbed in my worries over what all this means for us. Were I to admit my love for you, would anything change for us? You will still wage your battles against Troy. I will remain Priam's daughter. Will our love bring an end to the war? We know it won't."

He seemed to understand what I was saying, recognizing that we were both entrapped in a web that had been spun by others, yet he was remarkably unaffected by my words, which I thought peculiar. I detected no disappointment in him, only that he appeared embarrassed over having revealed his affection for me, knowing all along nothing would come of it.

"Oh, Achilles," I said in dismay, "I'm so sorry."

"Don't be," he said. "I had unrealistic expectations, even running counter to my reasons for having come to Troy. In speaking to you, I suddenly realized I can't take any measures that would negate why I came here."

"Why did you come to Troy?"

"To fulfill my destiny."

"And that is?"

"I've long believed, and have been told by some, that my destiny is to fall at Troy," he said somberly, peering at me as if seeking a verification to his assumption.

"What?" I was amazed. "You came to Troy believing this?"

In spite of perceiving my puzzlement—it had to be obvious—he said nothing more about this and instead gave me the oddest smile, almost as if he enjoyed that prospect and looked forward to it. Surely, I was wrong in thinking that.

"I do love you, Polyxena," he next said. "But I cannot let Aphrodite thwart what had been ordained for me."

What a strange thing to say. We rode on in silence, evidently preoccupied with our own thoughts, so neither of us felt any compulsion to say anything more. I was relieved that he was not upset over my uncommitted posture. If anything, he was gratified that I refrained from advancing my case and insisting our love lead us into proposals neither of us could fulfill. Had he rejected me? He expressed his love for me, but it was a conditional love, one that was not to interfere with the greater destiny he envisioned in store for him. The course of our conversation had imparted a state of confusion in me. I was unable to determine whether his confession was meant to please me or to keep me at a distance from him. No. He was truly attracted to me, and it gave me great pleasure to have him say so. I should have been more direct and told him how much I adored him, for in truth, I did.

Whatever befuddlement I felt during the rest of the day was readily dispelled that evening when I again seated myself next to him beside the fire. His nearness, the strength he exuded, so vigorous, so seductive, preyed upon my sensibilities. I was becoming obsessed with hopes that he might take it upon himself to sweep me up into an erotic embrace, distracting me from attentiveness to the subjects being discussed and, in this, probably making myself appear as poor company. Yet as the night before, nothing came of this, and we parted in our mutual longing for each other without having progressed in satisfying our hunger for more. I was unable to fall asleep in my regrets over another opportunity lost.

Two more days and nights were to pass without incidence, and I was becoming increasingly conscious of our journey nearing its end as we drew closer to Troy, the drier plains so familiar to me now around us. I dwelled on thoughts of how I would be received once I got home. Had I accomplished the objective under which I embarked on my journey? Achilles alluded to its failure, but how could he know? Would the Greeks still be there? But that did not make any sense; who would Achilles return to if they left? Doubts prevailed for me, and I turned my thoughts more toward my parents and family members, over how they would welcome me back, envisioning their happiness at seeing me. In a strange, indefinable way, I took little pleasure in this. Instead, I was overcome with bouts of recurring sadness, rueful that my time with Achilles would soon be over and fearful that I might terribly miss him. Did he feel the same way? I believe so, for his gazes reflected an impending sorrow. Like me, he wanted our companionship to continue indefinitely, perhaps also for the hope that we might yet engage in lovemaking, indulging in our most anticipated cravings.

That fifth night, Achilles and I remained seated beside the dying fire after everyone else had left to go to sleep, the burden of our journey's conclusion weighing heavily on us both. We saw no happiness in its termination, only the prospect of our separation, something neither of us wanted. I cuddled up to him, and he wrapped his arm around me, drawing me closer to him, our bodies meeting in warm contact.

"What happens next?" I asked him, my sadness getting the best of me and causing my voice to tremble.

He delayed in answering, due to feeling the same apprehensions that possessed me, I believed, for in truth, our worries bore deeply into our consciousness, engulfing us in gloom and depression.

"I would like to say whatever we decide," he finally said. "But it's not so simple."

"No, it's not," I agreed.

"Can we deny our destinies?"

"Not if the gods determine this for us."

"True. I was pondering if we have any say in this. Can we, by our own actions, create our own fortune?" He seemed utterly immersed in his contemplation, gazing at the dying embers, but his thoughts elsewhere.

The question was problematic. To acknowledge it was to deny any influence the gods exerted over us and place their entire existence in dispute. Yet great accomplishments are given to those who venture to take matters into their own hands. Do the gods look favorably upon them because they dared? Is everything preordained?

"I'm worried about you being back in Troy," Achilles continued.

"Because you think Troy will fall?"

"Yes."

I took exception to that, reacting adversely, saying, "Please don't tell me that. You're wrong. Troy will not lose this war."

"But if it does, how will I find you?"

"Will you ever know? I mean, if you believe you're destined to fall at Troy. I don't see how this can ever be, not when, as so many claim, you're immortal in combat."

"I'm not."

"I don't believe it."

"It's true. You haven't heard this? The way it was explained to me, my mother held me under the fires of immortality by my heel—my right one—leaving it untouched by the flames and thus vulnerable to injury, the only place I can be wounded."

"Your heel?" While I thought this unusual, it was also contradictory to his expectation. "I don't think you have to worry about falling over a wound to the heel, not if a physician is there to treat it. That type of injury is rarely fatal."

He reflected over my words, not appearing pleased over my observation, as if I had marred a deeply personalized vision he held for his future. I cannot believe he would not have drawn a similar conclusion or at least questioned the possibility before. Then he squeezed me closer.

"Perhaps the prognosticators are wrong," he said.

He focused his eyes on mine, the emanation from them penetrating me, enchanting me, and drawing me to him. We kissed, a kiss unlike any I have ever experienced before, wrapping me in warmth, a sublime happiness sweeping over me, and I never wanted it to end. I was overwhelmed with a desire to fully consummate our intimacy, but he abandoned this purpose when he released his hold on me, leaving me in perplexed frustration.

"Not here," he told me. "We have no privacy. When we're alone."

"Will we ever have such a moment?" I asked in my disappointment.

He merely smiled then stood up and extended his arm to me to raise me on my own feet. He kissed me once again—oh, the rapture!—clutching me to his body, until at last he let go of me, and I knew my contentment for the evening was ended.

"We shall see," he said. "Maybe we can ride off to a secluded spot, the two of us, away from the pack, tomorrow."

I had to give him due credit, for he excelled in keeping his ardor in check while at the same time elevating my hopes to frenzied heights in anticipation of the sweet contact he proposed. I nodded my approval and then we parted, I for my tent and he for the blanketed patch of ground amid his soldiers that marked his sleeping spot.

As I entered my shelter, I was startled to see Menodice standing there, her face clearly revealing her discontent even in the darkness. I was relieved that Achilles had decided not to press ahead with our affectionate exposition.

"Why are you looking at me like that?" I demanded to know, not at all pleased over what I regarded her intrusiveness on my privacy.

"Your conduct is disgusting," she declared, withholding no reservations about her obvious revulsion over what she had witnessed.

"What's disgusting is you staying awake to see what I do," I replied, much offended by her behavior, her spying on me.

"You betray Troy."

"I betray no one. One man, a subordinate captain, does not cause a city to fall or the demise of an empire."

"This one does," she decried, elevating the pitch of her voice.

"He is not Agamemnon. He takes his orders, just as I did on this mission, and carries them out. He does not determine what his orders are."

"He is our enemy, the most dreaded of our enemy. I cannot believe you. The man Who killed noble Hector—your brother! And now you throw yourself at him in your carnal lust. You are unprincipled, nothing more than a prostitute. You shame us."

I began to have worries over what Menodice might say once we got back to Troy. She did not understand my dilemma, the mutual attraction Achilles and I had for each other, the torment this was causing me, nor was she likely to grant me any sympathy, viewing my actions as next to treasonous. She did not know how we both were fighting against our deepest desires, knowing our relationship had little chance of succeeding, as all factors stood against us. Was I fraternizing with the enemy? Did my conduct pose a threat to Troy's survival? How could it? Whether I was with Achilles or not, nothing we did here changes what is happening at Troy at this moment. And if we are separated once we get back, what we have done has no more relevance and cannot influence what will then occur. But Menodice was bound to distort my behavior, depicting it in a most unfavorable light, requiring me to defend actions I am having difficulty explaining to myself let alone anyone else. That prospect was not pleasant.

"I'm sorry, Menodice," I finally said. "I am weak, a slave to my emotions. I'm unable to surmount my womanly passions. Please forgive me."

My having humbled myself into her adjudication had a surprisingly mollifying affect on her, and she suddenly had a great concern over my perceived folly, as if merely my youthfulness and the naïveté that goes with it was the source of my erroneous path.

"You must be careful," she counseled me, "not to be led astray by his wily charms. All he wants from you is his temporary pleasures, his sexual gratification. He is using you."

A remarkable estimation, I thought, since it was he, more than I, who deferred our sensual progression. But I was not about to deprive myself of her good graces or the compassion she presently bestowed on me and did nothing further to alienate her.

"I shall be alert to that," I said.

"I can ask no more from you, dear princess. We have a responsibility to protect ourselves, especially from this man who thinks Troy will fall."

So she overheard that. I was apprehensive over what else in our conversation she knew about. My worry centered on when Achilles revealed his vulnerable heel to me; did Menodice hear that? But how would I uncover this from her? If I drew attention to it, she would learn about it for certain, recognizing its potential importance. If I said nothing, she might forget it, but I would never know that. I had to assume she heard it. Accordingly, I deemed it best not to allude to it, even if meant enduring my uncertainty.

"Good night, Menodice," I said as I moved into my curtained division of the tent.

"Sleep tight, princess," she replied, smug in her belief that our discussion had drifted in her favor and that I was now compliant to her wishes.

The next day began as all the others, taking our time indulging in our meals and in packing our gear, until around midmorning when we were finally underway. We were now in the sixth day of our journey and expected to arrive at Troy tomorrow. The terrain assumed a familiarity I recognized and identified with home: a coastal plain interspersed with sparsely treed forests. Soon we would come upon the campgrounds of our allied armies, one after another, covering the inland expanse reaching to the city, while the Greek camps hugged the shoreline along the coast adjacent to where many of their ships were moored. My guess was that we were going to make our approach in the kind of no-man's-land existing between these stretches of inhabited areas, because Achilles expressed no worries about our party falling into the wrong hands. Just the same, I made sure my envoy standard was securely fastened to the royal cart and fluttered gracefully in the breeze.

Conflicting notions possessed me now that we were but a day away, the immediacy of our journey's termination now a preponderant preoccupation for me, and I had great difficulty in envisioning myself back in Troy's royal palace. On the one hand, I ached to see my friends and relatives, my absence from them more keenly felt as we got closer and closer to home, and I thought of my happiness at seeing them again at long last. Yet, on the other hand, I clearly sensed I would sorely miss Achilles, and not just him, but his companions as well, and the almost carefree lifestyle that had characterize my existence since beginning my mission.

I still craved to have a torrid encounter with him, imagining this as a sensual barrage of utmost ecstasy, but saw my chances for that happening growing slimmer by every league disappearing behind us. We found it a near impossibility to ride off, as we had discussed, without raising the suspicions, perhaps even hostility, of Menodice and Thalia. So we just paced our horses within eyesight ahead of the pack, as Achilles called it, and engaged in pleasant conversations, not doing anything that might have led to wild speculations, despite my wishes for more at this late stage of our time together.

That evening, Achilles and I again found ourselves staying up late, seated around a burned-out fire, the only light coming from a full moon. Sometimes it is nothing short of amazing how brightly an area can be lit up by such a moon. We perceived the emotions etched in our faces plainly enough without requiring a torch to intensify the sadness affecting us over our pending separation. We nestled closer, our bodies touching, a blanket over us for warmth.

"All good things must come to an end," Achilles said. "Isn't that the old saying?"

"I wish we had more time, another six days."

He laughed, "I was considering myself charitable for wanting just one more day."

"I can't believe it's almost over."

"Will I ever see you again?" he asked, his voice weak, a pained look coming to him.

"There has to be a way to arranging this. Supposing I can, how will I get the word to you?"

"Agamemnon has his spies, but I don't know who they are," he said and then chuckled as he continued. "They would be poor spies if we knew them."

"Dead spies. I'll figure out something. At this point, I have no idea what my father would think if he knew about us."

"I suppose he would be quite angry."

"More distraught, I think. He'll understand how Aphrodite can manipulate our lives, and he'll take this into account; he very much honors the gods. An ordinary Greek would be acceptable, but you? The death of Hector, his favorite son, devastated him."

Achilles did not add anything on the subject of Hector, probably because he saw a futility in this but also because he may have had recriminations about his abusive treatment of the slain hero's body. Maybe he, knowing Hector was my brother, had no wish to risk my alienation over a matter having no more relevance. He need not have worried about this; you have cast your spell over me, Aphrodite, and I could no longer envision Achilles as the cold, dispassionate slayer of the people I once held dear. Would my return to Troy rekindle the hatred and fear that I once had for him? That was unlikely, I thought, for I knew him now, as much as it was possible to know someone in the short time we spent together, and my awareness was sure to deter me from ever repossessing such previous convictions.

"I'm sorry," was all he said.

We then kissed, the sweetness of our joining as enthralling as before, soon followed by caresses and fondling, heightening my pleasure to delirious levels. I was not going to have this end short of its final climactic conclusion. Not caring whether anyone took notice of us—I did not think anyone had—we rolled over on the grassy edge bordering the doused campfire, laying one blanket down while covering ourselves with a second one, and brought to a closure the intense cravings that had overwhelmed us, an immense gratification of all my senses.

We remained locked in each other's arms long after having consummated our passions, savoring the lingering contact and happy in our company. Present realities once again asserted their claim over us, and we gradually rose to go our own ways to our sleeping places, all the while refraining from saying a single word. When I entered my tent, I saw that Menodice and Thalia were on their cots soundly asleep, not that it mattered to me anymore.

By midmorning the next day, we were well underway on what was to be the last leg of our journey. I directed Zephyrus to the head of our column, taking my place next to Achilles on his scruffy mount. The elation of yesterday's encounter remained with us for a while, and we both glowed over its recollection, relishing confiding our strong feelings for each other, but eventually the grim realization of our impending separation took hold of us, displacing our earlier joy with a somberness that quieted us. Neither of us saw the ending of our trek as that welcoming, cutting short the amiability we had discovered in ourselves and depriving us of our desires to perpetuate our condition. At the same time, other emotional highs surfaced for me, and I yearned to be back in familiar surroundings with people I had long known and loved.

As noon approached, I could make out the structures of Troy in the distance, its citadel jutting above the walls. We would be there by midafternoon. I also saw that we had passed a number of Greek camps along the shores of the sea and feared that little was changed since I had left. They were still here. My father's plan to render them a death blow had not materialized. Achilles was correct when he said I had failed in my mission. What went wrong? Can it be conceivable that everything that has happened, the lives involved, the events that transpired, all amounted to nothing? No. This was too horrible to contemplate.

When we got to within about five or six leagues of the city, now looming impressively before us, especially the Pergamus with its palaces, we noticed a group of about thirty riders approaching us from there. Achilles did not appear that alarmed, although I tensed up, thinking he and his soldiers might be in danger, facing possible captivity. We rode back to the royal cart and awaited their arrival, which soon came, and they quickly circled about us and had us surrounded. The leader of the group walked his horse toward Achilles and me—I thought I knew him—then stopped and slowly removed his helmet.

"Agenor," I greeted him.

"Princess," he said through his grin. "You had us worried. We were afraid that something terrible happened to you after we heard about

Penthesileia being killed." Then he turned sober as he addressed Achilles. "You killed her."

"So I did," Achilles calmly told him, not appearing the least ruffled over his predicament.

"I should kill you and your soldiers right now."

"No, Agenor," I interjected. "He escorted us back to Troy. He granted me the immunity of envoys as you must likewise accord him."

Agenor seemed momentarily to resent my intrusion, glaring hard at Achilles, but he soon recovered from his indignation, his smile returning to him.

"You shall live, Achilles," he said. "Thank great Zeus for that. I'm robbed of a prime opportunity to rid Troy of its scourge."

Achilles bowed his head slightly, acknowledging his appreciation to Agenor, then ordered his soldiers to assemble so that they could together ride off.

"Thank you for returning Polyxena to us," Agenor continued. "We shall take over now."

Achilles glanced my way, moved to pity at seeing my look of dismay, the suddenness in which our separation was thrust upon us tearing me apart. We lost our chance to finalize any scheme by which we might meet again. I had resolved, after Penthesileia's funeral, never to shed any more tears, finding them insufficient in depicting the true heartache I felt. Yet I could not help myself at present. The pain of leaving Achilles, perhaps never to see him again, struck me most severely.

"How can I ever forget you?" I told him, trying my best to keep from breaking out in sobs.

"Do not cry, Polyxena," he said, not doing that well a job in repressing his own feelings as his eyes moistened.

"I'm sorry. I want so much to—to be with you."

"Destiny will bring us together again," he answered, his voice broken. "It is meant to be, just as it was for this time we have come to share."

Achilles smiled at me and then prodded his horse ahead as he and his companions rode off in the direction of the coast. He never looked behind to see my grief.

Agenor observed our parting with concern, not too pleased with what he saw, judging from the frown he exhibited, but he was unaware of the extent of my remorse over this, not knowing of the relationship Achilles and I had developed, and would have perceived it as quite strange if not outright treasonous. How could I tell anyone? It hardly seemed possible that it ever happened. I became cognizant of my own attempts at denying it. I then noticed his eyes lighting up when they espied Menodice seated next to the cart driver.

Accordingly, he led his horse over to her. I was relegated to a place of secondary importance to him.

After a brief exchange of words with Menodice, Agenor directed his soldiers into a column, half of them ahead of us, half behind, and directed me to its head with himself.

"Come," he declared. "Let us enter Troy."

CHAPTER XI

S
O AFTER FOUR MONTHS ALMOST to the day, I had come home.
Four months! Had it only been four months? This seemed so
incomprehensible to me. I lived an entire lifetime in that short ·
duration. The people I came to know—Penthesileia, Lycus, lovely Antiope,
Achilles—were forever ingrained in my memory, never to be forgotten,
haunting me in my remembrance of their transitory presence in that
lifetime. The enormity of the events that took place—Otrea, Pedasus, and
Zelea, that last, terrible battle—the horror and exhilaration, would remain
as ephemeral relics of that lifetime. Did it all really happen? How like a
dream it seemed now that I was back, only a dream, nothing more. But
what a dream!

At first, I was astonished when we approached Troy's formidable walls.
I had forgotten just how massive they really were. It thrilled me to see the
crowds in the streets once we entered through the Dardanian Gates, their
differing, multicolored costumes denoting the many regions our allies
came from. All the structures I remembered were there, though seeming
larger than before, at least for a time. But then the chill of disappointment
came over me as the familiarity of the setting took hold of me and nothing
seemed to have changed. If anything, I was feeling claustrophobic—my
journey having inured me to open countryside—not being used to the
densely packed multitudes or, rather, having lost my affinity toward these

conditions. What could I have expected in only four months? The place was the same. It was my attitude toward it that had changed.

I became aware that everyone we passed by was staring at me. These were people I have never known and who could not have known me, as those of us living within the Pergamus, our palace complex, did not typically mingle with the populace at large. Some faces were familiar to me, and I smiled at the ones I thought I knew, but that would not have accounted for this overall seeming interest in me. I was becoming self-conscious over being so intensely scrutinized.

"Why are they staring like that?" I asked Agenor. "I find it very annoying."

"It's what you're wearing," Agenor replied. "You're dressed like a soldier, not like a woman, and definitely not like a princess."

I was reminded that I meant to change into my chiton before entering Troy. Had Agenor not come upon us so quickly, I could have discarded my Amazon attire, but as it was, I remained clad in my red tunic, tawny vest, and high boots. Never comfortable with being the center of attraction, I sensed my face becoming flushed in my uneasiness.

If I felt things congested in the lower city, I cannot say the same for the Pergamus. The citadel, consisting of our council hall, multiple palaces, and Apollo's temple, along with shrines to Athena and Zeus, was as imposing and grand as ever and loomed over the city in awesome magnificence. We left our horses in the inner corral below the complex and then proceeded up the steps. My heartbeat accelerated as I anxiously waited to see the members of my family.

My homecoming was bittersweet. At first, everyone was brimming with happiness over seeing me again, most believing, as Agenor said, that I had died along with Penthesileia on that northern plain. My father met me with abundant ebullience when we arrived at the palace, the joy any parent must feel at learning a child of theirs was safe and sound when the opposite had been feared and expected.

"Dear Polyxena," he greeted me, with tears of happiness running down his cheeks. "We believed you were lost to us. What hardships you must have endured."

He appeared considerably older than I remembered, his wrinkles more pronounced and hair thinner, undoubtedly the strain of the war imparting its effect on him, and his forceful, strong gait now seemed tottering and weak. How could that happen in four months?

"I did my best, Father," I said.

"Of course you did. We received the reports, so dismaying when Agenor told us that you were to accompany Penthesileia on her campaign. That you chose to do this, what dedication to your duties."

"You told me to do whatever was necessary."

"What a daughter. I am so proud of you." He then ended his hugging me and looked me in the eye, his demeanor turning serious. "It grieves me to tell you that we were unable to implement the plan we meant to carry out."

He confirmed what we had observed in coming here, that the Greeks were still around, no death blow had been dealt to them. His embarrassment was acute—he could scarcely look me in the eyes— for he had to concede that, where I had succeeded in accomplishing my part of the undertaking he entrusted to me, he had failed in his.

"Was that because Agamemnon sent too small a force against us?" I asked.

"No, it was because we were abandoned by one of our major allies. The Lycians withdrew their forces, no longer believing Troy can win this war. The timing could not been worse, just when you had talked Penthesileia into coming to our aid."

"You mean our cause was dead before it even began?" I gasped in my shock.

"I'm afraid so. Such are the fortunes of war, my dear. All the planning, the spying and scheming, the maneuverings, can disintegrate in an instant."

So what I had suspected was true. Everything we did was for absolutely nothing. The battles we fought, the casualties we sustained, the slaughter of the young Greek captives at Otrea, Penthesileia's death, all for nothing. This is what Achilles alluded to when he affirmed my mission had failed. Everything was a waste. I felt myself getting sick.

"Are you feeling all right, Polyxena?" my father asked after seeing my disillusionment. "You don't look well."

"I'll be fine," I reassured him. "Right now I'm heartsick. You don't know what we went through. All I believed we had accomplished is shattered for me."

"Ah, you grapple with the capriciousness war entails. My poor daughter, be comforted knowing that, in our eyes, you are a true heroine."

"I don't feel like a heroine."

"Oh, but you are. Very much so. You were sent to secure an ally for Troy, and you achieved this purpose. Who has done as much?"

I was not consoled by my father's words, preoccupied with the bitterness I felt over the results of our endeavors, all so pointless, casually dismissed as war's capriciousness. Perhaps I was being too hard on myself, I thought. After all, did I not undergo an experience of a lifetime? What kind of value do I place on having met beautiful Antiope? Or Queen Penthesileia? Or even Achilles? In truth, I would not exchange my encounters with them for anything yet lived. That my association with them should be of no benefit to Troy's cause did not alter the fact I enjoyed the time I spent with them, and I now cherish this above all else. I should thank my father for having granted me my opportunity, not hold this against him, for in exposing me to the fortunes of war, as he calls it, he has enriched my life in far greater measures than he can ever know. Through this sort of rationalization, I overcame my earlier despondency and started to feel better.

"I'm so glad you have returned safely to Troy," my father said. "You must see your mother and everyone else. They'll be overjoyed."

"Thank you, Father," I said, smiling at him; his happiness heightened when he saw this. I left him in his contentment, obviously feeling good over having seen me again, and proceeded for the residence hall, where I expected to meet the rest of our family.

Word of my return had indeed spread like a rampaging fire, for when I entered through the doors of our living area, everyone was standing there waiting to greet me: my brothers and sisters, my mother, Andromache, Helen. At first, my appearance seemed to come as a jolt—I think it was seeing me in my garb—but having overcome their astonishment, they then cheered and clapped their hands. I was a celebrity in their eyes. My mother broke out in tears as she rushed up to embrace me.

"Oh, Polyxena. My dear daughter," she wept profusely, and in her crying, she caused me to burst out in my own sobbing. I told myself I would not cry, but my determination abandoned me in that moment of our hugging. "You have come back to us. We believed you had died."

"No, Mother," I said after regaining my composure. "As you can see, I'm alive and well."

She was still in tears when she released herself from me and said, "When we got word that cruel Achilles had killed Penthesileia—we knew you were with her—we were certain you perished along with her. But here you are. Let me look at you."

As I conceded to my mother's indulgence, I glanced at everyone in attendance, smiling in turn at each one upon seeing their sparkling eyes and cheerful grins. I noticed that both Andromache and Helen were teary eyed, as were Cassandra and Cruesa. Everyone appeared deeply affected by my mother's emotional reunion with me.

"Your face is quite tan," my mother said after taking her full glimpse of me. "You have been in the sun too long."

"I have," I told her. "I spent most of my time in the field, with the Amazon army."

"What outrageous attire," she then added. "You're dressed like a man."

"It's what the Amazons wear, Mother. I assure you, nobody has mistaken me for a man." My reply elicited chuckles from the group.

"Undoubtedly," she answered. "Not with that much of your legs showing."

"Tonight we have a feast in your honor, dear Sister," said Helenus, my brother known for his ability to predict future events. "You will have to tell us about the Amazons. We are most curious to know what they're like."

"Men," Andromache said. "Expecting to hear erotic details about women who have no need of them. That's what fascinates you, isn't it?"

"Don't deny it, Andromache," said Helenus with a grin. "It fascinates women as well."

At this point, Paris, who had quietly stood next to Helen, gazed directly at me and drew attention to himself with a mild cough.

"So tell us, Polyxena," he slowly began speaking. "How did you manage to escape from Achilles?"

Stillness. Everyone focused their concentration on me, leaving me no time to deliberate over how I should answer. My fear was that more would be made out of what I told them than was necessary or appropriate.

"I didn't," I answered.

"He ravaged you?" my mother interjected, eyes blazing.

"No, Mother. Quite the opposite. He escorted me back to Troy."

Unearthly silence. If I had everyone's undivided attention before, now it was absolutely riveted on me.

"Achilles brought you here?" Paris said, astounded.

"Yes. We had no way of getting back after he defeated the Amazons. Penthesileia was going to bring me here, but when she was killed, her warriors rode off, leaving me and my servants to ourselves."

"Why?"

"I don't know. Well, no, I do know. I think he took a fancy to me."

"And what did you do in return?" my mother sounded off, her previous affection for me apparently diminished.

"I did nothing. He volunteered his services, without demanding anything from me or my attendants. We came to no harm."

Paris was intrigued by my comments. I was hoping he would let the matter rest, but he wanted to know more.

"From what you say, am I wrong in concluding that you came to know the man? You spent days with him."

"If by that you mean what he is like, then yes."

"And?"

"We became friends."

The uproar that followed startled me. First they, one and all, gasped in disbelief, and then they, particularly my brothers, unleashed a torrent of discord, shouting and grumbling, even hurling abuses, not only at me but among themselves as some of them defended my actions while others condemned it. I instinctively sensed that I had sabotaged my welcome arrival. Only Andromache and Helen gave me a sympathetic look. My mother, so happy moments ago, glared at me, her utter astonishment, if not outright hostility, much in evidence. Her reaction dismayed me, but I could understand it, for she had lost three of her sons at the hands of Achilles and could not be blamed for holding the man up to be the worst of monsters. With Paris, I was not as generous. I did not appreciate his having placed me in this position when he, of all people, ought to have empathized, or at least made sense of my situation. After all, his abduction of Helen was a far greater affront against Troy, in my opinion, than my mere friendship with its greatest antagonist. So what if I was not altogether honest and did in fact love Achilles; this still was a lesser offense, coming as a consequence of this war and not from having initiated the actions that created the war. Paris was out of line, and I resented that.

After the commotion died down—fortunately it was short- lived—and a calmer demeanor took possession of the group, as its members realized their conduct was quite unpolished, I became more resolute that I was not going to allow myself to be flustered or intimidated by the interrogations I had been subjected to. I had no reason to be disparaging toward my conduct with Achilles. Their judgment of me over this matter was unwarranted and based on ignorance.

"I'm sorry, Polyxena," my mother said, trying to ameliorate her previously exhibited displeasure toward me. "Were it anyone else but Achilles, I would be more kindly disposed in accepting it. I am wrong to fault you. You were in dire circumstances and, although you see him as a friend, the event was not of your choosing."

"He protected us on the way back, Mother," I emphasized.

She dismissed my comment, as if I had not said anything at all. "You must be tired after all you have been through," she said. "We have a bath prepared for you in your old chamber. Come, relax before this evening's affair."

I nodded my assent to the suggestion; a bath sounded extremely appealing at this time. Before leaving them, I once more glared at Paris, making my displeasure known to him with my penetrating stare. He was unruffled by this, no emotion revealing itself in his steady gaze.

"You will have to tell me more about your friend," he said. "I want to know as much as I can about him. Perhaps tonight."

Was he being sincere? If so, then maybe I misjudged him. Or did he have an ulterior motive? At this point, I no longer cared. I wanted only to luxuriate in a hot soaking to rid myself of the grime accumulated on the long journey back. I smiled at everyone on my way out. They still had the look of marvel and amazement about them, as if I had indeed returned from the dead. I could hear them talking among themselves, giving expression to their great astonishment at seeing me, their excitement over this, but also their joy—I must be fair in my appraisal—and genuine happiness. I was very much the star attraction at this particular moment.

Once I cleared the doorway, I took the familiar steps through the corridor toward its far end, where my chamber had been prepared for me. As I entered—it seemed so roomy to me—I saw the steam rising from the tub emplaced against the back wall. My mother's attendants waited on me, towels in hand, ready to assist me in every way. Menodice and Thalia were in need of their own rest, and I excused them from their duties earlier in the day.

It is hard to describe the immense pleasure I derived from a hot bath after going four months without one. The cold-water showers, plunges into rivers or diverted channels, and sponge rubdowns were all such poor substitutes for the real thing. For long stretches, I just lay in the tub, submerged up to my neck, relishing the warmth penetrating my body, so soothing, so satisfying. The tan I had acquired was limited to my head, arms, and legs, leaving the rest of me as light as ever, and the overall appearance of this struck me as almost comical; my body consisted of two distinct hues, their demarcation clearly defined. I took ample time in my immersions, making up for all my missed opportunities, basking in my relaxation; I am certain my attendants wearied of my indulgence. By the time I finally arose to be wrapped in the towels held forth by them, I felt truly clean. I would have wished to just sleep then, the bath having induced a tiredness in me, but I had to prepare myself for the evening's feast in my honor. I could hardly absent myself from the occasion.

As the evening approached, my vitality returned to me, eclipsing the fatigue that overcame me earlier, for I again eagerly anticipated meeting everyone and engaging in conversations with them. I put the final touches into my ensemble, checking in the mirror to see that my attendants had set my hair properly and that my chiton suitably enhanced my appearance. Overall, I was pleased with the way I looked. My attire exposed only my tanned area without revealing any of the lighter skin, so nobody could see my dual composition.

Helen and Andromache came to my chamber to see how I was coming along. Both indicated a mild surprise at seeing me. I think they saw me as very presentable, if not beautiful to behold, making me feel quite good about myself.

"Oh, my, Polyxena," Andromache said. "I've never seen you look so lovely."

"Do you think they'll like me?"

"If they don't, they're blind," Helen replied.

"Well then, let's go," I teased. "Let me dazzle them."

Helen laughed at this, as did Andromache. They were my true friends, and I preferred them to my own relatives when it came to sociable togetherness. We left my chamber and entered the main palace hall that had been converted into a dining facility with tables and chairs placed about. The guests were milling around when I made my entry. I could not believe the reaction I solicited as I walked in.

Everyone was truly taken aback, and their talking abruptly ceased. I drew admiring glances from men and women alike. My brothers gaped openmouthed; I swear I saw them drooling from the mouth. Obviously, they liked what they saw.

My father, on seeing me approach him, was, for an instant, stunned into silence, but then his eyes brightened, and he moved forward to greet me.

"My dear Polyxena," he remarked. "Is this really you? I can scarcely believe it. Your absence has been most kind to you. You look sensational."

"Accolades are always welcome, Father," I answered, smiling widely. "But I'm sure you say that to all women."

"Ask Hecuba," he laughed, looking her way. "Have I ever called you sensational, dear?"

"Not for a long, long time," she answered, glinting at Father.

"Indeed? Perhaps you were sensational—once." He twinkled back at her and chuckled.

Everyone laughed, and I admit that I enjoyed having been the source of their joviality. With Helen and Andromache standing still next to me, my brothers and sisters presented themselves and accorded me their salutations and fond respects.

"I'm happy to have you back, dear Sister," said Helenus. "Of course, I knew all along that you would return."

"Did you? And what else have you known?" I asked him in my curiosity over whether he had presaged the events as they played out.

He merely gave me a faint smile, indicating to me that he had foreseen more than he let on, perhaps even the affair I would have with Achilles. That was disconcerting for me, for I questioned whether my intimacy with the Greek could be kept a secret.

"Enough," he said after a long pause. "Let us just say that I anticipated your safe return."

"I was never worried about my safety, Helenus. Cassandra told me as much."

"Well and good," he said before walking away, leaving me with some reservations over his insinuations. I do not like seers; they have an awareness transcending what the rest of us apprehend, which subjects us to vulnerabilities implied or explicit in the interpretations of their prognostications whether they are accurate or not. Sometimes it is better not to know what is to become than to know this when all that you do will not alter the outcome.

Next to greet me was Cassandra, dour as always but genuinely pleased to see me. She did not linger long in conversation, aside from the congratulatory comments now all too familiar to me. She was followed by Deiphobus who was known, at least to the court ladies, for coveting Helen, even though she was married to Paris.

"What an extraordinary adventure you've had," said Deiphobus, glancing more at Helen than me, tactless to be sure and quite annoying to me. Even after four months, some things remain unchanged. "But you're here, and none the worse for it. By the way, you look fabulous in that tan."

"Why, thank you, Brother," I responded. "I'm glad you noticed in spite of the distractions posed by Helen."

"I have a weakness for lovely women," said Deiphobus, blushing. "You must forgive this foolish man his extravagance."

"You mean his lewdness, don't you?" I said, displeased over his conduct.

"Whatever. I am a slave to my passions."

"You need to be more respectful, Deiphobus," interjected Helen. "I am a married woman, deeply in love with my husband. Your attempts at acquiring any solicitations out of me are quite useless."

"As you say, dear Sister-in-Law. But remember, fortune has a way of rewarding those who are most persistent."

"Not in this case, I assure you," said Helen.

Deiphobus added nothing more and walked off, his face red with embarrassment. Helen had effectively, almost callously, put him in his place. I sympathized with his plight; he was afflicted with an insatiable craving for what he can never have, his brother's wife, which had to hurt. But I also had empathy for Helen; her exceptional beauty was so irresistible to men that they lusted after her even following her binding commitment in marriage. While this may be flattering at times, it also had to be tiresome, and I often sensed that Helen questioned if she had been blessed or cursed by her pulchritude.

"He cannot help himself, Helen," said Andromache. "It's sad when you think about it."

"Even if so, Andromache," answered Helen, unmoved, "he ought to know when a situation is futile for him. He reminds me of a puppy. He seeks your constant attention and does not know when to stop."

"Until he grows weary," I added.

"If only that were so," said Helen. "He never ceases in his trying. But quiet now—here comes Paris."

Paris strode up to us, leaving the cluster of friends he had been with, looking very dapper in his white cloak and beaming in his grin. Until I met Achilles, I believed no man was more handsome than Paris, and I was immensely proud of being around him just for his looks alone. He and Helen definitely made an attractive couple, turning people's heads wherever they went and maybe even arousing envy among the onlookers. But he lacked the strength of Hector, as well as the courage—some even claimed that he was somewhat cowardly—which detracted from his person and may explain why Aeneas rather than he was selected Troy's supreme commander after Hector's death. He made up for his deficiencies in combat skills by constantly practicing with the bow and arrow and was an accomplished archer, perhaps even the best one in our army. In summation, he was not as attractive as Achilles to me, another consequence resulting from having undergone my journey.

"I see you three remain in league with each other," he said, "just as before you left, Polyxena."

"We are good friends, Brother," I affirmed.

"As you speak of friends, how is your newfound enemy friend?"

"Paris," exclaimed Helen. "Your bluntness borders on outright rudeness. Polyxena has told us Achilles escorted her back to Troy when she was in need of that. Try to be more understanding."

I glared at him, but his smile told me he was not that serious, and I soon recovered from my initial umbrage over his cold remark.

"How should I know?" I said to Paris. "He brought me here, yes, but that's it."

"Excuse my ill manners. I meant, what is he like."

"Very handsome, if you must know. Indeed the handsomest-looking man I have ever met. He is what they say about him: the most beautiful of the Greek warriors."

"Beautiful? A curious choice of words."

"But apt. He is magnificent to behold, a true feast for the eyes. Of course, I'm giving you a feminine perspective."

Paris may have actually resented my depiction of our nemesis, in the sense that I challenged his opinion about himself being possessed of manly beauty, perhaps believing he had no rivals in that regard, a viewpoint reinforced by the fact that Helen fell under his spell and was now his. Interestingly enough, both Helen and Andromache were sufficiently intrigued over my description that I held their interest to a great measure, and their searching eyes indicated to me that they wished to know more about Achilles. I thought this amazing for Andromache, as she might have most despised the slayer of her husband; she was at last reconciled to his fate.

"So he is physically attractive," said Paris. "What else?"

"Very pleasant and courteous, even charming when he wants to be. He does have that temper he's known for, and sometimes he can startle you with the unexpected; he slew one of his men for insulting him right in front of me. I was very much afraid of him when he first entered our tent, as were Menodice and Thalia. But he soon let us know he wouldn't harm us. When he learned that we had no guards left to take us back to Troy, he chose to perform that duty for us. He values the warrior's code and honored Penthesileia at her funeral as a great warrior."

"Yes, we saw how he honored Hector."

"He regretted that," I was quick to point out, not appreciating his retort. "He said he was wild with rage over Hector having slain his best friend, Patroclus, and lost his reason."

"My suggestion to you, dear Sister," he coldly remarked, "is that you remember *that* instead of everything else you know about him. He had an ulterior motive for bringing you here."

Paris, at times, could be very intrusive, and I was rankled by what I felt was his disrespect for my suppositions.

"And what might that be?" I asked, sensing my pressure rising.

"You said before, he took a fancy to you."

"Then why didn't he force himself on me? He had ample opportunity."

Paris declined to state his opinion about that, and I was relieved that my conversation with him had evidently ended. He smiled at me, a gesture that perplexed me, and then left us to join Deiphobus at the opposite end of the hall, but not before telling Helen he would join her at the table for the dinner.

"How unlike him," Helen said to me. "He's still angry over Hector's death."

"He should not be pointing his accusing finger at me, Helen," I said. "It's not as if I just readily acquiesced and threw myself at Achilles. I censured myself, telling myself over and over that he was Hector's slayer and that I must hate him for this. I resisted, knowing he is our enemy, as much as any woman would, refusing to succumb to him."

This was a lie, of course, but not entirely. I did recall that, when I first met Achilles, I was horrified to be in his presence and vilified him for the suffering he brought upon our family, holding this against him. So it was not as if I felt no contrition over my subsequent behavior, enduring the pangs of condemnation and castigation that I hurled against myself. I was, in great measure, a victim of circumstance and should not have to bear any abuse or criticism for this.

"I understand," said Helen. "I'll talk to Paris. His insensitivity to your predicament is uncalled for."

"You have my sympathy, Polyxena," Andromache added, much to my comfort, for she, above anyone else, had justifications for denouncing my actions. But what could she have known about what I had done? I confided nothing in her other than to acknowledge that I saw Achilles as a friend. True, for her, this admission could have been painful to hear, and that she surmounted her distress over this said much of her character; she was a noble woman.

When the announcement for dinner was called, I learned that I was to sit next to Agenor who, although not of our family, had been invited to celebrate my safe return along with his father, Antenor. I was delighted to be once again in his company, especially now that we had a lot to talk about, having shared our adventure. As we dined, we spoke of the times we had spent together on the way to and at Themiscyra.

"I was saddened to hear about Queen Penthesileia," he said. "She took a liking to you."

"I saw her as a mentor. She was very good to me," I answered, my eyes moistening as the sorrow of her loss once more impacted on me.

"I'm sorry."

"No, it's all right. I'll get over it."

"What became of Antiope " he next asked.

Antiope. The very mention of her name filled me with a deep sense of regret over the manner in which we parted. My recollection of her last words to me, begging me to come with her, almost paralyzed me with the gravest misgivings that I had made the biggest blunder of my life, having denied myself a true turning point that can never be reclaimed. Yet at the same time, I took comfort in knowing that she had survived that last battle and managed to escape with much of her force, and my overall reaction was one of happiness rather than despondency. I smiled as I thought about her.

"My guess is that she now rules the Amazons," I said.

"Ah, she survived. I'm glad for that. She was a remarkable woman, and a rare beauty. I found it interesting that, after I got back, I missed her more than anyone else."

If Agenor only knew. How could I adequately describe what she meant for me, the joy she gave me, or how much I missed her as I now recalled her in my mind. I needed to distract myself from thinking of her, else my celebration would be ruined in my abundantly flowing tears that was sure to follow.

"Not Menodice?" I said.

"Well, yes. Her too. But she's here. How did you know?"

"You haven't been exactly discreet. You made Thalia jealous."

I think this flattered Agenor, which was not my intent, for he appeared quite smug in his grin. Men are so easily persuaded of their prowess and self-worth when their vanity is bolstered by complimentary assertions.

"Did I?"

"You did."

"I had no idea," he said, brimming in his aura.

"Stop it. I didn't tell you this so you can gloat."

He raised his eyebrows as he glanced sideways at me, his grin still very much in evidence, absorbed in his adulation and quite enamored with himself. But then we both saw the humor in this and began to giggle, to the curiosity of everyone seated around us.

At this juncture, my father stood up and, through this gesture, quieted the room. He raised a goblet of wine.

"I propose a toast," he said, "to the return of a daughter we thought lost to us. During a time of our protracted war, when our world is engulfed in never-ending sorrow and heartbreak over loved ones slain, we are blessed with an occasion for which we can rejoice. Join me in my happiness over having regained my daughter, looking more lovely than ever before. To Polyxena!"

"To Polyxena!" everyone voiced off and then downed their drinks.

I arose and gave everyone a bow of my head amid a wide smile, but I was happy that I was not called upon to give a speech. I would not have known what to say. Besides, my return had pleased my celebrants well enough and required no additional affirmation on my part. But I must say that the salute granted me made me feel quite good, and I thoroughly appreciated the praise given me. I had, in truth, come home.

CHAPTER XII

I N THE PASSING OF THE next few days, I tried to make the adjustments necessary to fit back into the former lifestyle I had led before being sent on my mission and found the going tougher than I had imagined. For one thing, the claustrophobic feelings that first struck me as we entered Troy now similarly affected me residing within the confines of the Pergamus. My months of living out of a tent, exposed to the vastness of the open plains of Phrygia and Mysia, as well as amid the widely scattered buildings of Themiscyra, had imparted a strong preference for spaciousness in me, resulting in a cramped, enclosed feeling that plagued me in my present surroundings. Adding to the pent-up consciousness was the besieged state of the city, impeding free movement to and from the seashore, my view of this from our walls never ceasing to remind me of our imposed restrictions, something that had never bothered me before but that now existed as an irritant to my desires to move readily about. Facing inland, to where the Dardanian Gates opened, we met no obstacles, as most of our allied camps were located there, and this is where much of our population dwelled in the houses that extended beyond our fortifications. We kept our horses in this area, mostly within a fenced-off section extending over a wide expanse, allowing them a lot of running room. We had also erected a smaller enclosure for them within the walls, where I kept Zephyrus.

Once the novelty of my return had worn off, things readily transformed themselves into a normality, and I soon ceased to be the luminary I had been. I usually woke up around sunrise and took a morning walk about the palace complex, the Pergamus, or the citadel, which was actually comprised of several palaces adjoining each other as well as the official buildings, where the councils took place. Also, there were three temple structures in this quarter, one to Great Zeus and another to the Goddess Athena, actually shrines, and the third, a true temple, to Apollo, Troy's patron god—Cassandra's place we called it, as she was his priestess and spent so much of her time there. By the time I finished my walk, the rest of my family members were up, and we typically ate breakfast as a group. After that, the women spent much of the remaining day in the weaving rooms or the residence hall, where we recited stories and poems. Much as on my journey, my favorite times of the day were the evenings after we had eaten our meals and remained together in the hall, relating our adventures and happenings of the day until it was dark. We had frequent visitors during this time who shared in our company, typically for another purpose, mainly to woo Cassandra and I, unattached as we were. Agenor was often a guest so he could make his overtures toward Menodice. It seemed such a mundane existence after my experience with the Amazons.

I livened things up by riding Zephyrus, typically inland toward our allied camps and back, usually twice a day, often with the companionship of one of my brothers or Agenor and, every once in a while, with Andromache who was also an accomplished horseman, or rather, horsewoman. Now and then, I rode by myself, seeking the solitude I needed to escape the confinement that prevailed over me on occasions. Zephyrus was such a salvation for me from the frustrations and boredom surrounding me; I felt a true sense of liberation in taking my rides, but he was also a reminder of a more enjoyable time, of Antiope and the rides I so often took with her.

Wearing a chiton while riding now seemed awkward, even ridiculous, to me, having to fold its pleads repeatedly up my legs, and I reverted, despite my mother's disapproving glances, back to donning my shorter Amazon tunic when going on my excursions. I also much preferred their enclosed deerskin boots to our delicate open-laced sandals; being much sturdier and more durable, they were far more practical, especially when mounting or dismounting Zephyrus. Before long, I was also wearing the leather vest and then also the rectangular cloak when it was colder. All that was missing was the metallic breastplate, crescent shield, and helmet and weaponry, and I would have been the complete Amazon warrior.

I thought a lot about Achilles during my solitary rides and increasingly longed to see him again. I kept wondering how I could possibly arrange a meeting with him, hopefully on a continuous basis, perhaps during the frequent riding periods I took. What if I just rode to the shore in the direction of the Greek camps? Would I be safe? I was tempted to take that step and, if intercepted by the soldiers, simply say that Achilles requested to see me. Surely the mention of his name ought to protect me from harm. I knew the approximate vicinity of the Myrmidon base. But how would I justify my actions to anyone here? The sentries on the walls were certain to see me. If I only knew what he was thinking, if he also desired to see me. With each passing day, my obsession to see him increased, and I knew it was now only a matter of time before I dared to take the measures I contemplated.

As luck would have it, we entered another period of lull in the fighting when both sides accommodated each other in a temporary truce, accepting the armistice in effect for an agreed-upon time, sometimes extending to as long as a month. These spells offered both Greeks and Trojans a respite in which they could move freely about and even fraternize with each other. Through these events, we obtained much of our intelligence on the morale and disposition of our enemy, as they did on us, I am certain. Rumor had it that this present lull was spawned by another rift occurring between Agamemnon and Achilles, primarily over Achilles having slain Thersites but also for having escorted me back to Troy, which the supreme commander viewed as a violation of his orders. My heart palpitated when I heard this, for I was again in his picture, and I knew he was thinking about me. With the intermingling of our soldiers with the enemy's, I saw that my approaching the Greek camps would not be conspicuous to our sentinels, and I chose to take the step I had long thought about.

So it was that, during one of my afternoon rides on Zephyrus, I directed my mount toward the shoreline and approached the camping area, where I believed the Myrmidons were located. When I got within approximately a hundred paces of the camp's perimeter, several soldiers guarding the grounds walked up to me. I stopped and waited on them to reach me.

"You are the Trojan princess, Polyxena," one of the soldiers addressed me.

"How did you know?" I asked.

He then removed his helmet, and I recognized him as having been among the guards who had brought us back to Troy.

"Do you see who I am now?" he said.

"I do," I said, smiling at him and, by that, making him a standout among his companions. "Thank you for what you have done. You must then know why I have come here."

"My lord will be pleased. We shall take you to him."

Once again, I had a benign escort taking me through an enemy camp, a sight that drew considerable attention from the rest of the soldiers standing about, me on Zephyrus, walking in the accompaniment of ten soldiers on foot, penetrating deeper and deeper into the heart of the foe's grounds. We arrived at a large tent adjacent to the beach, flying the banner that denoted it as a headquarters for the Myrmidons. Even before I could dismount, Achilles had emerged from inside his tent. He stopped on seeing me, quite surprised for a moment, then he stepped ahead, his eyes glowing and a broad smile brightening his face.

"Princess," he said as he lifted his arms to help me down. "My wishes are granted."

I was so happy at seeing him, nearly swooning in his embrace, longing for his touch, a warmth sweeping all over me. The poets failed in lending an adequate description for the sensations I felt.

"I've thought of you every day since we last parted," Achilles said, his joy at seeing me immeasurable, revealed in his shining eyes and irresistible smile.

"I had to see you," I said. "I missed you so."

"You coming here tells me that we have opportunities to meet, even if we are on opposite sides. The matter is of our choosing."

"If only that were so," I said. "We have the advantage of this temporary truce; it allowed me to come here unnoticed, I hope so at least. Otherwise, I wouldn't have dared."

"That means," he said in a subdued laugh, "that, if the war keeps dragging on, I will have to arrange for more truces." He then led me into his tent, out of the hot sun, where, at the far end of the enclosure, I saw his notorious concubine, Briseis, at least, I assumed that was her. She was not at all pleased over seeing me, glaring at me with hostile eyes, apparently regarding me as a rival for her lover's attention. Nor was I pleased at seeing her, for her presence told me Achilles and I would not be intimate with each other. She was an audience to our affair and inhibited me from yielding to my desires.

"This is Briseis," Achilles introduced her. "Given back to me by Agamemnon. She makes my lengthy stay here tolerable."

I rendered her my typical faint smile, used when I was not altogether happy over a situation but still surrendered to the customary requirement to be cordial. Was I envious of her?

"And this is Polyxena," Achilles said to Briseis. "She is the Trojan princess you have heard me speak of."

Briseis looked me over, scanning me from head to toe, her smile coming as difficult for her as mine did to me, and for an instant, she had me thinking I was a threat to her, an intrusion into the blissful context of her life, and I actually felt badly about this. That could not be correct, I checked myself; she was, after all, a captive in this war and obviously had no choice over her status. Yet I saw her as fortunate in that she could receive the love of a man such as Achilles, the most splendid of that species, night after night, something I could only dream about my desires. Having completed our acquaintance, Achilles and I sat down at one end of the tent and talked about the usual things lovers talk about: the joy of their previous time together, how they missed and longed for a return of this, the pain of their separation, and so on. He held me close to him, and we frequently broke up our conversing in favor of soft kisses and tender caressing. But he never asked Briseis to leave, thereby limiting our reunion to merely the pleasure of our company and nothing more. Yet I relished our time together, dismissing the intrusive presence of his mistress—no lord, Greek or Trojan, lived without one—and was quite content that I had come to visit him. All too quickly, the realization that I had to get back before my long absence would be noticed took hold of me and forced me into reluctantly disengaging myself from his embrace.

"I must return," I told Achilles. "They are sure to look for me if I don't."

We arose and together walked out of the tent, where Zephyrus was being held by one of the soldiers waiting on me. Achilles clasped me tight to him one more time and then lifted me onto my horse.

"We can meet again," he said, his warm eyes penetrating me. "The truce may last a while. Perhaps even in a day or so."

"I would very much like that," I said.

"Should I come to Troy?"

I was shocked that he would suggest that. Truce or no truce, that was too bold a measure to even consider and assured him no protection. His reputation, and the scourge he represented for Troy, let alone my family, heavily mitigated against such a proposition.

"No," I immediately reacted in my alarm. "It's too dangerous."

"Very well," he replied. "I must rely on your moves. Thank you so much for coming. You have truly cheered up my day."

I waved at him and rode away, not requiring an escort out of the camp, as word of my visit had spread through the ranks and guaranteed my passage back. I was worried that I may have stayed too long, for I saw the field between the coast and city now devoid of people, making me highly noticeable as I galloped along. I was the lone rider coming to the Scaean Gates, those facing the sea; fortunately, they were still open, as it was daytime. I thought about riding to the rear of the city, but that would have made me even more prominent, increasing my time before the walls. My hope lay in the guard being lax in their duties during this lull period so as not to recognize me.

It turned out that I was indeed spotted by the sentries as I emerged from the Greek camp, and I was met by one of their commanders when I arrived at the inner corral and dismounted Zephyrus.

"What's a woman doing out there?" he said, not recognizing me as a member of the royal house. I did not respond, holding on to the reins of my horse as I saw him fuming.

"Speak up, woman," the commander angrily demanded. "Why were you at the Greek camp?"

"I visited a friend," I said, unnerved over the aggressive manner in which he spoke to me.

"A Trojan woman has an enemy friend? You're a liar. I think you're a spy."

"Do not speak to me in that offensive tone!" I shouted at him. "I am the daughter of King Priam. You will treat me with courtesy."

He was quieted by my outburst, unsure if he should believe me or not. That I confidently rode into the city straight for the royal corral gave credence to my words and made him ponder if he might not have erred. He backed off, afraid of aggravating a situation that could have grave consequences for him, and I was prepared to dismiss his conduct, directing one of the corral keepers to see to Zephyrus, when Deiphobus walked upon the scene. My heart sank.

"Polyxena," he spoke out. "Where have you been?"

What could I say? If I lied and said I was merely giving Zephyrus his exercises, the guard commander would repudiate this. I hesitated in answering.

"She rode in from the Greek camp, prince," the guard commander said.

Deiphobus gave me the dirtiest look, obviously making more out of the circumstances than was warranted.

"So you saw Achilles," he remarked.

How was I to deny it? I had already confessed to regarding Achilles as a friend in front of all of them. Who else would I see except him? My first instinct was to plead with Deiphobus to keep this to himself, but realistically, there was little chance in the prospect; the guards had seen me and were sure to tell others.

"My, my," continued Deiphobus, "you are a shameless slut."

"What?" Now he angered me. I glanced at the guard captain and saw him smirking, taking pleasure in my deprecation.

"What else can I think, Sister? Even if I'm wrong, at best, your conduct is treasonous—you probably don't realize this—and subject to a tribunal. A lull in the fighting does not apply to the major warlords, and Achilles is one. Only lower-ranking soldiers are permitted to fraternize."

I was not aware of this but was also alarmed that my brother would even consider forwarding my case to any official judgment.

"Why do you hate me so," I asked him, "that you would call for a tribunal?"

"Not you, dear Sister—Achilles."

"I beg you, Deiphobus, keep this from our father. He has suffered much. This will not help."

I could see the wheels turning in my brother's head as he deliberated over my request. He studied the possibilities offered by my predicament, appreciating the sway he held over me.

"I won't say anything," he finally said. "But he'll find out. This is not the sort of thing that can be kept a secret. People love to gossip. A daughter of Priam visiting the enemy camp, that's juicy."

I was angry at myself for not taking the potential consequences of my actions into account, and I was suspicious of my brother's motivation. Deiphobus was a devious sort, not to be confided in, and if he offered conciliatory gestures, there was a reason behind his amenable facade. He walked away a few paces with the guard commander, and I saw him say something to the officer but was unable to hear what it was. I did not trust him.

"I told him to keep this to himself and to tell his guards likewise," Deiphobus said as he stepped back to me, easing my worries a bit. "It won't work, you know. But maybe it will postpone things. You owe me one, Sister."

"Thank you, Brother," I replied, relieved to some extent as I hurried away but also wary of whether I had not bargained with a viper. He was sure to tell Paris, I thought, as the two of them were the closest of brothers, then Paris would tell Helen, and Helen would tell Andromache. I should never have made my visit. What a mistake. But it was done, and no amount of wishing otherwise was going to alter the situation. Sometimes I am such a fool.

That evening, when we were all together for our supper, I was more tense than usual, as I felt myself under the constant scrutiny of Paris and Deiphobus who glanced my way repeatedly, adding greatly to my consternation. As I feared, the conversation soon turned to me, spurred on by my prying mother of all people.

"You were gone all afternoon, Polyxena," she said, her steely eyes stabbing me. "We couldn't find you."

"Why were you looking for me?" I reacted sharply. "I have need for my privacy."

"How touchy. You don't have to get sore about it. We merely wanted you to join us in our discussions."

"I'm sorry, Mother," I apologized.

"You must be more respectful to your elders, Daughter."

"I said I was sorry."

"Do not raise your voice to me!" she erupted in her exacerbation. "You have changed, Polyxena. Your trip has transformed you into a different person, not the loving daughter I once knew."

I was deeply shocked over her outburst, directed as it was straight at me, not even having been aware of the changes in my behavior she accused me of. Her anger caused me to focus on her insinuations, troubling me considerably, especially if they were true. Had I actually changed that much, to the point that my conduct was so evident and affected those around me? I could not believe it. Everyone sat about spellbound at our exchange of words.

"Forgive me, Mother," I said, feeling badly about having disturbed her so. "I had no idea. It hurts me to hear this."

Now it was my mother's turn to feel compassion for me. Whatever I said touched her to such a degree that she began to weep.

"Dear Polyxena," she whimpered. "I was too harsh. I didn't mean it. To undergo what you did at your tender age had to be a difficult ordeal. Excuse my indiscretion."

"I do, Mother, with all my heart."

I was again in her good graces, for she was quite satisfied, commenting repeatedly on what a fine, loving daughter I was. Her happiness, of course, affected the rest of us, enhancing our joy and leading to the gaiety we were used to on these occasions. But to say that I could readily dismiss the disturbance she had created in me was wrong. I pondered long over whether she had accurately described my disposition and groped for the ways in which I could improve myself. The notion struck me if it was not my introspection that led my mother to the judgment about having changed. If so, then I had no answer as to how I would mend my ways, for it was true that my journey had led me to question and think about things, things that never before had given me cause for reflection. In that sense, I had indeed changed.

My father, who sat quietly throughout the exchange, winked at me, elevating my spirits to such an extent that I almost forgot what transpired earlier. I truly needed that at this time, coming at a moment when I was about to sink back into the abyss of self-absorption. Silently, I thanked him for the gesture.

"We never did find out where you spent the afternoon," Paris then said.

Paris had a way of refocusing attention back on a problem that I wished had gone away, and I was not happy about this, sensing everyone's concentration directed back at me. I was sure Deiphobus had told him where I had been. Should I lie?

"I was riding Zephyrus and lost track of time," I said, anticipating a barrage of questions.

"Be more cautious, Daughter," my father said. "A royal princess riding alone exposes herself to potential dangers. I strongly urge you to have a partner when you do this."

"I will, Father."

To my surprise, no one else disputed this. My answer had satisfied them, much to my relief, and their conversations centered on other topics.

Deiphobus, to his credit, refused to linger over the matter, even though he could have made things hot for me, and, at present, won my admiration. I decided I would stay late, if he did also, and thank him for his shown discretion.

Soon enough, our gathering dispersed to their individual chambers, except for Paris, Deiphobus, and me. We remained in the hall after everyone else had gone, my intention in staying to thank Deiphobus for his prudence, but I had not expected Paris to be there, and that he was confirmed to me that Deiphobus had indeed told him about my visit to Achilles.

"So you know," I said to him.

"Very foolish of you," Paris said.

"What will you do to me? Threaten me with a tribunal as Deiphobus did?"

"Let me ask you this: how far are you willing to go to exonerate yourself of the crime you could be accused of?"

"What crime? I did nothing wrong."

"Treason. Spying. Fraternizing with the enemy. Name it, and so you could be charged."

"Wild conjectures—nothing more."

"We have the witnesses. A number of guards saw you."

I was at their mercy. My only recourse was to adhere to whatever they proposed and try to make my amends. I cannot believe I got myself into this mess.

"What do you want me to do?" I asked, fearing what they might say.

"We want to use you as bait, pardon the crudeness of that term," Paris proposed, "to lure Achilles into the open, so I might have a shot at him and bring him down."

I was horrified, stunned, so severely shaken that I could barely breathe, but then I was also outraged over the very suggestion that I should be an accomplice in a deed tantamount to the utmost betrayal of one's trust. No matter what the consequences, I was not going to be a part of this.

"I will not!" I railed at Paris. "Decide whatever you will. I'm not doing this."

Paris had anticipated my response, for he revealed no surprise over my declaration, and he kept himself quite collected as I refused him. I expected him to turn into a raging beast, but he evinced no strong emotion and instead resorted to calm reason in pressing his point.

"Think about it," he said. "You can be Troy's salvation. Achilles is the most dangerous of our enemy. If we can get rid of him, the war might still be won."

"I don't need to think about it. I will not assist you in this."

"You are so stupid," Deiphobus reproached me, irritated over my reluctance. "What is he to you? Before this war, you knew nothing of him."

"That is exactly the point, Deiphobus; I now know him."

"You're being selfish. Think of Troy, your brothers that he has slain, Hector! You have an opportunity most rare in anyone's life: to make a difference. You want to throw this away over ridiculous sentimentality?"

Paris became annoyed over his brother's loss of temper and motioned for Deiphobus to settle down, preferring his own approach to one of hostility.

"In a way, you have already done your part, Polyxena," he said. "In fact, we don't even need you. All we have to do is send out a herald to let Achilles know you wish to see him, whether true of not. That ought to be sufficient inducement for him to come within range. So you see, what you decide is actually irrelevant."

What Paris implied was that Achilles was doomed no matter what I did, and this reality bore heavily into my mind, as my own action had furnished the conditions allowing this to happen. But that was not quite true, for the same inducement could be applied whether I had taken my ride out to see him or not. He would respond likewise to their message based solely on the journey we underwent. A cold chill ran through me, and I suddenly feared for him. I attempted to dissuade my brothers from their purpose.

"It won't work," I feigned a scoff. "Achilles doesn't do a woman's bidding."

"Yes, he will. We know he loves you. Men in love do stupid things."

Paris was the last person to be telling me this. Bringing Helen, another king's wife, to Troy was anything but smart.

"What makes you think that?" I replied. "My own impression is that we are friends, nothing more."

"That's not what Menodice told us."

Menodice! She could not keep her mouth shut. I cursed the day I ever decided to have her accompany me on our mission.

"She's wrong," I asserted, my anxiety mounting. "We're only friends."

Paris eyed me curiously, perceiving that I was lying to him, but refrained from uttering another comment. Not so with Deiphobus who was very agitated with my overall stance on their request, regarding me as nothing less than a traitor.

"Unspeakable whore," he denounced me. "That you refuse to help Troy. I ought to turn you in. You deserve to be put on trial."

"How dare you!" I yelled at him. "I have risked as much for Troy on my expedition as you have around here. Don't play the loyal patriot with me, not when everyone knows how you covet Helen."

Deiphobus turned red and glanced at Paris, no doubt to ascertain whether his brother would take offense over his lecherous bent, but Paris took little notice of my remark, evidently having arrived at the same conclusion long ago; Helen was sure to have told him.

"I had hoped we could get your cooperation in this," Paris said, unruffled. "As we cannot, understand that we will proceed on our own. I expect we will succeed."

With that, Paris and Deiphobus departed, leaving me alone in the hall to fret over what had transpired between us. I was a wreck, unable to determine the steps I should take to avert the impending disaster facing Achilles. My first inclination was to run to the corral, get on Zephyrus, and ride out to the Myrmidon camp to warn Achilles. But sober reflection quickly dispelled that notion; the gates were closed, and riding in the dark, I would most likely be shot by the archers on guard duty. I could do this in the morning, but then everyone would see me, and I would surely be branded as a traitor. If I dared to take this measure, I would never be able to return to Troy. I was near tears in my indecision and nervousness. No sleep awaited me this night, not with my present emotional turmoil hounding me. What could I do? Feeling the worst of apprehensions, I slowly headed in the direction of my chamber, a depression spreading over me and filling me with gloom and despair.

After a distressing night of tossing and turning, I woke up somewhat later than normal, my sleep not having come to me until the early predawn. Still perturbed over the past night's gathering, my predominant thought was how to alert Achilles of the planned ruse. Again, further deliberation highlighted the difficulties entailed in this, and I decided to take my time over breakfast to think this through. I had to get word to him without jeopardizing my own safety.

"Are you all right, Polyxena?" Andromache, my companion as I ate, asked after detecting my agitation. "You're looking tense."

"I am tense," I hastily answered. "I slept poorly."

"I'm familiar enough with that."

"Is the lull still in effect?"

"As far as I know, yes. Why do you ask?"

Dare I tell her? No, not yet. Perhaps once the news reached her about what I had done yesterday.

"Just curious if I'm able to ride Zephyrus today," I replied.

"You must adhere to your father's counsel about riding alone. Come, I will accompany you."

"No," I quickly reacted, startling Andromache with my emphatic rejection. "I mean, I must be by myself, to meditate. Please understand."

Although she still demonstrated astonishment over my hasty dismissal of her proposal, Andromache was forgiving by nature, a feature of her personality I admired, and acceded to my request. Her quiet nodding affirmed her consent.

I proceeded to the corral and directed one of the keepers to prepare Zephyrus for his daily exercise. I hoped to find a solution to my problem while on my ride, the solitude being conducive to reasoning.

"Where's your partner, princess?" the keeper asked me.

"What do you mean?" I snapped at him, responding adversely to his question. "What concern is that of yours?"

"I'm not allowed to let you ride by yourself anymore."

"On whose authority?"

"Prince Paris gave us that order."

It had come to this. I was, for all practical purposes, a prisoner within the walls of Troy. My options had been taken away from me as effectively as if I had been confined to the royal palace. Whatever plan I might have come up with no longer mattered, as I had no means to implement it. I slowly walked back to our residence, feeling both angry and sad, utterly helpless in my dejection.

What was I to do now? Obviously, I could not ride with Paris or Deiphobus or Agenor, my usual partner, to carry out my intentions. What of Andromache? She was my only female companion on these outings, but she would surely oppose any effort I applied toward Achilles, the slayer of her husband, especially if I warned him of impending danger. I saw little that I could do and moped in my chamber for the rest of the morning, sulking in my depression and not seeing anyone.

Later that day, Andromache came by to check on me, concerned over my downcast state and wanting to ameliorate the gloominess I felt.

"You have not eaten since breakfast," she said. "Why are you so distraught?"

"Paris has issued an order that I am not ride Zephyrus by myself," I said.

"Because of yesterday?"

"So you know?" I asked, amazed that my visit to Achilles was now common knowledge.

"Helen told me."

"You're not mad at me? Deiphobus called me an 'unspeakable whore.'"

Andromache appeared genuinely shocked but was also surprisingly sympathetic toward me, which provided me some relief from my torment.

"He has a heart of stone," she said. "No, Polyxena, I'm not mad at you."

I loved her for saying that, for understanding, for being supportive of me when even I doubted my sensibilities.

"Oh, Andromache," I answered, restraining my emotions, "for you to tell me this, after what Achilles has done to you, to be so forgiving, you are truly a good person."

"Our fate is decreed for us, Polyxena," she said. "We must accept this, however painful that may be. Hector strongly believed in this. I think he knew when he confronted Achilles that he was destined to die."

She sounded a lot like Achilles and reminded me of the time when he told me that he believed he was destined to die at Troy. Frightened over how the setbacks presently facing me seemed to direct themselves toward this end, a coldness engulfed me, and I momentarily believed greater forces were at work here. This cannot be. Was I resisting what has been fated? I refused to accept that.

"This means nothing I do will make a difference," I pondered aloud. "No. How can it not make a difference? He would know what to look out for if alerted."

Andromache gave me a gentle hug, soothing my anxieties for the time, and then rose to make her exit.

"Don't miss supper," she advised. "Your absence will only add fuel to the rumors being said about you."

I adhered to her counsel and attended the meal, ever conscious of Paris and Deiphobus gesturing their ascendancy over my predicament, the glares they gave me emphasizing this to me. At times, I wished I could just run away, but I stoically endured my humiliation and determined that I was not going to allow myself to be daunted over this, to deny them the satisfaction of my deprecation. Besides, nothing happened on this day, so perhaps there would follow more of them when no harm came to Achilles, and I could yet send him some warning.

Again, fate intervened, for the next morning, it was obvious that the lull in the fighting had come to an end. The two armies once more faced each other before the city and waged their battle throughout most of the morning. To Troy's sorrow, another of our major allied kings was killed— by Achilles—that day. He was Memnon, lord of the Assyrians. Or was it the Ethiopians? I was not sure. Very much liked by my father, he had been at Troy for only a short period, a year at most, and was quite young. His loss was demoralizing to us and, accordingly, cast a melancholy shadow over our dinner that evening. He was one of those leaders who, by sheer strength of his personality, held his force together, and now that he was slain, my father feared his army would disintegrate and abandon its cause, because no one came forth to assume the helm. Once more Achilles dealt Troy a significant, if not devastating, blow.

The next few days were characterized by smaller skirmishes about the city, as each side probed the other for signs of weakness, the Greeks to ascertain the adverse impact Memnon's death, or rather, their anticipated crumbling of his army resulting from it, had on us, and the Trojans to make their point that the effect was minimal. Neither side gained anything through these clashes, and the only consolation was that the casualty counts were low enough so as not to undermine the ability to continue waging war.

On the sixth day after the lull, a major battle was in the offing as the bulk of the enemy army began approaching our outer walls at early dawn, prior to our force having come out to meet it. I happened to be standing at one of the upper ramparts of the Pergamus, observing the activity, when I spotted the strangest sight. A single charioteer rode forward, well in advance of the main force, heading straight toward the Scaean Gates. I recognized the golden-crested helmet and breastplate. It was Achilles. I instinctively sensed something was wrong. Even Achilles, intrepid as he was, would not be so rash as to expose himself in such close proximity to our line of fire. He stopped directly in front of the main gate and waited; on what? Slowly, the gates opened, and out rushed several of our warriors, one who I knew was Paris. Turning his chariot around, with the intent of escaping back to his units, I saw an arrow strike Achilles in his heel. He stooped down, reaching toward the wound, when another arrow struck him in the neck, causing him to fall off his chariot.

I froze in horror, my shock numbing my senses. I cried out, not knowing what I said, and fell to my knees, unable to keep myself upright in my weakness. When it all sank in, I was so torn with grief that I burst out in long sobs, unable to constrain the pain I felt. I knew he was dead—Achilles was dead!—and my heart was broken.

Helen and Andromache, who had viewed the proceedings from our observation post a few paces back, rushed up to me, both breaking into tears, seeking to comfort me when they saw me slumped against the wall in my agony. Helen remained the more composed of us and looked down upon the dreadful scene I could no longer watch.

"What's happening now?" I whimpered, hoping against hope I misinterpreted what I had seen.

She hesitated for a moment before answering, "They're fighting over the body. Oh, I see it being carried off, by Ajax I think. Odysseus is there. The Trojans have given up their fight over it and are allowing them to get away."

It was true. Achilles was dead. Gradually, I snapped out of my pitiful state and merely glanced blankly in front of me, saying nothing and quieting down. He was our enemy but also my friend. No, I loved him. He was so beautiful, handsome beyond belief. I will never again meet anyone like him.

The death of Achilles stopped the battle from commencing, and throughout the Greek camp, an eerie silence prevailed during the rest of the day. His passing must have come as a profound shock to them, leaving them in disarray as to what to do next. That quietness sounded more deafening than any clash of arms.

If quietude marked the enemy's disposition, the extreme opposite presented itself to us inside the dining hall that evening. Elation, bombastic revelry, joy, all the declarations signifying the highest of morale filled the room as everyone celebrated their pleasure and relief over the death of the greatest warrior who ever lived. Even my father, usually more sedate in his mannerisms, was caught up in the frenzy and bubbled in his enthusiasm over the event. Only Andromache, Helen, and I remained subdued, I in my remorse and my companions out of their empathy for me.

Paris, who was applauded as the man having fired the fatal shots that brought Achilles down, was loud and boisterous in his self-adulation, eager in relating his expertise at the bow to everyone and feeling sky high over his accomplishment. His joy was immense and also contagious, for he soon brought Helen under his buoyant euphoria and had her celebrating along with him.

"A toast," my father shouted out as he raised his goblet in the air.

"A toast," the men responded in unison.

"To Paris!" my father went on. "My son, you have nobly redeemed yourself for all your past transgressions and endeared us to you. I drink to you."

"To Paris!" came the collective response, and the drinks were gulped down.

"Speak, Brother," Deiphobus shouted out. "Tell us of your great deed."

"My deed could not have been achieved without the help of someone close to us," Paris announced. "And I propose a toast to her."

Her? What did he mean? I began to tense up as I sensed what my brother was alluding to. He would not do this to me.

"To my dear sister, Polyxena," Paris declared.

His toast left many in bewilderment, as few knew of my connection with the slaying, and had the assembly mumbling, not exactly knowing how to proceed. My father was among the befuddled.

"Explain yourself, Son," he said. "Why do we toast Polyxena?"

"None of you have heard?" Paris sounded off, quite inebriated at this point. "We learned that Achilles, to his lasting regret I might add, fell in love with Polyxena when he returned her to Troy. That's why we were able to get him to come so close to our walls."

My father was not amused by this, turning somber. He looked my way, as did everyone else, and saw me in my distraught condition, my teary eyes saying more about this story than any spoken words.

"We sent a herald to the Greek camp to inform Achilles that Polyxena had been banished from the city for fraternizing with him," Paris went on, laughing. "That he could pick her up by the main gate before the battle. What a fool. The ruse worked, as you all know." Paris did not solicit the response he expected, for all was quiet, and his laughing stopped. "What's the matter with all of you?" he bellowed. "I've gotten rid of Troy's scourge, and you mope over it. Where is your gratitude?"

"Tarnished," my father said. "You interfered with what Goddess Aphrodite contrived. We did not know. Yes, you got rid of our nemesis, but dishonorably. For us to celebrate such ignominy is an affront to the gods."

"Your principles be damned," Paris angrily replied. "It is our welfare and safety I have to think about. You've lost sight of that, Father."

"Paris is right," Deiphobus acclaimed. "All that matters is that Achilles is dead. Who cares over the methods we used?"

My father was clearly disappointed in hearing this, as if a new morality dictated the rules of warfare, of which he disapproved because of its lack of honor, something he highly valued. Also, he was agitated over the irreverence displayed by his sons and may have even feared that they had imperiled Troy to a greater extent than they realized.

"The gods are witnesses to this," he exclaimed, his vexation transparent. "They judge us by what we do. Ultimately, the fate of Troy rests in their hands. What you have done blemishes our standing with them."

The outburst threw a melancholy over the celebrants, dispiriting them in their awareness of the treacherous manner in which Achilles had been slain, and for all practical purposes, the party was over, as nobody was inclined to continue proclaiming what was now viewed as a disgraceful feat. What an incredible about-face from just a short while before. Paris had his life's most notable achievement almost entirely diminished by the manner of its execution, and he was extremely bitter over this.

"Ingrates," he scoffed. "Not one of you will credit my well-aimed shot at his heel, his one vulnerable spot."

How did he know this? I had told no one. It had to have come from Menodice. She overheard this when Achilles confided it in me. I suspected it all along but refrained from questioning her about it in my naïve supposition that she would forget unless I drew attention to it. How could I be such a fool.

"You did well, Brother," Deiphobus shouted. "No matter what my unappreciative relatives think, I salute you."

"Yes," Helenus added. "Honors to you, Paris."

"Honors to Paris," Polites, my youngest brother after Polydorus was slain, joined in.

Soon the chorus of adulation for my brother's accomplishment reasserted itself, although not to the degree exhibited earlier and not engaging some of the previous revelers who were bound to a more rigorous honor code and were soured over the perfidious method in which Achilles had been lured to his death. My father was among the disillusioned members, and he voiced no satisfaction in the proceedings, sitting by in stillness, a disturbed visage written in his face. Helen, likewise, revealed no inclination to continue celebrating; instead, she walked over to where I was seated and took her place beside me.

"I'm sorry, Polyxena," she said. "For what it's worth, I take no pleasure in my husband's achievement, not after hearing how he did it."

I was too despondent to give proper thanks over Helen's attempts to mollify me, until I recovered enough from my malaise to see my impoliteness.

"It's so sad, Helen," I then said. "He exposed himself to danger, thinking he was coming to rescue me. What a nightmare it must have been for him when I wasn't there."

"Did you love him?"

"I tried to deny it to myself, remembering the misery he brought to our family, telling myself I should be hating him. Oh, Helen, I couldn't help myself. Against my better judgment, he drew me to him."

Helen embraced me, and I found solace in her arms, comforted by the sincerity of her compassion. She understood Aphrodite's seductive guile, being herself the victim of the goddess's manipulations, and knew my pain more than anyone else. My father, ever respectful of the gods, also viewed me with pity and was deeply affected by the misfortune that had come my way, resulting from the assignment he had given me. He directed his sympathetic glances at me and, when he was about to exit from the room, came up to me, his sadness very prominent.

"When I should, by all accounts, share in this merriment," he told me, "I am instead quite depressed. Dear Polyxena, what have I done to you? You were the innocent, carefree child, and I plunged you into a world of cruelty, deceit, and sorrow, into a hasty adulthood with all its duplicity and hardships. But do not think I did not have my misgivings and regrets over this, agonizing over whether I did the right thing, and I was so proud of you, what you have done. Even with the knowledge that Achilles loved you and that you may have loved him, I cannot find it in my heart to fault anyone for this. Know that I love you even more having learned this."

His sentiments shredded me, tearing at my very soul, and my tears gushed from me as I tried to maintain a proper decorum, unsuccessfully, to be sure. He clasped me, quite shaken himself, and together we cried our hearts out, to the stunned paralysis of everyone in the hall watching us. What an ending to an evening meant to have an opposite closure. The assembly was, if not in tears, beset with noticeable contrition.

Chapter XIII

Poor Paris. I did not mean for my behavior to deprive him so utterly of his great moment of glory, but that indeed had been the effect, and he delayed in his forgiveness for several of the succeeding days, perhaps blaming me for the muted laudation he received. But I felt no guilt over this, for he brought it on himself. Had he never mentioned my name in his toast, nothing adverse would have resulted, and he might well have basked in the praises he so eagerly sought. I almost took pity on him. He portrayed the classic case of one's rash tongue getting the best of him and spoiling what he believed he was due. Still, I did not believe he deserved to be acclaimed for the manner in which Achilles was slain. It was treacherous by any standard and, even if defensible, certainly not admirable.

As the days passed, I slowly began to accept the reality of my condition, overcoming the deep sadness that dogged me. The irreversibility of death is most tragic and yet also, in a strange sort of way, consoling, because it forces one to come to grips with it and accede to its truth. The realization comes that one must move on. One thing I have learned from my involvement with Penthesileia, and now Achilles, is that the pain of their loss, the suffering, is transitory and, given time, can be surmounted. In this context, I gradually emerged from the shell I had sought refuge in. I had kept to my room for long periods of time, avoiding everyone, but I began to rejoin my family in its get-togethers and, through this, brought myself back into the present.

I was once again free to ride Zephyrus without restrictions imposed on me, and I made the most of this, reverting to my original schedule of exercising him twice daily, once in the morning and again in the late afternoon, more frequently by myself than before. I found my greatest peace in these solitary rides, when I had time to reflect over things, not always to my benefit, as I also grieved over the events that happened to me, but overall, they were conciliatory for me. Free may be a misnomer, for I was limited to the area east of the city, which was secured by us and not subject to enemy patrols; the war was still very much with us.

I had occasion to see Paris alone one day when I was recuperating from my sense of loss. He was standing by the corral when I arrived there after having run my horse. He met me with a smile—very conducive to instilling depths of warmth with him—as I dismounted and left Zephyrus in the care of a keeper.

"You're a skilled rider, Sister," he said, watching my horse being led away. "I never took notice of that before."

"With a horse like Zephyrus it's easy enough," I replied.

"A beautiful animal. Not one of ours."

"He was a gift from Antiope, an Amazon commander, a good friend to me."

Paris was fumbling over his words. I knew he wanted to tell me something more significant but appeared uncertain on how to express himself. I think he withheld telling me because of feelings of embarrassment, his face was a bit red, and I was touched by his modest restraint. He wanted to make amends to me, I thought, but had difficulties saying it.

"I'm not mad at you, Paris," I told him, trying to ease his ambivalence. "I regret what happened during your celebration party."

His eyes sparkled even if his expression remained sober.

"I was wrong to propose that toast to you, Polyxena. It was a cruel gesture."

"It caught me off guard and, yes, hurt me."

"I wish I could say that was not my intent, but—I'm so ashamed of it—the truth is that I meant to cause you distress. I knew you liked Achilles. Menodice told me. I wanted to rub it in. I deserved to have it backfire on me. I was justly punished for my maliciousness."

I stared at him, not knowing what to say, while at the same time being deeply moved by his confession. Obviously, his admission was burdensome for him, and I recognized that his coldhearted intent was troubling him in the worst way. I suppose I could have railed him for his cruelty, but this no longer seemed appropriate or relevant.

"If you want my forgiveness, Paris," I said to him, "you have it."

"Do you really mean it?"

"I do. Nothing will bring Achilles back, nor is that good for Troy. I know I must be dutiful to our effort in winning this war. I'm just sorry that this is the way things have to be, but these are matters beyond our control."

Paris placed his hands on my shoulders and looked me directly in the eyes.

"You are a good person, Polyxena," he said. "I'm honored to have you as a sister."

"Thank you, Brother," I answered, at last smiling at him.

Paris was cheered up significantly by my response, as if I had brightened his day, and he drew me to his body for a short hug, but then, just as quickly, he ended his embrace all the while flashing his wide grin at me. As I walked off I turned around and saw him waving at me. I waved back, happy that we had reconciled our discord.

I was less kind to Menodice and disengaged myself increasingly from her services, even finally requesting that she no longer be my personal attendant. She was considerably more upset over this than I would have expected, for I thought she comprehended my reasons for being disenchanted with her. It was not as if I suddenly told her I did not want her to serve me anymore, but rather, a sort of gradual withdrawal where, over the passing days, I called on her less and less, until I suggested that she attend fully to my mother.

She was with me in my chamber as usual, comb in hand and ready to brush my hair, when I decided to tell her of my intentions.

"I asked Mother if you could serve her," I told Menodice. "She consented to this."

"I've cared for you since you were a baby," Menodice replied in a broken voice, nearly on the verge of tears. "And now you discard me, princess. Why?"

"You don't know?" I answered, amazed that she failed to grasp my disappointment.

"I know I was critical of your behavior with Achilles," she said. "But I should not be faulted for that."

"Why not?"

"I was concerned about your loyalty to Troy. All your actions, your snuggling up to him at the campfires, riding off alone with him, being constantly in his company, had me worried that you were being manipulated by him, that you were going to betray us."

"What's this talk about betrayal? Our mission was over. Nothing I would have done at this point had any bearing on it. All was inconsequential."

Menodice paused for a moment as she digested what I had just said, the notion coming as somewhat surprising to her.

"I didn't see it that way," she admitted.

"You did not trust me."

"That's not true, princess."

"Yes, it is. I told you I was doing what I thought necessary to secure our safe passage home. You did not believe me."

"So I'm being dismissed because I was misled by your coziness with our greatest enemy? You were very convincing, princess. Indeed, I am guilty of fretting over what I was seeing. My concern was for you."

"You're not being dismissed, but reassigned, and not for that reason."

"For what then?"

"How did Paris know to shoot Achilles in the heel? I did not tell him this."

Menodice froze up, not able to give a ready response to my question, and I think she at last realized the crux of my discontent with her performance of her duties. Still, she resisted the idea that she should be castigated for what she believed was in the best interest of Troy and rejected my objection to this.

"I had to tell him," she affirmed. "For Troy. It was my duty to tell him."

"Why did you think that?"

"Because I knew you would not."

Was I being fair? Clearly, Menodice meant well, and who could condemn her for doing what obviously was in our city's defense? That is the trouble with these situations: they offer no clear cut answers as to what the proper course should be. Basically, I was reacting to my annoyance over her having spied on my conversations with Achilles and not informing me about what she had learned from this. I strongly believed I could no longer place any trust in her, and this would inevitably lead to a strained relationship between us, and consequently, it benefited both of us to keep our distance from each other. I was uncertain if this was the correct assessment of our standing but, for the present, regarded my actions as appropriate and intended to follow through on it. I suppose I could always make some amends later on if that were required.

"I will think about this," I told her. "But for now, I want you to devote your services to my mother."

The fact that I left the door open for a possible reconciliation between us mitigated the hard feelings Menodice must have gathered from our discussion to some extent. I felt badly over my decision but also somewhat relieved, as my affairs with her were definitely strained, and I needed to be away from her continuous presence. I would, of course, still see her in the palace, but less often as before and not in the intimate context that demanded the need for me to socialize freely, without in inhibitions, an exchange I no longer thought possible, at least for the immediate future.

Another aspect of my return here that I found demeaning to me was that I was not asked to participate in the council meetings affecting Troy's prospects. Penthesileia had involved me in her high-level command gatherings, where she discussed battle plans and strategies with me, even soliciting opinions from me. Through this attendance, I developed an absorbing interest in grand designs, the method in which plans were formulated, the debates entailed in selling the schemes to its opponents, the issues brought forth in arguing its merits, all phases of the decision-making process.

An excitement surrounded these affairs, and I very much took a liking to being engaged in them. I thought, perhaps naïvely, that the mission I had undergone qualified me for at least a voice in the proceedings of our council, but apparently, I was wrong. Ours was still very much a man's world, and women were relegated to the backwaters of the major flow of events generated by the decisions and actions of men. It dawned on me that the reason I was more valued among the Amazons was precisely because I am a woman, and the interesting thing about this is that I performed better in that environment than I now did in my present setting. My adjustment to my underappreciated role—commonly referred to as woman's work: weaving, sewing, caring for children, punishing the servants, the afternoon chats—was difficult for me, and my nature rebelled against this, causing me to often regret that I ever came back to Troy.

My frustration was alleviated somewhat by the curious behavior of my father who met with me frequently in private, usually in the courtyard, after having concluded one of his meetings, and asked me what I thought about some of the decisions that had been made. I was more than willing to state my views to him, often quite strongly, and he appeared genuinely interested in what I had to say. His regard for my opinions helped a lot in giving purpose to my otherwise meaningless existence—I am being hard on myself—and kept me stimulated and abreast of the current problems besetting our city. In time, I looked forward to my sessions with him, as they constituted the most impelling part of the day for me. The subject of Agamemnon came up during one of our encounters.

"Has Achilles ever spoken to you about him?" my father asked.

"I don't think he liked him," I answered, "but I'm not sure."

"He told you this?"

"No, but he did kill a man named Thersites for bad-mouthing him," I replied, recalling the incident as if it had occurred but yesterday.

"Thersites? I've heard the name."

"He was vicious in his condemnation of Agamemnon. Not only him, but all the Greeks in general."

"So he deserved what he got."

"I suppose. But I liked him. He had a sardonic wit."

"You met the man?"

"Yes, I spoke with him. He walked with a limp and had a crooked back, and his face was splotchy. He told me—you'll like this, Father—that the purpose of this war, Agamemnon's war, he called it, was to 'make rich Agamemnon richer.'"

My father thought this amusing and could not keep from smiling, even snickering for a brief instance. The more he thought about it, the funnier it became for him, until he burst out in a hearty laugh.

"You are full of surprises, my dear," he said. "I am remiss in not relying more on your knowledge."

I wished he would follow up on that, permitting me access to his high-level meetings, but was gratified that his visiting me gave him a bit of joy. I had not heard him laugh like that since before the death of Hector.

"Much took place in the short time I was with the Amazons," I said.

"To be sure. So Achilles killed Thersites over that remark?"

"Well, not just that. My understanding is it was the cumulative effect of all his derogatory insinuations over the total years of the war. Achilles accused him of undermining the morale of the Greeks."

"I wish Thersites were still around to do his worthy work. But I've heard enough to affirm what we all suspected all along: this is indeed Agamemnon's war. Helen was but a pretext for that man's greed. It would have made no difference had we returned her to Sparta; this war would still have been fought."

Father then rose to make his departure, rendering me that endearing wink that so elevated my spirits. I could not help but swoon in my warmth as I watched him walk away.

I think my father relished his conversations with me, as did I, contrary to my relationship with my mother, which seemed always artificial and belabored to me. A lot of this had to do with the more mundane aspects of life that were of paramount concern to her; she preferred to talk about the behavior of her children rather than the conduct of our relations in the war and with states. As I decidedly favored the latter, we did not have much in common in the subjects of interest to us. In truth, I was bored with the things that delighted her, which did not help matters any and usually kept me in the background when she monopolized our time during our afternoon get-togethers in the residence hall. She must have regarded me as the most noncontributing member of her flock, but that was fine with me, as it did not force a topic on me that failed to arouse my curiosity or interest, although occasionally, I had a feeling she did not appreciate my aloofness. I think that is the correct word to define my attitude, which was not intentional or indicative of ill intent.

Fortunately, Mother had eager adherents to her areas of engrossment in both Helen and Andromache, as well as Ilione and Cruesa. All of them enjoyed talking about family members and delighted doting on their offspring, and I learned through these talks that Helen had left a daughter she named Hermione behind when she fled with Paris to Troy, her one major regret in life, she called it. Cassandra, by contrast, was more like me in this respect. She likewise shunned the small talk and thought them tedious and, as a consequence, contributed little to them, preferring to observe from the sidelines rather than get immersed in an exercise that brought no satisfaction to her. Aside from that, I had nothing else in common with her, for she totally dedicated herself to her duties as a priestess in the Temple of Apollo and had no time for any other activity. She did not enjoy life, composed as she was of a rather dour disposition that did little to attract anyone to her, even though she was quite good-looking. In a way, she represented a paradoxical figure; she devoted herself to Apollo in spite of that god having, as some claimed, cursed her by making her prophecies unbelievable to anyone she related them to. Try to make sense out of that.

As for my brothers, the ones who were left, I generally fared better with them than I did with my sisters, usually having an enjoyable time when in their company. Even Deiphobus, whom I should have despised for his insults, had a knack for turning on the charm, especially when he apologized profusely for his tasteless remarks, and soon had me forgiving him for his rudeness. The difference was that I rarely saw them. They spent most of their day with the units they commanded and their evenings with their wives, except for the unmarried ones who were occupied with their women slaves who might as well have been their wives. Only at the evening meal were we together, and then only some of the time, because duties frequently kept them on patrols, commanding guards, and meeting other military requirements.

In an interesting turn of events, Paris and I became closer after his confession to me. He became my most consistent partner when I exercised Zephyrus, and together we rode our mounts to visit the various training grounds and the camps of our allies, usually combining business with pleasure. He took advantage of our need to keep our horses in condition to check on the morale and material needs of our supporting contingents and to pass important information to their leaders, thereby keeping them abreast of the situation. I think he liked my company while fulfilling these necessities. Can I ever forget the manner in which he led Achilles to his doom? Probably not, but this was war, and war has a way of superseding one set of priorities with another so that the new circumstances obliterate all that was, and I was no longer sure. Given enough time, everything can change.

"When will you ever get married?" Paris asked me when we rode toward the Dardanian Gates on our way back from one of his inspections.

I thought the question highly personal, but I knew his intent was not an intrusion into my private life but out of curiosity, if not true concern.

"I can't say, Brother," I answered. "You need to have suitors first."

"A woman as beautiful as you? No suitors?"

"There were a couple, some time ago, and both have been killed in this war. No one has come to me or my father since."

"I'm sorry to hear that. Love is the most gratifying of life's experiences."

I looked hard at Paris, astounded he would make such an assertion with me, especially when he knew of my major misfortune relevant to our subject of conversation. Just because I was not with a husband did not mean I had not experienced love, of which I was certain he was well aware.

"I *was* loved," I reminded Paris. "More than once."

He returned my stares with considerable regard, compassion exuding from his eyes, and seemed uncomfortable with the direction of our discussion.

"Yes, you were," he replied. "A love that could never be, sad to say."

He was correct, and I was as much aware of this as anyone. That we were talking about this revealed how much reconciliation had taken place between us in a relatively short period of time.

"I know," I admitted. "I blame it on this war. Not only was I deprived of any suitors but also of the man I truly loved."

"I have heard it said among the Greeks that Achilles came to Troy aware that he would die here. Did you know this?"

"Yes, he spoke about it."

"Indeed? So, to be truthful, Polyxena, your relationship with him was doomed from the start, wouldn't you agree?"

I thought about that for a while. Not that I disputed his conclusions, as it verified what Achilles himself had related to me more than just once, but that it ignored the conflicts this premonition had posed for us. Paris made the obvious deduction, not understanding the full dimensions of the problem nor the inner turmoil Achilles faced over this issue.

"Yes, in retrospect, it appears that way," I finally conceded "But…" I hesitated.

"But what, Sister?"

"He grappled over this, asking himself repeatedly if he could change his destiny by daring to go against what he thought was the will of the gods. He questioned if it were possible to create one's own fortune. The issue was problematic for him."

Paris was impressed by this, pondering, I think, over the same issue, and for the first time, he indicated an admiration for the fallen Greek.

"I had no idea he had a philosophical bent. Isn't this what wise men debate among themselves?"

"It is. I see no easy answer to the problem."

"Some say that my going to Sparta and bringing back Helen was preordained, in fact, it led my parents to abandon me after I was born. They meant for me to die on the slopes of Mount Ida, because it was predicted that I would bring ruin to Troy. The shepherd, Agelaus, took pity on me and raised me as his own child. You know the story. What is puzzling about it is that, in spite of all the precautions taken to avert the prophecy, it nevertheless came to be. I say this because it makes me think Achilles was wrong in debating whether we can bring about our own fortune. We are at the mercy of the gods. I am convinced of this. Nothing we do can change what is destined to be."

"Then we have no free will. Or if we do, it serves no other purpose but to affirm what is already decreed for us, which amounts to the same thing. Not a pleasant thought, Paris."

"No, it's not. I leave the matter in the hands of the philosophers."

I developed an increasing respect for Paris, because contrary to his maintaining that he saw no way out for what destiny had in store for us, he nonetheless, like Achilles, questioned this, meaning he demonstrated the quality I most admired in us as mortal humans: our capacity to think, to exercise our will, to challenge what is prescribed.

"You said more than once," Paris went on, changing the direction of our conversation. "Who was the other man?"

His question brought Antiope to mind, whom I alluded to from the start, but I was reluctant over how much of my personal life I should reveal. Still, she loved me, I was assured of this and I should not be ashamed to its admission.

"Not a man, Paris," I replied.

"Oh?"

"If you must know, the Amazon commander, Antiope, loved me. So did Penthesileia, for that matter, but in different sort of way."

"I had no idea."

"I won't say any more about it. I only meant for you to know that I am familiar with what love is about, its gratifications as you referred to. I agree, no other experience in life is as rewarding."

By this time, we had returned to the corral, where Helen was standing to greet Paris as he dismounted. They embraced and kissed, and I may have envied them as I walked beside them to the Pergamus. Paris and Helen were such a loving couple, without question the most engaging marriage there ever was, and their joy had a contagious effect on anyone fortunate enough to be a witness to it. You could not look upon them without sharing their happiness, being enveloped in the warmth they exuded, and simply relishing what you were seeing. No, I do not think this was envy, rather I would call it contentment, a satisfaction that such a deep love was possible, out of which sprang forth a hope that it could one day happen to you as well as them. Inspirational is the word that best defined their union.

The cruel war once more delivered its grim reality upon our lives in the following days, when the battles before the city resumed in full fury. The respite that had been in effect since the death of Achilles, not only for the granted twelve days allotted to his funeral, but for another two weeks after that because of the enemy's indecision over how to carry on without their best fighter, was over—its ending heralded by the blowing of trumpets and marching of armor-clad warriors. Aeneas assembled our army and those of our allies before the Scaean Gates, and their formation extended along the entire length of the city's walls, appearing as large as any ever put together.

I saw my brothers at the head of their complements. Deiphobus led the left wing, Paris was at the right, and Helenus was near the center, with Polites as one of his subordinates. We viewed them from the front wall of the Pergamus, the one facing west to the sea. Advancing from the beaches was the Greek host, likewise extending along broad lines covering the width of the expanse ahead of us. As they came closer, we recognized the banners of the various components comprising their army and presumed they were led by the same commanders as always: Odysseus and his men from Ithaca; Diomedes and his Argives; Menelaus and his Spartans; Clonius and his Boeotians; Eumenus and his Thessalians; and of course, Agamemnon and his Mycaeneans. These were the ones Helen identified to us. We did not know who now led the Myrmidons, but they were definitely arrayed against us, their insignia clearly visible above their ranks. I was with Andromache, looking at the spectacle from the wall, while Helen sat next to my father on his right and Cruesa, my sister and wife of Aeneas, was on his left, the seats of honor. I had the worst feeling about today. This was going to be a bloody contest. I sensed it and tensed up, my heart pounding inside me.

In conformance with battle etiquette, the generals met in conference in the middle of the field between the two opposing armies, presumably to make their threats and assessments, as Lycus once informed me. Their meeting lasted only a short while, and they turned about to take up their positions with their troops. Almost immediately following this, trumpet calls spurred the lines into an advance. In a horrific clash, they collided.

Everywhere across the field, men fought. One soldier went down with a spear point protruding from his groin, another had his arm severed from a slashing cut of his opponent's sword, still another took a javelin in his chest, and many dropped after their throats had been cut, clasping their hands over their wounds but unable to stem the flowing blood. Throughout the carnage rose the terrible screams from men with agonizing wounds, many dying even as they fell. I did not know where to focus on the slaughter, as it took place everywhere, to the very ends of the lines, chaotic and ferocious. At times, I could make out Paris or Aeneas or someone else I knew, but then they quickly meshed into the frenzied masses, and I was unable to identify them again.

Neither side appeared to gain a breakthrough, even when it looked for a moment that they might. I saw a column, spearheaded by Paris, drive into the Greek ranks, only to be enveloped by squadrons of reinforcements directed from one sector of the battle to counter the advance. Then I lost sight of him again, enclosed from all sides by enemy soldiers, only later to spot him once more when he managed to fight his way out of the trap.

Occasionally, a number of the embattled warriors temporarily ceased their fighting to watch a duel taking place between giants, those standout combatants known for their bravery and skill, who faced off in a one-on-one confrontation. For them, the battle, for the time being, rested in abeyance, depending on who was to fall. One such encounter occurred between Aeneas and Diomedes, clearly visible from our vantage point, but neither was able to bring down the other, and after an indeterminate amount of time had elapsed, both simultaneously withdrew, only to have their onlookers resume their attacks. This scene swept repeatedly into our view, often leaving us holding our breath. Even when we did not know by name who was fighting who, we recognized the more uniform attire of our soldiers and reserved our cheers for them, if not out loud, then in silence.

All day long, the battle raged and took on a tactical direction of its own as soldiers and units rotated themselves in the intense action, one sitting out to rest while the other continued fighting. Despite all the heroics and effort, by afternoon, it became clear to us that this struggle, like all the previous ones waged before our walls, would end in a stalemate, a horrible loss of life for no gain to either side. As if by mutual consent, both armies began to disengage themselves and started reversing their direction, spent of energy and needing a respite. Then we saw this, Paris was on a stretcher being carried from the field toward the Scaean Gates.

"Oh, no," I said to myself, feeling faint. Instinctively, I glanced at Helen who had risen from her seat, her face ashen. I will never forget her shocked expression. She quivered as she stood there, but she did not weep, being too stunned for that. Only after her initial paralysis had passed did she begin her sobbing. My father rushed to her side and held on to her as he began to lead her from the platform to the steps.

"I'm sure he is only wounded, Helen," he told her, "else he would be returned later with the fallen."

She took a momentary measure of comfort in that, but her despair was easily discerned, her eyes displaying a fearful countenance. I followed them as they descended the Pergamus and hastened to the main gate. By the time we arrived there, Paris had already been taken inside, and the bearers laid him down in front of us. He was conscious, and his eyes sparkled when they focused themselves on Helen. She dropped to her knees and stroked his head amid a tender smile that hid her pain. But then we saw the injury, turning us grim: an arrow had penetrated his chest cavity, the end of it sticking out from his left side, between his ribs. Helen tried to maintain her composure, but again burst forth in tears until he hushed her by caressing her face.

"I'm not dead yet," he told her, showing his typical grin. "Do not worry. The physicians will take care of me."

Helen tried her best to smile and appear soothed by his words, but the dread was there, her worrisome demeanor unaffected by his assurances. She and my father accompanied the bearers when they came back to take Paris to the infirmary.

I remained by the gate, looking out across the field, horror-struck at the extent of the slaughter that had taken place. The dead were all about, littering the expanse in front of me, greater in number than in any battle the Amazons had fought while I was with them, and all for no gain. It must have been one of the most brutal battles fought since the start of the war, for its cost was staggering. What a terrible waste. The medical teams were now in full swing, doing their grim work, treating the wounded—though there were not enough bandages to go around—and comforting those who were beyond help and destined to die. So were the disposal crews, carrying on their gruesome assignments, carting away the dead and amassing them in huge piles for later burning. The activity was in progress on both sides, as, I am sure, was the shock over the losses that must have equally struck them.

I found it incomprehensible how the leaders who decided to wage this war could still hold their units together after such an inconclusive bloodbath, with all the casualties they sustained, depleting the strength of their army, not to mention the adverse impact this had to have on the morale of their soldiers. I would have expected, at some point, the warriors to have rebelled over the uselessness of their exertions. The personal motivation of each of them had to suffer on this account. Yet they persisted, allowing themselves to be guided into one disaster after another, with no reward in sight for any of them, facing no other reality than deferring the death that eventually might come to them. Could it be that they now so personalized this war that no other priority existed for them except victory, even if it meant their death? How could any sane person still have hopes of winning after the magnitude of today's carnage?

Dazed, I slowly limped my way back behind our walls, unable to make sense out of the situation, mystified over the seeming obsession that war gripped us with, assuming a life force of its own that mitigated against sound logic and compromise. I was met by Andromache when I reached the entrance of the Pergamus. "How's Paris?" I asked.

"He lives," she answered, shaken. "But barely, clinging desperately to life. The physicians are afraid to remove the arrow, thinking this will aggravate the injury."

"But how can you just leave it in his body?"

"Why do you ask me that?" she snapped, agitated over my question. "Am I a physician? I must believe what they tell me."

She was very upset, pained nearly as badly by the suffering of Paris as by the death of her husband. I regretted my remark, even if innocently made.

"I'm sorry, Polyxena," she recanted. "I didn't mean to scold you. I feel so terrible. One setback after another, how much more of this can I endure?"

I understood her heartache, having often enough assailed myself with the same question, and was suddenly overcome with the stark realization that I might lose another brother, one I adored, and it sent a chill through me.

"Where is he now?" I asked, my eyes watering.

"With Helen, in their quarters."

"I should not intrude on them. Oh, Andromache, what will Helen do if ... if ..."

"Do not even think it! I cannot imagine what this will do to her. They are not only husband and wife, but best of friends as well. What an awful situation."

Together we entered the Pergamus, soon arriving at the residence hall, our gloominess distracting us from continuing our talking, and there I saw my father and mother in embrace, both of them weeping and seeking solace in each other's arms. I felt so sad for them, nearly on the verge of tears, their heartbreak penetrating me to the core. I chose to leave them to their commiseration not knowing what I could say or do to comfort them, and went to my chamber, leaving Andromache with my sisters, Cruesa and Ilione. Once inside my room, I threw myself on my bed and broke out in uncontrollable sobbing, the full weight of today's events having registered with me.

That evening, as we partook of our meal, depression prevailed over the gathering. No one was in a mood to talk, and we sat around in quiet, hardly even eating. Only once before—at the death of Hector—did such a darkness engulf our family. Our dejection was enhanced by the conspicuous absence of Helen who remained secluded in her quarters to be with her husband. Yet we knew that, as long as she was with him, he was alive and there was hope.

"Only one person can save him," Deiphobus said, breaking the silence.

"Tell me, Son," my father entreated. "I am relieved that you think he may recover."

"His former wife, Oenone. She is reputed to be highly skilled in the healing arts and once promised him that, should he ever need her services, she would assist him."

Oenone. Here was a name I had rarely heard mentioned for nearly ten years, although I knew about her. Yes, it was true, Paris had been married to her, a woman said to be nymph who lived on the slopes of Mount Ida. I did not believe this, of course; she was very much a mortal, but indeed excelled in medicine. Her reputation for this widely acknowledged, and because of this, she had no need to move from her residence by that mountain, as those in need of her services always came to her. I did not know about the promise she gave Paris.

"Paris spurned her for Helen," said my father. "Why would she live up to her promise?"

"That is so," replied Deiphobus. "Yet a promise is a promise. We must believe she will be true to her word."

"Can Paris make the journey to Mount Ida?"

"If we cushion the wagon, make things as comfortable for him as we can, I believe so."

My father remained skeptical, not as convinced of Oenone's commitment to her word as Deiphobus seemed to be.

"What else can we do?" he groaned. "If we keep him here, he is sure to die. Gods have pity on me. Very well, Deiphobus, make your preparations."

"We will leave first thing in the morning, Father."

"What about Helen? Do you want her to accompany you?"

"That would not be advisable," Deiphobus cautioned. "If Oenone saw her, she might get angry and renege on her promise."

"Yes, I can envision that," my father answered. "I shall tell Helen of what we plan to do. Go on with your dining."

My father then left to visit Helen, leaving the rest of us a bit more relieved, as his talk with Deiphobus afforded everyone a glimmer of optimism in an otherwise bleak perspective. I only hoped Paris was able to make the trip.

The next morning, all was in readiness for Deiphobus, and he surveyed the wagon that would carry Paris to Mount Ida. The vehicle was padded with several layers of blankets and pillows, making for a soft ride, and canopied to provide protection from the sun. Father checked it out as my mother, Polites, Andromache, and I waited for Paris to be set into it. He soon came forth, actually on his feet and supported by two servants who held him up as he stepped forward. Helen walked next to him, looking a bit fatigued but more calm than the last time I saw her. Paris was next carefully lifted into the back of the wagon and lain on his back upon the cushioning. Then another surprise. Neither Paris nor Helen wished to be separated from each other, and both insisted on taking the journey together, despite the cautions emphasized by Deiphobus and my father.

"Helen can stay in the wagon, hidden from Oenone's view," Paris informed us, in fairly good spirits considering his condition.

"Is this wise, Paris?" my father asked, opposing his son's decision but reluctant to deny him his wishes.

"To be honest, I don't know, but then, what have I ever done in life that can be regarded as wise?" he said, smiling at us and delighting my parents with his cheerfulness. I was not as assured of his exhibited composure, thinking it was feigned to mask his own uncertainty over the decision he had made. He glanced at me, and I would have sworn he read my mind, for his smile vanished and a frightened look revealed itself in his eyes. The image was haunting to me, stamped into my memory as it was, and I lowered my eyes to be rid of it. When I again looked at him, his buoyancy returned as he rendered us his farewell. I was happy for that, as I did not want him to feel the apprehension that beset me.

"Our hopes ride with you, Son " my father said, waving his hand as the wagon rolled away.

After yesterday's horrific bloodbath, neither army was prepared to resume any action for the time being, the shock of the enormous casualty count sinking in and deterring them from any further engagement. Consequently, it appeared to us that we were entering another one of those prolonged lull periods, greatly welcomed this time around, for I sorely needed the relief from anxiety it afforded us. This did not mean that everyone relaxed and enjoyed the respite. When I walked past the council hall that afternoon, I heard shouting emanating from heated arguments throughout the duration of the meeting. Things were not going well for Troy, I could tell. The battles outside our walls with the enemy were matched by those occurring in the councils among ourselves. When my father met with me in our usual courtyard setting later on, he was clearly agitated and in need of venting out his frustrations. I served him nicely in that capacity.

"Both the Carians and Phrygians are threatening to leave us," he lamented. "Our alliances are falling apart, the result of this protracted war. Victory is as distant from us as when the war first began. Even Antimachus cannot persuade them to stay, but then he is so obnoxious that he offends more often than he does any good."

"Is this because they see us losing the war?" I asked.

"A better way to phrase it is because they do not see us winning it. Nothing is so dreary, or detrimental to morale, than continuing in a fight that does not produce a seeable outcome. Lives and funds are depleted, and for no satisfactory result. Eventually, they ask themselves, why are we doing this? Is anything to be gained?"

"Troy's riches are not sufficient to keep them here?"

My father gave me an inquisitive look, perhaps amused that I would touch upon a topic I knew nothing about, for he smiled, more to himself than to me, as he peered at the floor.

"What riches?" he said. "Our wealth was based on the trades we controlled, our access to the sea and land routes permitting us to impose levies on caravans and shipping. Nine years of war has ended that. Oh, sure, we still have huge reserves on hand—gold, always in demand—but even these are rapidly dwindling."

"Why not expend it all?" I kidded. "That way, if the Greeks do win, they'll have nothing but empty coffers. Our allies would stay, receiving better compensation."

My father's smile widened. I am sure he did not think I was stupid, but maybe quite ignorant.

"Believe it or not, that thought has also occurred to me," he mused. "The problem is that, when you pay them more, they will want to spend it. Being in war is not conducive to that. You could get killed."

I respected my father's sardonic observation but saw that it also pained him, even though he made light of the situation. He seemed to value, or should I say, tolerate, my opinion, despite my lack of knowledge in many of the subjects we talked about, and I think I assuaged his woes sufficiently enough to cause him to seek out these meetings time and again. As we spoke, his demeanor turned very grave, a moroseness enveloped him that gave me reason to worry.

"You are thinking of Paris, Father?" I asked.

He briefly paused, impressed that I accurately expressed what he had been thinking, and then held my hand.

"I am afraid, dear Daughter, that we must prepare ourselves for the worst. Hearten yourself for this."

"You can't mean it," I said, dismayed.

"Oenone will not help him. I know it. Why should she? He abandoned her after he met Helen. She will never forgive him for that."

"Please don't say that, Father."

He detected my consternation and pressed me to him.

"I see that you love your brother, and it distresses me to heighten your fears. Forgive this old man his lack of trust. I did not want to frighten you so."

He told me what he felt inside, and I ought to be more considerate of that, but I desperately wanted to believe that Paris would recover from his wound. Of all my brothers, I liked him the best, despite our occasional discord, and the thought of losing him was upsetting to say the least, even unthinkable. Yet my father was correct in his alerting me to prepare myself for the worst that could befall us. The worst? I have endured one worst setback after another ever since being asked to go to Themiscyra. Was it even possible to undergo more tragedies? I had to block such notions out of my mind and concentrate on the positive, be optimistic, else I feared I might go mad.

"At this point, I only wish to think about good things, Father," I said. "Sometimes I fear what I think will actually bring it about. I know this doesn't make sense, but my fear is real."

My father lovingly glanced at me, touched by my words, perhaps even relating to them, and continued to hold me tight until, gradually, he let go and arose to make his departure. He gave me that understanding, sympathetic gaze that so warmed me.

"You are a treasure to me, Polyxena," he said. "Never let it be said that parents cannot learn from their children." Then he walked off.

In my subsequent rumination, I was struck over how much I missed Helen. She had only been gone for two days, yet her absence was conspicuous to me, as well as to Andromache, I am sure, for our usual afternoon gatherings in the residence hall were somehow less engaging without her company. To me, she had become as much a member of our family as someone born into it, and I loved her equally well, no longer seeing her as the foreigner she once was or the cause of the misfortunes that befell Troy. Andromache was even closer to her than I, the two of them having become best of friends, so remarkable, as she had lost her dear Hector in this war.

I was not able to gauge my mother's actual regard for Helen. Outwardly, she was friendly enough to her daughter-in-law, accepting her as the one true love of Paris, but she retained a certain aloofness that deterred her from exhibiting the warmth she displayed to others in her household. This may have had nothing to do with her believing that Helen brought this war upon us but, rather, that no children had been produced in her marriage to Paris. Mother's priority was family. Having offspring, carrying on the lineage, these were the things that most mattered to her, and in connection to this, Paris and Helen did not live up to their obligations. In that sense, Helen was a disappointment to her, as I am sure was Paris. More than ten years together now and no children. That was discouraging, perhaps even disgraceful, to Mother. It could also be that Mother was not the gregarious, outgoing personality that characterized my father, and being naturally more reserved, she withheld her displays of affection and thereby demonstrated a greater detachment than she actually possessed. Whatever the reason, she left us ambivalent about her actual feelings for Helen, fluctuating between moods of pleasure and indifference when with her.

Our worries over Helen and Paris hung like an oppressive cloud over our afternoon gatherings, and we sat in silence much of the time, absorbed in our anxieties, disinclined to speak on the subject while, simultaneously, being in need of voicing our concern. The atmosphere was depressing and tense. If only some message would arrive.

"I can't remember Oenone," I said during our latest such get-together. "What is she like, Mother?"

"Small in stature but attractive," my mother replied. "She had brown hair and eyes, an angular nose, pointed like an arrowhead, I thought, very gentle, almost frail-looking. I liked her. I was saddened when Paris left her."

"That must have been before he went to Sparta."

"It was. She had the gift of prophecy and knew that Paris would forsake her for Helen, so even before his departure, she returned to her home at Mount Ida. Regrettably, this had no effect on Paris who did not mind her leaving. Yet, before she left—it shows how much she loved him—she told Paris she would help him if he was ever hurt. She is a good physician."

"What a sad story."

"It is sad. Very sad. Who can make sense of these things? It's not as if Paris was unhappy with her; they made an endearing couple."

"The seers are correct," Andromache interjected. "Aphrodite contrived this."

"I wish she had picked on someone else," my mother moped. "How different things would be now." She then shrank back and looked frantically about, fearing that the goddess may have heard her.

"She must keep her promise," said Andromache. We all agreed.

On the fifth day after having left for Mount Ida, we received word that the wagon carrying Paris and Helen was spotted approaching the Dardanian Gates. My heartbeat pounded heavily within me as I rushed from my quarters to scurry down the steps descending from the Pergamus to the lower grounds. Andromache joined me after observing my flight. Together, we anxiously awaited inside the gate for the wagon to arrive. *Gods be merciful. Let it be the news we desperately want to hear.*

My optimism faded as the cart entered the gate, the gloom of its occupants telling me that things had not gone well. Helen looked forlorn, downcast in her deep depression, as did Deiphobus and the two attendants that had gone with them. Paris was lying inside the wagon, covered with blankets, his face pallid, looking much worse than before, with a deathlike glaze in his eyes. A stretcher had to be called to transport him. He was too weak to even be propped up by his servants. I was too afraid to talk to anyone, but there was no need to. We all knew what happened. Oenone had denied him her assistance, for him, the only chance left for life, and he came home to die. To be aware of one's imminent death, what can be more horrible than that?

As Paris was being carried to his chamber, Helen, trembling and weak in her legs, fell into the arms of Andromache and me, and we lifted her up as we proceeded to take her upstairs.

"She would not help him," Helen cried. "I pleaded with her, begged her, on my knees, to no avail."

"I'm so sorry, Helen," I moaned.

"I can't believe it. What a bitch! How can I live without him?"

As we continued through the corridors of the residence hall, I once again saw my father holding my mother in an embrace, the dismay written on their faces, tears flowing, such a pitiful sight that so magnified my sorrows. I could not keep from openly weeping. The gods had dealt us another devastating blow. What a cruel world this is.

Paris lingered in his agony for two more days. Knowing there was no hope for him accentuated the grief we felt over our helplessness that much more. What could anyone say? Near the end, he became delirious, his excruciating pain getting the best of him, causing him to scream out in repeated intervals. I heard his cries even in my chamber. The medicine given him to relieve the suffering had only a minor effect. Helen stayed with him throughout, but the rest of us were unable to bear the ordeal for any length of time and wished only to be away from it. The last time I was with him, he did not recognize me, or gave no indication that he did, and I was almost as much discomfited by this as by his torment.

When death came to Paris, late on that second day, it descended upon him more as an act of mercy than an unwanted guest, blessing him in its release from suffering and furnishing us with greatly sought-after relief. I was not in the room when it happened, but I knew from the quiet emanating from it as I made my passes by it that he had at last found his peace. And when its reality imparted on me, I was nonetheless torn by it, even as I told myself that Paris now rested in sweet repose and was no longer in torture. I staggered outside the doors of the Pergamus and slumped down in a seated position on the steps. I had no wish to be inside with all the crying and hurt, knowing the futility of providing any solace to Helen or my parents. I think I am better in facing grief by myself than in the company of others. The loss of Paris deeply hurt me. I was closer to him than any of my other brothers, and he would always have a special place in my heart.

As I sat there, when it was almost nightfall, a woman with an attendant hurriedly ran toward my direction, winded from having nearly exhausted themselves in an effort to get here. She saw me in my bereavement and halted, a shocked look coming to her face. She appeared just as my mother had described her, petite with brown eyes and brown hair and a small, pointed nose. I knew who she was, even though I had never met her before, and why she was here.

"You're too late," I said in a whimpering voice. "Paris has died."

I shall never forget the look of abject horror that came over her. She nearly turned white. She was too dazed to speak and, as I did earlier, slumped down on the steps next to me, her tears gushing profusely from her.

"I am Oenone," she gradually told me, recovering enough from her grief to speak. "I have just made the worst mistake of my life."

"Because of Helen?" I asked.

"Because I was envious of her. I am justly punished for it."

I looked at her and saw a pitiable figure indeed. Her sorrowful comportment evoked my deepest sympathy as she kept on weeping, inconsolable in her despondency. She had a pretty face, and I could see how Paris might have been quite content with her before Helen came into his life.

"I'm so sorry," I said. "I think I understand."

"As deeply as I loved him—how could I have done this?"

"Could you have helped him?"

"I'm not sure. His injury was severe, but I should have tried."

So it was not known if Oenone could have saved Paris. She could not be blamed entirely for being the cause of his death. She was afraid to see him and yet also wanted to look on her one-time lover and husband once more.

"They will condemn me for this," she sobbed. "How can I face them?"

"I shall come with you," I said, wanting to console her.

Although she did not say anything, Oenone nodded her consent to my offer, lacking, I think, the courage to confront my parents, brothers and sisters, and, most of all, Helen by herself. I afforded her the support she needed. Together, we walked into the chamber, where Paris lay. At first, only hostile glares met her, but when everyone saw her profound sadness, she was soon seen as the tragic figure she was, and the anger directed at her turned to pity. When she stood beside my brother's body, she burst out in uncontrolled weeping and had to be held up by Deiphobus. With his head resting on a pillow and his eyes closed and his body covered in a white shroud, I was struck at how serenely Paris lay in death, the same impression I had when looking at the slain Penthesileia.

Gradually, Oenone's open crying reduced itself to soft whimpers. I saw that she could not look Helen in the eye; that was just as well, as Helen's unforgiving bitterness clearly revealed itself in her intense stare. I escorted her outside, where my father, moved to compassion, told her she could stay overnight in the guest quarters. I took her there. I was not sure why I was kind to her, except maybe that I sensed her regret and could relate to it, and I liked her.

"I thank you," Oenone said as I was about to leave and then hesitated, wanting, I think, to say my name, but not knowing it.

"I am Polyxena," I informed her.

"Polyxena," she repeated and then added, "You have a good heart."

I bade her a good night and returned to my own chamber to retire for the evening. It was now dark, and the day had been long and enervating for me. Although I anticipated that I would soon fall asleep, that was not to be. I lay awake for what seemed an interminable length of time through the night, trying to come to grips with the reality of my brother's death, disputing it and wishing it were not so. Typical of nights when I am awake most of the time, sleep does eventually come to me, but not until early in the morning, causing disruptions in my normal pattern of rising on the following day.

As a result of this, I woke up later than normal, and by the time I joined everyone else at breakfast, they were nearly finished with theirs and ready to leave the table. I noticed that our guest was not there.

"Where is Oenone?" I asked.

"Still asleep, we think," Andromache replied. "She has not eaten yet, at least not here."

"I should check on her," I said. "She might still be too ashamed to face us."

"She ought to be," my mother scowled, "after what she has done."

I left them and proceeded for the guest quarters, a separate structure about a hundred-some paces from the residence palace, and saw that the door was closed. I knocked, but there was no answer.

"Oenone," I spoke out. "Are you there?" Still no answer. Did she leave Troy early to avoid us?

I pushed on the door, and it readily opened. I entered the room and, to my horror, saw Oenone swinging from a lintel. She had wrapped a bed sheet from it around her neck and tipped over the chair she stood on.

"No! No!" I screamed out. My cries brought several guards and attendants into the room just as I emerged from it, trembling from my jolt.

Benumbed, I slowly lumbered my way back to the palace dining room, torn emotionally by another shock heaped upon me, startling everyone still there.

"Polyxena," Andromache exclaimed. "What's wrong?" I paused, unable to give words to my despondency.

"Say something, child," my mother demanded. "You look ill."

"It's Oenone," I said. "She has hanged herself."

"What?"

"She is dead."

Until this moment, nobody at that table had grasped the depth of Oenone's remorse over what she had done. Everyone fell silent. Even Helen had a shocked expression. To their credit, no one took any satisfaction in the news—I would have reacted very angrily to this— and Mother even shed tears. She, of course, had once loved Oenone as a daughter-in-law, and I am sure these feelings resurfaced for her, nullifying the anger she had for her denying Paris treatment. Nothing in life seems clearly defined. Our relationships are intertwined and convoluted, and so we react to these.

I would have preferred for Oenone and Paris to be resting side by side upon a pyre for their funeral, a fitting closure to their once-happy life together. But my parents, in deference to Helen, I think, decided only Paris deserved to be immortalized by sacred fire. Oenone, having taken her own life—viewed as dishonorable—was to be buried in the cemetery on the outskirts of the city, the appropriate internment for her method of death. And that is how the rites were accomplished. We all attended the funeral of Paris, although the laudations were significantly less in coming and more subdued than when Hector was honored. Paris was still regarded as the prince who brought about this war, not necessarily by the royal house, although, at times, I felt, even by some of them, but by the populace at large, the praises rendered him for having slain Achilles not being enough to remove this stain from him. Yet it was still quite moving, and an aura of dignity surrounded the proceedings, enough to make an impressive spectacle that was worthy of a royal son of Troy.

Not so with Oenone's funeral. In a quiet gathering, only my parents, Andromache, and I present, she was laid to rest without as much as a speech given on her behalf. Even though I hardly knew her, she touched me deeply, and I mourned for her. I was glad that I met her. Of all the stories that might someday be told about this war, I think none is sadder than that of Oenone. She reacted so normally to a situation she was confronted with that was injurious to her, angered over having been forsaken by a lover and husband, and made a decision she did not mean to. More than anyone else, she is representative of what personal responsibility entails, the finality of a regretted judgment that, having been made, cannot be taken back. What can be concluded about this other than to say she did nothing differently than any of us might do? That is what haunts me about her.

CHAPTER XIV

N O ONE WAS WORSE AFFECTED by the death of Paris than Helen. Her world, in every respect, was destroyed, so thoroughly demolished that she must have felt herself cast into an orbit of strangeness, residing among foreigners, an outsider. She had been so intrinsically linked to her husband, tied to his affiliation with the family, championed and defended by him, that no one could even conceive of her having her own identity. The closeness of their bond deterred her from attempting any measures that might have secured another friendship for her, especially among Troy's men, rendering her untouchable in their eyes. As a consequence, she isolated herself from their attentions, very much aloof to their overtures, and came to be regarded in almost mystical awe, virtually sacrosanct.

She had risked it all for the sake of her love of Paris. She had abandoned her husband, Menelaus, her daughter, Hermione, her parents, her friends, even her status as Queen of Sparta, everything over this love, and I am sure she had to be fraught with the worst torment of whether it had all been worth it. If ever a person had been smitten by Aphrodite's spell, Helen was her, and all these things she gave up in surrender to this enchantment existed as its proof. But what had she to show for this now? Emptiness. Not even a child had been born to them that might have forged a closer bond to our royal house. Paris was her life, and without him, she was very much the out-of-place figure, having no visible ties to the rest of us in Troy, and some of my remaining brothers even doubted her continued loyalty to us.

For our people, the death of Paris accentuated the woes he and Helen had brought to Troy, or so I gathered from the reports my brothers related during our evening meals. With the primary instigator of their hardships gone, they regarded themselves having been forsaken and left to undo the chaos that the couple had inflicted on them. That they naturally resented Helen all the more, instead of rendering her the sympathy she was most in need of at present, was understandable, but also very cruel. She was held in disdain, openly derided, and perhaps outright despised, and this hostility isolated her further within the Pergamus. She could not walk freely through the streets as she used to out of concern she might be harmed by some offended malcontent. Even my mother cooled toward her, her earlier prejudices over Helen having brought the Greek host to us reasserting themselves, and because no grandchild existed to attach her to the family, an alienation had risen between them. It made us believe that only a recognition of her son's love for Helen elicited her amiability rather than her ever acquiring an actual love for her daughter-in-law. The situation was not pleasant.

Had it not been for Andromache and me, Helen might have gone mad in her anguish, perhaps even killed herself. In the two of us, she had her only friends left, and when are friends more necessary than when one is overcome with grief? We did our best to console her, feeling deeply for her loss, understanding her predicament, and kept her company so that she might have some occasional diversion from her bereavement. Not easy at first, for Helen's lamentation was so distressing, we did eventually succeed in ending her self-imposed exile within our quarters and got her to rejoin our evening meals and get-togethers. Our concern was facing the existing reality presently confronting her and making her accept the adjustments that had to be taken into consideration if she was to have a future at Troy.

"You must end your loneliness among us," Andromache told Helen. "Nothing good can come of this."

"I know this, Andromache," replied Helen, very downcast in her depression. "But I feel I am a such a complete stranger now, like I don't belong here."

"There's only one way to get over this. I suggest that you consider another marriage, to another of Priam's sons."

"So soon? Please don't give me that counsel. Besides, I'm not in love with any of them. No one can replace Paris in my heart."

"Be realistic, Helen," Andromache advised. "You can learn to love again."

"But you yourself have not taken that step."

"I have a son, Astyanax, to comfort me and also to keep me connected to the royal house. That makes all the difference."

Helen was not convinced that Andromache's suggestion was a solution, admitting to us that she feared she might not be an appropriate wife, as she lacked any affection for my other brothers, at least not to the extent that merited a commitment to marriage.

"That's a drastic step," she mused. "What do you think Polyxena?"

I was not certain what the correct answer was in this situation and questioned if I, were I Helen, would consider such a proposal. "Loneliness can be oppressive," I responded. "Maybe worse than marrying someone you did not love. I don't know."

Helen looked thoughtfully at me, pausing as she contemplated her dilemma, and, like me, not sure what was the proper answer to her plight.

"You are a precocious child," she then said. "I can learn from you."

I was not clear over how to take this. Certainly, I was no longer a child in my eyes, but I suppose from Helen's perspective, being, I think, twice my age, I might well be considered as such, and I had to conclude that her intention was magnanimous.

"Were I even to submit to this," Helen went on, "who would have me?"

I could not imagine her saying this. Nearly all men, my brothers among them, drooled at the mouth on seeing her while married to Paris. Now that she was single, their salivation was a raging torrent, an obvious exaggeration, but not that far off.

"I think the question is, who would *you* take?" I said. "Both Helenus and Deiphobus have no wives. Polites and the rest are probably too young."

"Then the choice is between Helenus and Deiphobus," replied Helen.

"It appears that way."

Helen was not enthusiastic over either candidate, although I think she favored Deiphobus more, as he led her to Mount Ida and assisted her in doing the best for Paris. They would have gotten to know each other during the journey. Helenus was of a sober mold indeed, an augur who, it was said, had warned Paris that he would bring disaster to Troy if he sailed for Sparta. Although occasionally able to exude some warmth, he was mostly composed of a serious demeanor and very straightforward in speech and mannerism, to the point of being blunt. But he was also a strong commander and led his troops admirably in battle, his valor and stamina being undisputed. I suppose I would like him more if I knew him better, but he avoided our family dinners as much as he could, spending a lot of his time with the slave women and captives he retained as concubines.

"I need to think about this," Helen said. "I don't have to rush into this."

I was convinced that what Helen wanted was an indefinite postponement to a problem she deemed unpleasant in spite of the reprieve it offered to her alienation believing, in time, the answer would come to her.

Helen may have thought she had time to think about marrying Helenus or Deiphobus, but my father did not, as he was telling me during another one of my courtyard meetings with him.

"There is envy among my sons," he told me, "over Helen. She is seen as fair game now that she is single, and this is disruptive to their willing cooperation, causing dissention among them."

"Them?" I asked.

"Well, between Helenus and Deiphobus. What a mess. What am I to do? Helenus is a year older and next in line for the kingship, but Deiphobus has long craved her, even when she was still with Paris. He is depraved. I fear what he may do if she is denied to him. Who is more fit to claim her?"

"We have talked about it with Helen," I said. "Andromache suggested a new marriage so that Helen may not feel as such an outsider, as she now does."

"You are ahead of me. What did Helen say?" he said, an enthusiasm returning to him.

"She understands that may be inevitable but thinks she has time to ponder on it."

"Not really. The people are not as willing to accept her as a justifiable excuse for pursuing this war if she has no more affiliation with the court, especially our allies, already strained in their commitment to us. A new marriage will strengthen their resolve, improve their morale, and provide for them a cause to continue their effort. Indeed, the matter has every aspect of immediacy about it."

"So she has no time?" I asked.

"Not much time. I would like to get this over with. Once a husband is chosen for her, I expect things to improve for everyone concerned, the bickering should stop, hopefully their harmony will be restored."

"You said chosen? Helen must submit to what is decided for her?"

"Is there another way?"

"What if Helen were to decide?" I proposed, somewhat demurely.

"If she were able to, at the soonest time, I agree there's an advantage in that. But you said she was hedging. In such cases, it is prudent to make the judgment for her, as this will rid her of her indecisions and expedite the process."

I perceived what my father was saying. Between two equally loathsome prospects, as Helen appeared to view her options, the simple and direct approach was to announce the selection to her, eliminating her voice in the matter altogether. Once the issue was settled, there remained no more reason for further reservations, everyone would be satisfied, and the acceptance of this was to our mutual benefit. If only things were that easy. My intuition told me that hard feelings would ensue out of this.

"Do you know who she favors?" my father asked.

"I believe Deiphobus, but I'm not sure."

"Can you find out?"

"I'll try to," I said. "My feeling is that if I bring up the subject, she will reject my inquiries and want to speak about something else."

"Find out, Polyxena. It may make things easier for me. That this should happen, as if I were not burdened with enough problems," he groaned, his anguish getting the better of him.

I related to my father's anxieties. This was one of those situations where, no matter what selection was made, the choice was bound to lead to anger and resentment with the loser, and we were likely to all suffer on this account. The death of Paris, unanticipated as it was, left us with no peace. He could have solved the entire problem by declaring his wife's future husband and thereby eliminating all doubt and competition. In spite of lingering in his dying, that he did not do this told me that he himself had no desire for anyone to claim Helen after he was gone. Very selfish of him, I thought.

The current lull in the fighting remained in effect despite the passing of the prescribed days accorded a funeral of a notable, such as Paris, and neither side demonstrated any inclination to resume the struggle, owing, I think, to the enormity of the casualties sustained in our last battle. We also received reports that both Menelaus and Agamemnon had been wounded in that confrontation, which probably resulted in a significant deterioration of morale among the enemy ranks. If only Agamemnon had died. That would lead to a permanent end to our hostilities.

I took advantage of the current calm and resumed my habitual rides on Zephyrus, if not alone, then with Andromache who likewise discovered the release of stress such a diversion provided. It was during a time when I was trotting along by myself across the fields separating our allied camps from the Dardanian Gates when I saw Andromache galloping toward me at full speed. I stopped Zephyrus to wait on her.

"Is something wrong?" I asked, worried over what caused her haste in seeing me.

"I just left the scene of a most violent argument," she replied, visibly shaken, "between your brothers—over Helen."

Not the thing I wanted to hear while seeking relaxation from the pressures brewing within the palace, but I cannot say I did not expect such a blowup. Still, the news came as an annoyance to me, bringing to a forefront the seriousness of the problem my sister-in-law now presented to us. My father was correct in saying a resolution had to be found at the earliest opportunity, before the situation gravitated to open antagonism.

"Both Helenus and Deiphobus claim she should be theirs," Andromache continued. "And they want us to side with them. I want no part of this."

"Was Helen there?" I asked.

"She was, but she ran into her room when things got out of hand, upset at both of them. I had no idea things would get this bad."

"She's going to have to choose one of them."

"Who? Helenus says he is the oldest and, as heir to the throne, has a legitimate right to her. Our laws decree this."

"What does Deiphobus say?"

"He claims he is the one who has most consistently befriended Helen and done more for her than anyone else."

"That may be true, but his motives have always been lecherous."

Andromache seemed surprised that I would say that, mainly because, I think, my views substantiated what she also had long suspected but refrained from talking about, not being a family member and thinking this impolite.

"We need to speak to Helen " I added.

"We do. The last thing Troy needs is a division arising within its own rank, especially now, with its hold over the allies very tenuous."

"My father's major worry. Come, let's ride back and see her."

We headed back to the city, an urgency in our pace, seeing our situation as critical and demanding some action be taken. We left our horses at the inner corral and hurried into the Pergamus then scampered up the steps to the residence quarters, where we met other family members, still shaken by the confrontation that had taken place.

"Helenus has gone mad!" my mother exclaimed when I greeted her. "He has become utterly obsessed with Helen. Indeed, he means to have her as his wife, even if it means going against his father's wishes. Self-centered, that's what he is. He cares nothing of what this will do to our unity."

"Where is Helen?" I asked.

"In her chamber. She should well hide from us, all the grief she has brought upon us. I curse the day she ever came to our shores." Mother could not hide the disdain she presently felt, nearly shrieking at us.

"Mother, please."

"So you also oppose me in her favor? Ungrateful one. I gave you life, and you show me no respect."

I hated it when she was like this, the unreasonableness of her position, as if the past can be returned to us, permitting us to alter the course of events that had transpired. Everyone of prudent thought recognized that Helen was nothing more than a pretext for the ambitious and greedy Agamemnon. Helen had offered to surrender herself to the Greeks more than once in the time she had spent with us, only to be swayed from this by our leaders. The issue had been discussed over and over, and each time, the same conclusion was arrived at: she was not the cause of this war. Mother, of course, was not persuaded by this, maintaining that the findings were determined by men, robbed of their sound judgment by the physical beauty of Helen and biased toward her. I did not help matters by ignoring what she said.

"Rebellious child," she shouted after me as I proceeded to Helen's chamber.

"Who is it?" Helen asked after hearing my knock. "Polyxena, with Andromache," I answered.

"Leave me. I wish to be alone."

"We have to talk," Adromache responded. "Let us in."

We heard nothing more and waited. Helen then opened the door and invited us in. She looked forlorn, having just wiped away her tears with the sleeve of her gown.

"I'm sorry," she apologized. "My nerves are on edge. You heard this morning's argument between Helenus and Deiphobus."

"Yes," affirmed Andromache. "That's why we must talk."

"I don't know what to do," Helen moaned. "They're fighting over me as if I were theirs for the taking. My time with Paris has granted me no privileges in their eyes, no special status meriting any approbation out of them."

"Did you think that would happen?" I asked.

"Yes, I did," she replied, still whimpering. "In honor of his memory."

She should have known better, I thought. No raving beauty like Helen was going to avert the competition to possess her that would result out of her being single again. An ordinary woman might have been left to her own devices, and even this was doubtful in a male-dominated society, but never Helen, the most sought-after woman that ever lived. Men craved her; they always had. What other woman could claim to have had forty suitors seek her out in marriage? I had my strong opinions on how to advise her, but deferred to let Andromache do the talking, as she was closer to Helen's age and was more inclined to be listened to.

"You must decide—this very day!—who is to be your next husband," Andromache urged.

Helen shuddered, not prepared for any such commitment and obviously disinclined to have either one of her prospects.

"That's easy for you to say," she said. "You don't have to share your bed with them."

"They're not as bad as you make them out to be."

"No? So tell me, Andromache, who would you prefer making love with?"

Andromache was quieted for the moment, grasping fully what was demanded of Helen and averse to declare her own preference or lack of such, whichever was the case. I had no idea my two brothers were perceived in such low esteem. Their uninspiring personalities and somewhat uncouth mannerisms aside, neither one was bad looking, in fact, they were quite handsome; I don't think my father sired any ugly children. I had difficulty understanding Helen's resistance to the notion of bedding down with one of them and Andromache's seeming concurrence over this subject. Did I really know them?

"It's no longer a matter involving only you," Andromache stressed. "Troy's stability is at stake here. Whether you like it or not, your choosing a husband is tied into the welfare of others. Consider it a duty requirement."

Helen understood this, I think, and made no attempt to deny Andromache's assertions, realizing that any postponement now entailed inherent risks in our continued ability to sustain the war, what it meant to our alliances. Yet she remained hesitant, as if unwilling or unable to voluntarily consign herself to a fate viewed as quite disagreeable to her.

"If you like, Helen," I broke in after seeing her reluctance, "I can have my father make the choice for you. Would that be amenable to you?"

Helen appeared to ponder a while on the notion, then nodded her agreement.

"I should prefer that," she muttered. "It would absolve me of blame should the selection be badly received by the one not chosen."

"Do you want the choice to be totally his, or do you wish to have him name whoever is preferable to you?"

"I suppose I prefer Deiphobus. He did comfort me on our trip to Mount Ida and can be nice when he wants to. I hardly know Helenus."

"Thank you, Helen," Andromache said. "Our burden, as well as yours, is lightened."

I think Helen was somewhat more relaxed now that she had made her choice, taking comfort in knowing she did not have to announce it, leaving that distasteful task to my father. I did not envy him his duty, for we both sensed that Helenus was not going to be satisfied, but exactly how he would react was open to speculation. My belief was that he, while not pleased, would accede to it once its inevitability was established. Generally, such issues are contested only as long as they are in abeyance. Once finalized, they readily dissolve into acceptance. Certainly, I hoped that would be the case here.

When I met with my father that evening at our usual setting, prearranged this time, as he required a speedy answer to his inquiry, and passed on what Helen had decided earlier, he appeared likewise relieved initially, until he pondered over what consequences might ensue out of this, at which point his countenance assumed a troublesome perspective. He obviously did not relish the task facing him and had to bolster his flagging determination to see this through with words of self-encouragement, trying to be optimistic as best as he could under the strain.

"As my oldest remaining son," he reflected, "I must believe Helenus has acquired the wisdom one associates with maturity. If I did not think this, I should be loathe to make the announcement tomorrow. Why am I so tense over this?"

His question was rhetorical, and I felt no reason to respond to it, which eased me of the need to give an answer I was unsure about. But it clearly revealed the aversion he retained for his declared intentions, and I sympathized with him, recognizing the weight of responsibility his kingship imposed on him.

"What if I'm wrong?" he continued in his deliberation, still directing his concerns more to himself than to me.

"Do you fear Helenus, Father?" I interceded in his rumination, curious over what he would say. He welcomed my intrusion.

"Fear? A strong word, but not entirely off the mark. Let's just say I fear what might result if he is embittered or, rather, remains so over my selecting Deiphobus."

"What can happen?"

My father thought long over this, showing no inclination that he might answer my question, and left me bewildered over his hesitation.

"I worry needlessly," he then said, deferring from replying to my inquiry altogether. "He ranks among our most valiant leaders and has fought bravely in Troy's defense. I can't see him betraying our cause."

"Betray us?" I asked, alarmed at the suggestion.

"Never! He is a noble son of Troy. Forget what I said. I thank you for your information, Polyxena. At tomorrow evening's gathering, I shall bring this disruptive matter to a close. You will then see that Helenus loyally serves us."

Father may have alleviated his own anxieties but admittedly did little to ease mine, and when he left me sitting by myself to reflect further over our conversation, troublesome notions persisted to hound me, significantly adding to my discomfort. That he contemplated the very possibility of a potential betrayal by Helenus meant that there was a basis for holding such fears, although I had no idea what that might be. But now that its plausibility had been implanted within me, I could not dismiss it readily as my father was able to do, and I, at present, possessed the fears he seemed to rid himself of. This night's meeting had not helped resolve my apprehensions; quite the opposite, my worries were greatly enhanced.

I spent the next day overwhelmed with tenseness in anticipation of our evening's gathering, where the truth of my worriment would reveal itself. Like Helen, I wished the decision could be indefinitely postponed, and I fumed against my brothers for their intolerance toward this end and for forcing the condition on us. The more I cogitated on the problem, the more I began to believe that Helen could have simplified things considerably by choosing Helenus rather than Deiphobus. Helenus was a seer, known to have the power to predict things, which made him a formidable figure, especially if he was to become an adversary, a foe of greater dimensions in generating difficulties for Troy. Also, he was a strong warrior, his courage unquestioned, and, as such, was held in greater esteem than his brother, and he was the older, granting him the legitimacy he claimed. I could not see Deiphobus in the same regard; he may have been more likable than Helenus, actually charming at times, but he was also weaker and therefore less threatening. Were he to lose Helen, the expectation was that he would pout and mope over this, but that would be it. With Helenus, we did not know what to expect.

Word had circulated through the palace that this was the day Helen's future husband was to be announced, tantamount to a wedding ceremony, news received with the deepest foreboding for some and eager anticipation for others. I definitely fell into the former category and, strangely enough, appeared to be in a clear minority, at least within the palace, aside from my father and maybe Cassandra, being the only persons around to see things that way. Most of the household expected tonight's decision to bring an end to the divisiveness that had marked our recent times, and they were happy to have the matter closed. The rest of my sisters, my mother, and Andromache maintained our problems were now over. Helen, while still ambivalent to a situation she considered being forced upon her, reconciled herself to the inevitable and perhaps sought the relief that the end of the contentious issue provided. As she already knew who was to be chosen, her eagerness for the gathering was subdued. Still, she must have been apprehensive to some extent over whether her preference would indeed be met. I doubt if she looked forward to the coming nights in store for her.

Needless to say, that evening, the residence palace was filled to capacity, every member of the family and their in-laws being there in addition to special guests, the most notable among them Antenor and his son, Agenor. I had not seen Agenor for some time and seized this opportunity to update myself on his activities, walking over to where he was standing. He was as charming as ever.

"You look lovely," Agenor said, flattering me, "as I remember you."

"I know you, Agenor. You say that to all women."

"No, it's true. I am sincere."

"Never let it be said that your approach is not appreciated. So what have you done with yourself lately?"

"The usual. Defending Troy. However, I have found time to woo a certain woman I've taken a liking to. I mean to have her as my wife."

For an instant, I thought another potential suitor had slipped away from me, but then the realization that Agenor and I were not really meant for each other took hold of me; for one thing, royals were not permitted to seek out commoners as marriage partners. Besides, he demonstrated no romantic interest in me when we journeyed to Themiscyra, nor had I reciprocated in kind.

"How fortunate," I replied. "Do I know her?"

"Well enough, I think."

"You mean Menodice?"

"She's the one." His eyes lit up as he said this. "It was obvious to me since I first met her, when we went to Themiscyra. You saw that, else you would not have guessed it. She very much loves me."

Yes, I saw that and remembered how Thalia felt herself slighted over all the attention he heaped upon Menodice. But that was then, this is now, and I honestly was quite pleased over hearing Menodice had found her happiness in him and wished her the best in this regard. The grievance that led me to dismiss her from my services evaporated for me, and I was comforted that at least one long-term benefit had resulted from our Amazon venture.

"I'm happy for you both," I said.

"Thank you, princess. Can I ask a favor of you on her behalf."

"I know what it is. Yes, I will take her back."

"This means a lot to her. She really misses you."

I suppose I had been too hard on Menodice. After all, she had devoted her entire life to caring for me, and for me to be inconsiderate of that may be callous. If I had retained her services, I would not have been surprised by Agenor's announcement, for she certainly would have mentioned this to me. Yet she revealed Achilles's vulnerability to Paris, which led to his death only six weeks ago. Already, it seemed ages. So much has happened to me in the past half year that I cannot measure it in the normal passing of time. All the events existed in their own seemingly lengthy time span, and it felt as though each was a life unto itself. I am now feeling as if I am living in separate lifetimes, each defined by its own particular set of circumstances and problems. The question of whether I should forgive Menodice over what she did in one of those past ages faded, as it now seemed to be no longer problematic for me. Only the present has relevance. That is the lesson I have learned out of my experiences: what is gone is gone, never to return, and one's behavior should be adjusted to what presently matters. I can be unforgiving, remembering my past, and make myself miserable in the process, or I can forget and move forward from this point on.

After we had eaten and done much of our socializing, my father stood up at the head of the table, his reserved place of honor, and, goblet in hand, quieted us in our eager anticipation as he rose. He stood there, a bit nervous, I thought, looking at every one of us in turn, his glances shifting from one end of the table to the other, as if making a prolonged evaluation over when to start. The moment was at hand. He was about to divulge the news to us, the naming of Helen's next husband.

"A toast," he proclaimed. "But first, I must speak. I have thought about this, torturing myself over what is the right thing to do, so that everyone might be satisfied with the choice I have made. I request, no, I insist, that my decision be accepted by you, as it is for the greater good of Troy. Be respectful of it and also understanding of the difficulty this posed for me. In other words, behave as men."

The suspense was killing me. This in spite of knowing who it would be. My heartbeat pounded in my neck, and I held my breath as I waited for my father to end his pause.

"Now, as to Helen's husband," he continued, "I have chosen Deiphobus."

For an instant, a hush overcame the gathering, but this was quickly followed by outbursts of congratulations.

"Well and good," shouted Pilatus. "A toast to Deiphobus."

"To Deiphobus!" a chorus followed.

"Lucky man," proclaimed Aeneas as he drank from his goblet in his toast.

I looked at Helenus and was shocked at the horror depicted in his face. He froze in his stunned amazement, and I could tell he was about to unleash a torrent of abuse against all of us, but at present, he stared, an intense, wild glare, at his plate and kept himself under restraint.

Deiphobus, of course, was elated and gave Helen an lascivious smirk that left her shaken in its evocative suggestion. She maintained a dignified mannerism in spite of this but hardly once smiled throughout the duration of the celebration, feeling obligated to uphold her end of the bargain, even if distasteful to her. There was little doubt this marriage was forced on her, arising out of the necessity to stress a unity in the royal household, especially in connection with our allies who were faltering in their allegiance, a show of cohesion and cooperation, if you will, and she was less than thrilled over its consummation. My brother's smug drooling did not help her situation.

All of a sudden, Helenus jumped to his feet, tipping over his chair, and riveted our eyes on him.

"This is outrageous!" he shouted as loud as he could and threw his goblet across the floor.

Everyone stood aghast, most of all my father who had expected his plea for understanding to prevail among his sons, and the gathering fell into stone silence. The explosion I anticipated was in progress.

"Shut up, Helenus!" my father yelled back.

"I will not!" Helenus raged. "For the greater good of Troy? Is that what you said? You will have to explain that one to me, Father."

"I asked you to abide by my decision. Why are you doing this?"

"I want an explanation!"

His insistence rankled my father, and I could see the anger in his eyes. He should not have been put in a position demanding a defense of his selection, especially not in front of the entire assembly. Helenus was out of line.

"If I tell you," Father angrily replied, "you will find yourself humiliated. I suggest you let the matter rest."

Helenus was not about to let this persuade him, perhaps because he was unaware of what could possibly be said that might debase him. In his agitation, he ignored my father's warnings, refusing to take the cue, and persisted in having his answer.

"I will not," he declared. "Tell me."

"I had hoped to spare you the painful truth, but as you persist, I now inform you that I adhered to the wishes of Paris. Yes. Paris, before he died, made me swear to him that I was not to let you have Helen but, rather, Deiphobus. *He* chose your brother, not I. There you have it, plain and simple. Do you feel better in knowing this?"

I thought the answer brilliant, but also a lie. Yet who could dispute it? We all knew that Paris and Deiphobus were very close as brothers, in constant companionship with each other, and that he would make such a dying request seemed a natural enough consequence out of their friendship. My father had neatly averted the challenge railed against him, at an expense to his persecutor. True or not, it was a masterstroke.

Helenus stood dumbstruck, his face flushed, utterly disarmed in his aggressive posture, standing in clenched fists, ready to pounce on anyone opposing him, and feeling most awkward. To persist in his claim now amounted to a show of open contempt for his father and family, an imprudent step he was not about to take. Bitterly, he replaced his chair and slumped into it, resigned to the loss of Helen, almost pitiful in his quiet self-reproach. We were to hear no more from him for the rest of the evening.

My father took no delight in his triumph; in fact, he appeared unnerved over the encounter—you could see this in his eyes—and it clearly pained him that he had to overtly discredit Helenus in front of all of us. As he was to explain it later to me, cruel necessity forced him into making his calculated deprecation, and while it succeeded in resolving the temporary conflict, he saw no virtue in congratulating himself. He worried that, in the long term, a smoldering resentment would manifest itself in Helenus and lead to horrible consequences for us. I was hoping the opposite, that, given the time, my brother would overcome his current dejection and accept the condition imposed on him this evening.

After the confrontation had ended, rejoicing resurfaced among most of the guests, and their carousing continued on through the remainder of the evening until, finally, weariness, greatly accentuated by drunkenness, overcame them, and they filtered out one by one until only a handful of us, myself included, were still left. I was about to go and felt obligated to bid my well wishes to Helen and her besotted Deiphobus who remained to see everyone off. As I looked at Helen, I noticed a definite alarmed, even frightened, expression in her gaze that gave me the chills. It was as if she was reaching out for me in a desperate call for help. I was struck with the odd notion that she purposely prolonged her stay in order to get Deiphobus so drunk that she could avoid what came next. Not exactly a blissful thought.

CHAPTER XV

THINGS RESUMED THEIR FAMILIAR NORMALCY soon enough after that tension-filled evening, to the relief of all. Of primary concern, of course, was the matrimonial state between Helen and her new husband, and that seemed, from outward appearances, to proceed pleasantly along. Helen, for her part, applied the effort to make the arrangement work, not speaking ill of her husband or denying him his pleasures, I surmise, and this solidified her standing within the family, namely, placing her once more in my mother's good graces, a prerequisite to our harmony. As a result, she performed her functions as a dutiful wife to full, also surprising, measure, as far as we could tell, and while not the perfect loving couple, at least no open strife marred their relationship.

Deiphobus obviously came out the best in their conjugation. He was in possession of the most beautiful woman known. Being the lecherous sort that he was, this ought to have satisfied his lust for feminine flesh, gratifying his depraved nature and fulfilling a lifelong dream of his: to bed down with the most ideally fantasized woman existing anywhere. Whether this was actually happening, I had no way of knowing—it's not the sort of thing openly discussed—but he had a smugness about him that had me thinking it was. I would not call theirs a happy marriage, but then neither was it sad; rather, I classify it as a sort of matter-of-fact affair that characterizes most royal unions, held together more by a sense of duty and obligation instead of true love.

Helenus, as far as I could tell, had reconciled himself to his loss and drew no further allusions to his disappointment or anger over it. He may have still envied his brother the good fortune that befell him—Helen had that effect on men—but did not communicate his feelings to anyone and went about his business as usual. Nevertheless, I detected a change in him. Always the dour sort, he had become even more so, his sober introspection impacting in a negative way on the rest of us so that we did not wish to be in any prolonged presence with him, preferring the time spent with him to be minimal. He did not snap out of the dolorous state he dwelled in, and indeed, it became more pronounced as time went on, which, in turn, made us shun his company to an even greater extent. Consequently, he imposed an isolation upon himself that left many concerned over his intentions, to say nothing of his well-being. Yet by what we saw, this did not appear to trouble him any, and the performance of his duties was not adversely affected by it.

I had occasion to see Helenus in other than our family setting, which always elicited the brooding side of him, usually at the inner corral when I was preparing Zephyrus for his daily exercise. Admittedly, in a one-on-one encounter, he could put on a favorable front, behaving cordially and d spelling the darkness that hovered about him.

"You're not like the others, Polyxena," he said on seeing me stroking my horse's face. "You enjoy riding horses, don't you?"

"I enjoy riding Zephyrus. We're kindred spirits."

"So I see. Perhaps you know the answer to this. I implore you to be truthful. Has my father gotten over my disagreeable conduct the other day?"

"Why go through me? Ask him yourself."

"At present, I am too embarrassed, ashamed that I lost control of my emotions. I don't know what got into me."

"I do. It was Helen."

"She's a curse."

"She has that affect on men, that much I know. She causes them to lose their reason in their passion for her. I don't believe men can just erase that desire, no matter what they say."

Helenus gave me a suspicious glance.

"Say what you're thinking," he said.

"I'm questioning if you have gotten over it," I replied.

"You're a smart one. Correct, though. I will never get over it."

I regretted hearing that, for Helenus made it plain he fostered a lingering resentment over his perceived grievance and was unwilling to let the affair rest. Or was it simply that he craved Helen so much that he could not stand the thought of Deiphobus getting pleasures from her that should have been his? Whatever, the point was that he possessed no inclination toward conceding a right he claimed he had and pressed ahead with his conviction that he had been wronged.

"You admit to jealousy," I told him. "As my eldest brother now, you should be beyond such pettiness. Set an example for us, for me, of the wisdom that is said to come with age. Give me reason to look up to you."

"My head agrees; my heart does not."

"Your head must prevail."

Helenus paused. I am certain nothing I said had not been mulled over abundantly by him, and he readily recognized my recommendation as the proper advice, even if he was reluctant to openly acknowledge it. He was wrestling with emotions that fought for the domination of his mind, depriving him of his better judgment.

"So much easier said than done," he determined. "Helen preys on my intellect, robs me of sound logic."

"Father understands this."

"If only that were so. I should do as you recommend and seek his forgiveness, even give him my apologies." He winced as he said this, suggesting the notion was disagreeable to him.

"You owe him that, Helenus."

"Why? If I apologize, I do it because I want atonement for my ill-mannered behavior, not because I owe it to him. I have already done him a favor."

"What favor?"

"He lied when he said those things about Paris, his dying wish that Helen go to Deiphobus. I knew it all along, but I refrained from making a point of this. Not easy for me, as it amounted to a concession Helen was his, the last thing I wanted."

If this was true, then I may have judged Helenus too harshly. He, in fact, had exercised some restraint that evening, contrary to what we all thought. That does not excuse his actions, still perceived as abusive and inflammatory, nor does it provide him with a justifiable defense, for his conduct was malicious. Indeed, the best that can be inferred is that he might have made things worse than they already were, and he chose to avoid a further escalation of the tensions he had inflicted on us. But at least that was something. In confirming my own suspicions that Father had lied, I was curious who else might have reached the same conclusion. Can it be everyone knew?

"No, Helenus," I told him after mulling it over. "You do owe him an apology. He is our father and properly deserves our respect. You had no right to challenge him, not in front of all of us the way you did. That was more than just bad manners. You insulted him."

"Did I?" Helenus responded, seemingly surprised.

"That's how we all saw it. So what if he lied? You put him on the spot and, in effect, forced him to say whatever was going to get him out of it. He deserves an apology."

Helenus pondered on this, not saying anything for the present. His absorption manifested itself in his penetrating glance into the distance, concentrating on his inner being rather than a faraway object. When he finally decided to give his response, he still seemed engrossed in his contemplation.

"He would get satisfaction out of that," he said. "I'm not about to give him the pleasure."

So I failed to reach Helenus. How obtuse can one be? What appeared as a trivial imposition to me apparently posed a major obstacle for him. I was unable to comprehend the source of his resistance in giving his apology. This was our father, not some foreign potentate to whom such an accommodation amounted to groveling. I am at a loss to figure out what is behind men's thinking.

"I'm saddened to hear that," I said. "Your reluctance makes no sense to me, but then, what do I know?"

"That's right. Don't let it bother you."

"It *does* bother me. It bothers me a lot. I've tried to give you my best counsel, what I felt deeply within me, believing you valued it, to no avail. If what I say means so little to you, why even speak to me?"

I was angry at Helenus and made no pretensions over any attempt to disguise the frustration he aroused in me.

He smiled, evidently finding my agitation amusing, which incensed me even more, inciting me nearly to the point of openly yelling at him. But I checked myself, aware that that kind of overt display of irritation only fed into his trifling with me, which I now believed he was doing. He was not a brother to look up to, nor did he aspire to be that; that much was obvious.

"You've helped," he then said, his inconsistent words leaving me in befuddlement.

"If only I could believe that, Helenus," I replied as I mounted Zephyrus and prodded him into a gallop, away from my brother who still had me fuming. He was a strange man, I had to admit, and applied no effort in seeking my, or anyone else's, good graces, and he operated in a mystifying fashion that did not fit any conclusive description. That must be the nature of seers. Cassandra, who also possessed this ability, was likewise a difficult person to penetrate and get to understand.

As I rode my circuitous route around the city, leaving the Dardanian Gates and covering the area of our allied encampments and then moving along its northern edge to the west side for my return through the Scaean Gates, I noticed the increased activity indicative that the hostility would soon be resumed. Soldiers were sharpening their weapons, honing their fighting skills, checking the fit of their armor, training the new recruits that had arrived as reinforcements. Both sides were engaged in similar exertions, and I suspected that, in a day or so, another battle faced us. I had to enjoy today's unrestricted ride while it lasted.

When I later returned to the Pergamus, I noticed that I became more tense as I ascended the steps leading to the residential palace. My heartbeat pounded heavily within me. How odd that this should be so. Was it because the friction between my two brothers over the hand of Helen had caused its weight to be felt among us all? Certainly, I found greater relaxation in my rides, my escape from our grim reality, and the return to the palace again brought me into the less pleasurable present.

There was more to it. Since the death of Paris, a lot of the joy that once permeated the palace walls had diminished. Not that Paris was the cause of this former elation, although, when together with Helen, he greatly attributed to it, but because in his passing, the last of my more confident and gregarious brothers that included Troilus, Polydorus, and Hector, who most added to merriment, were gone. The joking and kidding was now absent from our dinners, with only our more sober brothers remaining, who had no bent for the rollicking. If I was keenly affected by this, think of how much more my parents must have been aware of it. For them, the loss had to be omnipresent, as well as heartbreaking.

Outwardly, Helenus and Deiphobus were reconciled to the decision my father had imposed on them. To say imposition applies only to Helenus, since, for Deiphobus, as the beneficiary of the judgment, the word hardly fits. They communicated well enough with each other but averted drawing attention to the source of their friction: Helen. So our evening gatherings remained seemingly congenial, on the surface anyway, and that made up for the lack of joviality that once characterized them.

But inside, I am sure Helenus seethed, remaining constant in his bitterness over losing Helen, having to forego a claim he regarded as his birthright, and somehow we picked up on his concealed resentment, or at least I did, although I suspected that the others did also, which added to an underlying tension that, though never expressed, was there. Deiphobus, to our disdain, appeared to intentionally aggravate the situation by flaunting his triumph over securing Helen. He did this by fondling her whenever in our presence, making sure in his leering that we all noticed it, especially Helenus who was hard-pressed to constrain himself. I was upset with Deiphobus, thinking his overt displays of affection as unnecessarily provocative, and told him so one day when I met him as he was standing alone in a corridor.

"You have Helen," I said. "Why do you need to slap us in the face with it?"

"Is that what you think I'm doing?" he smirked.

"It's plain to see."

"I love her. Can I help myself if I am unable to contain my rapture? She does that to men, you know."

I was not impressed by his response. That might have been a justification when seeking her hand, but not once having acquired her.

"No, Brother," I said. "Nothing requires you to emphasize your love, as she is your wife. You just want to rub it in, to endlessly remind Helenus of your victory."

"That's my business. You don't have to like it."

What a low person Deiphobus was, having no regard for anyone, his own selfish interests all that preoccupied him. I think I loathed him as much as Helenus at present.

"Show some concern," I entreated. "Helenus is not the only one offended, so are the rest of us."

"Is that so? Why should my love for Helen be offensive to you, Sister?"

I pondered over his question, debating what reply would actually reach such a self-centered individual, who was too callous to grasp the pain his actions inflicted on others or, worse, meant to distress them. I decided to make this personal, thereby imparting a lesson he was much in need of.

"You know I have no lover," I said. "No suitor has recently come forth looking for my hand. Am I to take comfort in seeing you dote on Helen in my presence? You shout out to me, 'I have my love; you do not.'"

For a moment, Deiphobus gave all the indications that my words had touched him, and he waited in answering, needing the time to study them, and had me thinking I had made my point.

"Sorry, Sister," he then responded. "Not good enough. Helen manipulates me. I can't help myself."

Deiphobus was scum. His lame excuse made it clear to me that he had no wish to end his public exhibition, because he knew the irritation this caused Helenus, and he was not about to stop on my account. So much for appealing to his rational side. I made no additional attempt to get him to demonstrate greater consideration for me, which would have been futile, and just walked off. Needless to say, he gained no respect from me on this day. I think my sympathies were shifting toward Helenus.

I chanced to speak with Helen later that same day, and in the course of the meeting, our conversing began to direct itself toward the same subject matter I had discussed with Deiphobus. She was more conciliatory to my complaint than he, and I think she wanted the problem resolved as much as I.

"I've tried to get him to stop," Helen said. "I hate the way he gloats."

She did not try very hard, I was thinking. It seemed to me all Helen had to do was remove his hands whenever they touched her in front of us or strongly urge him to desist in this; she had as yet done neither. What could be more damaging to a selfish person than to have his actions publicly railed against?

"Can't you just scold him?" I asked.

"A humiliation for him. Sure to increase the resentment he bears Helenus even more. I thought about it but worry over insulting him."

"What then?"

"Whatever I do, it has to be in private. He is a slight man, given to outbursts of fury, as well as tears, not at all like Paris. I never know how he will react to things."

Helen told me that she was not in a comfortable relationship with Deiphobus, that she had to be wary over his responses to her, unsure if he would misinterpret her meanings, even fearing his anger. Also, she regarded him as weak and perhaps even held him in actual contempt, the sneer she exhibited denoting this. We had not talked about Deiphobus since their marriage, and the revelations she gave me stood at variance from my expectations. But then, as was becoming increasingly evident to me, I never really knew Deiphobus. The more I was finding out about him, the less admiration I had for him.

"Please get him to stop, Helen," I said. "I fear he is pushing Helenus to the brink. That is dangerous."

"Agreed. I'll handle it."

When I left her, I mused over how she was going to amend his ways, but I felt reasonably assured Helen would somehow manage it. In many ways, she was a strong woman, she had to be to give up all she had to come here with Paris, to endure the pain of his loss. I could not see her as being controlled by Deiphobus; if anything, she led him, despite her worries over his reactions.

True to her word, at the next evening's gathering, we conspicuously noticed that Deiphobus refrained from his usual exhibited surrender to his lust. I have no idea what Helen said to him, but whatever it was, the effect was immediate and appreciated, coming at a juncture when I was questioning how much longer I could stand it. My relief was heartfelt. I glanced at Helen, and she winked at me, inducing a smile out of me. I also saw that Helenus appeared in better form than was typical of him, even cheerful at times. Success, at least for this night.

Skirmishes broke out the next day along the entire front, extending over the length of the coastline to the inland areas, where our allies were camped. These confrontations involved a number of smaller units and patrols coming in close proximity to each other, lasting only a short duration, ending when the casualty count was enough to impede the progress that was believed to be occurring by their leaders. For each individual unit, the numbers were small, but with all of them taken together, the accumulative toll was significant, again resulting in a cost that had no gains for either side. We saw these encounters as a prelude to a major battle that was in the making, expecting it to commence in the coming days, and kept our force on full alert.

After the council meeting was concluded that same day, my father again met with me in the courtyard and updated me on the proceedings that had taken place. Our meetings became an established routine for him, and for me, and I think we both looked forward to them. For me, they kept me in touch with all that was happening. For my father, I believe he appreciated my own views on the proposed tactical plans, my experience with Penthesileia having provided me with some insight into such matters. But conforming to the usual pattern, our talks soon drifted upon other than battlefield subjects. I suppose even this had value, for we both learned about the latest news circulating around the household, things we frequently were not aware of. So, in summation, they were fruitful for us. Besides, I got to know my father better through them, as he did me, and we discovered we enjoyed our company.

"Thank you, Polyxena," he said, gladness in his voice. "Your speaking to Helen produced results. I was increasingly annoyed by Deiphobus."

"How did you know?"

"Eventually, everything reaches my ear," he answered with a weak smile. "I heard it from Andromache. I'm sure Helen told her. For a while, Deiphobus nearly jeopardized my hopes for harmony with Helenus."

"Does this depend only on Deiphobus? I blame as much on Helenus."

"I suppose, but he did see me to apologize for his boorishness. I thought that was quite big of him."

So Helenus had listened to me after all. I was pleased to hear it, knowing how distasteful he considered doing that. But he remained inscrutable in his behavior, and I was not entirely convinced about his motivations being that altruistic. Yet that he did this at all deserves a kinder word for him. I should be more appreciative.

I looked at my father and was deeply struck by what a singular pitiful figure he seemed to me. The death of Paris had a horribly detrimental effect on him, much as if the last vestiges of joy had been snatched from him, and he not only seemed significantly older, but considerably sadder, no longer finding happiness in the little things that once added a lot to his pleasure. Only a few of his many sons were still alive, the more prominent others, the charismatic ones, having been slain in this protracted war, and it bore heavily on him. He had several grandchildren and knew Troy's royal line would endure through them, but somehow that no longer appeared sufficient for him. I think, more than anything else, with Paris gone, so also went the causal grounds for the war, now transformed into a struggle with no other purpose than sheer survival. That is not to say this is a lesser motivation, far from it, but only that it lacks the brashness and swagger of our former spirit, and in combat, that can be a crucial quality.

"Dear Polyxena," he went on, nearly on the verge of tears, "things are not as they once were. My resolve is badly weakened. I must bolster it constantly, reassuring myself over and over that we will triumph in the end, but the truth is, I don't think I believe it anymore. I try to mask this—you cannot infect your subordinates with such defeatism—but the charade is exacting its toll on me, demoralizing as it is. What do you say to this?"

"You can't be blamed for feeling depressed, Father."

He merely glanced ahead, no particular emotion demonstrated through this, but I realized the spark was gone from his inner self, replaced by a dark, introspective brooding that cried out in anguish of a desire to be free of the burdens his office imposed on him.

"Depression?" he said. "Yes, I suppose that's the proper word."

"We can't capitulate, can we?" I asked.

"You understand," he answered, his penetrating eyes focusing on me. "No, not without forfeiting our lives. The war has been too long and brutal for everyone to be simply dismissed if one side surrenders to the other. Vengeance will be sought and taken out on the loser so that none will be left alive, at least among the leaders We are now engaged in a struggle for true survival: life for the victors, death for the defeated."

I had known this for some time, and what my father said came as no surprise to me. Our only remaining option was to hold out behind our walls as long as we could, living only in the hope that the enemy would become so exhausted, depleted in numbers and morale to the point where it was no longer possible to persist in attacking us. But we had thought this for over nine years, and the Greeks remained. What motivated them to continue in their efforts, with no victory in sight?

"I guess it's wishful thinking expecting them to leave," I went on.

"The war has become personalized for them. It's no longer a question of just defeating us, of controlling our trade routes, of ruling over us. We must be punished for our insolence in refusing to surrender, for our resistance, for their heroes we have slain. They mean to mete out their punishment, even if it means fighting to the last man."

"How long can this continue?"

"Only the gods know for certain," Father declared somberly.

"We have been able to replenish our provisions from season to season in spite of this siege, because we control the interior lands. Possessing the sea has not prevented the enemy from stopping this. A greater problem is that of replacing our expended warriors. The reinforcements are dwindling, especially since many of our allies are losing heart in sustaining the fight."

"But aren't the Greeks faced with the same problem?"

"Yes, but by controlling the seas, they have greater access to lands for reinforcing their strength than we do. I don't think anyone could have predicted it would come to this when it all began. We are entrenched in a struggle that can have only one end: victory for one of us, defeat for the other. Compromise, a conditional surrender, is out of the question." He paused, then continued, "Excuse me if I expound defeatism. I did not wish to upset you."

"What you say is that no alternative exists for us but to fight on and on. More than half my lifetime has been taken up by this war. I despaired over this before, but now I feel outright gloom and doom."

"Forgive this old man his careless tongue," my father sadly declared. "Yet I sense that nothing I have told you was not already known to you."

"It was. But to think it and to have it said to you are very different. The former allows for hope that I might be wrong. The latter affirms it as certain."

"Nothing is certain, even to the gods."

"It's so sad," I said, dismayed.

"Forgive me, Polyxena."

Of course I did, and I deeply cared for the difficulties my father grappled with, especially when he conceded to me that he lacked further conviction in Troy's eventual success in this war. That truly had to be burdensome. I leaned into him and kissed him on the cheek, hoping this be a gesture that I consented to his plea and exonerated him of any guilt he retained over having confided his fears to me. I saw tears trickling down his face when I left him.

The battle we had expected came on the following morning when, once again, the enemy's trumpet calls spurred its units into formation for an advance against our walls. In response, our own battalions marched forth from the Scaean Gates to take up their battle configuration before the city. Aeneas commanded our center, with Helenus and Deiphobus heading each of the wings, and soon our allied contingents joined them to take up the usual broad front that countered the opponent's equally extended line. I also saw Polites and Agenor, each standing ahead of their unit in the center section. This was going to be another slug match, as most of the recent battles had been, and I worried if we could sustain the kind of losses we incurred in our last major undertaking.

The enemy line steadily moved forward until it came to a stop about five hundred paces from our line. In the usual prebattle format, the commanders, accompanied by their leading generals, from each army rode ahead to meet in the middle of the field dividing the sides. Aeneas was with Helenus and Deiphobus, and Helen identified the Greek commanders with Agamemnon as Menelaus, Odysseus, and Diomedes. Their conference lasted for quite a while, not like before the last big battle, but eventually, they turned about to return to their respective positions. It would have interesting to hear what they had said. Did anyone actually believe that this day was going to be different from all the others?

Shortly after the commanders had returned, the call to action reverberated across the field, and the Greeks initiated their drive, advancing as a solid line spread over the length of the coastal plain in front of us. Suddenly, they shifted their formation, deploying their winged elements toward the center so that a heavy mass of troops was concentrated in this middle ground, clearly outweighing our strength at that location. Aeneas, on seeing this, directed Deiphobus on his right to move toward our center and bolster it. He arrived there just as the armies met in a collision of arms, their clashing shields resounding as one continuous crushing crunch. The battle was on.

Again, the shrieks of the warriors arose over the din, cut down in the ferocious fighting taking place in the center of the field, and blood flowed in abundance as soldier hacked at soldier, parrying swords and thrusting spears, trying to gain the upper hand. The momentary advantage of the enemy's massed drive was halted by the merging of Deiphobus's wing on our beleaguered center, and together, they were holding their own against the aggressor. While the struggle was being played out in that section, Aeneas apparently held his left wing under Helenus in position, uncommitted to the battle at present. Neither the extreme wings of the Greek army nor ours, comprised of the allied contingents, were engaged in the fighting; all the action took place in the compressed center. This is also where Polites and Agenor were positioned, and try as I might, I could not make them out in the intensity and constriction of the battling combatants. What a bizarre sight. Half the warriors of both armies were just looking on while the other half were fighting for their lives.

The Greek drive, having been stalled, was gradually forced backward, at a high cost in casualties, slowly at first and then turning into a mad rush as soldiers tried to escape the slaughter. Soon, everybody was running from the main battleground. At this point, Helenus—he must have received an order from Aeneas—directed his left wing into an assault upon the fleeing Greeks. Shouting out wildly, the Trojans ran ahead, striking at the Greeks fleeing the carnage. Some turned around to face their attackers only to be hastily struck under, dying amid agonizing cries, clasping their hands over gaping wounds to stem the flow of blood that spurted forth. Next, Helenus and his unit were lost to me, engulfed by hordes of soldiers, both ours and the enemy's, in one confusing entanglement of fighters.

The extreme right wing of Greek warriors then chose to enter the fray and mounted an assault upon the place where Helenus had advanced moments earlier. It appeared to me that Helenus was now entrapped, for all I saw were Greeks about the area where I last spotted him. It suddenly appeared as if the entire left side of the battlefield was now heavily engaged in combat, locked in deadly contact, just as the center had been a short while ago. This was not the typical battle, the fighting shifting from one part of the field to another, equally intense in both sections.

I had almost given up hope for my brother when I saw his Trojans returning toward our own lines, embattling their assailants from every side but managing to make it back, although in reduced numbers. I did not see Helenus leading them, but he could have easily been hidden among the swarming masses that impaired my view as my eyes searched for him. By now, more than half the day had been spent, and the battle, for all intents and purposes, was at its end, with the combatants disengaging themselves and returning to their respective sides. As our soldiers filtered back to the city, my father sent a messenger to fetch Aeneas once he arrived. I was standing next to where my father was seated in his observation post, where he always viewed the battle, when, sometime later, Aeneas came up, looking very haggard, blood splattered over his armor, still breathing heavily from the fight.

"You called for me, lord?" Aeneas addressed my father.

"I could barely believe what I was seeing," my father sternly reproached him. "Why, in the name of the gods, did you order our left wing into the battle? I thought the maneuver suicidal."

"I did not order it, lord," Aeneas replied, very irate. "I am as angry about it as you."

"What are you suggesting?"

"Helenus took it upon himself," Aeneas raged on. "He evidently assumed, when he saw the enemy fleeing from the center, that this was an opportune time to launch a pursuit."

"The fool! He had best give a good explanation for this. Where is he?"

"He did not return with his unit, lord."

"What?" My father's demeanor switched from anger to worry.

"Has he fallen? I pray to the gods he did not."

"He was taken captive, my lord."

"A major commander captured? Where were his bodyguards? How could they allow this to happen?"

Aeneas grimly looked at my father, his eyes afire, and hesitated for the moment, not saying anything. He was clearly in an irritable mood, but being of strong character, he was not intimated by the grilling he w s subjected to.

"Well?" my father fumed on. "Why are you stalling in your answer?"

"My answer will not please you, lord."

"Do you imply they were remiss in their duties?"

"No. I fear the truth is more sinister, great king. His soldiers have reported that Helenus intentionally permitted himself to be taken. I know—I can scarcely believe it myself."

My father turned white. He sank deeper into his chair in his dismay, unable to come to grips with the news just received, the shock and disappointment patently etched in his face. The death of his son would have been less devastating. This was a betrayal of the worst kind, no royal personage ever having turned against Troy. I was as stunned as my father, as I had sincerely believed that Helenus had overcome his animosity over losing Helen. He had fooled us all.

"The traitorous wretch," Father shouted out. "We must get him back."

"A difficult task, lord," Aeneas replied. "He is surely well protected, as a royal son."

"He is a seer," my father muttered, more to himself than anyone around him. "He will inform the Greeks on how to defeat us. That I should live to see such a day."

How painful it was to see my father so despondent. No one could have foreseen this. So deep was this injury to us that we could not even conceive of any countermeasure we might take, still in shock.

"Do what you can, Aeneas," my father directed. "I don't have to tell you the gravity of this situation. Helenus, long a champion in our cause, has suddenly become the greatest threat to us."

With that, Father dismissed his chief commander to go about his business, leaving the rest of us to share his misery. And in truth, I was distressed, empathizing with my father, sensing his despair, and questioning how many more setback he could endure. Surely, the gods must see this and take pity on him.

Helen. I was trying my best to look upon our present predicament in as objective a manner as possible, but she, more than anyone else, had a lot to do with all that happened in the recent days. Yes, I know she cannot be faulted for the obsession men feel over her—you, Aphrodite, have seen to that—but her wanting Deiphobus rather than Helenus, whose claim for her was more legitimately based, directly led to this consequence. I was not about to exonerate her of her complicity in this. But how could I hold that against her? Would I be content to have Helenus as a husband? I hardly think so. Besides, Helen expressed no desire to marry either of them and wanted to delay that prospect as long as possible. I don't know what to think anymore but have to wonder if things might not be totally different had she never arrived at our shores.

Deiphobus, when the truth of his brother's desertion became known to him, was likewise astonished over the treasonous act. He seemed to have recognized his culpability in the matter, especially since he so enhanced the animosity of Helenus with his consistent flaunting of his envisioned conquest. Conquest? If he only knew how Helen resisted the proposal and that he was but the lesser of two undesirable candidates for her. He was an ignorant man. I suppose he could be excused to some extent in the sense that no one ever imagined what might ensue out of the affair. That was unpredictable, which accounted for the awful shock imparted on us all.

As for Helenus, his treachery cannot be forgiven. Never. To think he actually had me convinced that he had reconciled his differences with Deiphobus. His seeming accord was a sham. Evidently he planned his revenge all along, pretending he was past his resentment. I should have known better.

Chapter XVI

I T IS SAID THAT TIME heals all, but that did not apply to the pain afflicting my father since Helenus became a renegade to our cause. Nothing helped in alleviating his downcast spirit, and he increasingly avoided seeing us, staying mostly in the council hall long after his meetings were terminated, sitting alone in his throne, brooding. He sat quietly by during our evening meals, contributing little to our discussions, even when they solicited his response, his glazy eyes peering blankly into space, seeing nothing. He also had aged considerably in just this past month, his gaunt face more crinkled than ever, the strain of events taking its toll on him. I thought I was imagining this, but it was true. In addition, I noticed that he had problems looking at Deiphobus, averting eye contact with him, and every so often revealing a contemptuous sneer toward him. The sight was pitiful, and it tore at my heart. I felt helpless, unable to allay the pessimism that now possessed him.

Despite this, he was ever cordial to Helen and never once alluded to her having contributed to the misery that plagued him. She had that effect on men; they were endlessly willing to forgive her—for everything!— and sought to endear themselves to her. That is how it has always been, from the very beginning to the present. Can this be solely attributed to her sheer beauty? If so, where does that leave the rest of us when in her presence? She was beautiful, without doubt the most beautiful of women, but that is not to say that we were left out in the cold in winning the affection of men. A few men managed to resist her: Agenor had his eyes set on Menodice as an example of this, and Achilles favored me. It is fortunate that things are so, else there would be no hope for us. At any rate, Helen was absolved of any transgressions in the fate befalling Troy, the responsibility being continuously attributed to the gods instead. Can I deny this?

The meetings I longed for with my father in the courtyard became less frequent, and I was presently often left sitting there by myself, waiting on his arrival, which did not come. I dearly wished that his depression would end, for I blamed my circumstance on this, and the pleasure of our conversations would resume. Fortunately, on this day, he chose to make his appearance, most likely because he needed to confide his deepest concerns in somebody, a role I willingly performed for him.

"Things have never looked so bad," he told me. "Troy's prospects are bleak. True, our walls will protect us, as eve, but we cannot endure this siege without our allies. I fear their resolve is being sorely tested. It's only a matter of time before they desert us."

"I've heard such talk before, Father. You thought the same thing when Hector died."

He glanced at me, my comment having provided him with inducement for contemplation, and for the first time in days, he exhibited a glint of satisfaction.

"You know, you're right," he then said, vigor returning to his voice. "I'm thankful for your reminder. I've lost sight of that. Hector. What a fine son I had in him. Killed less than a year ago, and it seems as if it has been ages."

Nostalgia can be crippling. While I admit that we all at times succumb to it, I strongly resisted this and kept my thoughts relevant to the present and avoided delving into the past as much as I was able to. If I did not, I would surely go mad with grief. My hope was that my father would do likewise, and for the most part, he has. I felt uncomfortable when he allowed himself to be preoccupied with things that can no longer be.

"I try not to think about that," I said.

"Why is that?"

"It hurts too much. All that has happened to me so far this year, the people I've known and loved, if I think about them, I can't help crying, and the melancholy I feel is so painful. It's not good for me." I nearly broke out in tears as I said this but checked myself. My father was touched by my sentiment. I saw him repress his emotions, but his eyes moistened, giving evidence of his discernment.

"Your words are profound," my father said. "Sending you to the Amazons has indeed changed you. You've acquired wisdom. Do you ever feel regret over my having done that?"

"Never," I replied without hesitation. I would not have exchanged my experience on that journey for anything, in spite of the painful memories it left with me. I lived during that time of my life, undergoing trials that tested my true being, with its highs and lows, reaching to the depths of my soul. I lived then more than in all the accumulative years before, a happening irreplaceable for me.

"Then I have done well," my father concluded.

"You have, Father."

"You have brought an element of joy to this old man, Polyxena. I very much needed that. Let's meet again tomorrow. I'm finding that I benefit from this."

I was enthralled to hear him say that not only because I derived wholesome pleasure out of our get-togethers, but because I truly believed I was helping my father in overcoming the moroseness that seemed to preoccupy him recently. If I accomplished that much, my purpose was well served. I nodded my consent.

A lull was somewhat in effect again following the last battle. By that, I mean that, while no major encounter faced us, minor confrontations continued, typically involving units no larger than squadrons of less than a hundred soldiers. These conflicts engaged mostly our allied contingents, as they occurred more in the outlying areas, well away from the city, often along the shoreline, where the Greek encampments were located adjacent to their anchored ships. They usually arose out of a reconnaissance mission conducted by one of our patrols having come face-to-face upon an enemy patrol, their contact frequently leading to reinforcements being committed by both sides but stopping short of a large-scale deployment of units, and lasting of short duration. So, while we were reasonably safe within our immediate vicinity, the skirmishes existed as a reminder that things were not entirely secure for us and that precautions had to be exercised.

Accordingly, I was restricted in my rides with Zephyrus to the eastern region extending from the Dardanian Gates, where our allied encampments dotted the landscape, keeping it safe from enemy movements or observation. I did not risk making my usual wide circle around our walls, where I came in close proximity to the coast, which might have exposed me to enemy archers. Had a complete lull in the fighting been in effect, with its mutual understanding that a temporary truce prevailed, I would have had no qualms in covering my normal route, but at present, that was too dangerous.

As I was returning to the inner corral after completing one of my excursions, I saw Deiphobus standing nearby, watching my movements. He came up to me after I had left Zephyrus in the keeping of a handler and was about to ascent the steps leading to the Pergamus.

"You know you shouldn't be riding by yourself all the time," Deiphobus began. "Father doesn't like it, neither do I."

"I'm safe enough," I answered. "But I appreciate your concern."

"Even if you're not worried, Father is. Show some regard for him. He is old and ought to be spared unnecessary stress."

I thought it paradoxical that Deiphobus should suddenly have consideration for our father's well-being, never having previously taken that into account. Certainly, his behavior with Helen in our company did not suggest this.

"My riding is essential for me," I informed him. "I am subject to the same stresses as anyone else, worrying about how the war is going, how Father is feeling. I need my diversion to relieve me of this."

"Find another way. A woman should not be exposing herself to gawking soldiers."

I took umbrage over his insinuation, more in the manner that he spoke, authoritatively and assuming he had dominance over me.

"What do you mean expose? I'm not riding naked in front of them."

"Don't get smart with me. You know damn well what I mean. Your behavior is improper for a royal princess."

"Who are you to speak of improper behavior?" I snapped back angrily. "Fawning over Helen in our presence. You, more than anyone else, are responsible for Helenus deserting Troy."

That shut him up, for the moment. Then, having recovered from his astonishment over my reprimand, he hurled his abuses on me, his usual recourse when anyone countered his argument.

"You're a slut," he declared. "You always have been. Others may be favorably impressed with you, but I know you for what you are. What I do with my wife is nobody's business."

My first impulse was to inform him how little regard Helen had for him, but on reflection, I thought this rash. He might take it out on her.

"You ignorant bastard," I yelled back. "Too stupid to see that any time you make a public exhibition of your lust, you *make* it our business. It's offensive and rude, distasteful to anyone looking on."

"Call me that again, and I'll bash your head in."

"Oh, you really have me scared. My knees are trembling in fright." I grossly amplified my feigned dread, aimed at offending him. "If I'm a slut, then I am proper in calling you a—"

"All right. Your point is taken. But be warned, you are on a dangerous footing. It's unwise to antagonize someone who may one day hold your future in abeyance."

"What's that supposed to m an?"

"Our father is old, and with Helenus out of the way, I stand next in line to inherit Troy's throne. You'd best think about that."

Deiphobus as king of Troy? What a ghastly notion. He had neither the emotional stability nor the talent to make a suitable monarch. In fact, if anyone was singularly unqualified to fill that position, it was he.

"Let me by, Brother," I next said. "I have no desire to prolong our discussion."

"As you wish," he said as he stepped aside. "When I'm king, you'll come to regret what you said."

"Thanks to you, Troy may never have another king. Had you treated Helenus with respect, he wouldn't have forsaken us. You knew how offended he was over losing Helen to you, yet that did not stop you from rubbing it in. You sought to irritate him. We may all pay the price for your idiocy."

"You speak treason."

"The truth hurts. For your information, Deiphobus, I'm not the only one who thinks this; everyone does."

My words had a sobering effect on Deiphobus, his contemplative gaze very pronounced. He probably did not realize how obvious his conduct was communicated to us, and in becoming aware of this, he suddenly recognized why we all blamed him for his brother's defection. He did have a conscience and was undoubtedly troubled over the revelation. In spite of his threats, I had little worries about being harmed by him. He was simply not a strong man, and if you boldly stood up to him, he was the one who would back down.

When I entered the residence hall, I saw my mother and sisters, as well as Andromache and Helen, engaged in their usual afternoon gathering, where they passed their time chatting and doing the things women were expected to do: weaving and other artistic endeavors such as flower arrangements. My mother, typical of her, did not respect my absence from these affairs and let her opposition be known.

"You were riding again," she scoffed. "That's what men do. And by yourself. You know how we dislike this. I should not have to remind you that, as a woman, you should be spending your time with us."

My relationship with my mother was never that warm. Actually, that's not quite true; it was fairly affectionate until I left her on my Amazon quest. Ever since returning from that venture, it seemed as if a rift had risen between us. Perhaps this was more my fault, but I developed a distaste for the mundane womanly things expected of us, a legacy the Amazons imparted on me.

"I'm not into weaving, Mother," I answered.

She glared at me, not appreciating my response at all, and had me nearly reeling under her icy penetration.

"That explains your failure as a woman," she snapped. "No wonder you're still single. You have nothing to offer a man."

I suspected that Mother was trying to rile me and told myself I was not going to let her achieve her purpose.

"Oh, I have lots to offer a man," I teasingly said.

Helen and Andromache were amused by my insinuation, looking at each other and smiling; my mother was not.

"You are a rebellious woman," she replied. "I caution you, mind your manners. I have your interests at heart, Polyxena. Instead of deprecating me, you should be more considerate. I'm your mother."

"I'm sorry."

"No, you're not. I know you. You've changed. You're not the daughter I so lovingly raised. It's Priam's fault. He should never have sent you on that mission. Your stay with the Amazons has given you a distorted view of womanhood."

There was no denying this, and often I wished I had stayed with them. But that would not have worked out either, for I saw no merits to a world without men. Maybe the truth was that I indeed no longer fit in anywhere, a disturbing thought.

"I didn't mean to be unkind to you, Mother," I said with sincerity. "I apologize. Forgive my rudeness."

"See? You can be gracious when you want to," she said, mollified. "Now won't you join us and learn more about being a woman?"

That was not what I wanted, but I consented to her request, as I had no desire to further aggravate her. And so I spent the rest of the afternoon in my place as a woman, conversing with my peers and trying to maintain an interest in thing that did not excite me. It's not that I did not know how to weave; the skill had been taught me since early childhood, and I was actually quite adept at it. But how can that pastime compare with the thrill I obtained in galloping across the plains on my magnificent Zephyrus? Surprisingly, our talks, on this day anyway, turned toward a subject matter I was interested in: the status of Helen's marriage to Deiphobus. Andromache started it off by asking Helen how things were proceeding between them.

"Paris he's not," she said, acknowledging what we presumed to be true. "But are you getting any pleasures in your relationship?" We thirsted to hear Helen's response.

Helen hesitated, reluctant to expose the nature of their conjugation, and my feeling was that she would only reveal as much as she meant for us to know and no more. Yet I admit to a curiosity in hearing what she had to say.

"Some," she conceded. "You're right in saying he is no Paris." Tears welled in her eyes at the mention of his name, touching us deeply. She had so loved him.

"But is Deiphobus a good husband?" Andromache asked.

"He is kind enough to me," Helen answered, "and capably performs his function as a man. But regretfully, it is but a chore to me."

We all understood what she meant by that. No love existed on her part, and it expressed itself in the bedroom. Yet I had to give Helen credit in that she nevertheless submitted to his advances and lived up to her responsibility as his wife, something I was not sure I could have done. Her confession just confirmed what I had long suspected. She admirably put up with Deiphobus, even though she had no true feelings for him.

"Has my son done nothing to endear himself to you?" my mother asked, disturbed over what she was hearing.

Helen knew she was treading on delicate grounds. Her response had to be tactful, even a lie, if she was to retain my mother's good graces. I was wondering how she would handle the situation.

"Oh, to be sure, he has," Helen appeased my mother. "He is the gentle sort, always doing things to please me. I used to think that was because he felt insecure over having me, but in time, I realized this was his true nature. He has a good heart."

This was not the Deiphobus I knew. And it brought to light the contradictory behavior that can be manifested in a person as related to his exchanges with others. To me, Deiphobus seemed possessed with trying to assert his dominance and acted the role of the bully, forcing his way upon me, not that this worked for him. But I knew he could also be very charming and that he was not lacking a conscience, being often troubled by his own performance on matters. Who was the real Deiphobus? My rationalization led me to conclude that Helen knew him better than I, and I was prepared to give him the benefit of the doubt and accepted what she said about him.

Certainly, my mother was gratified that her son had some positive qualities in Helen's eyes, even if her daughter-in-law's concession was small, and I think she drew encouragement from that, empowering her to stress the benefit of their union.

"Given enough time," she said, "you can learn to love someone. You'll discover this, Helen, and eventually will be pleased with my loving son."

Loving son? That may have been a bit of a stretch. He clearly demonstrated no affection toward me, holding me in apparent low esteem as revealed in his abusive name-calling and threatening posturing. Helen also glanced strangely at my mother, as if not knowing what to make of her supposition.

"What does he say about us?" Andromache inquired. "Do you talk about that?"

I was glad that Andromache asked that instead of me and must confess that I eagerly anticipated Helen's response to that, curious to see if my brother's hostility was something they discussed in private.

"Sorry to disappoint you, Andromache," Helen answered. "The truth is, we rarely speak about you, or anyone else, in private."

Instead of looking at Andromache, Helen gazed at me, which convinced me that she had been dishonest with us. It seemed unrealistic to me that they would not talk about us, especially when their relationship seemed strained, and that would have been a natural outlet in holding it together. But I was not going to press the point. Besides, whatever Deiphobus had to say about me, while probably not flattering, was inconsequential. As far as I could tell, my conduct was not detrimental to Troy's interests and posed no dangers to me.

"So what do you talk about?" Andromache asked.

"Aside from personal matters, the war mostly. Things discussed in Lord Priam's council meeting. His opinion on these. The Greeks. That sort of stuff."

That made sense to me, so perhaps my previous conjectures were wrong. Enough material surrounded these subjects that it could occupy their time, fulfilling a need to keep up their communicating with each other. Still, my feeling was that Helen skirted the issue—very neatly, I might add—telling us only as much as she intended. Following this, our conversation drifted to the trivial and insignificant, making the imposed time I spent with the group intolerable for me. Somehow, I managed to cope and endured my ordeal, but my joy was immense over having it end.

How different was my conversing with Father in our courtyard, nearly always on subjects of importance that had significance, informing me on the progress of the war. I increasingly admired him for the confidence he had in me, the worth he placed on my opinions, his seeming evaluation of what I related to him, and his soliciting my understanding of things, acknowledging an appreciation of my counsel. Our talks were stimulating and challenged my thinking process, in all respects the opposite of the residence meetings my mother insisted I attend. My views mattered to my father, and that made all the difference.

When I spoke with him later that day, he was eager to release his pent-up concerns to me and had no qualms about relating what most troubled him.

"The worst thing about Helenus being with the Greeks is that he can inform them how they might win this war," my father said.

"Augurs can be wrong, Father," I replied. "They speak in generalities that can easily be misinterpreted."

"True, but Helenus has been correct in his prognostications, else I would not have these misgivings. He warned us that sending Paris to Sparta would have dire consequences for Troy. The man can see future things."

"So can Cassandra, but no one pays attention to her warnings."

"Cassandra?"

"Have you forgotten about her, Father?"

"I admit I have. But for good reason. Her predictions are questionable at best. I lack any confidence in them."

"They are accurate. I once kept track of the things she foretold and was amazed that she had faithfully reported these."

My father was astounded over hearing this. I don't think he ever took Cassandra seriously and minimized her contributions in this regard accordingly.

"Can this be true?" he asked.

"It is true. I couldn't believe it. Like you, I'm inclined to dismiss anything she says, but after that, I had second thoughts about her. She also told me I would be successful in getting Penthesileia to take up our cause before I left Troy."

"She did?"

"Her words comforted me, especially at times when I thought I would fail."

I could almost see the wheels turning inside my father's head. He had resisted seeking my sister's counsel from the beginning, assuming, as so many others, that she was on the fringes of madness, but had he ever truly listened to her? Not so. And now that I revealed my observations to him, he became aware of his recalcitrance and questioned if he might not have passed up prime opportunities available to him.

"Have I been wrong all these years?" he pondered aloud. "Do me a favor, Polyxena. Speak to her and find out what she foresees for us. I want to know what Helenus will say to the Greeks, or has already told them."

"Of course. But wouldn't it be better if you saw her?"

"Soon enough I will. For me to suddenly do an about-face is sure to arouse her skepticism, even distrust my sincerity. Seers are sensitive to that. I am told doubt impairs their ability to conjure up the images we seek."

This was going to be tricky. I was convinced that Cassandra had always been suspicious of my motivations and never confided in me some of the things she had seen. I remember all too well her message that implied, while no harm would come to me on my Amazon mission, a chill surrounded my future prospects. You never forget something like that. But as I already consented to my father's request, there really was no way out for me. I suppose it was time that I spoke to Cassandra anyway. We had avoided contact with each other, not intentionally on my part, for she never seemed to be around any place when I was there. I couldn't understand why I was reluctant to meet with her. Did I fear what she might say, what she knew? Or was it that she was not that easy to talk to and my natural inclination was to shy away from such people? Whatever the source of my queasiness, I was determine to suppress it and became resolved that I should visit her. Perhaps if I pretended that I had sorely missed her presence and desired to compensate for my remissions. But as a seer, wouldn't she know that? My best approach was simply to be honest with her and, through this, attain her appreciation and cooperation.

The following morning, after having had my breakfast, I undertook the step that harassed my thoughts and walked to Cassandra's place, the Temple of Apollo, standing at the eastern edge of the Pergamus. An imposing structure, its columns ascended five times a man's height to the capitals holding up the entablature. This was the largest building in Troy, nearly twice as large as the Temple of Athena. As Apollo was the god of prophecies, in addition to youthfulness, music, archery, and medicine, it was proper that Cassandra should serve him, owing her gift to him, even if, as some claimed, he cursed her when she supposedly consigned herself to a chaste life so that no one would ever heed her words. I was skeptical over that explanation, blaming the neglect she elicited more on the ineffectiveness of her elocution.

An eeriness enveloped me as I proceeded into the temple's portals. The interior was dark, with only the fires from braziers spaced at specified intervals along the walls furnishing any light, flickering off the awesome statue of Apollo, in size reaching from floor to ceiling. The place was scary, yet awe inspiring in its starkness, projecting a somber mood that made one pause and actually contemplate the presence of the god. Here was where Cassandra spent nearly all her time. How could she stand the bright daylight after leaving this place?

"What are you doing here?" a voice I recognized as Cassandra's suddenly broke the silence, startling me. She spoke out of the darkness behind the statue, not revealing herself to me.

"I wanted to speak to you," I said. "I never see you at the palace."

"Oh, I'm there often enough. You just haven't tried."

"Really? You haven't been conspicuous."

"That's what I always hear. I've seen you, Polyxena, but you rarely look at me, acknowledge my presence."

If this was true, I had not been aware of it.

"You need to be more assertive," I said. "I certainly didn't intentionally avoid you. But you know this."

"You spend too much time with Andromache and Helen, not enough with the rest of us, including Mother. You're right. I do know. Just as I know why you've come to me: because Father lacks the backbone to see me, having discounted everything I've told him."

Her insight made me uncomfortable, as if I was speaking to someone who knew ahead of time what I was going to say. Why should I bother relating anything to her when she already was aware of it?

"Be more considerate, Cassandra," I said. "He has regrets that he ignored you for so long and wants to atone for it."

At last she came forth into the dim light to peer into my eyes, refraining from saying more for the moment. She gave no hint of being glad to see me, no joy emanating from her, instead retaining the grave composure I always associated with her. Little wonder I avoided her, no pleasantry surrounded her, and if I may be faulted for my delinquency in recognizing her, I saw this as a natural tendency for anyone in the same situation.

"Maybe," she said. "Whatever I say to him will be discarded. I am wasting my time."

"Let me be the mediatory," I pleaded. "Tell him what he wants to know through me."

Cassandra delved on my proposal. I don't think she took satisfaction in it, but it was better than not heeding her warnings at all. The question was if I would believe her words.

"He wants to know what Helenus has told the Greeks," she said. "If he has jeopardized Troy's future."

Seers give me the creeps. They leave me at a loss over how to address them. I am the one who is wasting time in trying to speak to her.

"He has told them what they must do to win this war," Cassandra went on. "Mainly, its outcome hinges on the arrival of a young warrior not presently here. Agamemnon has sent Odysseus to fetch him from the island of Scyrus."

"Who?"

"Originally, he was named Pyrrhus, but he has more recently been called Neoptolemus ."

"Neoptolemus!" I exclaimed. A name like that can never be forgotten. "You mean the son of Achilles?"

"You are familiar with him?" Cassandra asked, surprised.

Why didn't she know that? Evidently, prognosticators do not perceive everything that goes on.

"Only by name," I answered. "Achilles mentioned him."

"Ah, yes. You and Achilles," she sneered, offending me with her derision.

"Don't say it," I snapped at her. "I'm not here to discuss what has been, but what will be. I need no reminders of things done."

Cassandra's steely gaze unnerved me, rattling my resolve to see this through, and made me want to run away. She saw something in looking at me, and whatever it was did not settle well with her, for her eyes momentarily expressed an abject fear. However, she soon regained her composure, resuming the somberness I identified her with. But her initial alarm had done its damage, impacting adversely on my senses and leaving me with the gravest misgivings over its meaning. I wished I had never come here. I determined I was better off not knowing what she had seen, thinking I could easier cope with the doubt than the certainty of a negative future prediction, and I avoided prying into the matter.

"He is on his way to Troy," Cassandra said, "to take command of the Myrmidons."

"Troy will fall because of him?"

"No. But beware of him, Sister. That's all I will say about it."

So Troy's fate was not tied to Neoptolemus. That is the inference I drew from Cassandra's answer. If that is so, then Helenus did not pose the threat my father envisioned. But she had an ambiguity in her phrasing of things that gave me no assurance about my conclusions.

"Answer me directly," I entreated. "Will Neoptolemus bring about Troy's destruction?"

"No," she answered.

"Then we're safe, in spite of what Helenus has done."

"I did not say that."

"Stop being so enigmatic," I demanded, getting flustered over her obscurity. "First you imply the outcome of this war depends on Neoptolemus coming here, then you say he will not be the cause of our ruin. I consider myself to be reasonably intelligent, but you leave me in a quandary over your meanings."

"A combination of factors will determine if Troy is to fall. Someone else, not Neoptolemus, will have more to do with this. We are not given access to all these. Our visions come to us in fragments, often with no correlation to each other, and we also are left in doubt as to their exact interpretations. I can positively give answers to some, but not others." She studied me, as if in search for assurances that I fully comprehended what she had said.

I paused, feeling the weight of her examination, then continued, saying, "I think you know much more than you are willing to relate to me. If you mean to spare us the truth because it is detrimental to our hopes, I can accept that. But let me know that is the case. Don't be so dubious about it."

"So you say, but if your future was accurately revealed, you may not find it so acceptable. That applies to everyone. Be grateful I am exercising my restraint. Now, leave me. I have said enough for one day."

I walked from the temple, feeling considerably more insecure than when I had entered it, deeply troubled over my talk with Cassandra, besieged by my perceived implications, if not certitude, of her words. Troy was going to lose this war, that much I gathered, for all her declarations alluded to that despite her attempts to obfuscate the point. That in itself was discouraging enough, but for her to suggest that I faced a threat in Neoptolemus, a man I did not know nor saw any possibility in ever getting to know was quite depressing for me. Unnecessarily so, I had to keep telling myself, doing my best to minimize the worry she had inculcated in me. I strongly believed that augurs were, for the most part, charlatans, and one ought not place much value in what they announced, but my awareness that Cassandra had a record of accuracy in her predictions mitigated against this, which did little to alleviate my apprehensions. My mistake was to ever suggest to my father that my sister could be useful to us. I would not have incurred an obligation to meet with her and could have avoided all the tribulations that now hounded me. Nothing in life comes easy for me anymore.

Lucky for me, my father pooh-poohed everything I passed on to him, my words coming more as a confirmation of the distrust he retained for his clairvoyant daughter than a warning of any impending threat. He did concede that he professed some concern— indignation is a more adapt description—over Helenus advising the enemy of what steps had to be taken in order to triumph over Troy, but thought it absurd that one man's arrival could have such an impact on this. His skepticism was contagious, bolstering my inclination toward dismissing my sister's prophesies as ludicrous, although not entirely.

"What can Neoptolemus do?" he scoffed. "Jump over our walls? So much for heeding Cassandra's words."

"She should not be ignored altogether, Father."

"No? Then she must say things of use to me. I'm glad she spends her time in Apollo's temple, saving me from justifying my rejection of her counsel."

"You're not worried about what Helenus said?"

"How can I know what he said? Cassandra telling me is not convincing evidence. Even if true, I find his words not that crucial to our survival. Our walls will protect us. Nothing I have heard leads me to believe they can be penetrated."

I considered reminding my father of the declining morale among our supporting armies, resulting from the war's protraction, and that a continued siege undermined their commitment to us. Can Troy stand without its allies? I did not think it could, for our strength in soldiers was being depleted by the recurring battles confronting us. We were relying more and more on replenishing our losses with the reinforcements provided by our neighbors. But how much longer were they willing to keep this up with no prospect of victory in sight? My conviction was that my father was quite aware of this and needed no emphasis from me on the subject. In front of his subordinates, he openly displayed an optimism despite all the setback sustained over the years of warfare: the death of so many of his sons, the inability to expel the enemy from our lands, the abandonment of allied support, but mainly the seeming hopelessness of our situation in which no relief appeared in sight. With me he was more truthful and dared to confide the certain inner weaknesses that troubled him, revealing the doubts to his own resolutions in facing the obstacles confronting him. Yet Father put up a solid front, surmounting the pain endured, his fortitude enhanced by the trust he placed in our walls, and strived to see a positive side in our strife. This was leadership at its best, although I suspected inside he was being torn apart and in a constant struggle to present himself as a pillar of strength.

One of our main justifications, one we relied on increasingly as the war went on, was our strongly held view that the struggle had to be as trying on the enemy as it was on ourselves, with an equally undermining effect on their morale as well as an erosion of their confidence. We used this argument to convince ourselves that eventual success favored us, and the requirement on our part was to outlast the Greeks, breaking their resolve to extend the siege. The contest tested our mettle, evolving into a battle of wills as well as physical exertions, and whoever was the strongest in both regards was going to be triumphant. I confess to becoming less assured in the legitimacy of that argument. On the surface, it seemed sound, but it ignored a reality posing an obstacle for us that exempted the enemy. Simply put, the Greeks had greater access to reinforcements than Troy. In controlling the seas, there existed no barriers to their search for additional support, the matter being one of persuasion rather than security, and this gave them an advantage over us, one that could be decisive.

Although rising worries predominated my assessment of our present condition, I was not about to let my negativism deter anyone from our purpose and kept my deductions to myself. My father may have picked up on this, for he gave me a comprehensive gaze that suggested he knew my skepticism.

"The gods must favor us," he said to me, grave in manner. "We have suffered too much to be abandoned by them. I have to believe this, else I would go mad with grief and loss of hope. I must have faith in this."

He told me this faith was lacking, his words desperately trying to boost his flagging confidence in the assertion. I had no desire to raise a cloud over what he already doubted, further impairing his purpose, and nodded my agreement.

"I long to ride freely about," I said, "with no more restrictions imposed on me. Nearly my entire life, since I developed an awareness of the things around me, has been associated with this war. The only time I felt truly liberated was when I was with the Amazons, even though I could not escape its influence."

"The war brought you to them."

"I meant liberated in the sense that we could go anywhere we wanted. The land was ours to roam, no barriers, no infringements. We did as we pleased, choosing our targets at will. A feeling of independence took hold of me. I relished it."

"So you shall again," my father assured me. "Trust me. Troy ill once again reign over the region. Believe in this." His strong assertion negated my earlier misgivings.

When we parted, I did sense an elevation in my spirit, Father's optimism working its charm on me, and was gratified to have the meeting close this way. I told myself I should share in his hopefulness, recognizing its beneficial attributes, and was encouraged to the point that I may actually have thought this war might soon come to an end. Was I in denial?

I should also mention that, by this time, I had reacquired Menodice's services, adhering to Agenor's wishes, but this did not go as well as I had expected. The alienation that had arisen between us was not as easily dismissed, as her assistance to my mother transferred back to me. While appearing outwardly happy over the change, Menodice was not as engaging and open in her conversations with me as before, which I attributed to the misgivings she might have retained over her betrayal of my trust. Either that, or she bore a lingering resentment that I requested a termination of her duties to me, that she cater to Mother instead. For my part, I still delayed in my forgiveness over the injury she inflicted on me, which resulted in the death of Achilles. It surprised me that I could not overcome this reservation, as that aspect of my life seemed long gone and increasingly remote to me. But that was the case; I can offer no other defense for my reluctance, and it persisted in driving a wedge in our relationship. At best, we spoke cordially to each other, respecting our individuality and trying to improve the less than satisfactory division now existing in our association. At worst, I tolerated her, unable to erase from my mind the grief she brought to me. I suppose I am equally at fault for our intransigence in resolving this estranged affiliation. Fortunately, my relationship with Thalia, whose services I had retained all along, remained as affectionate and strong as ever.

Chapter XVII

N EARLY A MONTH HAD PASSED since Helenus deserted Troy, and while most of this time was marked by minor engagements between our forces and the Greeks, there presently appeared to be another complete lull in effect, with the understanding truce this entailed. This afforded me the opportunity to resume my more circuitous route around the city when with Zephyrus, which I enjoyed more, because it kept me closer to the coast, where cooler winds coming off the water made things more comfortable. Admittedly, the riding also brought me nearer to the enemy camps scattered along the shore, but I viewed this with ambivalence, not feeling particularly threatened by it. I had no recollection of anyone coming to harm whenever a truce was in place and, accordingly, gave little thought to the potential of that happening to me. As I was approaching the Scaean Gates, although still some distance from there, I saw a singular riding figure coming toward me from the Myrmidon camp. He was waving his hand and shouting, entreating me to stop. I halted, curious over his apparent attempt to see me and secure that, if I had to, I could escape him on Zephyrus.

When he came within a few paces of me, the rider stopped and glanced long at me, quite transfixed, as if he was smitten by my appearance. His piercing eyes, very blue, exuded a warm glow and a friendly demeanor was revealed in his wide smile. He had flaming red hair, such as rarely seen.

"You're not afraid of me," he said. "A woman riding by herself in a war zone, not very smart."

"If I thought I was in danger, I would have fled," I replied. "My horse can outrun yours, I'm sure."

"What brashness. But I pardon you, ill-chosen as your words were," he clumsily blurted out, a smug grin flashing across his face.

Who did he imagine himself to be that I should be pardoned by him? He was very young, certainly no older than I, and fairly handsome, although I was not attracted to him, thinking him as agreeable and nothing more. But his attitude was arrogant and deterred me from taking an immediate liking to him.

"Destiny brings me to you," he continued. "I have just arrived here, eager for battle, and the first Trojan I come across is a woman."

"Sorry to disappoint you."

"Do you see me complaining?"

"I see you slavering from the mouth. Stop staring at me. You behave as if you have never seen a woman before."

For an instant, I was frightened that I may have been too abrasive in my response. Both ours and the enemy's societies were patriarchal, and men were not kindly disposed toward being reprimanded by women. And indeed, the youth's initial reaction, expressed clearly in his eyes, was one of hostility, but he quickly regained his composure and kept himself in check.

"Who else should I look at?" he snarled. "You're the only one here."

Still a bit distressed over my previous outburst, I felt a need to ease the tensions I evoked.

"So I'm the first Trojan you have come across," I said. "Do you like what you see?"

That calmed him, and a radiance returned to his eyes, but he hesitated in answering my question, as if at a loss over how to express himself.

"For being a Trojan, you look pretty nice," he then said. "Not what I expected."

"You expected us to be ugly harpies?"

"Well, no. But not as beautiful as Greek women."

I smiled over his bumbling mannerism. He had flattered me but somehow failed to grasp an awareness of that, at least so it appeared to me, in that he more or less blundered into his reply than giving any thought to it.

"I'm Polyxena, daughter of King Priam," I informed him.

"You're her?" he gulped.

"You know me?" I was alarmed over his shock.

"Only from what I've been told about you. You're the Trojan princess my father fell in love with. I am Neoptolemus, son of Achilles."

I was stunned, glaring open-mouthed at him in my astonishment that I should be face-to-face with the man Cassandra had cautioned me to avoid. The probability I thought absolutely unlikely now boldly confronted me. So much for averting a potential adverse situation. For being only fifteen, perhaps now sixteen, he was very much a man, fully grown to that size, in fact, even bigger than most of them.

"You were also responsible for his death," he exclaimed, denouncing me with his vehement tone.

"I had nothing to do with that," I said.

"You lie. I was told he rode into an ambush trying to rescue you from—what was it?—your supposed banishment from Troy. You're still here. Try to deny that."

"The ambush was done without my knowledge. The story of my exile was fabricated by it perpetrators."

"You expect me to believe that?"

I became angry over his obvious mistrust in what I was saying.

"I loved Achilles," I snapped back, the recollection of our affair bringing me near tears. "As much as he loved me. What do you know about it? You have no right to deprecate the love we had for each other. Your father would be the first to censure you for that."

My outburst moved him, and I detected a noticeable trace of sympathy emanating from his eyes. His hostility abated, and I sincerely believed that he accepted my words as true. I had no idea what Achilles had said about me to him or to others who related this to him, but I never doubted that it would be disparaging or unfavorable to me. He still glanced strangely at me, as if captivated by me, but the intimidation I felt earlier over this was greatly diminished, and I presently sensed that I faced no harm from him.

"That's not how things were related to me," he said.

"The reports were distorted."

"So you say. It's not that I don't want to believe you—I think I do—but I must deny to myself what has long been said and what I had assumed true. I know my father loved you, and that cost him his life."

"To this day, I am grief stricken over that."

I think he was beginning to trust me, and why shouldn't he? Nothing I told him was false or exaggerated. True feelings cannot be easily disguised. They reveal their sincerity in numerous ways, especially through the eyes. I was also starting to develop an interest in him, not in the romantic sense, but out of curiosity over what it was like to be the son of the acclaimed greatest of all Greek warriors.

"Were you close to your father?" I asked.

"Not really," he said after some pause. "To be truthful, I have no recollection of ever having seen him. He had an affair with my mother—her name is Deidameia—when he was at Scyrus, but he never married her. She told me a lot about him though, of his manhood and boldness. And his reputation as a fighter was heard everywhere. I have always admired him, although at times, I feel that I live in his shadow."

"He was also beautiful," I added.

"Beautiful? Men are not beautiful."

"Yes, they are. In the sense that they present the ideal portraiture, perfection, in physique and stature. Your father was beautiful."

He gazed oddly at me, not particularly impressed by my description, thinking it demeaning to manliness, at least, that is what I surmised at first. But when he again spoke, I was amazed how wrong my perception had been.

"Great," he said, scowling. "Another image to live up to. Trying to be the warrior he was is not enough. I must also strive for his— perfection."

So the truth had come out, Neoptolemus lived in envy of his father, jealous of his glory and prowess, belittled by the greatness bestowed upon him, and apparently insecure having to live up to him. Perhaps even worse, he may have regarded himself inferior in appearance as well as abilities, and my comments contributed nothing to dispel this perception. I could see the annoyance this created for him.

"We have to be ourselves," I said. "You should not try to compete with your father."

"Easy for you to say. I'm expected to fill his shoes in this conflict. That's why I was brought here."

Obviously, this posed a burden for him, and it was understandable. Shamefully, I agreed that he was no Achilles. He was certainly strong enough, with his bulging muscles and rock-solid frame suggestively outlined through the short, white tunic covering him, all that he wore,

I'm sure he possessed his father's courage, but no real beauty defined his features. He lacked the exquisitely proportioned body and attractive face that characterized his father. He was handsome but in a different sort of way, and a less appealing quality, one that struck me as austere rather than refined, delineated the comportment in which he carried himself. In short, I felt no immediate attraction for him, unlike his father, but that is not to say I was repulsed by him. I was merely indifferent to him, and it mattered little to me whether he liked me, as he seemed to, or not. At present, anyway.

"You know that it was your brother, Helenus, who proposed I come here, saying this was a prerequisite for our winning this war."

"He is contemptible."

"I rather like him. A Trojan who's on our side, there's nothing wrong in that."

Why did I get the feeling he was trying to agitate me? Finesse was not one of his better attributes.

"Don't count on his prophesies," I cautioned him in an attempt to deprecate my brother. "He's been wrong before. Troy will endure, whether you're here or not."

"I guess we'll just have to see," he smirked.

He had a talent for offending people, I thought, and yet I was intrigued by him, though I could not figure out why. Maybe I was fascinated by his seeming lack of concern over what he said to me. I wasn't sure, but I knew it had nothing to do with his seeming admiration for me. I should have been flattered by that, but in actuality, it had no dramatic effect on me, and I had no problem dismissing it from my thoughts.

"I have to get back," I said, tiring of being gawked at. "They'll be looking for me."

"Will I see you again?" he asked.

I demurred in granting my consent, not wishing to encourage any unwarranted hopes in him over our meeting, thinking it best to keep my distance from him, Cassandra's warnings ever present in my mind. And yet, something about him aroused my interest, even if I was presently unable to define it, and I viewed another encounter with him as worthwhile for me, to learn what beguiled me about him.

"Possibly," I answered, "as long as the truce remains in effect."

I waved him good-bye and prodded Zephyrus into a gallop toward our walls. Looking back, I saw him remaining in place, watching me depart, causing me to speculate over what he might be thinking. Then it hit me why I knew Zephyrus could outrun his horse, thereby minimizing my fancied threats from him. He was riding the same scruffy mount that Achilles rode, although it looked somewhat more presentable now, but not by much. I had to laugh as I dwelled on this.

I had met my nemesis, according to Cassandra's premonitions, and if I were smart, I would avoid further contact with him. Somehow, seeing Neoptolemus as a future menace was difficult to grasp, especially as he was quite enamored with me. I'm not suggesting he was harmless, but after having spoken with him and seen him, my fears were significantly diminished, if not outright vanished, and I had trouble visualizing him as a destructive influence. Still, I could not ignore my sister. Her admonitions were now preying more intensely on me. I had to get greater clarification, mainly about my continued visits with him, in order to decide whether this represented, or would lead to, whatever evil consequences she envisioned for me.

After giving Zephyrus my affectionate strokes—he remained my one great joy during these trying times—and turning him over to the corral keeper, I presented myself, again late, at the usual afternoon women's gathering, where my mother met me with her habitual scowl meant to show her disapproval of my conduct.

"It's not my fault," I said. "I was unexpectedly detained."

"You are an incorrigible child," my mother caustically replied. "It's useless to discipline you. But I have given up trying. I cannot let it upset me."

I truly resented being called a child. After what I have been through this past year, that was demeaning to me. I merited the respect being called a woman entailed. I suppose, from her perspective, I may have been just a child, but I strongly felt that would only be applicable if she disregarded the passage of events that had transpired. But I was determined to avoid any confrontation. I took my place upon the cushions strewn about, ready to contribute my part in their afternoon chats. That is when I noticed the bruise on Helen's face.

"What happened, Helen?" I asked.

Helen looked at me, her eyes moistening, but she hesitated to respond.

"We've all been over that," my mother answered on her behalf, indicating in her frown that she not eager to pursue the subject. "If you were more attentive, you would not miss out on learning about it."

Mother could be so annoying. Why would she try to keep this from me? I examined the discoloring running from just below Helen's left eye to the edge of her lips. Clearly, she struck her face on something.

"Did you fall?" I inquired.

"Please, Polyxena," Helen said, glancing briefly at my mother. "Forget about this ."

"What's the matter with everybody?" I snapped, peeved that no one was willing to tell me. "Why keep this from me? I'll find out anyway."

"Go ahead, Helen," my mother said. "Let her know."

I could not believe their reluctance. You would have thought I was creating an intrusive imposition on them, as if I should not be privy to seemingly confidential information that belonged exclusively to them.

"Deiphobus hit me," Helen said, her glassy eyes penetrating me.

I was floored but should have guessed this. It explained my mother's aversion, as she did not want her son cast in a bad light, even if he deserved it.

"Don't act so shocked," mother exclaimed when she saw my surprise. "I'm sure he had an excuse. He was provoked."

"Provoked? What kind of provocation justifies him striking Helen?" I angrily responded.

"Don't raise your voice to me, Daughter," she countered, equally irate.

"It's all right, Polyxena," Helen said. "I had it coming."

"No, it's not all right. It may be true that men rule over us and that we are to submit to them, but we are royalty, not animals or disobedient slaves that should be beaten."

Momentarily, I silenced our gathering, perhaps because I voiced an accord among each of its members and they identified with it. But soon after that, the customary and accepted practices prevailing overuse counteracted my protestation, and the realities facing us came to the forefront. This led them, I think, to a quiet concession that the blame for the assault on Helen was ultimately her fault, even that she probably invited it, much to my dismay. Helen herself pronounced no support for me. Instead, she excused her husband of his misdeed, acknowledging, as everyone else, that she was responsible for the punishment he inflicted on her.

"I was out of line, Polyxena," she said. "I insulted his manhood, making fun of his inability to satisfy me in bed. I knew this would enrage him, but I persisted in mocking him."

So Deiphobus indeed had provocation, as any man so assailed would have, but that did not, in my opinion, give him the authority or right to physically assault Helen. Was I wrong? Even Helen herself had me thinking so. What I knew for certain was that no Amazon would have ever stood for that. Again, I came to realize how my attitudes had changed as a result of having been with them and that, in a subtle but certain way, I had submitted to their indoctrination. I said nothing more to Helen, feeling, in some measure, that she had negated my attempts in backing her. So much for trying to stand up for solidarity behind womanhood.

I looked around to see if Cassandra was present and saw that she was not. This was the usual situation for me. Whenever I tried to search her out in our gathering, she was not there. I do not know what she meant by saying I just I fail to notice her. She's never there.

Frustrated, I got up to make my exit, which elicited a negative reaction out of my mother.

"Where are you going now?" she growled, her disapproval much in evidence. "You just got here."

"I have to see Cassandra," I said. "I came thinking she would be here."

"My other disagreeable daughter. You're becoming more like her every day, Polyxena. She hides from me in Apollo's temple, you in your riding. Why can't you two behave as normal women?"

"I'm sorry I haven't lived up to your expectations, Mother."

"I bet you are. I see your regret in your reluctance to leave us. Go if you must. Do not let our undesirable feminine existence detain you."

Sometimes I felt that Mother would not be happy unless she had something to complain about, and if I fulfilled this requirement, then I was satisfied that I contributed to making her day. But to compare me with Cassandra? Not to deprecate my sister who was, in fact, quite beautiful and even had a suitor, a Phrygian named Coroebus, which is more than I can say for myself, but she was not a person to hang around with. Her sour disposition deterred you from that. What was wrong with Coroebus?

I rendered my mother a small curtsy as I backed myself away from her. I noticed Andromache exchanging smiles with Helen, perhaps in mutual concession over my failings at womanhood, which apparently struck them as humorous. Once I got sufficiently distant from her, I turned around and hurriedly proceeded for Apollo's temple, my thoughts now dominated over what my encounter with Neoptolemus meant for me. My major concern was whether I had inadvertently exposed myself to a danger she knew about or if an absence of specificity offered me hope for misinterpretations in whatever was foreseen about me.

Once more, I was surrounded by the eerie darkness of the temple's interior, but this time, I was not as intimidated by it as before, mainly because of my eagerness to meet with my sister, which had a greater urgency for me than the last time.

"Cassandra?" I spoke out. "Are you here?"

"I hear you," she answered from somewhere. I did not see her as yet. She then stepped forward from behind some shrouds and ambled up to me. "What is it you want, Polyxena?" Her tone was one of annoyance, as if regarding me an intruder into her busy schedule.

Again, I thought it paradoxical that she did not know. I became increasingly convinced that seers could only know of things they concentrated on rather than everything that goes on around them as I previously believed. Only the gods know everything.

"I may have made a mistake. I need to know what this signifies for me."

Cassandra gave me that penetrating gaze now familiar with me but nevertheless just as unnerving as ever. It told me she was focusing her attention on me, concentrating so she might know what troubled me.

"I told you to avoid him," she exclaimed after some pause. "He is bad for you."

"Do you mean Neoptolemus?" I asked, wanting assurance we spoke of the same person.

"Of course," she replied, vexed that I would question her. "Who else would I be talking about?"

"If you can truly see things, you should know that my meeting him was by accident. I had no idea who he was when I first saw him."

"That is unfortunate for you."

"Don't scare me like that," I reacted in alarm, not appreciating her threatening message. "What can happen if I stay away from him from now on? I know who he is, so I ought to be able to keep my distance from him."

"Yes, but he also now knows who you are. He will seek you out given the opportunity."

"What opportunity? All I have to do is confine myself to our city and the areas under our control. That should preclude any chances of him seeing me."

She hesitated and, in her pause, created a consternation in me that was distressing. I sensed that she comprehended Troy's future to a greater extent than she was willing to concede. What else could place me in danger of Neoptolemus except the fall of the city itself? Otherwise, I obviously would be able to shun him. But that would have horrible consequences for all of us, not just me. This told me that, while I may be in danger, my peril was no worse than anyone else's. I did not expect Cassandra to tell me of Troy's demise, everyone already regarded her as quite mad, and that would only affirm what was alleged.

"Just stay away from him," she said. "Promise me that."

Having rationalized that the danger posed to me was no greater than that facing others, I no longer viewed her warnings as that critical to my security. So even if I gave her my word that I would accede to her wishes, whether I would adhere to it was another matter. I was not going to let it disturb me to the point that it would dictate impositions on me. Better to just let circumstances occur as they may.

"I'll do what I can," I replied, being evasive.

"Don't minimize the threat," she announced bitterly, angry over my inconclusiveness. "Neoptolemus will hurt you."

"I quote you what Father told me: 'What can Neoptolemus do? Jump over our walls?' If you can truthfully tell me that Troy is doomed, the only condition I can see exposing me to a risk from him, then say so. Otherwise, spare me your frightening posture."

I knew she was not about to openly declare Troy's fall—that was tantamount to treasonous conduct, aside from placing her sanity into further question—and I fully expected her to desist from additional prophesies. My confidence was rising over my ability to avert the impending disaster she foresaw in any relationship with Neoptolemus, seeing myself as the controlling factor in promulgating such an affair and quite capable of managing this. Increasingly, her admonitions seemed less and less relevant to my safety. I do wish she was less dramatic in her presentations.

"I have given you my warning," Cassandra said. "You can make of it what you like. It's dismaying to see what is in store for us, as much for me as anyone, and sometimes I envy people who are able to discount it and go about their lives as usual. Overall, life is happier not knowing what will happen. You won't be burdened with the worries this entails."

Her words were touching. Having been affected by her exhortations, inflicting anxieties in me which may have been unnecessary, even if well intended, I had to agree that knowing the future did not lead to a happier situation. It would be far more burdensome than rewarding, I think, especially if it was preordained and could not be averted.

"Do you regret having that gift?" I asked.

Cassandra appeared surprised that I expressed an interest in the dubitable nature of her endowment. She probably had never been asked that question before. Her demeanor softened and the hard glare she usually emitted changed to a warmer glow.

"At times," she answered, "especially when it touches me closely. I have to block things out of my mind that I don't want to know about. Once the image comes to me, I can't shake it, even if it is detrimental to me. That can be so difficult. You know about Coroebus?"

"Andromache told me."

"He loves me, and I'm also very fond of him. Every time visions of him appear, I try hard to dispel them for fear that an undesirable future image may come to me. You can't imagine how hard that can be."

For the first time in my memory, I had deep compassion for my sister, recognizing that she was far from blessed in her clairvoyance. She made it clear to me it was a talent I had no desire to possess.

"I think I can," I said. "You make me grateful that I'm just plain me, without any extraordinary powers beyond my own sensibilities."

Cassandra broke into a rare smile, and I must say, that smile utterly transformed her face, greatly accentuating her beauty so that I could readily comprehend how suitors might flock to her. She was very alluring when seen in a chirpy context. She should carry herself that way more often; everyone would have a more favorable view of her.

"Why, thank you, Sister," she said, still beaming. "You understand."

What a different person she was when pleased. I was actually enjoying conversing with her and being in her company. Who would have thought it? But her indications were that she was finished with me. She glanced toward the side of the interior wall, as if being called upon to go there, and since I felt my own business concluded, we made our departure, but not before exchanging smiling glances that warmed me.

A disquietude beleaguered me as I strolled out of the temple, pain coming to my eyes as I squinted in the bright sunlight. My own uncertainty over my encounter with Neoptolemus, what this portended, remained unanswered for me, but I found some relief in that. I was reasonably assured about one thing: whatever destiny was decreed for me regarding the Greek, it was connected to the fate of Troy itself, and as long as Troy stood, I was safe from his reaches. A more compelling question was, did I face a threat from him in my rides about our city? Should I be tempting fate? Somehow, after my previous encounter with him, I could not see it as potentially dangerous to me. After all, he now already knew me. One more visit was not going to make me a stranger to him. I would have to think about that.

As for Cassandra, I had never seen her in an agreeable disposition before, and I have to admit that worked wonders for her. She always was beautiful, but when she smiled, she greatly highlighted her attractiveness, even becoming seductive, dispelling my earlier convictions that no man in his right mind would want her. Clearly, I had a more favorable image of her, and that could actually work to my advantage. If we got along better with each other, I might get her to reveal what she perceived about Troy's future—do I really want to know this?—and about mine, if I wanted it told, and at this point, I did not. I realized she was not that comfortable in her precognitions, regarding it as a significant hardship occasionally. Her assertion that she fought to keep some of the images from implanting themselves in her mind had a haunting aspect to it. I saw how it could seriously impinge on one's serenity, making things miserable. It is interesting how I could be around people all my life only to learn that I have never really known them. That's how I felt about Cassandra.

When I returned to the residence palace to rejoin the "feminine" group, I discovered that they had terminated their session and probably retired into their own respective chambers for an afternoon nap. This appealed to me, the fatigue and boredom of the day affecting my alertness, and I decided a short snooze was beneficial to my well-being. Accordingly, I headed for my chamber. As I entered it, everyone in the group was there and greeted me, cheering me, for what, I don't know. I was amazed.

"Congratulations, Daughter," my mother gleefully announced, gravitating to the head of the gathering. "You have turned eighteen." My birthday. I had completely lost sight of it in all the flurry of activities that had taken place during this last tumultuous year. So now I was eighteen. It did not feel much different from being seventeen. All I could think of was that, if this year was going to be as eventful as my last one, I was not going to survive it. So much has happened to me in the recent months that, in reflecting on this, I scarcely comprehended how I had come out of the year in one piece. I bowed my head repeatedly to acknowledge my appreciation.

"Have some wine, Polyxena," said my mother, handing me a goblet. She was grinning from ear to ear.

"Thank you, Mother," I responded, energized by her obvious enthusiasm. "Thank you all."

"A toast, everyone," Andromache declared. "To Polyxena!"

"To Polyxena!" everyone replied in unison.

We all gulped down our wine, draining our goblets, and I must say, the wine was actually quite good, one of our better vintages.

As for being the center of attention, I cannot say I was well suited for that, my natural tendencies directing me toward a quiet, rather than effervescent, comportment. Still, as the honored celebrity, I was expected to say something, however trivial it might be, and I was not going to dampen the affair by neglecting my duty.

"I'm honored," I said. "I know I haven't been the best example of womanly virtues, but I promise to do better this year. So forgive me for my past failings, accept my present efforts, and wish me future successes. I hope to make you all proud of me."

Everyone cheered. My mother was particularly pleased, her joy obvious, gushing as she was in her ebullience, although I was at a loss to explain why. I fully expected her to get in the last word in our stormy relationship. I was not disappointed.

"Now you must have a husband," she said. "Single women have no place in our society."

I always thought it strange that others should concern themselves more with my marital status than I. Yes, I was now four years past the accepted age of nuptial arrangements for our gender, but I possessed no real worriment over this. The thought only occasionally crossed my mind, and then only momentarily, and I was easily able to dismiss it. Had I a fear that no men would be attracted to me I would perhaps be more disturbed over this, but I knew such was not the case. Achilles fell for me, and so, it appears, had his son, Neoptolemus. Why was I unable to name any Trojans? Was I ignoring them? No matter. In spite of my mother's incessant demands, I felt no pressure to adhere to them. I was quite content, at this stage of my life, to remain in my unwed condition.

"I must have suitors first," I told my mother, trying to avoid being sarcastic.

"That should not be a problem for a woman as beautiful as you," she replied.

"So where are they?"

"We can arrange for that, Daughter. We shall announce to the noble families that you are available."

Whenever my mother called me Daughter rather than by my name, I knew I was beginning to get under her skin. Believing that she was now upset with me, I had no compunctions over maintaining my civility any further. So much for my promise.

"Don't bother," I said. "I'm not ready for it."

That was the last thing she wanted to hear, and she reacted instantly in the negative, her eyes revealing her scorn. She walked closer to me, stopping directly in front of my face.

"Get ready for it!" she shouted. "I'll not have a self-indulgent daughter in this household who will not incur the obligations of adulthood. Even Cassandra has a suitor."

"Cassandra is twelve years older. You've given her ample time, why not me?"

"Cassandra is a priestess. She has dedicated herself to a chaste life in service to Apollo. Only recently has she decided to balance this with a more rewarding marital life. You have no excuse for your deferment."

Things were heating up, and I saw that I had to diffuse the situation and modify my stand if I was to prevent an all-out confrontation that would have both of us regretting our actions. What better way than to accede to her wishes.

"All right, Mother," I said. "Go ahead. Make the announcement. Let's see what happens."

"That's more like it. You have to change your behavior to make yourself more appealing to potential suitors. I suggest you start by spending more time in our domestic gatherings. And stop riding that horse of yours."

Stop riding Zephyrus? Not a chance, I said to myself. My rides offered me the diversion and release of tensions that I needed to make my existence tolerable. These distractions from my daily routine were not seen as an option for me, but as a necessity. Without them, I would surely go mad. So while I was willing to participate in the womanly assemblies, I knew full well that concession was not going to apply to my time spent with Zephyrus. Accordingly, my response was intentionally evasive.

"I will try to be the daughter you want me to be, Mother," I said. "You'll see."

Everyone present, most of all my mother, breathed easier, and after another few rounds of toasting, they gradually filtered out of my chamber until I, at last, obtained the solitude I had sought in the first place. But by this time, I was too inebriated to make anything of it and soon, without being cognizant of it, entered into the realm of Hypnos.

So opposite was my relationship with Father. None of the things that so preoccupied my mother about me seemed to matter to him. Best of all, he had no problem with my single status, never once alluding to it, accepting it a perfectly normal, even making me feel quite good about it. He saw me as a true individual, tolerating my idiosyncrasies, whatever they were, recognizing the boredom my womanly gathering might pose for me, and understanding the pleasure I derived in my excursions on Zephyrus. He actually admired my skill in horsemanship, thinking it worthy of a royal princess. In every respect, his views vividly contrasted those of my mother's concerning me. That is why I looked so adoringly upon him. And although he diligently avoided making references to my mother, he ignored her designs for me as much as I did, dismissing these as not applicable to me. The importance this had for me, not only in elevating my spirit, but in stimulating my interests, was immeasurable.

The next day, when we again met in the courtyard after he had concluded one of his staff meetings, I told him about having met Neoptolemus. He responded as I anticipated: inquisitive and perceptive.

"He is not Achilles, from what you say," Father said.

"Physically he appears as strong. He's as tall and muscular, but he doesn't have his father's charm or charisma, nor his commanding presence."

"That can be attributed to his youth. Gaining confidence will lead to that. Where you in awe of him, you know, in an intimidating sort of way?"

"Actually, no. I thought him an arrogant young man. I got the impression that he is very much envious of his father."

"Indeed? But then, who can live up to Achilles? That has to be a weighty load to carry for a son, especially if that is an expectation people have of him."

"He said as much himself."

"Your overall assessment of him, do you see him as a significant threat to Troy?"

Personally, I could not see him as such, but I was somewhat unsettled over his conviction that he was fulfilling a destiny and would make a difference and the eagerness in which he embraced his duties, wanting extremely badly to fight us.

"Not as much as Achilles was," I said. "He is very enthusiastic in wanting to get into combat with us and has a strong belief that the Greeks will triumph in the end ."

"Newly recruited warriors always believe that, until the stark realities, their impotence in the greater scheme of things, dawns on them. One hard-fought, but inconclusive, battle will dispel such notions quickly enough."

"He also is grateful to Helenus for bringing him here. I think he gets along well with him."

This did not go over well with my father who openly demonstrated his contempt for my brother—ex-brother is more appropriate—with a sneer.

"He shall pay for his treachery," he growled. "When all this is over, I may personally slay him."

"There's one other thing," I continued and then hesitated over whether it was worthwhile mentioning.

"Yes? Go on."

"I think Neoptolemus may have taken a liking to me. He couldn't keep his eyes off me. I felt uncomfortable being scrutinized like that."

Seeming to dismiss the notion at first, my father peered at me askance, drawing his head backward as if thinking it silly. He then brought his hand to his chin and pondered over it at length, sitting quietly on the bench as he appeared to probe the possibilities entailed in my observation. I was not sure how he would respond, thinking he might berate me for having an inflated view of myself. To my surprise, he wanted to explore the idea further.

"Are you deluding yourself into believing that?" he asked.

"No. I thought it quite obvious," I answered.

"How do you feel about him?"

"I find him intriguing. He's different, but in a way I can't properly define. If you mean it in a romantic context, no, I'm not interested in him."

"I'm pleased to have you say it. One such infatuation is ample. If he is smitten with you, I see potential in extracting some useful intelligence out of him. Have you cut off further contact with him?"

"No, I left the door open for future meetings. He requested as much."

"If you do this skillfully, we can learn what Agamemnon plans next: which allied city he may strike, how many soldiers he will use for such raids, when, perhaps even his next move against Troy. Meet with him again. In his youthful naïveté, he may inadvertently reveal what we wish to know."

"Willingly. But I should tell you that Cassandra has told me to stay away from him. She sees him as a threat to me."

"Oh, she sees a threat in everyone. Don't listen to her. But be careful, Polyxena. If you suspect the slightest danger, don't go through with this. I don't want you to think you have to do this. It has to be on your terms. Another day is just as fine."

I nodded my agreement, again gratified that my father expressed such confidence in me. Add to that the assurance he bolstered in me over, if not outright disregarding, at least greatly lessening, the dire insinuations of Cassandra's prognostications. But what I liked best about my talk with him was that, while not explicitly stated, he gave me his authorization to continue my usual rides with my graceful stallion. How else would I meet Neoptolemus? Let Mother try to stop me now. Unlike Mother, he presented me with tasks I definitely favored doing, that I believed were more in tune with my abilities, and that had the thrilling aspect of a challenge about them. As I left him, I could hardly conceal the excitement I felt in anticipation of meeting Neoptolemus again, this time as an agent of Troy.

CHAPTER XVIII

FORTUNE CAN BE SO CAPRICIOUS. Little wonder one is prone to believe that the gods directly intervened in the affairs of mortals. The very next day, when I meant to meet Neoptolemus so that I might test my cleverness at espionage work, a task I eagerly embraced and looked forward to, the lull in the fighting came to an abrupt end. I was told the conflict began when ours and an enemy patrol made contact and initiated the fighting, and it soon escalated into a major skirmish as additional units entered the fray. Before long, more reinforcements were committed to the action, and that led to their augmentation by backup forces, including most of our squadrons from Troy, so that, by midday, nearly the whole of both armies was engaged in the struggle, which had transformed into a major battle.

The battle raged relentlessly on for the rest of the day. We viewed it spellbound from our observation station. Aeneas still commanded our army, with my brothers Deiphobus and Polites his major subordinate generals. Agenor now also led a division, a significant promotion for him, which he deserved, as no one fought more courageously in defense of our city. As for the Greeks, we learned that Neoptolemus, despite his youth, had assumed command of the Myrmidons, the other leaders remaining Agamemnon, Menelaus, Odysseus, and Diomedes. I had difficulty spotting the individual commanders amid the mass of battling warriors but did manage to occasionally see Odysseus. He wore the gold-crested helmet that once belonged to Achilles, which glistened in the reflected sunlight, revealing his position. He was the one who had been given the armor worn by Achilles, so our spies reported, a prestigious award.

By sunset, the combatants slowly disengaged themselves from the fighting and began to withdraw to their own sides, leaving the field between them strewn with the bodies of the fallen and the severely wounded who were unable to stay on their feet or get assistance from their peers. This battle had ended, as all the others, at a horrible cost of life over no gains to anyone, another stalemate. Once more, the medical and disposal crews entered upon the scene, doing their grim work amid the cries of the suffering and the dying. If I ever came to believe that eventually I would get accustomed to the slaughter and inure my sensibilities against its horror, this notion was eclipsed every time the reality of the situation confronted me. It always impacted with severity upon me, never easier the next time around, afflicting me with the same pain and dismay I felt after my first introduction to the cruelty of war. At times, I shied away from facing the situation, thinking I could not endure it, but then a sense of duty took possession of me, and I again answered the call for help from the medical teams and assisted the physicians in dressing the wounded and seeing to their needs Most of our work was being done in makeshift shelters set up within our outer walls, the infirmary building being filled to capacity, and that's where I was performing my services when Deiphbus, sweaty in his gore-stained armor and spent of energy, came up to me.

"Why are you doing this?" he asked, his tone of voice denoting that he disapproved of my efforts.

"My help is needed. Ask the physicians."

"This is the work of commoners. You are a royal princess. There is a decorum you must maintain. As royalty, we must carry ourselves in a manner that precludes us from getting too familiar with them. An aura of mystique must surround us so that people look up to us in awe and reverence."

To some degree, that may be true, and I would have concurred with him if we were in a conventional circumstance, but our situation was far from normal, and I based my actions on necessity rather than niceties of protocol.

"I'm not doing anything that jeopardizes our standing with our people, Deiphobus. If you don't like it, talk to Father."

"You are the only member of our household here. That ought to tell you these chores are inappropriate for your station."

"Go away. You're interfering with my work."

"I insist that you go back to the palace. Leave this work to others."

Now he offended me, mainly over his presumption that he was the master ruling over me, exercising an authority beyond his realm of powers. Age alone did not grant him dominance over me. Only the title of king could do that.

"You insist?" I snapped at him. "Just who do you think you are? Priam—not you!—rules in Troy. I've helped before, and no one ever objected to it. The physicians are grateful for it. Only you, being the insensitive brute that you are, oppose it."

"You insufferable slut," he snarled in typical fashion, resorting to profane insults when things did not go his way. "There will come a day when you will sorely regret ever having crossed me."

"What will you do to me? Strike me as you did Helen?"

I could see the fires raging within him and momentarily worried if I had not overstepped my bounds. A problem existed when assailing a man's sense of self-importance, his vanity, and I knew I was subjecting him to severe provocation. This was not my intent. Sometimes I wished I could better control my acerbic tongue.

"She had it coming," he said, calming down a bit. "As will you one of these days."

"Talk to Father about me," I told him, trying to amend things with him. "If he shares your view that what I'm doing here is wrong, he will tell me, and I will stop. But until then, I feel my services are useful and wanted."

"I'll do that," he replied, tiring of my recalcitrance or perhaps respecting that I afforded him an exit from his obstinacy. Either way, I was glad to see him depart and continued to perform the duties I was assigned by the doctors. Perhaps I should be more concerned about my disagreeable encounter with my brother, but for some unknown reason, I had difficulty in regarding him as inimical to my well-being. Was this wise? If he could actually hit Helen, the obsessive love of his life, what was to stop him from venting his fury on me? I simply could not conceive of Deiphobus as king of Troy, a notion so preposterous it defied contemplation, and that I should disregard any threat I faced from him. That may have been a grave mistake, but at present, I doubted it.

As the day's casualty count was calculated, the true magnitude of the carnage unveiled itself, not for the numbers that were slain, but rather, the important personages who had met their fate. We received word that Neoptolemus had killed Prince Eurypylus, commander of one of our major allies, the Mysians. Later, we learned that he had also killed the Phrygian leader, Coroebus, Cassandra's lover—*Oh, no, the news will crush her*—in addition to several other high-ranking allied officers. He certainly gave a formidable account of himself in his first major battle, and we may have underestimated his importance to the enemy's effort. The son of Achilles obviously possessed his father's prowess in warfare. We lost Eussorus, commander of the Thracians; Mygnon and Otreus, both Phrygian commanders; Epistrophus, the leader of the Halizonians; and Antiphus, a co-commander of the Maeonians, all leaders of our allied contingents. Among our own forces, we lost Medon, Orthaeus, and Polydamas, major captains who could scarcely be replaced. A brutal day by any measure, ending in another stalemate, serving no useful purpose for anyone.

Certainly, the day could not have been any easier on the Greeks, although we received no reports about which of their major commanders had fallen. What must have shocked them most, as it did us, was that an unplanned, disorganized, and unanticipated minor confrontation should evolve into a battle of greatest proportions, leading to the loss of so many noteworthy and high- ranking officers. They had to be likewise concerned with the control they exercised over the situation, that things should slip so violently and unmanageably from their grasp, to assume a life force of its own, unregulated and unconstrained. I think this, more than anything else, was what alarmed and frightened our leadership. They exercised no command over the events that descended on them and magnified in intensity, reaching beyond the conceptions of their tactical plans.

Fortunately, no one in my immediate family was a casualty on this day. I became ever more worried over how my parents would cope with additional setbacks and was relieved that none presented itself this time around. In fact, the reports coming to me applauded the valor of Deiphobus who had slain many of the enemy warriors and distinguished himself in the battle, so did Polites and my more distant brothers, namely, Agathon and Pammon, all giving a credible performance of courageous and heroic action. I thank the gods they are still with us. They provided the comfort my parents needed in these trying times.

The same could not be said for my sister. When the news of Coroebus's death reached Cassandra, she was so disconsolate, wailing and tearing at her hair and pacing aimlessly to and fro, that no one was able to provide relief to her agony. I was torn with remorse in seeing her extreme grief, afraid to say anything, because it might only add to the misery she felt, unsure how to give voice to the tragedy. She was at an age when suitors were increasingly harder to come by, and to lose one of them portended a lonely, singular life, undesirable for anyone, even if a priestess. When I chanced to talk to her outside the Temple of Apollo, I tried to give her my condolences as best as I could, perhaps being awkward in my effort, as I was never assured of what was the proper approach in these matters.

"I'm so sorry, Cassandra," I said, deeply distraught.

She glared at me, her intense anguish visibly pronounced in her face.

"What do you know about it?" she groaned. "No one can feel my pain, the severity of it."

That was not fair to me nor to Andromache nor Helen. We had all undergone the horror and despair of losing someone dear to us, the terrible suffering that it entailed, being unable to find relief for it. We knew about it. All too well. But I was not going to make comparisons for Cassandra. The grief she felt was now, ours had passed, and she was the one who presently needed comfort. By saying "passed," I did not mean to suggest we had gotten over it. That will never happen, especially when we recall our loves in our mind. But if we avoided thinking about it, we could suppress our torment to the point that we can surmount our loss and go on with our lives. Coping with grief did not come easy for me, whether my own or someone else's, and my sister's current sorrow touched me deeply. I could not hold back my tears as I spoke with her.

"I know about love," I said in my broken voice. "I'm no stranger to it. I was loved once. I know how much it can hurt."

She peered directly into my eyes, silent for the moment, and then burst forth in convulsive sobbing, unable to control her emotions.

"Oh, Polyxena," she said amid her weeping. "Please forgive my callousness. My own loss makes me lose sight of my better judgment. What am I to do? I shall never meet another Coroebus."

She probably knew this, being the seer she was. This placed me in a quandary over how to respond in a way that provided solace for her.

"Nor will I ever find someone to replace my fallen love," I said. "It's a sorrow we must bear, difficult as it is."

She understood, and while I don't think I alleviated her distress by any significant amount, when we parted, she was somewhat quieted, at least, the intensity of her anguish seemed less intrusive. Still, she was a pitiable figure, and I truly was affected by her despondency, finding it hard to keep from crying. And I am saddened to say this, but I was never again to see Cassandra smile.

After such key losses in that last battle, it was to be expected that another respite would mark the ensuing days, and that indeed was the case. Neither side demonstrated an inclination toward more fighting, at least for the present, as each assessed the damages incurred and, hopefully, the fruitfulness of sustaining its operations. With all sincerity, I wished that was happening, but I had no way of actually knowing this and could only speculate upon my desires. Obviously, I was pleased to have a lull in effect. Life resumed a more casual semblance, making everything nicer for us. I spent most of the next two days still attending to the wounded, doing my part for Troy, as I rationalized it, and appreciated not having any interference in work I thought important.

On the third day, I decided I needed to take Zephyrus for a ride, not merely for his sake, but for mine as well. While I waited for the corral attendant to bring him to me, Deiphobus strode up to me, looking rather pleasant instead of exhibiting the usual disapproval he held for my activity. He was difficult to gauge, his composed exterior often masking a turbulent inner nature that could explode in an instant, and I alerted myself to be prepared for that so I might not be surprised if the worst was to happen.

"Riding again, I see," he said.

"Will you stop me?"

"No. It wouldn't do me any good. You'll do it anyway, stubborn as you are. I just want to say be careful. Enemy observers are everywhere."

What was this? Niceness coming out of Deiphobus? I was not about to let this moment go by without comment.

"Why, thank you, Deiphobus," I said, smiling. "I'm glad to see that you care for me."

"Don't make too much of this, but I did want to apologize to you."

"For what?"

"Father agreed that your work with the wounded was good for our household, that you endeared yourself to our people, and he approves of what you're doing. I was wrong."

This concession had to be awkward for him, as it countered his nature, which precluded him from admitting that a woman could ever do the right thing. Yet I appreciated the gesture and strove to further amend the strain that had marred our past association.

"As we are in a complimentary mood," I said to him happily, "let me say that I have heard of your daring feats in our last battle, your bold leadership and courage. I'm impressed."

A faint smile came to Deiphobus. He was obviously flattered by my words, and justifiably so, I thought, for my praise was sincerely based.

"I must say, Sister," he said, "you excel in making a person feel good about himself. Kudos are nice."

"They are. But you did well, Deiphobus, and deserve recognition for it. Even Helen was proud of you."

Now his morale was sky high, greatly in evidence by the smirk on his face that almost had me believing I was laying on the acclamations too thick. My intent was not to fuel his vanity, although, in this case, he probably merited it, but why shouldn't I? Certainly, it made me feel better to be on a more cordial footing with my brother, and that had its own rewards. Amity was far preferable to animosity. By this time, Zephyrus had been brought to me. Deiphobus even helped me mount him by cupping his hands so I could lift myself more easily upon him.

"Are you going to ride along the shore?" Deiphobus asked.

"I'm hoping to run into Neoptolemus. Father wants me to extract information from him that might be useful to us." I had no need to identify the Greek other than by name. He had left such an indelible mark on our forces in his initiation to combat that everyone knew of him.

"He wants you to be a spy?" Deiphobus said, astounded.

"Well, not exactly. Father believes I should take advantage of his infatuation with me to grill him into revealing details about Agamemnon's plans. I'm unclear how to proceed on this, but I find the whole idea intriguing."

"What makes you think he's enamored with you?"

"He convinced me. He asked if he could see me again last time I saw him. I've only seen him once before, but that was enough to draw my conclusion about him."

"What faith Father has in you. You enjoy doing men's work, don't you?"

In honesty, I never saw it as work confined exclusively to the male gender; rather, I viewed it as in the best interest of Troy. Whoever performed it was inconsequential. Yet I admit that, as a woman, I possessed a distinct advantage that was not transferable to men. Being the object of a man's love afforded me a leverage that, if used smartly, enabled me a means to extract the information I was after. With sufficient cajoling and guile, a man in love was likely to fall for my charms and manipulations to tell me things not intended. I felt reasonably confident that I could hold Neoptolemus under my sway.

"I enjoy doing something productive in service of Troy," I answered. "Father trusts me. I love that. His confidence in me is inspirational. It helps my self-esteem."

"Yes, I can see that. Just the same, watch yourself. Unforeseen dangers abound in doing this sort of work."

"Wish me success, Brother," I said as I prodded Zephyrus into a steady trot away from the Pergamus, leaving Deiphobus standing there looking after me. He was not the man I feared for the most part, not on this day anyway, and I found him relatively engaging. In actually revealing a regard for my safety, he did a lot to soften the hard image I retained of him and made me fairly willing to forgive all his previous transgressions involving me, but not entirely. I demurred in accepting him as a sudden reformed person ready to let bygones be bygones who now saw me in a positive light. I needed more time before taking that plunge. Also, at this moment, my concerns dwelled on my anticipated meeting with Neoptolemus. What would I say to him?

At first, I did not see Neoptolemus, even though I had galloped for some distance along the coastal stretch between our walls and the Greek encampments. I was thinking this was just as well, for the more I envisioned our meeting, the less confident I became over whether I could credibly pull off a convincing performance as an inquisitor, for that is the role I would be playing. Finally, I discouraged myself enough that I no longer felt up to the task. Instead, I decided the best course at present was for me to return to Troy and forget about any ideas of patriotic duty and helping our cause. I was about to goad Zephyrus into a speedy run when I heard a voice calling out to me.

"Polyxena. Stop, Polyxena!"

I turned Zephyrus about and saw Neoptolemus approaching me at full gallop on his scraggly mount. I waited until he arrived, my earlier worries dispelled from my mind as I was now in his presence.

"I knew you would come," Neoptolemus said, gleaming. "I'm so thankful."

"Let's keep this in perspective, Neoptolemus," I said. "These are regular excursions for me. I'm just glad that I can resume them after what has happened."

"You're not happy to see me?"

"I didn't say that. But I don't want you to make more out of this than is appropriate."

"So you are pleased to see me," he concluded, grinning widely. "I want you to know I really missed you."

"Did you?"

"Very much. I'm worried that I may not see much more of you, if Agamemnon has his way. In spite of our victory the other day, he deems it a loss. I'm not sure why?"

He alluded to a significant change in the offing. Unbelievable. He openly declared as much with me not having to apply the slightest exertion in squeezing it out of him. This would be easier than I imagined.

"Well, he should," I replied. "You had no victory."

"What's this you say?" he reacted angrily. "I drove back the Mysians. I killed Eurypylus, their commander. We beat them."

"That's happened countless times before. Yet Troy stands, as do its allies. They will regroup and face you again."

"No, I won the battle. I saw it."

"You did not. Your Myrmidons may have driven the Mysians from the field, but they will again oppose you. Nothing has changed. That's the way this war has been fought for the past few years. Agamemnon is correct in saying the battle was a loss, for both sides. Nothing is gained in a stalemate."

He had difficulty in accepting that, and I expected him to shout out his denials, but instead he turned introspective, hashing out in his mind the reality I unfolded on him, a disbelieving look in his eyes. He still had a lot to learn.

"So you say all my efforts amounted to nothing," he moaned. "My dreams are shattered."

I can't say that his lamentations touched me. He seemed to fail in grasping that he was speaking to an adversary, although, from his continuous stares, he may have thought otherwise and that I found no thrill in having him expound his heroics to me. But he said something earlier that caught my attention, and I meant to have it clarified for me.

"Why did you express worry about seeing more of me?" I asked.

"Agamemnon is fed up. The older veterans are clamoring to return to their homes, to see their wives and children. They're worn out. They have no more stomach to keep the war going."

I could scarcely contain my excitement. At last, at long last, there was hope that the war was going to end.

"You mean they're going to leave?" I said, wanting absolute assurance I had heard him correctly.

"He's talking about it."

Oh, blessed joy! News we so long yearned to hear. News my father would absolutely relish.

"With all my heart, I wish this to be true," I said.

Neoptolemus's face blanched. My displayed exhilaration over the prospect of the Greeks leaving did not please him.

"But that means we may never see each other again," he moped. "You act as if you like that."

"I want this war to be over," I replied.

"Even if it means we'll forever be separated?"

I became alarmed. He was reading far more into a relationship that I believed casual at best. Relationship? We had no relationship. We were not even friends but only two people who had met once before and struck a temporary accord with each other. Nothing more.

I had to dispel any notions of romance, which is what he obviously considered in me, that possessed him, but I did not know how. If I cut it off abruptly, in a harsh manner, I ran a chance of invoking his hostility, which was undesirable at this time, mainly because I might still have need of his openness to me as a source of acquiring extra information. His was an unrequited love. I had no amorous regard for him, and that posed a delicate situation for me. If I led him on, pretending I loved him when I did not, it would one day explode in our faces and lead to extremely hard feelings. What was I to do? I determined that honesty was the prudent approach.

"You worry me, Neoptolemus," I said, mincing my words. "You're a Greek. As a Trojan, I have different aspirations. Do not get too personal in your association with me. I see you as a potential friend and request you see me in the same context. Don't delude yourself into believing anything more than that."

His demeanor hardened. He took offense to my words, but I think he repressed his agitation as best as he could, although his glaring eyes made his discontent apparent.

"By your own admission, you loved my father," he said, his face flushed. "Your different aspirations, as you call it, posed no encumbrance for you with him."

"We understood each other," I reacted harshly. "We recognized that an uncommon destiny guided our paths. Achilles believed all along that his destiny was to fall at Troy. Our love was conforming to our present passions. We made no long-lasting promises to a future neither of us had confidence in."

"Why can't you grant me the same concession you gave my father?" he entreated. "That's all I ask."

"It doesn't work like that. Aphrodite manipulates us. She concocts the feelings we develop for one another."

I desperately wanted our meeting to be over, fearing that he was going to erupt into an outburst of uncontrollable rage. My tenseness was heightened by his intense stare bespeaking his inner turmoil. I prepared myself for prodding Zephyrus into a full gallop should things get out of hand.

"You're going to be mine," he fumed. "Deny it as much as you like, but someday, you'll come crawling to me, wanting me. Make no mistake about that." His face was ablaze, matching the color of his hair.

The nerve of him. Who did he think he was? His talent was in offending people, and he was succeeding admirably in that. I had no desire in protracting our conversation and chose to terminate it. At this point, it mattered little to me if I was being tactful or took care in my regard to his sensitivity.

"How dare you!" I angrily denounced him. "You have no claim on me. You are fantasizing a romance that does not exist. Be cautioned, Neoptolemus. That can only lead to tragedy."

"Forgive me," he hastily recanted. "I was wrong to say that. I didn't mean it. Tell me you accept my apology."

"I think I had better l have," I concluded. "Good-bye, Neoptolemus." I turned Zephyrus toward the Scaean Gates.

"Wait. I said I'm sorry. What more do you want?" His mercurial shift in temperament was of extremes, first utterly irritated, then greatly elated, then back. He truly alarmed me.

"I want you to get a grip on reality. You have created an illusionary affair between us that is mainly in your imagination. There is no romance here."

"All right, I agree, but we can still be friends, can't we?"

Friends? Can I accede to that without rising his expectations to levels belying our truthful association? My situation was problematic. If I disallowed this minimal imposition on me, I precluded any possibility of future contacts with him, which may not be to my benefit. I had obtained useful information from him. And despite his impertinence, he was not altogether so offensive that I should avoid him entirely. Who can know what destiny has in store for us?

A friend among the enemy may one day have its importance. Yet his evident fascination with me had troublesome aspects to it. He might misinterpret my gesture of courtesy as having far greater significance than was appropriate, accelerating a threat I was already facing. Is it possible to reduce infatuation to mere friendship?

"Yes," I concurred, reluctantly. "We can be friends."

A broad grin lit up his face. Admittedly, he appeared substantially more appealing when he smiled.

"Shall we meet again, as friends?" he asked.

"We'll see," I answered as I urged my horse into his gait. The relief I sensed as I rode off was overwhelming, outweighing all other considerations, and that was probably not a good sign. It suggested that my immediate impulse was to shun him, but then I remembered that a similar reaction met me when I first saw Achilles, and look what happened there. But then, Neoptolemus was not Achilles. He possessed none of his father's magnetism or his physical beauty or his charisma, and I seriously questioned whether he could ever be more than just a friend to me and then not even a good one. The fact that I was more nervous about having met him this second time than in my previous encounter did not portent any improvements being in store for us. So as I headed back to the Scaean Gates, my resolution was to not visit him again.

A great commotion met me when I entered the Pergamus. Father was in a near frantic state, his alarm extending to several of the other members of the family, including my mother. Something serious had happened.

"What's wrong?" I asked, their anxiety bouncing off me.

"Someone has stolen the palladium," Father exclaimed.

"You mean the statue of Goddess Athena?" I only had a vague conception of what this denoted. As it was once explained to me, the palladium was a wooden sculpture, in size, coming up to my shoulders, of Athena, or was it her friend, Pallas, whom she had accidentally slain? I couldn't remember. At any rate, it somehow came into the possession of Ilus, founder of our city, who built a shrine to Athena and placed it there. A sacred object, the palladium was said to come from heaven and was not created by mortals. It was guarded by our leaders from one generation to the next. Strangely enough, I don't have a clear image of it. I remember having seen it once as a young child but never since then, as it had always resided in an inner chamber of Athena's sanctorum. Only her priests had access to it.

"Who would dare?" my father asked himself. "No one in Troy would do this. But how could the Greeks get in here? It had to be them."

"Maybe Cassandra can tell us," I said.

Father dismissed the idea, waving his hand away from him, as did the others, not deeming it worthy of pursuit. Instead, he bemoaned the loss as a dire circumstance that proposed drastic consequences for us, and he was profoundly disturbed over this.

"We are in trouble," he groaned. "Athena's protection over us is compromised."

Not to disillusion my father, but the general consensus among our augurs was that Athena was in the Greek camp, favoring them over our Trojans, and if that was the case, I saw no reason to despair over the palladium being carried away.

"I always thought it was Apollo who protected Troy," I said.

Father peered obliquely at me, as if in recognition of the contradictory nature of Athena's blessings, which I alluded to.

"It is," he declared. "Yet on the subject of gods and goddesses, we are better off acknowledging all their contributions rather than placing our trust in but one of them. Don't you agree?"

"I suppose, Father. But it seems Athena's contributions are dispensed in greater proportions to the Greeks than Troy, according to the majority of our priests. If that is so, why fret over the theft of the palladium?"

I spoke heresy, I knew this, but at the same time, I believed there was a legitimacy to my question. I really could not comprehend all the fuss that was generated over the palladium's pilferage, but I may have naïvely perceived this, being ignorant in many of the matters relating to our deities. My father, interesting to say, was significantly mollified of his fears after hearing me, even flashing a smile at me, and expressed a mild amusement over my befuddlement.

"It's just that we have always borne that responsibility," he answered. "We have assumed we are obligated to guard it. Tradition, you know. Nobody can conceive of us not doing this."

"If you have time, Father, I need to speak to you in private." My entreating eye struck an immediate chord with him. He responded by looking about the room, as if in a pause over how to make an unobtrusive exit without alarming anyone further. He then directed me to follow him into the council hall, currently not occupied, and together we strode from the residence area, to the annoyance of everyone there, mainly my mother who, I suspect, gathered that I had been on another of my "unauthorized" rides. In the hall, Father took his place in his royal seat while I stood in front of him.

"Go ahead, Polyxena," he motioned. "What news have you?"

"I met with Neoptolemus. He mentioned something noteworthy. He said that he may not see me anymore if Agamemnon has his way. When I asked him what he meant by that, he told me Agamemnon is considering withdrawing. He says the old veterans have lost their stomach to continue fighting and are pressuring him to give up their cause."

Father was dumbstruck. For an instant, he sat openmouthed, staring blankly into the wall behind me, as if I were not there. Disbelieving me initially, in a remarkble transformation, he ran the emotional gamut from despair to jubilance, still finding my word inconceivable.

"Can this really be true?" he asked.

"Neoptolemus was frustrated over hearing it, resenting that the subject should even be considered."

"The impetuosity that comes with youth. Bless you, Daughter. You've made this old man very happy. Happy indeed. But why tell me this in private? Shouldn't these news be shared by all?"

"I was afraid, just in case I may have drawn an erroneous conclusion, that I might raise false hopes. I wanted to be sure you agreed with my assessment."

"Oh, I do. Indeed so. But your prudence is wise. Let me think it over before revealing it to anyone else. Keep it to yourself for a while longer. Let me be the one to decide."

I nodded my consent. If my mother ever discovered that I was having liaisons with the enemy, I would never hear the end of it, even if Father approved of it. Fortunately, as far as I knew, Cassandra had not mentioned this to the others. But Deiphobus now also knew. Was I deluding myself in thinking Mother was not aware? Still, it was better if Father disclosed the news. He had the authority lending greater credence to his words.

"Will you see him again?" Father asked. I shuddered over the prospect.

"I don't think so," I replied. "He scares me. He assumes I should love him because he loves me. If I see him again, he's sure to misconstrue it. I don't want to add to his delusions."

"Perhaps one more time, Daughter," Father urged. "To learn who stole the palladium. He might be able to identify them."

"So what if we knew them? Can we do anything about it?"

"Probably not, but I need to discover why. I suspect Helenus had something to do with it. Only he could have told them where we housed it."

I still did not comprehend why this mattered anymore. Helenus had defected from us. No amount of information he related to the Greeks was going to change that. But if Agamemnon truly considered leaving, why did this have relevance? Yet here was another test of my skills thrust upon me, and that had an enticement all its own, one more challenge presented to me. And on top of everything else, I was infused with a personal curiosity over who the culprits were who absconded with our sacred object.

"All right, Father," I finally yielded to his request. "One more time. Just for you."

His delight was pronounced, marked by his ebullience, and had its contagious effect on me, pleasing me that I held such prominence in his scheming, convincing me I was performing useful work for Troy. When we returned to the residence hall, only a few of the original members remained, among them Mother, Andromache, Helen, and my brothers, Deiphobus and Polites. Father called on the men to accompany him to the outer court of the Pergamus, leaving me alone with the women.

"You've seen the Greek, haven't you?" Mother said.

I glanced at her and noticed her dismay. There was no point in denying it. I was not about to lie above all my other transgressions.

"Yes," I answered. "I'm sorry."

"Your sorrow is plainly seen in your tears," she sarcastically retorted. "When will you stop this foolishness? Priam is wrong in assigning you men's work. I'm going to have a long talk with him."

"He wants me to see him once more."

"This nonsense has to cease. You are a woman. Riding alone along the beaches has inherent risks. I'll not have my daughter endangering herself. You could easily be taken for ransom, or worse, raped."

"I'm safe enough when a truce is in effect, Mother, else I would never chance it. Where is Cassandra?"

"In Apollo's temple, where else? I hardly see her since the death of her suitor. She avoids me."

"Not intentionally, Mother. She is taking his loss badly. I tried to console her, but I'm not sure I succeeded."

My mother was deeply touched, with her eyes moistening, her concern over a daughter coming to the forefront. She did love us in spite of her objections to our independent nature, which she often blamed on herself.

"Why endure grief in silence?" she asked. "Wouldn't it be better for her if she spent more time with us? In togetherness, we find the comfort we seek."

"That may be true, but sometimes we don't see it that way when adversity strikes us. We think we don't want to burden anyone else with our sorrows."

"It's hardly a burden relieve someone's depression. I see it as compassionate."

"There may be an embarrassment in it."

"How can that be?" she questioned herself, I think, more than me, legitimately puzzled.

"Cassandra feels she has lost her one chance at true love. At her age, additional suitors are unlikely to come for her. She is reluctant to confide this in anyone and yet realizes everyone actually knows this. She's embarrassed that she might be an object of pity or scorn, neither of which she wants."

Mother just sat there in a somewhat stunned comportment. I think what surprised her was that I told her about an aspect of Cassandra's tribulations that she herself had overlooked or not considered. Whatever the reason, my observation quieted her, although she continued her penetrating gazing at me.

"She told you this?" Mother asked after a considerable pause.

"She didn't have to," I answered. "I saw it in her. Her apprehensiveness was alluded to in speaking to me."

"Well, you could be wrong, Polyxena. Sometimes we misread these things, although I do admit your assessment may have an element of truth. At least you have spoken to her since then. I can't say that for the rest of us."

I detected a legitimate worry in my mother. She was quite teary eyed, despite a show of outer calmness, and in her disquietude, I acquired a sudden feeling of tender regard for her. She was not the cold, insensitive mother I too frequently beheld her as. Her care for us was heartfelt and sincere. A mother's love for her daughters, that is what I was seeing, and I was deeply touched by this.

"Are you going to see Cassandra?" she then asked.

"I am," I said. "I have to discuss something with her."

"I'm glad you are talking to her, Polyxena," she said. "Perhaps you can convey to her the message that I also long to speak with her."

"I will, Mother," I replied as I rendered her a loving smile, to which she responded in kind. On reaching the doorway, I looked behind to see Andromache and Helen rushing to Mother's side in an apparent attempt at alleviating the downcast spirit that all at once overcame her. She had broken out in open weeping.

When I came to the Temple of Apollo and entered its dark interior, I was met by Cassandra cloaked in a black robe, her hair disheveled and looking utterly forlorn, although I think she was actually pleased to see me, no doubt being much in need of talking to someone.

"You saw him," my sister spoke first. "You discarded my warning."

"I didn't mean to," I answered. "I'm drawn into situations despite my intentions, as if destiny is orchestrating my moves."

"Someone forced you to see him?"

"Well, not directly. Father did ask me to solicit information from him. I don't suppose that qualifies as a forceful situation."

"No, but it can be a subtle form of pressure on you, an imposition of sorts, if not an actual demand. I understand this."

"He wants me to see Neoptolemus again, but I'm afraid to."

"Because of my threatening words?"

"In part, but more because I had a less than desirable meeting with him. The man truly frightens me in a strange way. I can't identify exactly why. He's in love with me and expects me to reciprocate by loving him. I'm unable to do this."

"So you fear that your actions are inflammatory, giving rise to an expectation in him that is unwarranted, or misinterpreted," she concluded, her interest into my problem appearing to assuage her own despair to some degree.

"Yes. He makes inferences that alarm me. Not only are they presumptive, but invalid. I have done nothing to lead him to his conclusions, at least, I don't think I have, and yet he acts as if I were the cause of his conceptions, of our supposed love."

"Ah, an unrequited love on his part. You must be careful, Polyxena. My advice is to stay away from him. You should have done that last time. Why does Father want you to see him again?"

"He wants me to find out who stole the palladium. He thinks Helenus was behind it and that Neoptolemus might know."

"Helenus was behind it. He told Agamemnon that three conditions had to be met before Troy would fall. A bone of Pelops had to be brought here, the palladium taken from us, and, last, Neoptolemus had to come. All three conditions have now been met."

"Yet Troy stands. Neoptolemus suggested that Agamemnon is planning to leave. What do you know about that?"

"I suspect it is a ruse," Cassandra said.

"You're not sure?"

"I don't see everything. Some visions are very imprecise and even readily forgotten when I snap out of my trance, not much different from dreams in that respect. But I would not trust anything said by Agamemnon."

"Supposing he does leave, wouldn't that negate the three conditions Helenus spoke of?"

"Yes, it would."

"Well, then, it's just a matter of waiting to see if it happens," I said, relieved. "Do you know who stole the palladium?"

"No. I have to concentrate on that and, at present, cannot bring myself to do it. Coroebus still preoccupies my mind, a major distraction." She trembled as she said this.

"I know you want me to stay away from Neoptolemus, and I want to comply. But if I do see him, wanting to please Father, succumbing to the subtle pressures, as you describe it, will this be a problem for me?"

"The threat I saw was in him knowing you. As he already does, another visit won't make a difference one way or the other. Still, I think it's best that you avoid him altogether."

She implied that I was beyond redemption, not the most comforting of thoughts, and that I had taken the steps that spelled a future disaster for me. My inclination was to dismiss her as an alarmist, as everyone else did, but that did not rest well with me, for the seeds of doubt had been firmly implanted and could not be so easily dispelled. While she was amply cooperative, the terseness and soberness in which she responded left me feeling a coldness. Our conversing was very businesslike, without the warmth that marked the previous meeting. I contributed little to my sense of security by coming here. I even forgot to convey my mother's sentiment to her in my total self-absorption. Worse, as I departed, I fully expected to ignore her advice and do what I meant to do all along: see Neoptolemus.

Chapter XIX

T HE LULL REMAINED IN EFFECT the next day, permitting me to ride to our previous rendezvous spot, where I simple waited until Neoptolemus would arrive. My stay was of short duration. As soon as he espied my presence, I could see him getting on his horse, and he proceeded to approach me. As I watched him coming, a myriad of emotions gripped me, all of them adding to my consternation over whether I was doing a wise thing. For the most part, I worried that our get-together was going to lead to the same stressful result as before. How would I extricate myself from that situation when I invited it? Yet, inside me, I had an insatiable curiosity in discovering what Neoptolemus knew about the palladium. My inquisitive nature was getting the best of me, and soon, an eagerness replaced my reservations over seeing him. He met me with a bubbling smile extending from ear to ear.

"Hah," he exclaimed. "I knew you couldn't stay away from me. I just had that feeling."

The very thing I did not want him to think. I was off to a bad start.

"I came because I need your help," I said. "I need some information I'm hoping you can provide for me."

"Nice try, but I know it's untrue. You wanted to see me."

"Please, Neoptolemus," I entreated. "If you won't do me this favor, say so. I have other things to do."

"Can't you just once say that I am the object of your visit?" he reacted, disappointed. "It wouldn't hurt to be nice, you know."

I offered him a close-lipped, broad smile, meeting my obligation in courtesy. He looked altogether pleased in receiving it, as if I had implanted an actual kiss on him, surprising me. I was never going to be able to figure him out.

"All right," he said. "What is it?"

"Our palladium was taken from the Temple of Athena. Father thinks that the Greeks may have done this. Do you know anything about it?"

"Yes, I do."

He was stalling with me. I was not happy about that.

"Well?" I said. "Aren't you going to tell me?"

"Odysseus and Diomedes stole it. They entered your gates dressed as beggars during the day and remained until darkness. Your brother, Helenus, told them where it was located."

The suddenness in which he blurted out the information I sought took me aback. He was so easy. I could extract anything I wanted from him.

"One day, he'll pay for his treachery," I said.

"I like the man. We're quite good friends. There's something else that might interest you," he said and hesitated.

"Yes?"

"Helen saw them. She recognized them."

"What?"

"It's true. She raised no alarm, did not yell out. She was content to let them go. What do you say now of her loyalty to Troy?"

I could not believe it. Surely, he was lying to me. But why should he? That didn't make any sense. He had no motivation for deceiving me. If anything, he would try to please me with his honesty, to ingratiate himself to me.

"That can't be," I said, stunned.

"Deny it all you want, but both Odysseus and Diomedes will vouch for it. They said they were indebted to her. She allowed them to get away."

"Why would she ever do this?" I said, more to myself than Neoptolemus, unable to comprehend her actions.

"It's obvious why. She wants to make it clear her allegiance is still with us in spite of all that's happened. She's courting our favors in case Troy falls. She's no fool."

"I thought you said Agamemnon was considering leaving."

"He is. More than ever now. Yes, I know what you're thinking, why bother to steal the palladium if you plan to leave? It makes no sense, an exercise in futility if you ask me." He shook his head in his apparent confused assessment of the seeming paradox.

How was I going to tell this to Father? What would happen to Helen if he knew? Why should I care about her? This was very upsetting news. Not only was my confidence in her faithfulness shattered, but her actions presumed that Troy was going to lose the war. A total negation of the hopes we were clinging to. What was she thinking?

"I'm getting sick," I told Neoptolemus.

"Sorry to spoil your day."

"I have to get back. I need time to digest this."

"Are you going to tell Priam?"

"I don't know."

"Then do me a favor. I did not tell you this so Helen would get in trouble. Menelaus would kill me if any harm came to her, if he found out what I said. If you want to inform Priam about it, make sure you never mention what we discussed to anyone else. Will you agree to that?"

I was reasonably confident that Helen would not be censured over this, shocking as it was. Men were prone to forgive her for whatever transgressions she committed, eager to accept her apologies so long as they remained in her good graces. She had amazing power over them in that regard. I was more dismayed over the faith I had in her being so abruptly shaken for me. I had considered her a true friend. Now I did not know what to think.

"Did you hear what I said?" Neoptolemus asked when I did not immediately answer him.

"Oh, sorry. I'm lost in my thoughts. I won't tell anyone else. At this point I'm not even sure if I should tell Father."

"Well, whatever you decide, I hope it works out best for you."

A kind approbation coming from Neoptolemus. He could be considerate if he chose, and I was not immune to its effectiveness and quite willing to show my appreciation for it.

"Thank you," I answered. "I have to go now, think things through. I admit that I'm somewhat hurt by what you told me."

"About Helen?"

"Yes. I looked up to her. She was a friend. Good-bye, Neoptolemus."

"I'll see you again sometime, Polyxena." I heard him remark as I prodded Zephyrus into a gallop toward the Scaean Gates.

I wish he had not said that. The implication was that he controlled the circumstances under which that might occur, and I, at present, had no notion of such an event coming about. And yet I was gratified that our parting was on a better standing than last time. My fear of him had dissipated to some extent, and I was thankful for his information, even if it was troubling. Now I faced a more pensive situation: should I inform Father on what I learned? How can I shy away from this when it was he who prompted me to make my visit? Perhaps if I saw Helen first and got her side of the story, I might properly judge her and understand the reasons behind her actions.

Upon returning to the Pergamus, early for a change, I went directly to the residence hall after seeing to some private matters, where I was cheerfully greeted by the other women entering about the same time. My mother beamed widely on seeing me, pleased that I was there, and wasted no time in getting to the task at hand: today's project, the painting of vases placed in front of us by the palace attendants. I took my seat on a cushion next to Helen so that I might avail upon the opportunity to speak to her in private when we were done with our assignment. Unable to keep from glaring at her, I was scanning her face as if it could somehow reveal the cause of her duplicity to me. I overdid this, for she soon became self-conscious about it and tried to avert her own glances at me. I think she suspected that I knew.

"What's wrong with you?" Helen finally said. "You keep staring at me."

"I found out something today," I said. "I don't want to discuss it now. Can I see you in private after we're done here?"

Helen's eyes widened, and a perturbed countenance imbued her. She turned pale and failed in any pretensions at composure.

"All right," she said, her voice nearly trembling. "In my chamber."

She obviously was alarmed, perhaps resulting from the graveness in which I addressed her, and I'm sure her concentration on the lessons at hand suffered as a consequence, as did mine. I was in such eagerness to learn her side of the story that I likewise failed to pay due attention to my instructions. For both of us, this was going to be a prolonged ordeal. Soon enough, our distraction toward our project—I accidently tipped over the vase I was supposed to paint— was noticed by Mother who became increasingly annoyed over this until, at last, she was moved into giving voice to her objections.

"Polyxena," she suddenly snapped. "Is there anything about women's duties that might appeal to you?"

"What do you mean?" I asked.

"I can clearly see your lack of attention. It's apparent you are bored. Everything we do here bores you. You should have been born a son, not a daughter. All your interests seem to be those of men."

I heard giggles coming from the group. Andromache just smiled, but Creusa and Ilione could hardly keep from laughing.

"I can't help myself," I replied. "Blame it on Father. He spawned those interests in me."

"Yes, I see it. But I'm sure Priam had no idea his tasks given you imposed an irreversible condition. If he had, he would never have done it."

"I'm glad he did, Mother, despite the bad outcome."

Mother was not offended by this. Quite the opposite, she thought it amusing and responded with a warm glow, smiling broadly. I think she was at last reconciled to the fact that I was never going to fulfill her expectations at proper womanhood, but for the first time, I sensed a pride in her over that. She finally accepted me as an individual being.

"You may go, Polyxena," she said. "Do the things you like, but join us when you see us doing something engaging. I'm sure not *everything* we women do is abhorrent."

This was an exaggeration of course. Abhorrent was too harsh a description for my views on this matter. Under ordinary circumstances, I would have found the painting of vases stimulating. Only my anxiousness in speaking to Helen deterred me from enjoying the pleasures that might have been derived from today's session. But my problem was not solved by me alone leaving the group. Helen needed to come as well. As I rose to depart, my impulse was to ask that she go with me, but I hesitated, thinking that was out of line, and I questioned if I might not be better off remaining in the class as the time might pass more quickly if I occupied it doing something rather than nothing. Fortunately, Helen ended that problem for me.

"May I also be excused, Hecuba?" she asked.

"What's wrong, Helen?" Mother said.

"I'm not feeling well. Something I ate, I think."

"Yes, you do look rather pale. I suggest you get some rest. Let me know if you require the services of our physician."

What a relief, a temporary one. Now we were to have the tension-loaded face-off that disrupted our calm, and I admit to being very nervous as the two of us proceeded for Helen's chamber. How was I going to handle this without incurring hard feelings? I liked Helen a lot and had no desire to alienate our friendship, although my disappointment over her nefarious behavior was keenly felt. Once inside the chamber, I relaxed somewhat, the quietness and comfort of its interior contributing to an overall sense of security in that we were alone and could freely voice our concerns. She then extended her hand, beckoning for me to sit beside her on the cushions next to the window. We sat down. I saw Helen's chiton quivering before she took her place. She was clearly nervous.

"You found out," Helen spoke first. "That's it, isn't it?"

"About Odysseus and Diomedes?"

"Yes."

"Who told you?"

"Neoptolemus. Father wanted me to see him, to learn what happened. Oh, Helen, how could you let them just go?"

"It's not so simple, Polyxena. I have known them since childhood—Odysseus was one of my suitors—and as frequent guests in Sparta. They were close friends to us. If I had turned them over to the guards, they would surely have been executed."

"Not necessarily, Helen. As lords, we would more likely have held them for ransom."

"My mind did not think fast enough for all the possibilities when I saw them. I stumbled on them by accident as I walked about the Pergamus in the dark to seek relief in its solitude. All I could think of at the time was that two friends I had long known suddenly stood in front of me. I didn't know what they were carrying; they wrapped it in a blanket. When Odysseus placed his finger over his mouth, motioning me to be silent, his eyes shining, I was numbed into quiet obedience, under the shock of so abruptly seeing them."

I understood what she was saying and could relate to circumstances that might induce an inability to respond appropriately to a situation such as she described. In a way, I was glad it was simply this, what I saw as a normal reaction to that sort of unexpected encounter, and not the more sinister act of disloyalty that Neoptolemus alluded to. Her explanation seemed so credible to me that I was inclined toward accepting it wholeheartedly, yet an element of doubt arose to prevent me from doing so.

"They never told you what they were carrying?" I asked.

"No. Had I known it was Troy's sacred object, I would have sounded the alarm. No, I don't know. If you spotted Achilles within the Pergamus, what would you do?"

I had no definitive answer to that and recognized the quandary such a situation would place upon me. It astounds me how seemingly simple answers should evolve themselves into complicated entanglements of befuddlement and uncertainty.

"I can't answer that," I replied. "Rather, I wouldn't know until facing that problem."

"Then you understand predicament?"

"Yes."

"Since you say Priam sent you to Neoptolemus to find out what happened, are you going to tell him about me?"

I had to deliberate over this. I was so assured of Helen's probity that I was convinced that anyone else hearing her would be similarly persuaded. This led me to believe that no problem would ensue out of telling Father about what she had done, but I questioned the wisdom of this, thinking that even if there were a remote chance I might be wrong, the risk was not worth taking. Besides, Father wanted me to discover who did this, and this I did. There was no need to expound further on it. The important thing was that I believed Helen. In my mind, she had exonerated herself of any intentional betrayal.

"Probably not," I answered slowly. "Even if I did, he won't hold it against you. You know how men react to you."

Helen smiled, but not a smile of gratitude, I thought. Instead, her smile seemed to affirm the power she swayed over men in awe of her beauty. I may have been wrong in concluding this, but so it appeared to me.

"I thank you, Polyxena," she said. "Given another chance, I'll prove my loyalty to Troy."

What a strange thing to say. Was she implying that another such circumstance was likely to happen? I was making too much out of nothing, I said to myself. She merely meant that she would do the proper thing the next time, a simple promise of atonement.

"I'm glad I spoke to you first," I said. "You've erased the suspicions I had. Neoptolemus had me believing you cooperated in their escape."

"I can see how it can be construed that way, if by being stunned into silence is interpreted as cooperating. I assure you, my perceived assistance was unintentional."

"I believe you, Helen," I answered confidently, rising to leave. When I left Helen's chamber, I radiated in a glow of satisfaction, congratulating myself for not jumping to conclusions and having taken the step of seeing her first before anyone else, which might have caused me to inadvertently incriminate her. She was still my friend, as I was hers, and I delighted in the assurance of knowing this. I could not adequately explain why I felt this way. Was I captivated by her as men were?

That evening, when I met my father in our courtyard setting, I related my discovery to him. I told him about Odysseus and Diomedes being the culprits but mentioned nothing of Helen's part in the scheme. In typical fashion, Father concentrated on the more demonstrative aspects of the episode.

"Dressed as beggars, you say?" he remarked. "Troy has always been a rich city, and that wealth has extended to its citizens. Poverty does not exist, or is very rare, among them. You would think that, as beggars, they would have been conspicuous to our guards. I'm going to have to talk to their commanders."

"Maybe poverty is more prevalent now than before the war," I said.

"I haven't noticed this. Have you?"

"No, not really."

"They should have stood out. The guards are assuming the enemy is only going to appear clad in their armored military garb, ridiculous when you think about it. We must issue orders requiring them to search any person of suspicion, in dress as well as behavior. This was a clear lapse of responsibility."

"They were lulled into a false sense of security."

"More like into complacency. We'll take care of that. So Neoptolemus said that Helenus was behind it all. I curse the day I sired him. Did he know why?"

"No, but Cassandra did."

Father winced, and I immediately sensed that whatever I told him about Cassandra was going to be ill received, if not outright dismissed.

"All right," he said, "let's have it. What does she say?"

"She said Helenus told Agamemnon of three conditions that must be met if Troy is to fall. One of those was taking the palladium. She said stealing it fulfilled the three requirements."

"I know about Neoptolemus. What is the third one?"

"A bone of Pelops was brought here. I have no idea what that means," I shrugged.

A hesitation came to Father. He appeared to wrestle with his thoughts for a moment, then proceeded.

"Pelops was the conqueror of that region of Greece named for him: the Peloponessus. This was generations ago. He sired many notable heroes and was the great grandfather of the famed Heracles. He is highly revered among the Greeks. Perhaps for this reason, a bone of his is sought by them so the magic of his prowess and success might transform itself unto them. But how would Cassandra ever know about him? I have no recollection of ever telling her this."

"This confirms it, Father," I replied, eager to have him embrace my convictions. "She can see things."

He was not about to accept that, his negative regard for Cassandra overriding all other considerations. This amounted to compromising a long-held position that he was unwilling to change, something I was unable to grasp.

"I must have talked about Pelops," he said. "I just can't remember when."

I got the distinct impression that, as time went on, my father developed an increasingly greater disdain for Cassandra, and as a consequence, his intransigence in discrediting her words became more pronounced. It was useless for me to sway him from his persistence in deprecating her. I would never accomplish this. Trying to comprehend this was a fruitless proposition. Once an attitude is entrenched in someone, nothing can release its grip on him, and no amount of logic or persuasion will change his mind or deter him from thinking otherwise. This is what defined the relationship between my father and Cassandra. I had to concede to its reality and cease in my efforts to alter the condition.

"Did Neoptolemus say anything else about the Greeks leaving?" Father then asked.

"He thinks it's going to happen, now more than ever."

"Ah, you see, Polyxena?" Father sighed. "What worth are the three conditions Cassandra spoke of when Agamemnon plans to leave? It has no relevance."

"But Father," I reminded him, "she did not specify the conditions. She said Helenus did."

This gave my father pause. He stroked the beard of his chin with his hand and gazed at the floor, his concentration clearly discernible. In his contempt for Cassandra, he had already distorted what I told him earlier. I loved my father dearly, but I must say, he disappointed me at present with his prejudice.

"She is speaking for him," he said. "That does not confirm what he himself would say."

"Father," I exclaimed, getting flustered. "Neoptolemus also said Helenus told Odysseus and Diomedes where to find the palladium. How would he know this if it was not true? Helenus specified those conditions. I'm certain of it."

"No matter. We can dismiss it just the same," he determined, getting annoyed.

"But you told me you feared what Helenus prognosticated. You said he was accurate in his predictions."

He was becoming agitated over my persistence in pressing the issue. I could detect this from the frown he now displayed. I was upsetting the appeasement he obtained in presuming Cassandra's conjectures to be false, and he was not pleased over this, intrusive as it was to his presumptions.

"I think we've talked enough for one day, Polyxena," he next said, attempting to extricate himself from my incessant probing. "I'm weary. Perhaps also discouraged. I realize my tendency directs me into denying the things I do not cherish to hear. This is not good. As king, I should be open to sound advice and questions rather than seek an escape from what disrupts my tranquility or is unsettling to hear. A sign of age, I'm afraid. Forgive this old man his indulgence."

What a sad figure. My heart went out to him. I felt badly over my earlier disparaging thoughts, ashamed that I would ever even contemplate anything like that, and he had me at the verge of tears.

"Were Hector still with us," he went on, his mournful look deeply moving me, "I should have turned over the kingship to him by now. What a noble son I had in him. Even with Paris, I might have considered that.

But Deiphobus? Although next in line, he lacks the emotional stability for exercising such power. What am I to do?"

"What of Polites?" I asked. "Or Agathon? Pammon?"

"Polites is a mere youth. As Helenus taught us, we run grave risks when we make a unwise choice. As for Agathon and Pammon, they are not my sons by Hecuba. Old enough, to be sure, but a problem if I granted them a legitimacy superseding that of my in-laws. I would never hear the end of it."

"Deiphobus has changed as of late, Father. He has shown me he has a greater perception of his responsibilities, I think."

"True, but he always appears to be at the cusp to me, capable of losing self-control at any moment. I lack confidence in his judgment."

I found nothing in his statement that differed from my own views on my brother and may have been too optimistic in my estimations of him, but I was more willing, I suppose, to give him the benefit of the doubt. Would I have taken the risk of empowering him with the throne of Troy? Perhaps not yet, but probably in due time. In short, my assessment was close to the same as my father's.

"What of Aeneas?"

"Out of the question. I love the man. He is the most competent and best fit to rule. But that would mean the end of our dynasty. Troy would become a Dardanian city."

"Deiphobus is it then," I concluded.

"Do you see my problem? I am old, my bones creak, and I walk in pain. I long for a stress-free life. Yet I cannot surrender my leadership to anyone I deem incapable of ruling judiciously, with the wisdom and skill that's required."

"Oh, Father," I moaned, his predicament tearing at me. "I'm so sorry. The pressure I put on you. Forgive me."

He clasped me close to him, tears trickling down his face, his voice broken.

"In many ways, Polyxena," he said, gazing at me, "you are most able to rule. You question things, as people having true wisdom do, and you have compassion. I see an inner strength in you, the ingredients making a good monarch."

I rather enjoyed that compliment, although I doubted its veracity. I could not conceive myself as leading anyone, being too insecure in the astuteness of my judgments, as much of my actions derived more out of trial and error proceedings, I thought, than true insight. Yet I loved my father for thinking this, the confidence he had in me once more clearly exhibited, and that certainly is a boost to one's self-esteem. Am I admitting to possessing a vulnerability toward flattery?

When I left my father after our discourse, he seemed to be in a somewhat better frame of mind than on entering it. He smiled and winked at me before walking off warming my heart by his gesture. I was debating whether I should have said anything about Helen's role in the theft of the palladium, not really wanting to keep anything from Father, but I gradually accepted that my prudence was the proper course to take. With all the problems confronting him, what good could come out of adding an additional one on top of his other tribulations? I spared him the increased frustration this would have caused. I had done the right thing.

Tensions mounted in waiting for the Greeks to leave. Strange that this should be so, but by having the knowledge they meant to do this, its anticipation took hold of us, making things worse for us, the expectation becoming an unendurable imposition on our greatest desires. By this time, Father had informed the council members of what I learned from Neoptolemus, and their eagerness toward that end was difficult to keep under restraint. The question foremost in everyone's mind, I'm sure, was when. When would they leave? The possibility of them changing their minds was no longer considered, being too distasteful to even contemplate, now eclipsed with only wishes of their departure. This posed a significant problem for me. Should things not turn out as everyone now anxiously hoped, would I be seen as the ultimate villain in this cruel drama? The instigator of false promises? That notion was extremely disturbing for me, and I craved for something to happen, anything, one way or the other, so that I might be vindicated, absolved of the misguided declarations that led to our impatience.

As more days passed and no noticeable changes surfaced along our shores, I felt myself increasingly persecuted by feelings of guilt I felt over possibly misleading everyone. Even worse, I started believing that Neoptolemus may have intentionally deceived me and that I had foolishly fallen for his ruse in my naïveté, and this obviously ruffled me. How could he do this to me? I thought the man loved me. Was I also wrong in thinking that? My impulse was to meet with him again, a measure I had diligently avoided since our last encounter, but I was reluctant to, worried that he might once again draw unwarranted conclusions about my motivations over such a visit. I was losing sleep in my consternation over what went wrong. I had to do something. The anxiety was killing me.

Fortunately, the lull seemed to be holding, now in its fourth week, having lasted longer than all previous ones, giving further evidence of the enemy's aversion to continue the conflict and credence to Neoptolemus's intimations. I decided my only recourse was to confront him once more. Accordingly, I hastened to the corral and directed its keeper to prepare Zephyrus for my ride. As I waited on him, Deiphobus came by—was he waiting on me?—and stood next to me, his arms resting on the corral's wooden railing. I really was not in a mood to talk to him. I had to tell myself to remain calm and not let anything bother me.

"Going to see Neoptolemus?" Deiphobus asked.

"I have to," I replied, "even though I don't want to."

"Yes. I imagine you feel he's let you down."

"He should have been truthful or said nothing at all instead of instilling a nonexistent hope in me."

"You're taking this too personally."

"Can't you see how everybody glares at me these days? I detect their hostility. They're mad at me for my false reports. I don't blame them, but at the same time, it's not my fault. I just passed on what Neoptolemus told me."

"You only told Father, the sensible thing to do. You can't be held responsible for what he did with the information."

Has Deiphobus changed so much? His sympathetic overtures to me seemed quite out of character, and I confess to perhaps under-appreciating his effort, but suspicions still clung to me, and I may have held back in expressing this. Still, it warmed my heart that I had no more cause to regard him in a villainous context. He was definitely trying to be nice, and I ought to show consideration for that.

"Thank you, Deiphobus," I said, "for your kind words."

By this time, the corral keeper has brought Zephyrus to me, readied for my ride, and I stroked his face repeatedly before mounting him, again using my brother's cupped hands as a stepping stone.

We waved each other good-bye as I prodded Zephyrus onward. Prodded was too forceful a word for how I led my horse. All I had to do was pat him on the neck or smack my lips, and he received my intent. Occasionally, I rubbed him on the side with my lower legs. He seemed to understand instinctively what I wanted, giving me total control of him with minimal exertions. He was my joy, in appearance and action, the noblest animal in Troy. The other horsemen envied me whenever I rode by them, I was convinced of that. I suppose I could be accused of having a swelled head, but that was the feeling possessing me when on Zephyrus. It felt good.

I decided to make my usual circuitous route about the city, despite my impatience over meeting Neoptolemus, owing to the pleasure I derived from my riding, which always reduced my stress level and left me savoring the moment at hand rather than thinking about the many problems afflicting me.

When I arrived at the coastal strip, my path was blocked by a number of Greek sentries who had posted themselves in the vicinity. As this was an unusual situation, I grew alarmed, thinking I might be in trouble, and I cautiously approached them, walking Zephyrus in a slow gait, but ready to reverse him into a full gallop if I had to. The guards appeared as much surprised over seeing me as I was at seeing them.

"A woman," the man in charge said when I stopped in front of him. "What's a woman doing here?"

I was too intimidated to answer, especially when the rest of the soldiers surrounded me. My situation was suddenly extremely dire. I could easily be cut under, even though I was mounted.

"Speak, woman," the commander bellowed.

"I came to see the Myrmidon prince, Neoptolemus," I told him in as authoritative a tone as I could muster up in my predicament.

My words clearly registered in their faces. An immediate recognition focused itself in the commander's eyes, and the rest of the sentries uniformly backed off a bit. I breathed easier, my earlier worries somewhat dispelled.

"You're a bold one," the commander said. "But we know who you are. Still, you could have been shot. My archers are under orders to prevent anyone from coming here."

"Has the truce ended?" I asked. "It's always been safe for me to come here while we were under the truce."

"No, it's still in effect."

"So why am I being stopped "

"To keep you from coming any closer. Those are our orders. You'll have to turn back."

"I can't see Neoptolemus?"

"You cannot proceed," the commander emphatically declared.

My initial impulse was to just get out of this threatening situation as quickly as possible and consider myself lucky in my escape. Consequently, I was not about to ask him to send one of his men to fetch Neoptolemus, thinking this unwise. I had not dispelled my fears sufficiently enough to go about directing the guards what they should do. A woman placing such a demand on them was a major risk in itself.

"As you say," I told the commander. "Thank you for restraining your archers."

I smiled at the guards as I turned Zephyrus around. They responded in kind, flashing their wide grins at me, and appeared altogether cheerful over having engaged in this brief encounter with me. Women apparently were a rarity in their lives. While the lords and other top leaders may have seized their concubines, this privilege did not extend to the lower-ranking soldiers, and they undoubtedly missed seeing or talking to us.

In riding back, I pondered on why I should be prevented from coming any closer, and the reason for this dawned on me: the Greeks were making their preparations to leave and did not want anyone observing this. That had to be it. What other purpose could promulgate such an application of security measures? The realization gratified me in more than just one sense. I had discovered its truth without having to personally meet with Neoptolemus. In truth, I may have been fortunate in that regard. But at present, I was most eager to pass my conclusions on to my father so that he might share my excitement over this, as well he should, considering the restiveness this situation had imposed on him. I raced back to the Dardanian Gates at full speed, my joy boundless.

After getting back to the Pergamus, I searched for Father, wanting desperately to speak with him, and luckily caught up to him in a rare private moment when he was sitting by himself in the council hall. I stopped before its open front door, waving at him. Upon noticing my enthusiasm, he invited me in, and I related to him what happened along the shoreline this morning.

"Don't you see what this means, Father?" I beamed in my exhilaration. "They must be leaving. Why else would they stop me?"

Father was more composed over the news than I would have expected, perhaps because he had received one setback too many and was determined not to let another one disappoint him further. Yet there was a spark in his eyes, hinting that he believed my assumption to be correct.

"The gods be praised," he said, my enthusiasm spilling over to him. "That I should live to see this." Then his more cautionary side took hold of him again, reigning in the exuberance exhibited an instant earlier. "We must be sure of our surmises," he next said, "before we repeat past mistakes. Have you talked to anyone else about this?"

"Only you, Father."

"Let's keep this to ourselves for the time being, until the evidence positively confirms our conjectures."

Difficult as that might be for me, I concurred with the decision, not that I questioned my ability to keep things under wrap if I was conscientious about it, but rather, if in an unmindful moment of extreme bliss, I might inadvertently make allusions I would be asked to explain. The request was not as easy as it appeared on the surface. My emotions, as well as my voice, had to be kept in check. But for the present occasion, with only my father and me here, our jubilation was irrepressible, and we made no attempts in denying it to ourselves. How good it felt to see Father happy.

The inner pleasure possessing me when I left Father in the warmth of his rapture was indescribably rewarding for me. Our mutual agreement that I correctly assessed the meaning behind my brush with the guards made both of us giddy in our elation, and I never felt such contentment as when I walked from the council hall. I loved to see Father in good spirits, a sight so often lacking in my life. Its effect was contagious, filling my own consciousness with utmost satisfaction.

I should perhaps also say here that my relationship with Menodice had greatly improved in the past few weeks. I attribute this to the effort applied by both of us toward ironing out the conditions leading to the estrangement existing between us. The death of Achilles, even though occurring but five months ago, had been superseded by so many other happenings that it was becoming increasingly remote in my thoughts. I realized that I was attempting to revitalize a continuing fading recollection of him, and that awareness had me thinking of the futility inherent in such persistence. It had no more relevance to my present situation and was best discarded. Once I surmounted the inclinations that bound me to him, I found it easier to open up to Menodice, the barrier inhibiting me from doing this now removed. Our conversing became less restrained, soon acquiring the natural flow of earlier times, and we were again delighting in our company as a result.

For her part, Menodice abided my reservations without complaint and worked at pleasing me through her diligence and loyalty. She seemed to have overcome the resentment she once felt over my having dismissed her from my care, undoubtedly through the same conscientious effort that I applied in dispelling Achilles from my mind. I was happy to see an accord reestablish itself between us, mending our alienation and contributing to making both of us feel much better in the process.

CHAPTER XX

"T HEY'RE GONE," I HEARD A sentry shouting from one of the watchtowers flanking the Scaean Gates after the morning sunshine had illuminated the coastal shores, his outcry entering my chamber. "The Greeks are gone!"

"The Greeks are gone!"

Over and over these words reverberated throughout the city, spreading at lightning speed into its most inaccessible corners and reaching our ears within the Pergamus. I could not believe it. Was it really true? I hastily sprang out of bed, flinging a chiton over me, and rushed toward the outside wall, where other family members had already congregated. We instinctively directed our glances to the shore, scanning the beaches up and down. The ships were gone. But what fixed on our gazes was a strange site, obtrusive in its solitude as a singular object upon the emptiness of the strands: a sculpture of what looked like a horse, odd in proportions, standing upright in the distance. Even from our viewpoint, we saw that it must have been of extraordinary size up close, despite looking rather small at present.

"What can it mean?" I asked Father.

"An offering to the gods, I believe," he replied. "But why speculate on it? The beaches are ours again. Let's go there and see firsthand what it represents."

All of Troy's gates were opened—I think for the first time since the start of the war—and as we prepared ourselves to visit the enigmatic object, happiness and excitement defined our mood. I flung a shawl over my shoulders, the morning chill still encompassing us, and could scarcely withhold the exhilaration I felt in at last being able to walk freely about the seashore without fear. My exuberance was shared by everyone in the household. Even Cassandra, the most aloof in our family, got caught up in the frenetic atmosphere. We all wanted to roam at will outside the confines of our walls.

The opening of every gate symbolized our hard-won freedom, and the people took full advantage of it, flocking in droves from the city to frolic in the open space, along the beaches, breathing in the fresh, unimpeded breezes coming off the waters, enraptured in their exultance, a site nearly driving us to tears in our happiness. So many had given up hope that such a day would ever come again, and to now see it, what joy!

I walked beside Father in the direction of the statue that now loomed ever larger as we steadily approached it. All the members of our family came along, including Helen, Andromache, and Mother, despite the aches and pains she often complained about. With our group came also the chief priests and advisors that comprised my father's ministry and war council. Escort soldiers kept the populace from swarming over us, their formations clearing a pathway for us as we proceeded along. Finally, we arrived within the abandoned Greek fortifications and stood at the foot of the object that both mystified and intrigued us, even amusing us in the peculiarities of its dimensions. The statue was not by itself. A solitary Greek soldier, hands bound behind him and dressed in rags, stood under guard at its base awaiting us.

Clearly it was a horse, made of wood and shaped into an obvious representation of that noble animal, unmistakably a horse in anyone's eyes. Yet its proportions were strange to say the least, with overly thick legs, a somewhat bloated belly, and an irregular shaped head that seemed undersized for its body. I would estimate that it stood about the height of six, maybe seven men, no mean sculpture, making it the largest statue I have seen, even bigger than that of Apollo. For having been hastily assembled, it was surprisingly well constructed, its wooden planks securely fastened together by nails and twines without even the smallest aperture existing between them, a very solid piece of work. But Zephyrus it was not, resembling more the battle-scarred horse that Achilles rode, in a stylized sort of way, than any steed of consequence. An inscription was engraved on its chest; it read, "For our return home, we dedicate this thank-you offering to Athena." Father had correctly surmised the purpose of the statue.

"An appeal to Goddess Athena," brash Antimachus told my father, "to assure them a safe passage home."

"Appropriate that they should use a horse for that," Father said. "The symbol of Troy as well as the goddess."

"The owl is Athena's symbol," Cassandra corrected my father.

"Is it? I always thought it was the horse," Father responded, miffed over having his error announced. Cassandra said nothing more, sensing that Father was rather displeased over her intrusive remark. I also questioned Cassandra. Why would the Greeks thank the goddess with a horse if it had no relevance?

The lone Greek left behind was brought to my father. His demeanor was remarkably calm, considering he had been abandoned by his peers, and confidence exuded from him despite his predicament, which placed him entirely in our captivity.

"Who are you?" Father asked.

"I am Sinon, cousin of Lord Odysseus," he answered.

"Why is he bound?" Father addressed one of the guards. "Is a single man so threatening to you that you must tie him up?"

"No, lord," a guardsman replied. "We found him like this."

"Indeed? Well, cut him loose. He's no danger to us."

The guard hastily complied, using his sword to slash through the rope that bound the Greek's hands.

"Then they meant for us to take you," Father then said. "Why?"

"Not so, lord. They meant to kill me," Sinon answered. "I had offended Odysseus, as much as he offended me. He had slain Palamedes, my commander, whom I deeply admired, an act which I opposed, for which I incurred his wrath. He concocted a story, along with his conniving friend, Calchas, a seer, interpreting an oracle from Apollo as meaning that I should be sacrificed in order to ensure everyone a safe journey home. They fully intended to do this, but I managed to escape. I'm grateful your men found me."

"Why did Odysseus kill Palamedes?" Father's curiosity was insatiable.

"There was a long-standing animosity between them, going back to before the war, but I don't know exactly what spawned it. I was told it had something to do with Palamedes tricking him into getting involved in the war, which he wanted no part of."

"Odysseus did not want to get involved in our war?" Father said, much astounded.

"That's what they say. I don't know if it's true. All I know is that I had great respect for Palamedes, feeling honored to serve under him. I was outraged when he was slain and let Odysseus know it. That was a mistake."

How could anyone doubt Sinon's story? Being left on our shores, deserted and bound. He paid a severe price for antagonizing his master. I think Father took a liking to him.

"Such loyalty to your commander, very commendable," he said. "If it pleases my lord," Sinon said, "I should like to fight alongside your soldiers in defense of Troy. I have no more allegiance to the Greeks. They're my enemy as much as yours."

"That can easily be arranged, young man," Father beamed. "I shall see to it."

Our guards welcomed their new comrade-in-arms quite willingly, shaking his hand and congratulating him. Now that Sinon had satisfied everyone as to his sincerity, our attention focused back on the statue, and Father was interested in learning all about it, questioning the Greek to extract as much information out of him as he knew.

"Who built this?" he asked.

"Epeius, son of Panopeus, did. He's a skilled carpenter."

"Yes, I can see that, considering he erected it almost overnight."

"Our honor to Athena. We wanted to appease her wrath over what we had done so that she would not imperil our journey home."

I became suspicious over Sinon's phrasings. If he loathed the Greeks to the point of even joining our forces, why didn't he project this resentment to his expressions? Shouldn't he have referred to his former compatriots in a negative context, as enemies or as Greeks rather than as we? His loyalty appeared very intact to me, and it was not to us.

"What did you do to anger her?" Father asked.

"We stole her sacred image from your city. Some of our leaders reported that they saw fire coming out of its eyes."

"The palladium?"

"I believe that's what it's called. Calchas said we now had to sail home but had to build this horse first so that we would appease her anger."

But where was the palladium? Why hang on to it if it represented an irreverent act?

Overall, it seemed to make sense to us. Certainly, there was a coherence to it that we felt would be absent if it had been wholly fabricated. That he should know about the palladium was remarkable in itself. It's not the sort of thing that would be discussed openly among the rank and file, at least I didn't think so. But was he of low rank? His rags made that readily apparent. Something about him did not settle well with me. The ease in which he related his story suggested to me that he had been coached on, or maybe rehearsed, the words he spoke. A distinct uneasiness prevailed upon my sense, arousing my skepticism to the point that I no longer trusted him.

Didn't Father feel the same way? He gave no indication that he doubted anything in Sinon's story, especially when he spoke of the palladium as if it offered the proof of his veracity.

"What are we to do with it?" Father asked, glancing at each of us, solicitous of anyone's counsel.

"Burn it," Cassandra said emphatically. "The statue represents Troy's doom. Soldiers are hidden inside it."

"Be quiet, Daughter," Father reproached her and then turned to Laocoon, one of his chief advisors. "What do you say, Laocoon?"

"I'm with Cassandra on this," Laocoon said. "Destroy it where it stands. We are none the worse off for it."

"That is profane," Antimachus interjected in his booming voice. "A sacrilege. The horse is dedicated to Athena. As mortals, who are we to deny her this gift? She will vent her fury on us if we desecrate the honor rendered her."

At this point, Laocoon took a spear from one of the guards and walked underneath the statue's belly. With a strength I had no idea he possessed, he hurled the bronze shaft into the underside planking where it struck in a loud thud. Deathly silence. His action aroused near panic among the other sages, most notably Antimachus.

"Are you mad?" he angrily denounced Laocoon. "How dare you endanger us by your desecration? Athena will avenge herself for this."

Clearly his alarm was shared by several others in our group. You could see the fear in their eyes, and they mumbled among themselves in their agitation, affecting Father with their frightened countenance.

"That's enough," he cautioned them. "Calm yourselves. We must think this through and do what is proper."

He quieted the fearful sages, but I saw that he remained visibly shaken over Laocoon's rash act, evidently as worried over its potential aftermath as the others, and he gave the advisor a hostile glare denoting his disapproval. After some semblance of serenity was restored, he then directed his attention back to Sinon.

"Why was this horse built so large?" he asked.

"To assure its place on these shores, lord," Sinon answered. "Epeius wanted to make it large enough so that it would not fit through your gates."

"Rather presumptuous of him. What made him think that?"

"Calchas warned him that if the horse were taken into the city, the Trojans would invade our cities."

Father laughed when he heard this. While that was a plausible explanation regarding the statue's size, it obviously failed to take into account the exhaustive toll the long war had taken on everyone. Troy was in no condition to launch any kind of offensive operation.

"Calchas has an imagination," he said, "to think us as an aggressor."

"He is a seer of great repute, lord," Sinon replied. "I cannot question the nature of his visions. That's what he told us. He also said that if any Trojans harmed the horse, Athena's wrath would be directed against them, that Troy would be destroyed."

"We must protect it," Antimachus exclaimed.

Father was momentarily silent as he mulled over what he heard.

Sinon's story had all the aspects of logic and consistency to it and appeared to make a lot of sense. Clearly, the horse was not intended to be towed into the city, its dimensions precluding this, and yet it offered a tantalizing promise if we were to do so, that we would exact vengeance on the Greeks for what they had done, and while, at present, nobody knew how we could accomplish this, there were many in our city who relished that idea. And to top this off, we also incurred an obligation of sorts to assure the statue its safety. Sinon scored his points well, and that was precisely the problem, too well in my estimation. I walked over to Helen, wanting to solicit her opinion on all this.

"What do you think, Helen?" I asked her. "Is the story credible?"

"It is," she answered, "if you know about Calchas. He is a diviner of high regard, said to be flawless in his predictions. The Greeks, especially

Agamemnon, I've been told, will not do anything without his endorsement. That is the power he holds over them. Whenever he says something, everyone listens."

This was not the response I wanted out of Helen. Somehow I had the expectation she would cast doubts on Sinon, viewing him in the same suspicious regard as I did. She left me without a clue whether she believed him or not.

"And he told the Greeks to leave," Father interjected to remind us, apparently having overheard us. For a man his age, his hearing was remarkably acute.

Then an event occurred that left me confounded, mainly in the manner it was related to me and comparing this to what I saw. It seems during the course of our discussions, Laocoon and his two sons had moved to the water's edge, where the breakers struck the beach and set up a makeshift altar. I was later informed it was to make a sacrifice to Poseidon. I saw his sons wading in the water, thinking nothing of it, and shifted my glances back to Helen. I next heard a loud commotion coming from the people on the beach, and when I again looked there, I thought that the boys were getting too deep into the water, as they appeared quite a distance from the shore. I next saw Laocoon hastily entering the water in an apparent attempt to go after the boys. He was swimming out to them, but all disappeared under the waves. That was the last I saw of them. Much alarmed, I thought I had just witnessed three drownings taking place. I was speechless.

But that was not what happened, according to those who stood closer to them. The people around them continued their yelling and screaming. Panic-stricken, they rushed back to where the rest of us were standing and stopped before my father, their faces ashen and barely being able to speak.

"What is it?" Father cried out, startled by their frightened countenance.

"Laocoon, lord," one of the lot declared, gasping. "And his sons. We saw two huge serpents coming out of the water. They attacked his sons and crushed them. When Laocoon tried to fend them off, they turned on him and also killed him. Then all three were dragged out to the sea by the snakes."

"What's this you say? Laocoon killed by snakes?"

"We saw it, lord," another groaned in abject fear. "I swear before Apollo."

I could not believe it. But I had not seen it all. What I had witnessed was evidently the last portion of this episode, although I have no recollection of noticing any snakes there, nor would I have guessed that. Everyone stood aghast.

"This can't be," Father moaned.

"Athena's vengeance," Antimachus bellowed forth. "For throwing the spear."

I saw them in the grips of cold, unmitigated, horrifying fear. Not one of them cast an element of doubt over what had been related to them, even I was having second thoughts and wondered if I had accurately perceived what transpired, thinking that perhaps I had erred in my earlier assessment. Had Laocoon's death occurred in a more extended passage of time, no one might have made much of it, despite the cruel manner in which it descended upon him, but coming, as it did, within the briefest interval after he had committed his heresy upon the horse, the connection between the two events was not only compelling, but utterly convincing. End of discussion. No amount of reasoning or appeal to logic was going to deter anyone from the certainty of his persuasion.

To make a further claim on our actions, the sheer boisterousness and willpower behind the voice of Antimachus drowned out any opposition that might have yet asserted itself, and soon, everyone appeared to be of one mind on what to do next, openly declaring or nodding their consensus. My own hesitancy was overwhelmed by the magnitude of the assurances facing me, that I was unable to sustain the resistance I may have previously clung on to.

"Very well," Father determined. "Bring the horse into the city."

A hearty roar of approval resounded through our ranks, affirming the decision as popular and correct. Only four of us—Cassandra, Helen, me, and, interestingly enough, Deiphobus—withheld our applause and refrained from joining the multitude in its exultation.

Cassandra probably knew with exactness what this meant. I could only guess at Helen's or my brother's reason for their reservations. Helen understood the Greeks better than any of us, and this awareness may have contributed to her doubts. As for me, I did not have any trust in Sinon's story, thinking it contrived and too perfectly related to be true. His words lacked a spontaneity I would have expected under the circumstances. I had the gravest misgivings about Father's directive, an insecure feeling telling me something was wrong here, but I was unable to give proper description to it and feared, if I were to draw attention to it, I faced certain humiliation in being regarded a hysterical woman, perhaps even mad, as Cassandra.

As we walked back to our walls to get out of the way of the work crews, which would soon plunge upon us, Cassandra came up beside me, and we both proceeded in quietness, neither of us wanting to speak for the moment. Before long, however, the silence intensified rather than eased our suppressed discomfort and the need to speak prevailed over us.

"You're not celebrating, Sister," Cassandra said. "Like me, you sense we are making a big mistake."

I looked into Cassandra's eyes and saw her fears patently revealed in them. She was highly distressed, overcome with the deepest apprehensions of our impending doom. That is what I thought.

"I only feel it, Cassandra," I answered. "But I can tell from looking at you, you know what will happen."

"It's a curse. How more content I would be if I were as the rest of you. Ignorance has its rewards."

"Be honest with me. You don't really believe that."

"It does," she said, absolutely positive in her assertion.

"How? Knowing means you can prepare for things, thereby properly arranging for your safety, and future."

"But at what price?" she challenged me. "To be ceaselessly tormented with anxieties over whether you can alter things from happening or if they will occur just the same. To be deprived of hope that things might not come out as seen, to live in terror of not being able to stave off the inevitable. Tell me, Polyxena, where is the comfort in knowing what you cannot change?"

"I'm tormented with anxieties in not knowing what will happen, Cassandra. So what's the difference? Why is my insecurity over not knowing less than yours in knowing?"

"It's less because your ignorance gives you hope, and the promise that somehow things may not be as you believe. The certainty in seeing the future steals that from you. Yes, you can prepare for it and protect yourself and others—if they believe you—from it, but there is no relaxation in this. You agonize over it just the same."

I had some doubt if Cassandra was correct in her assertions, but I suppose that, given the choice, I probably favored remaining ignorant of the future as a better alternative to a clarity of it, especially if there was no way to alter its course. I guess it depended on whether one's future was good instead of terrible. Well, maybe not even then. Cassandra was right; I'm better off not knowing. Still, the temptation was present in apprehending if we faced a disaster over what we were about to do.

"Will this spell our doom?" I asked Cassandra.

She hesitated, as if grappling with her indecision over whether she should confide the truth in me or leave me to my speculation.

"You haven't listened to what I told you," she then said. "Live with your hopes, Polyxena. You'll fare better."

She was not going to tell me, and at this juncture, I decided not to press the matter, even though my uneasiness still plagued me. In putting all she ever said together—the warnings about Neoptolemus, repeatedly conveyed to me with alarm, and about the horse portending a serious problem for us—there was little to take comfort in. Combine this with the fearful expression in her eyes, alluding to a catastrophe of major proportions, how was I expected to be relaxed? Troubled by thoughts like these, I continued the rest of my way back to the city with her as I began it: in silence.

An enthusiasm engulfed our people, brought on by their zeal in getting the statue inside our city, and they seized upon the work with eagerness and fortitude. Crews began chopping at the stones above the Scaean Gates, slowly dismantling them and the lintel they rested on, thereby removing the impediment these posed for the statue. As this laborious work progressed, other teams of men tied ropes around the sturdy legs of the statue and placed logs in front of it as rollers. Additional ropes were flung over its back and held on to for lateral support so that it would not sway sideways and topple over. Slowly but steadily, the massive horse was being pulled ahead, under the tow of fifty to sixty soldiers who were rotated in shifts after completing about a hundred paces each. Women and children brought water and nourishment to the men toiling under the hot sun. Spirits were high, making the task easier for everyone. I think they believed Goddess Athena looked upon them with great favor, and that gave them the extra inducement to perform their duty with vigor and optimum exertion.

By the time the horse reached the gate, its upper masonry had been completely removed, and because the ground was now paved and flat, there was no difficulty in getting the statue through it. Once inside, the horse was dragged to the open plaza in front of Athena's shrine at the edge of the Pergamus. Nearly the entire day had been expended in the effort, and when the statue stood at its final resting place, we were ready for our afternoon respite, which normally followed the residence hall gatherings we held. In looking out over the walls of the Pergamus, I was struck by how obtrusive this colossal statue appeared in its setting, crowding out everything and making the plaza smaller than desirable. I wondered how long it was to stay there. Surely not forever. My expectation was that, once we were sufficiently secure in our coming peace, we would start to dismantle it and again open up the plaza to its full dimensions. Was I thinking heresy?

A sudden roar emanated from the crowd that had gathered about the statue, bringing me back to the citadel's walls after I had started to walk away from there.

"What's going on?" I asked Deiphobus who watched the proceedings.

"Father has declared today a day of feasting," he said. "As you can hear, the people wholeheartedly approve."

"That means a lot of partying tonight," I replied. "A drunken bash. Our wine stock will be depleted."

"Who can blame them? It's been years since we had one. Certainly, we are entitled to let loose on this of all occasions."

"Do you feel good about that?"

"What do you mean?" he inquired, his suspicion seemingly aroused by my misgivings.

"Aren't we going to let our guard down? Shouldn't we wait a while before we start our celebrating?"

Deiphobus rendered me a curious look, as if I had touched upon an accord that we both held in common, or so I thought. But when he spoke, he shattered that illusion.

"Polyxena, the Greeks are gone," he said. "The war is over. We have prevailed. There is no more threat."

"I didn't see you cheering on the beach this morning, Deiphobus. You're worried about this just as I am. Don't try to deny it."

"What are you thinking?"

"Same thing as Cassandra. That bringing the horse into the city was a mistake. Maybe we should have burned it as she suggested."

"Athena's vengeance doesn't trouble you? Didn't you see what she did to Laocoon?"

"I saw no snakes if you're referring to that."

"Yet we know Laocoon died, as did his sons. An amazing coincidence, wouldn't you say? It's hard to believe Athena had no hand in this."

I was getting nowhere with my brother, which greatly disappointed me. I was convinced he shared the same suspicions that preoccupied Cassandra and I, and to discover this was not the case deeply distressed me, for it amounted to one more confirmation that perhaps it was I, not others, who saw the situation as dismal. Was I turning into Cassandra? I surely was starting to feel that way.

"Keep in mind," Deiphobus went on, "we do keep a guard force on duty at all times, even when everyone else parties."

So Deiphobus did have a concern, or at least he did not outright dismiss the idea that something could go wrong. In back of his mind existed an element of doubt. I was glad to hear that.

"That's some comfort," I said, somewhat relieved. "At least we won't be altogether inebriated, unable to function."

"If it makes you feel any better, Helen and I are going to go down and walk around the horse. She will talk to it, addressing it by the names of Greeks who might be hiding within it, as Cassandra seems to think."

"Then Helen also suspects that?"

"I don't know about her, but I do. She is doing this at my request. You are welcome to come along."

Again, I had misjudged Deiphobus. His suspicions paralleled mine. I was not alone with Cassandra in seeing a threat in what was done. And I appreciated his invitation to accompany him and Helen, which I was not about to refuse, as my curiosity got the best of me and filled me with an eagerness to discover what might happen.

"Thank you, Brother," I replied. "I think I'll take you up on your offer. When?"

"I'm just waiting for Helen to arrive. She went to get a shawl."

No sooner had he said this when Helen came forth from her chamber, wrapped in her shawl, and joined us at the upper parapet. When Deiphobus told her that he invited me to join them, she reacted coldly to the idea and was not at all pleased. I detected a bitterness in her curt consent. No matter. Together, we descended from the Pergamus and approached the plaza, where the statue was parked. We found we were by ourselves, as most of the people had gone home to prepare for the evening's feasting.

"Why am I doing this?" Helen asked in her aversion to what she regarded an imposition.

"I told you why," Deiphobus answered. "If anyone is inside the horse, he might be enticed to sound off. Be convincing. I leave it to your womanly wiles how best to perform."

"I'll mimic their sweethearts," she said, "as much as I'm able to." As Deiphobus and I stood between the forward legs of the horse, Helen slowly ambled under its belly and looked up.

"Odysseus," she began, changing her voice into a slightly lower pitch. "You might as well answer me. I know you're up there. Only you could have dreamed up such an outlandish scheme. And I know you too well to excuse yourself from your own participation in it. Please answer me. I so miss you. My own life has been very sorrowful since I last saw you. Please tell me you miss me too."

We heard nothing. Helen moved to the hind legs, leaning against the right one, and once more looked up.

"Oh, Anticlus," she said in a somewhat higher pitch. "Dear Anticlus, most beloved of my friends, tell me you cherish my friendship as I do yours. Let me hear your sweet voice. Speak to me."

For an instant, I thought I heard something, and I was ready to declare my impression, but when I saw my brother straining to make out any sounds and giving no indication that he had, I questioned my own sensibility and concluded that I must have been mistaken. In my additional concentration, I only met silence.

"My dear husband, Menelaus," Helen continued, this time in her regular voice. "Please forgive me. I am so sorry for what I've done to you. Our daughter, Hermione, I long to see her, and you. The sorrow I felt in leaving you has been terrible for me. My separation is harder and harder on me. If you are there, please say you love me still. Please ease my heartache." She sounded so convincing, her face looking so authentic in her sincerity that I scarcely believed she was faking it.

Nothing. No sound whatsoever. Try as we might, we heard absolutely nothing, an eerie quietness, eerie because the stillness seemed amplified under our intense effort to detect a sound, any sound. But we did not hear a thing.

"You can stop now, Helen," Deiphobus said. "I'm convinced it's empty."

He was more assured of this than I, and I had no intention of bringing our investigation to a close just yet.

"Let's stay a while longer," I suggested. "If we remain very quiet, we ought to detect some movement. If anyone's in there, he's bound to move sooner or later. Staying in one position will be straining."

"Forget it, Polyxena," Deiphobus said. "Nobody's in there. Besides, it's getting close to feasting time. This place will be crowded."

Already we saw activity increasing around the plaza. Crews were bringing in the tables that were to hold the amphorae of wine. The noise was building up in the vicinity. We had no chance of picking up any faint sounds coming from the horse. I nodded my agreement, and we returned to the Pergamus to make our own preparations for the gala, or should I say, the drunken revelry. On my way to my chamber, I met Father who was in a euphoric state, savoring the moment he thought he would never see: Troy's regained freedom.

"Ah, my dear Polyxena," he said. "You will join our celebration, won't you?"

"Of course, Father. Let me get ready for it. Are we to gather by the horse?"

"Oh, that's for the people. You may if you wish, but we'll do our own partying here, in the residence hall."

I could see the advantage of feasting within our quarters. If I overindulged in drinking wine, I was in close proximity to my chamber. Someone could just dump me there if I was unable to make it myself. Still, engaging in the revelry with the people held a fascination for me, just to see how boisterous and bawdy hey might get, and I thought I would do as Father proposed, but only for a while and not alone. Maybe I could talk Andromache into accompanying me.

"I'll be there shortly," I said to him as I proceeded for my chamber.

As I searched my wardrobe for the proper chiton to wear, the realization struck me that in my anticipation toward having a good time, I had readily dismissed, even forgotten, the concerns plaguing me earlier about the possible mistake we made in moving the horse into the city. Again, a feeling of unease came over me. Did everyone else react in a similar way? If so, where will this leave our security? Stop it, I censured myself. My bad propensity for deterring me from relishing the moment was reasserting itself, to my dismay, and I was determined to suppress this. I would enjoy myself tonight. I selected a blue chiton for the occasion.

After preening myself, helped by Thalia, I returned to the residence hall, where almost everyone else had already congregated, though I did not see Cassandra. As dusk settled on the city, we began our rejoicing when Father raised his goblet.

"A toast," he declared in elation. "To our courage, skill, and perseverance, which brought us the victory we now celebrate."

"To our victory," Deiphobus shouted out.

A chorus of applause ensued. Everyone raised their cups and drank heartily, the scene was charged with exuberance. Our spirits soared, the exhilaration we felt was unrestrained, the pleasure of the moment overriding all other considerations. I began making the rounds to meet and talk with everybody who was there. All my father's chief advisors and priests were present, among them wise Antenor and greedy Antimachus. Aeneas and Creusa were looking the perfect couple. Agenor was with Menodice who was exempted from her service duties as his wife. Poor Thalia could not claim that exception and delivered our goblets on a tray. Polites and my other brothers bunched together at one end of the hall. Ilione, with her husband Polymnestor, whom I rarely saw, was there. My best friend, Andromache, gleamed in her wide smile. Deiphobus was with Helen who was absolutely striking in her maroon chiton. And of course, my mother clung to my father, both happy in their company.

When I came to where Andromache was standing, conversing with Ilione and Creusa, I grabbed her arm and nudged her to my side.

"Come, Andromache," I said. "Let's go to the plaza and see the people in their carousing."

"Aren't you having a good time here?" Andromache said.

"I am, but I've heard the partying is more raucous there. I'd like to see what that's like."

I could see the wheels spinning in Adromache's head. She was obviously enticed by what I proposed, her curiosity as fervid as mine, and it did not take long for her to acknowledge her agreement.

"All right," she said. "But promise you'll return with me when I get weary of what goes on."

"I didn't plan on being there for long. We're not going to participate, only to observe."

That did it. Andromache eagerly accepted the initiative I had offered, her propensity for an adventurous undertaking getting the best of her. We cordially disengaged ourselves from the group and stealthily headed for the exit. I'm sure Father noticed us, but he already knew what my intent was. I saw a smile on his face before leaving the hall. We descended the steps leading from the Pergamus to the plaza and were already assailed by the tumultuous roar emanating from there. My excitement mounted at every closer step I took in approaching the square. I looked at Andromache and saw the same anticipation in her eyes and the smile that engulfed me. Then we arrived to witness firsthand the source of all the commotion.

What a wild bash! I could scarcely believe it—the clamorous, disorderly, rambunctious, rowdiness prevailing everywhere about the plaza. People discarded their inhibitions, unleashing the long-repressed urges that now cropped forth to dominate them, and drowned themselves in an orgy of excessive drinking and debauchery. All the pent-up frustrations and restrictions imposed in ten years of war were released in this one night of extreme joy and intoxicating lust. Amphorae of wine—I was amazed how much of it was still in stock—were distributed among them, and no effort was applied in limiting the amount of intake indulged in. The supply seemed inexhaustible. Their imbibing was uncontrolled. No finesse displayed itself amid this uncultivated crowd in consuming the cherished liquid. It was guzzled, gulped down in huge swallows and in ample quantities. It hardly took any time before their previously restrained behavior led to open depravity. Musicians and drummers contributed to the mayhem, continuing their playing as long as they were able to before likewise succumbing to the deleterious effects of excessive drinking. Inhibitions broke down. In their drunkenness, men tore at the clothing of willing or equally inebriated women whose resistance could not avail itself against the advances. Some women, stripped of all clothing, danced to the chorus of applauding men, spilling over themselves to fondle their entertainers. Soon, as much sex as boozing predominated the scene. I had never seen anything like it.

If at first Andromache and I were excited and amused by the spectacle, this reaction was next replaced by feelings of alarm and revulsion when the situation turned ugly on us. With the loss of inhibitions rose a corresponding incidence of violence, especially as it also involved sex. Men began to fight over certain women and among themselves over perceived injuries, as much as anything can be properly perceived in a drunken state, to their self-image and prowess, particularly as it pertained to their sexual performance. How can anyone perform when soused? Things were getting out of hand, and this frightened us, for we now saw ourselves in a threatening situation. We had not taken any drink since leaving the Pergamus, and all our sensibilities remained intact, but we were being accosted by thoroughly bashed sots and had to fend them off.

"Let's go," I told Andromache, "before something happens."

"We stayed too long. I'm scared."

Just then, a particularly obnoxious man planted himself directly in from of me, very much out of it, and blocked my passage. He was staggering about and could barely keep on his feet, but he was a powerfully built individual, of huge size, and I was very much afraid of him, of what he might do.

"Get out of our way," I shouted at him, fear depriving me of my better judgment.

"You surly bitch," he countered angrily. "Nobody yells at me like that. I'll teach you some manners."

"I am King Priam's daughter," I hastily responded in a near panicky state, hoping that this would register with him. "Keep away from us."

"Hah," he roared. "You expect me to buy that? No daughter of Priam would party with us. You're just saying that to get out of having sex with me. It's not going to work, you know."

With that, he lunged at me and, despite his clumsiness, caught hold of the section of my dress covering my left shoulder, tearing it away. I was horrified, frozen in place, incapable of responding to the assault.

Andromache and I clung to each other as he recovered from his near stumble and faced us again. At that moment, fortune intervened on our behalf. The exertion of his thrust had so weakened him in his stupor that he began to drop to his knees, oblivious to what he had done, and he did not have the strength to get back on his feet. Without hesitation, Andromache kicked him in the chest, causing him to yell out as he fell on his back. We hurriedly scampered by him and rushed up the steps to our sanctuary within the citadel. The experience was most harrowing for me. Never again was I going to mingle with the masses, at least not when they were immersed in a drunken orgy.

"Well, you wanted a raucous party," Andromache said, able to smile in her tenseness, "and you certainly got it. Are you disappointed?"

"Not really," I replied, composed again after the ordeal. "Admit it, Andromache. We both enjoyed ourselves before it got wild."

"Wild is an understatement. I've never seen such perverts."

"Don't tell anyone what happened. I've no wish to see anyone punished over this, even if it might be warranted. He was drunk. He didn't know what he was doing."

"You're too lenient, Polyxena. He attacked you, a royal princess. Under any circumstances an unforgivable offense. But I will do as you ask, even though I disagree with it."

By this time, we had arrived at the residence hall, where our own party was still very much in progress in its more sedate formality, the mingling and conversations more congenial than the depraved orgy of excess we had just come from.

"I'm going to change dresses before joining you and the others," I told Andromache. "I'll see you shortly."

I bypassed the residence hall through a side corridor and scurried into my chamber, where I slipped out of my chiton, deeply regretting that I had worn my favorite blue one to the plaza. Almost all my other chitons were the usual white ones. As I was in a hurry to get back to the party, I was not about to take the time to pick out and sample what looked best on me, so I merely flung a white one over me and returned to the festivity as soon as possible. This is the strangest thing, not one of the men seemed to have noticed that I changed my chiton, or they failed to mention it, this despite the sharp contrasting color blue and white represented. I questioned what purpose it served for me to dress up to draw their attention when it had all the appearance of a lost cause. I must say, this awareness came as a major disappointment to me. The women, by contrast, indicated a greater awareness of this, some of them commenting on it, but I did not dress up to impress them. My discernment, of course, did not apply to Mother; she noticed everything, particularly when it involved me.

"What happened to your blue outfit?" she asked me when I was back in the company of Andromache and Helen.

"I'm such a klutz, Mother," I answered. "I spilled some wine on it."

She gave me a faint smile as she tried to hold back from laughing.

"We're going to have to teach you the social graces, Polyxena," she said. "You must be more womanly, else you shall never acquire a man."

Mother meant well, and I suppose I failed to give her much encouragement in my progress at acquiring the gentle feminine attributes she sought in me. But I was not the hopeless case she suspected me of being. If I were, how would that explain the infatuation Neoptolemus had for me? My problem was that I was more attractive to enemy lords than Trojan ones, and I had no answer why that should be. I noticed that Mother viewed my shortcomings more humorously now than she had in the past, actually being amused over my plight, which lightened my cares about the problem significantly, to the degree that I may have even lacked the incentive to try to please her. I'm not sure if this was good or not.

We kept up our socializing into the late evening, for rarely had there been occasions that so satisfied us and filled us with such delight, adding drinks as we went along, although mine lasted for a long time, because I did not want to get soused. My encounter with the drunken man left a sobering impact on me. The obnoxiousness resulting from inebriation was not worth the temporary gratification derived from indulging in the drinks. There wasn't even that much gratification. The wine tasted worse at every swallow after a certain point. But gradually, we tired of our feasting. The fatigue of the long day exacted its toll on our endurance powers, and add to that the lethargy induced by the wine we drank, so that soon, one after another exited from the hall. Although not the first to leave—I think Antenor and Agenor with Menodice left the earliest—I may have been one of the leading ones just the same, but I was utterly worn out. I did not care what anyone made of it. In my grogginess, due in greater part to my weariness rather than excessive drinking, I slowly staggered into my chamber and, upon reaching my bed, simply fell into it, clothes on and all. In an instant, Hypnos took hold of me, and I was lost to the world.

CHAPTER XXI

T HAT HORRID NIGHT! THAT UNBELIEVABLE, unforgettable, awful
night! I was suddenly awakened hearing the screams of people
and smelling smoke. Startled, I jumped from the bed and rushed
to the window and looked out over the city beneath me. It was in flames.
Panic seized me. In my shock, I ran back and forth for a moment, unable
to decide what to do, my mind failing me under my duress. *Be calm*, I told
myself. Regaining my senses, at least to the extent that I managed to reason
things through without fear's intrusive predominance, I dashed from my
room and ran into the residence hall, seeking the protection of my family.
Only my mother was there, sobbing hysterically.

"Where's Father?" I shouted at her. She did not tell me, her crying
preventing this, and I grabbed her shoulders and shook her. "Tell me,
Mother. Where's Father?"

"He went to the altar of Zeus," she got out between her wails. I let go of
her, intending to go after Father, but she clung on to me. "Don't leave me!"
she pleaded. Just then, Thalia entered the hall, with Helen directly behind
her. I placed Mother in Thalia's care.

"Take her," I said. "I'm going to look for Father. Where is Deiphobus?"
I asked Helen.

"In bed," Helen answered, much in shock. "Still out of it."

"Pour water on him. Do something. Waken him."

They were all too dazed to immediately grasp the directives I issued. That I was able to give out instructions at all, while they were incapacitated in their fright, so impressed my will upon them that they responded involuntarily, without thinking, and complied. Thalia embraced my mother, both weeping uncontrollably. Helen grabbed a water bowl and headed back to her chamber. I rushed out of the hall for the altar of Zeus located at the edge of the courtyard, where I so often met with Father. Once outside, in the darkness, my fears were accentuated, the screams and yelling more pronounced and ever closer. It was as if the building itself had afforded a sanctuary. My heart palpitated at triple pace. I could feel it pounding in my neck. I was terrified someone would assail me. I saw helmeted soldiers, carrying shields and brandishing their swords and spears, approaching the courtyard from the opposite end at the same time I entered it.

Father was standing before the altar, entreating Zeus for mercy, when I rushed toward him. Simultaneously, the soldiers ran toward him.

"Father," I yelled out. He glanced at me, terror in his eyes—I will never forget that dreadful look!—when the lead soldier accosted him, striking his sword deep into Father's chest.

"No!" I screamed out, breaking out in sobs as Father fell to the floor. I rushed to him, not thinking about my own safety, and knelt before him, lifting his head with my hand. Blood tricked from his mouth, and he looked at me in his pain, wanting to say something but unable to give expression to his intentions. As I held him, a momentary warm glow emitted from his eyes, and then they glazed over, the spark within forever gone.

I lost all self-control in my grief, weeping profusely and unrestrained in my anger over the killing of an unarmed, defenseless old man. I rose to look at the assailant, holding his bloody sword in his hand. The soldiers stood around silently for the time being as they observed how the slaying affected me. When I looked the killer in the eye, I was dealt another jolt.

"Neoptolemus?" I said in my astonishment. "You killed Father?"

"I killed the King of Troy," he snarled, "leader of our enemy, the man most responsible for the lives this war cost us."

"You've taken Troy!" I shouted at him. "What purpose did killing him serve? Father was your captive."

"Call it revenge. Whatever you like. Bloodlust. Rage. I'll make no apologies for it."

"We're wasting time here," one of the Greeks said to Neoptolemus. "It's Helen I seek."

"You'll get her, Menelaus," Neoptolemus replied. "Where's she going to go? We control the city."

So this was Helen's former husband, the king of Sparta. He was a powerfully built man, somewhat taller than the average man, and his bearded face accented his lordliness, giving him that distinguishable quality associated with royalty, an aura of confidence combined with a commanding presence. Yet his eyes revealed a sensitivity, not the cruelty I detected in Neoptolemus, and although he was bent on retrieving Helen, I could not see him as exacting any harsh vengeance on her.

"This Trojan woman will show us where she's at," Neoptolemus then said as he grabbed me by the arm and prodded me forward.

"We don't need her for that," another soldier said. "Let's take our pleasure with her now. Give her to us."

"This woman is mine!" Neoptolemus roared. "Any of you touch her, and I will kill you."

I was safe, for a while anyway, if I can call seeing my life turned upside down safe. Neoptolemus pushed me along into the residence hall, where Polites and Deiphobus, clad in their armor, waited. Quickly, the Greeks pounced upon them, outnumbering them and assailing them from all directions. In the ensuing fight, Polites fell under the sword of one of the soldiers before he could inflict any damage, but Deiphobus killed two of them and seriously wounded three more before Menelaus thrust his dagger into him. Moaning in pain, my brother collapsed to the floor near where Helen crouched in fear with the other women. She moved over to him, falling to her knees, and cradled his head in her lap. In his dying breath, Deiphobus gasped out his regrets over their parting.

"I'm sorry, Helen," he said amid blood spurting forth from his mouth, "for everything." He died in Helen's arms, fulfilling, I think, his deepest wishes if given a choice over how to exit from this life.

Helen was in tears, touched by her loss. Despite their less-than-perfect union, which could never measure up to the marital bliss she enjoyed with Paris, it nonetheless created a bond of its own, a familiarity found in a partnership that left its mark on both members. She gently lowered my brother's head until it touched the floor and closed the lids of his eyes. Through it all, Mother could not contain her open wailing. The last of her sons left in Troy was gone.

Menelaus strode up to Helen, bent on avenging the injury and humiliation she caused him. He raised his sword—did I misjudge him?— and for an instant there, I thought he might indeed kill her. But then she looked up at him, tears streaming from her face, and if ever there was a sight to melt a man's heart, it was that of Helen in grief, peering into his eyes, her lovely face at its pitiful best, amplifying her suffering. He paused in his observation and then sheathed his weapon. Helen's future was secure.

"Come," Menelaus said as he reached his hand out to Helen. "Let me take you back to Sparta."

She took a hold of his hand and permitted him to raise her to her feet, and while no show of affection revealed itself in their gesture, a quiet understanding was in place, and whatever hostility might have existed between them was readily eclipsed in their reunion. Even under our present duress, I was able to feel some happiness for Helen, however slight. She was my friend after all, and I had no desire to see her come to harm.

Bleak tomorrows faced the rest of us. Mother was inconsolable in her sorrow, especially over the death of Father. We could not keep her from crying, loud and mournful, becoming increasingly annoying to the many Greek leaders who now were gathering in the residence hall.

"Shut that woman up!" a Greek lord—I later learned it was Odysseus— finally yelled out, reaching the limits of his patience.

We tried desperately to calm Mother down, but she would not cease her wailing. All at once, Odysseus strode toward us, drawing forth his sword, and glared directly into Mother's eyes, his vehemence most apparent.

"Queen of Troy you may be," he stormed, "but if you don't stop your incessant blubbering, I shall run you through. Do you understand, woman?"

Though horrified, he succeeded in getting Mother to control herself, her loud wailing now but whimpering soft sobs. There's something to be said for a direct approach. I no longer cried. I was caught in the same situation as on the day Penthesileia was slain, where events of dire consequences superseded each other, and my emotions became drained in my reaction to each of them so that only the latest one prevailed upon my senses. Accordingly, I was, at present, more preoccupied with what was to be my future status than with my remorse over the loss of family members. This is not to suggest that my loss did not bear heavily on me, but only that my current worries mattered more.

All the heavyweights of the Greek leadership congregated in the residence hall, arriving in their blood-splattered armored tunics and headgear. They removed their helmets and set these on our dining table along with their shields. Besides Odysseus, Menelaus, and Neoptolemus, there were also Diomedes, Calchas, and others whose names escape me, and these were soon joined by their supreme commander, mighty Agamemnon himself. An awesome personage, to say the least, tall and sinewy, his short-cropped dark beard streaked in gray. The powerful Greek exuded strength and dominance, and when he spoke, his authoritativeness manifested itself to all, the force of his personality placing him clearly in charge. He was a man born to lead. Only he could have held the Greeks together for that many years. What courage Thersites must have had to rail against such a man.

"We've done it," Agamemnon said, gloating. "Troy is ours, what's left of it."

"There won't be anything left of it before long," Odysseus declared. "The fires are spreading fast. We have to get out of here."

"A shame. We can't luxuriate in the comforts this citadel gave Priam. Put the men to work. Get as much treasure from here as we can, while we can. Take everything that might have value."

Odysseus bade one of his subordinate captains to carry out Agamemnon's directive, then he, Agamemnon, and Neoptolemus ambled over to where we were huddled together. By this time, Andromache, holding her infant son, Astyanax, had also been brought to us by a guard. Only Cassandra and Creusa were missing.

They looked us over for a lengthy period of time, saying nothing.

Then Odysseus spoke.

"Which one did you claim?" he asked Neoptolemus.

Neoptolemus pointed his finger at me and said, "That one. She is Polyxena, a daughter of Priam."

Odysseus scanned me thoroughly from head to toe, as did Agamemnon, both grinning broadly, liking what they saw, I think.

"Aaah," Odysseus sighed. "I must say, Neoptolemus has good taste."

"Indeed so," Agamemnon said. "I sort of fancy her myself. Why should I permit a mere stripling to have her?"

Neoptolemus tensed up. An intense, fiery glare emanated from him, frightening to behold, and I almost thought he might actually strike his commander in his bottled-up rage.

"Oh, let him have her, lord," Odysseus said after taking note of the young man's mounting anger. "We have ample women for the taking. Restraint should guide us. What will our wives think if we overindulge ourselves?"

Odysseus was an interesting man. Even under my present tribulations, I was able enough to make an assessment of him. Of average height but sturdily composed, with sandy hair and light eyes, he had a charm about him that hinted at great intelligence and the craftiness he was renowned for. To me, he appeared more easygoing, in both speech and mannerism, than the others, a calmer, more methodical approach delineating his actions. Helen told me that he, alone among her suitors, did not court her with any gifts, recognizing that the rich Menelaus was going to win her hand, so he dispensed with the formalities of courtship. She also said it was he who encouraged her husband to secure an oath from her suitors, acquiring their allegiance to come to her defense should anything ever happen to her. Yet he was known to be ruthless at times, and in a cold, calculating fashion, which made him a dangerous man. Still, if I had to be taken captive by any of these Greeks, I should have preferred him to all the others present.

Agamemnon snorted, which I took to mean that he consented to what Odysseus said, and continued peering over us. His attention was next focused on Andromache who was cuddling her baby to keep it from crying. Both he and Odysseus neared her.

"And who might you be?" Agamemnon asked.

"I am Andromache," she fearfully answered.

"Just Andromache? Andromache who? Another daughter of Priam?"

"Daughter of Eetion, king of Thebe."

"Thebe? Ah yes, one of the many cities I sent Achilles to capture. He killed your father, if I remember right. So you must be the Andromache who married Hector."

"I am—or was—great Hector's wife," Andromache reluctantly conceded.

Agamemnon and Odysseus glanced at each other, then Odysseus took hold of the cloth wrapping covering Astyanax and parted it just enough to reveal the baby's face. A graveness came over the Greek.

"So this is the son of Hector," he said.

Andromache said nothing. She was very much afraid of what inference the Greeks might make of that, a worriment that extended to Mother as well, for she grasped her daughter-in-law in her arms in an attempt to comfort her. By now, Mother had recovered from her earlier distress, accepting the reality of her fate, and lent her maturity and purpose to relieving the fears still possessing many of us, especially the servant women, among them Thalia.

Throughout this conversation Neoptolemus kept staring at me, filling me with both dread and annoyance. I tried to avoid looking at him, only doing so periodically to verify if he still stood transfixed in his gaze, and when I saw such was the case, I again averted my glances. The scowl he exhibited was disconcerting for me, and I fear I may have aggravated his scorn for me by not giving him the attention he sought. I could no longer stomach him, not after the vicious manner in which he killed my father, and I think I was more afraid of him than any of the other Greeks.

Just then, several more soldiers entered the hall, dragging one of their members with them. Cassandra, in disheveled and torn clothes, walked alongside them.

"What's this?" Agamemnon asked, displeased over their intrusion. He, Odysseus, and Neoptolemus walked back to where the rest of the soldiers were gathered.

"We caught this man raping that woman," one of the guards said.

"You interrupt us for that!" Agamemnon raged. "What concern is that to me? Everyone is raping women. The spoils of war."

"This woman is a priestess, lord."

Suddenly, a silence ensued the group, the problem more serious than initially presumed. I looked at Cassandra who was severely shaken by the incident and still trembling from her ordeal. She had a horrible bruise mark on her cheek from evidently having received a vicious blow to her face. Her dress was badly torn, revealing nearly the full of her legs. She seemed to be in a state of shock.

"So she is a priestess," Agamemnon growled. "How was this man to know?"

"He raped her inside Apollo's temple, lord, under a statue of Goddess Athena that was placed there. The statue fell to the floor and shattered into several pieces."

The Greeks stood aghast. No longer a minor problem but one of major significance that portended potential disasters for their voyage home.

Neither Agamemnon nor Odysseus took a dim view of the report given them.

"You idiot!" Agamemnon shouted at the suspect. "In your bestial lust, you could not exercise proper restraint? Who are you?"

"Ajax, son of Oileus, king of Locris, lord," the man answered, quivering in fright.

"I know of you. You fought bravely for us."

"A noble," Odysseus interjected. "He bears the name of the great Ajax from Salamis, a man we both greatly honored, before he killed himself."

"I remember, because we gave you the arms of Achilles. You are not free of guilt in the matter, Odysseus.

"You know I regretted the affair as much as anyone. I pleaded with you to have him properly buried when you were reluctant to do so."

"Well, this Ajax is lacking the brains of our Salamis friend," Agamemnon hissed.

"He must be punished," Odysseus said. "The penalty given to anyone offending the gods: death."

"Come now, Odysseus," Agamemnon calmed his friend. "Is this how we reward great warriors? An imbecile he may be, but I am indebted to Oileus for supporting our venture. He is a good friend. Besides, Athena granted us this victory. She will understand the passions unleashed in savoring the fruits of our triumph. For all I know, this Trojan bitch may have deserved what she got."

"As you please, lord," Odysseus relented his hard stand. "I sincerely hope you're right about Athena understanding his transgressions against her."

"Go, Ajax of Locris," Agamemnon bellowed. "Get out of my sight before I forget myself. Thank your father that I pardon your crime."

Ajax hurriedly scampered away while Agamemnon studied the object of the warrior's lust, taking a lengthy view of Cassandra, checking her out in detail, apparently liking what he was seeing. He raised his eyebrows while perceiving her and was quieted in his concentrations of her features, being noticeably enticed by her. He placed his hand under her chin and rose her head.

"I must say," he said, "Ajax gave you a good smack. I should have had him flogged just for marring that pretty face of yours."

Cassandra stood there stoically, allowing the supreme commander to scrutinize her. I thought there was a serenity in this. She did not shed any tears or shrink back from his touch or even try to cover her legs. Her quiet submission had an aspect of dignity about it. What a scene it might have been had she wailed as Mother did earlier.

"Is your chamber near here?" Agamemnon asked Cassandra.

She hesitated, fearing, I think, that she might be assaulted by the king himself, but as she had no way out, she nodded.

"Get into some other clothes," he directed to her great relief. "All of you. Go to your rooms and fetch some extra belongings. Be quick about it. Only what you can carry under your arms."

We required no prodding to comply with that and hastily ran into our chambers to gather up whatever was readily available in the short time we had. The smoke was starting to build up within the Pergamus, giving more immediacy to the threat facing us. I grabbed two of my chitons, a shawl, and a blanket. Fortunately, in falling into my bed after the partying, I had left my sandals on and didn't have to take the time to lace them. I also took a belt and comb with me. I could not see my Amazon boots or vest. The looters had already ransacked my chamber, taking any items I would have wanted as keepsakes, and I made no effort to look for anything they missed.

"Hurry up," a voice shouted through the corridor. "We must evacuate the place."

Frantically, I rushed back to the main hall. As I took my place with Thalia and my mother, I saw Odysseus talking to Neoptolemus in the doorway. I did not hear what they said, but a cold pang shot through me, telling me that something horrible was being contemplated. I was fraught with anxiety over what this meant. Within the briefest time, the rest of our group had reassembled, Andromache carrying her infant son, and we awaited our next instructions.

"You will be taken to the shore," Agamemnon said, glancing frequently at Cassandra. "A tent has been set up for you. You'll stay there until we decide your further disposition."

I just wanted to get out. The smoke was now burning my eyes, and ahead of me through the open doors, I saw the fires nearing the palace, blazing red, surging forward in hot gusts. Quickly, we followed the Greek leaders as they proceeded from the palace into its courtyard and along the upper wall of the Pergamus toward the descending stairway, our passage lit up in the glow of the flames. I was next to Andromache in our flight, helping to carry some of her items. Suddenly, we had our way blocked by Odysseus and Neoptolemus, standing formidably in their grimness before us. We stopped, a look of terror coming to Andromache.

"I regret having to tell you this," Odysseus said to her. "A decision has been reached among us about your son." He uttered his words without passion, cold and calculated, exhibiting neither pleasure nor sorrow.

Instinctively, Andromache tightened her clutch on her baby. She began sobbing, knowing what was to happen.

"Please," she wept. "Don't hurt him. I beg of you."

"He is the son of Hector," Odysseus said. "The man most responsible for our injuries. We cannot allow his lineage to continue."

"What harm can a baby do?" Andromache entreated, now near panic.

"The fates decree what destiny is in store for us. We fear his destiny will be to avenge great Hector's death. If not him, then his sons."

"No! No!"

"Give him to us," Odysseus demanded.

"No!"

All at once, Neoptolemus grabbed the infant and wrestled it from Andromache's arms. To everyone's shock, he flung the screaming baby over the wall. I was stunned, numbed in my utter astonishment, unable to come to grips with what I had just seen. The incredible swiftness in which in all happened. In one moment, Astyanax was crying in his mother's arms. An instant later, he plummeted from the wall, never to be heard from again. After I regained my senses, my first impulse was to provide some comfort for poor Andromache whose terrible sobbing tore at me, filling me with the greatest grief. Mother already held her, likewise weeping, the loss of her only grandchild by Hector equally unbearable for her. I was deterred from my attempt. This was just as well, for I had no faith in my ability to ease the pain Andromache felt. Pitiful situations were difficult for me. I was never able to adequately cope with them, afraid that I might do more harm than good.

I glared at Neoptolemus, unable to conceal the disdain in which I now regarded him. He looked at me, apparently sensing my hostility, for he was shaken by it, turning his eyes away in shame.

"You're a monster!" I shouted at him.

I could tell he took no comfort in my berating him, but neither did he have any respect for being criticized by me, and typical of the impetuosity that comes with youth, he was not about to take any abuse from a woman.

"Shut up, Polyxena!" he yelled back in his contemptuous sneer. "Be grateful you live. You're going to be mine, a captive, a slave, whatever I choose to call it, but your future rests in my hands."

"You killed a baby. Only a beast—not a man!—could do that."

"I executed a decision made by my lords. There is no honorable way or painless way that can be done. I took the most direct approach, ending the squabbles over which method to apply. Would putting it to the sword have been better?"

I had no answer to that. All I knew at this juncture was how I loathed him and that I was indeed at his mercy, the reality of our situation implanting itself in me, and if I was to live, I had to be more accommodating to his demands. Offending him was obviously not the proper course to take, tempting as it was. I had to exercise prudence and control the emotions that presently gripped me. I did not reply, instead hugging Andromache as I helped her move on.

Overcoming the horror of that unspeakable event, we steadily moved ahead, descending the steps of the citadel until we reached the lower section of the city, where we passed by the inner corral. Another shock assaulted my senses when I saw a number of dead horses lying within the compound, one I recognized as Zephyrus. In their unbridled fury, the Greeks had not even spared Troy's royal animals. Tears ran from me. My greatest joy, my adored, noble Zephyrus—we were such kindred spirits—my sole pleasure in the times of my worst distress, whose presence invoked my cherished memories of sweet Antiope, also slain. Heartsick, I lumbered along, no longer caring what would happen to me, benumbed of all sensations that gave me cause to live.

The dead were strewn all about the square, where the wooden horse once stood. It had burned down in the fires that consumed the city and was now a heap of smoldering embers. Nearly all the bodies were those of men and boys. Only a handful of women lay among them, as their lot was to be that of slaves serving the conquerors as mistresses, concubines, or menials, the fate typical of all women. The Greeks were merciless in their slaughter, sparing no one of male gender they came across, at least not in this plaza, and I think the only ones who may have escaped where those sober enough to grasp the situation and able to flee before they were accosted. The gods had deserted Troy.

We were led through the main avenue leading to the Scaean Gates, seeing more signs of the savagery inflicted upon the Trojan people. Corpses lay along the entire route, cruelly slain, with horrible gashes from sword thrusts covering them in blood. We took care not to step on them and had to avoid the collapsing walls from buildings weakened by fire. We covered our faces with the cloth from our dresses to keep from inhaling the thickening smoke. Amazingly, we arrived at the gates unscathed, not one among us being hurt. How good it felt to breathe fresh air once we got outside the walls. Our lines were also getting longer as more women were added to them from different sections of the city, but we now proceeded in silence, our grief having expended itself in the futility of our condition.

When we arrived at the shore, we were divided into groups, the royal household members and their servants being guided to the tent Agamemnon had mentioned. Ours was not the only tent pitched. Other women had been placed in adjacent ones earlier, perhaps the wives and daughters of other nobles or our allied leaders, none that I knew. Our tent was sufficiently large, and we had no problem finding our particular spot within it. Cots and blankets had been placed within it and were available to us. In addition, water bowls and vases were furnished. A canvassed off annex allowed for our private functions. Austere accommodations to be sure, but it could have been worse. We could have been left out on the beach, without cover or privacy, under a burning sun and exposed to cold night winds. *Make the most of it*, I thought to myself. This would be home, for a while anyway.

Daybreak. As we settled into our quarters, the sun broke over the distant mountains, casting its brightness over the shore, at times clouded over from the dark smoke still rising from smoldering Troy and then clear and shining. It seemed incomprehensible that, at this time just yesterday, we gazed over our walls to look upon the vacated beaches, our hearts light and full of joy, with only a statue of a horse remaining of our enemy. That horrible wooden horse. Against the advice of our most renowned seers, we dragged it into our city and, as Cassandra had said, it meant our doom. We had the choice, if you can call it having a choice when those in authority decide, contrary to your own judgment, what is best for you. I cannot blame Father for what happened. He was old and much influenced by counselors he trusted. The treacherous Greek, Sinon, lying from the start, cannot be faulted either. He merely carried out the instructions he was given, and in a most convincing way. More than anyone else, Antimachus is the man most responsible for the fateful decision. In his aggressive tone and boisterous, loud voice, ever seeking to dominate any situation, his opinion prevailed. But what use is it to dwell on what has been? We were now captives, and this tent was our present setting. We must adapt ourselves to our situation and cope.

I felt such pity for Andromache. She bore her grief with great dignity, quietly weeping at times, but mostly just lying on her cot, dazed and lost in her contemplations, not speaking to anyone. I tried to get her to eat after the guards brought in some food for us, but she declined, thwarting my attempts to assuage her grief. I refrained from insisting on it, placing the matter in her hands. Eventually, she would recover from the pain presently engulfing her. In the meantime, it was perhaps best to leave her to herself.

Mother, for all the commotion she created at first, had settled into somberly accepting what the fates decreed. I think, in great part, this had to do with her realization that, as the queen and leading woman of Troy, she had to set the example for the rest of us in adjusting to our condition. She did this quite effortlessly, soothing us with words of encouragement and gentle hugs and being there to console us when we broke out in crying. And yet her emotions betrayed her when she occasionally shed tears, even though she tried to suppress these feelings. I think this resulted primarily when she was overcome with pangs of pain over the loss of Father rather than over our misfortunes. I admired the fortitude in which she endured her hardship. Her strengths came to the forefront when most needed. We became closer as a consequence of our ordeal.

Cassandra remained as steady as a rock under our duress, never complaining or even lamenting our fate, which she undoubtedly regarded as preordained, the inevitable outcome contrived by angry gods. I was drawn to her constancy, her poise significantly alleviating the fears dogging me, and spent a lot of my time with her, seeking out the reassurance she instilled in me. We talked frequently, usually outside the tent, away from prying eyes, most of our conversation centering on our predicament and future prospects.

"King Agamemnon has his eyes on you," I told my sister. "You're lucky."

"Why would you think that?" Cassandra asked.

"No one will compete for you. His claim on you is unchallenged. You know in whose palace you will reside."

"He gives me the creeps."

She surprised me with her harsh assessment, principally in how it contradicted my own evaluation of the man. Agamemnon was not that handsome, to be sure, but he could not be considered ugly either. He possessed that indefinable quality bespeaking of his kingship. A commanding presence dictated his actions, bold and resolute, mannerisms belonging to the realm of those in power who, by training and inclination, are driven to dominate.

"I hear Mycenae is the richest of the Greek cities," I said. "You will be surrounded with opulence."

"Troy was a rich city. Its wealth did nothing for me."

"You secluded yourself from it, Cassandra. Spending all your time in Apollo's temple. But you still enjoyed the warm baths, the fine meals, our wine, and the easy life provided by our servants. With Agamemnon, these pleasures will still be yours."

"Maybe, but he has a jealous wife. I've been told about Clytemnestra. She will not be enthralled by my presence. So is it Neoptolemus who claims you?"

"Yes. The prospect frightens me. He is not the man his father was. He enjoys cruelty."

"War makes beasts of everyone."

"Do you still see calamity for me in him?"

Cassandra's reluctance to answer told me that she did, and I was afraid to probe further into the matter, fearing I might be completely unnerved over my discovery.

"You can avoid it," she finally said, "if you submit to his desires. He is infatuated with you. Acknowledge this and do your part to please him, reciprocate."

"I can never love him, not after what he's done."

"Make him believe you do."

"No, I won't," I indignantly replied, the notion repulsive to me.

"If you don't," Cassandra sternly cautioned me, "a terrible fate awaits you."

I chose not to pursue the matter, being relieved in some measure that Cassandra implied I had control over the situation. My fate hinged on my behavior toward Neoptolemus, whether I responded in kind to his advances and deceived him into believing I shared the affection he held for me. On the surface, this seemed a simple enough task, requiring no undue effort on my part, but there remained an underlying problem: how long could such a deception be kept up before one's true feelings would assert themselves and reveal the projected falseness? I questioned if I could maintain such a charade for any length of time, never believing myself to be good at lying. I have been accused of being honest to a fault. I determined that I would allow the situation confronting me dictate what step to take.

In speaking with many of the other women in our company as well as those in different groups and also the guards who were surprisingly free of inhibitions in relating what they knew, I was able to reconstruct what had happened last night and learn of the disposition of known personnel affected by its advent. Here is what I discovered.

Odysseus was the mastermind behind the ruse to employ the wooden horse in gaining access to our city, and he also concocted the story Sinon was to relate in convincing us of his desertion. While the horse was left on the beach, the Greek fleet sailed to the western side of the nearby island of Tenedos, where it remained until nightfall. In the moonlight, the ships returned, making landfall under blackout conditions, and the Greeks awaited the signal they expected from their compatriots. Odysseus and nine others, among them Neoptolemus, hid inside the belly of the statue, patiently waiting for the carousing to end.

Sometime after the revelry had dissipated among its participants, with most of the people having returned to their homes, although some were lying in their drunken stupor about in the plaza, Sinon had entered the square and given a go-ahead for the occupants within the wooden horse to come down. Once on the ground, Odysseus and Neoptolemus rushed to the wall and used a torch to signal the main force. They then assisted the remaining Greeks, who had slain the few guards left on duty, in opening the Scaean Gates. Once the enemy was inside, the slaughter began, and buildings were set on fire. In the chaos that followed, townspeople rushed through the streets to escape the rampaging soldiers, most fleeing through the east Dardanian Gates, and many fled into the distant hills. But the majority of the Trojans, caught unaware in their sleep and insufficiently recovered from their drunkenness, were incapable of mounting any resistance and met their fate where they lay. A handful managed to assemble themselves and put up a fight, but these were hopelessly outnumbered and readily slain. They never had a chance.

I learned that Aeneas had escaped, but tragically, his wife, my sister, Creusa, did not. As it was explained to me, the commander spearheaded a unit that clung together and fought off the Greeks until the situation became hopeless. He then gathered up his family and carried his aged father, Anchises, on his back, and with his son, Iulus, and Creusa beside him, led his group from the burning city. In their flight, Creusa got separated amid the mob and disappeared. She was not seen or heard of since. I think she might have been among the dead we saw lying in the streets. I was relieved that Aeneas and Iulus got away with his band but also dismayed that Creusa was not with him.

Wise Antenor was also spared, as were his sons, Agenor among them. It turns out, the advisor once saved the lives of Odysseus and Menelaus when they arrived at Troy as envoys before the war began to request the return of Helen. When the rest of the Trojans wanted to kill them, Antenor prevented them from doing so and protected the Greeks, giving them the sanctuary of his house. The two Greeks returned the favor by protecting him from the fury of the soldiers, extending this safety also to his sons. Consequently, Agenor and Menodice, as far as I know, likewise falling under this shield, managed to also get away. It pleased me to hear this. They were a loving couple and deserved their happiness together.

By contrast, no mercy was given Antimachus, the greedy, loud-mouthed warmonger who had advocated killing Odysseus and Menelaus when they performed the duties of envoys. All three of his captured sons were killed, as was he, when the Greeks stormed his household. I would like to be more sympathetic to him, but he was such a despicable individual and also the man I most blame for our fall, so I have difficulties doing that. It is regretful that his sons should pay the penalty for their father's offensive behavior, but their own behavior was not much better. These were people who browbeat everyone else into their line of thinking and, in the process, invoked the anger and resentment of all. I felt no sense of loss in hearing of their fate.

Ilione, my oldest sister, and her Thracian husband, Polymnestor, and their son, Deipylus, also managed to flee Troy, but I had no other word on where they went. I think they fled for Thrace, but it would take some time to get there. The good thing was that they got away, which is more than I could say for my other brothers, Agathon and Pammon. Both were killed by the Greeks, as were all the other male relatives of Priam. Agamemnon was committed to wiping out all descendents of my father.

As for Helen, I had not seen her since Menelaus took her from the palace. I assumed the Spartan king had her lodged in this royal tent along with his captured concubines and was making up for lost time with her. How she would respond to that was open to speculation. My suspicion was that she would quietly submit to his demands, although she probably held him in greater disdain than ever. Having forsaken Menelaus, and her daughter Hermione, for Paris speaks for itself. It is very unlikely she could rekindle the warmth she may have once possessed for him, especially when all the intervening years and events are considered. Yet aside from the personal scars inflicted by her losses, she came out better than the rest of us, her position and well-being secure, and this might have caused me to envy her. She was my friend, and I wished the best for her, but at times, I felt indignant that she should emerge so unscathed from our misfortune.

Thalia and our other servant ladies kept on attending us, even though we placed no such requirements on them, finding it awkward under the circumstances to insist on being served when we were all in the same situation. In a way, I thought this somewhat sad. They reacted to their lifetime of servitude to us, as if unable or unwilling to comprehend the circumstances that had made us equals in our captive status. Maybe I was misinterpreting their intentions. They may have simply persisted in their labor to pass the long hours more quickly and make them endurable. And truthfully, there was not that much to do, aside from preening us. We had no bathing facilities, no need to fill tubs with hot water, no abundance of towels to wrap ourselves in, no cleaning of rooms, not even cooking necessities. We ate the rations our guards provided for us. I allowed Thalia to brush my hair and otherwise see to some of my needs, not because I required any services, but rather out of her insistence in continuing to please me, although I could have easily done this myself. I think she assessed her self-worth in being of assistance to us, a lifetime effort that was now habitual instead of obligatory. I thought that, if I denied her service, she might be hurt, thinking I no longer desired she do this. Such is the power of inurement once instilled in us.

Chapter XXII

A WEEK HAS PASSED SINCE WE fled burning Troy. By all appearances, the Greeks were far from departing our shores, busy as they were in emptying the city of all its treasures, digging for it under the stones of collapsed buildings, sifting through the deep ashes of once-glittering palaces, and looting the few standing private residences for anything that might be of value. A lot of their work entailed restocking the ships with depleted storages of food, an arduous and time-consuming task that included filling barrels with water drawn from the Scamandrus River, some distance away, and hauling the loads to the shore to be hoisted into the vessels. Troy's granaries remained intact despite the fires that enveloped the city and were the primary food source for replenishing the ships as well as feeding us while we languished in our tents. The city's arsenals were stripped of their contents, most of the weaponry deemed to be of good quality and useful as trade merchandise. Also, by now, disposal crews had amassed all the dead and burned them, a necessary task, as the gods looked with great displeasure upon corpses lying unburied to rot in the sun.

Another major task occupying the conquerors was that of consolidation, securing new alliances and oaths of allegiance from the former allied lords of Troy, many of whom were still fielded in their encampments east of the city. Agamemnon hosted these kings and generals with aplomb and courtesy, daily accepting a number of them into his tent in order to solicit their future cooperation and trade. Not that they had much of a choice, the supremacy of the Greeks now established, but from what I heard, the king had lost his taste for additional wars and was in a conciliatory mood, offering generous terms and enticing them to accept the hegemony of Troy for that of Mycenae. Most acceded to his demands and promised to support the new order in place.

A procedure of sorts fell into place among us as we accustomed ourselves to life in the tent. We arose at sunrise, cleaned ourselves with the water bowls available, and ate a small meal, after which we spent most of the morning engaged in conversations and roaming about the containment area comprised of numerous tents, each with a dozen or so occupants, speaking to our guards. I often visited women located in the other tents to find out as much as I could about our prospects. Sometimes, through contacts of their own, they knew more than we did, although I frequently questioned how much stock to place in what they said. Then we had another small noon meal, brought to us in earthen-made bowls, plundered from our city for the most part, along with cups of water or wine. After this meal, we related various stories or memorized poetical works, each of us taking turns in reciting the ones familiar to us. By late afternoon, boredom overtook us, and we usually napped for a while until our evening meal, which usually was provided near dusk.

When it got dark, we simply went to sleep on our cots. Thalia and her compatriots washed our clothes and dishes apart from our own schedule, or lack thereof. Not exactly thrilling, but neither was it free of stress, for we spent much of our talks expressing our worries over what was to become of us and which of the Greeks would claim us. Speaking about it helped, but only in the sense that it fortified each person's realization we were in this together. None of us was exempt from the apprehensiveness the unknown future presented.

I became closer to my mother and Cassandra than I would have thought possible. Aside from sharing our misfortune and austerity, we learned about each other's concerns, things we would never have bothered with before, and in our attempts to comfort and console ourselves, we acquired a deeper understanding of one another. For instance, one of Mother's fears was that, at her age, she would be discarded altogether by our captors and left to fend for herself all alone in the wilds. Her fear was so valid, not having occurred to us younger women, for she had no more relatives or friends left who would take her in should this happen. In that respect, the rest of us were better off. Only Cassandra's consistent assurances gave relief to Mother. I think my sister knew what was to occur and projected her confidence to the frail woman, giving her the incentive to go on. But Mother remained embittered over Helen. She hurled abuses upon her former daughter-in-law at every opportunity, blaming her for all the ills that had come upon us, and made us most uncomfortable in her vituperations. Sometimes, I had to leave the tent just to escape her tirades, as did Cassandra.

"She is unforgiving," I said to Cassandra in our meeting outside. "I'm so tired of hearing her. This is where our close quarters are starting to drive me crazy."

"I don't think she means what she says," Cassandra said.

"She's so unreasonable about it. Helen did not cause her abduction. Paris did. I wish she would remember that. I can understand how, in her grief, she might want to seek out someone to ascribe this to, but to lose all objectivity in the process, it comes across as so unintelligent and offensive."

"She is old and has lost it all: her husband, her sons, her home. And having spent her entire life surrounded with family members, she is now very alone. Only Andromache seems able to abide her. I try to be empathetic but like you, am driven to seek escapism from her endless ravings."

Cassandra was more comprehending, or perhaps a better description would be tolerant, than I over Mother's antics and made me feel ashamed of my behavior. She won my respect in her steadiness and perspicacity, and I increasingly looked upon her with admiration as I came to know her better. How sad that this enlightenment should come to me now rather than years ago when it might have made an actual difference. I could have insisted that Father listen to her instead of all the hedging I did, which only affirmed his low regard for her advice. It's one of life's mysteries. We learn too late the things we should have known earlier. I think the gods arrange for this, to keep us forever in our low standing with them.

"What will happen to her?" I asked Cassandra.

"She will be secure enough, but she will never truly be happy anymore. Odysseus will take her."

"Odysseus?" I could not hide my amazement. "I thought he was going to kill her when she didn't stop crying. He's the last man I would have suspected."

"The workings of the gods are most mysterious. I think Mother left her mark on him with all her weeping. If you do something that is remembered, you're ahead of the game. People take note of it."

Her answer befuddled me. Being remembered for excessive blubbering, as Odysseus called it, did not strike me as a particularly noteworthy achievement, certainly not one that denoted anything desirable. But then, who am I to judge what motivates some men. Maybe she reminded Odysseus of his own mother.

"It's best not to tell her," Cassandra added. "She does not think highly of Odysseus."

"After the way he threatened her, who can blame her?"

"At least she won't be left to the wolves. I'm going inside to relieve Andromache. By now, she'll need it. Are you coming?"

"Not yet," I answered, thinking I needed more time to myself.

I was glad that Cassandra showed consideration for Andromache who still deeply mourned Astyanax, the commonality she had with Mother's lamentation of Father. She was doing what I lacked the courage to do: consoling two women horribly beset with extreme grief. I was deterred from taking that step by a dread I possessed over botching things, fearing I would make things worse instead of better. Painful sorrow was a source of terrible discomfort for me. It left me with a loss over how to express the heartache I felt, and I truly did feel it, but to give voice to my anguish was a problem for me.

My natural inclination was to endure sorrow in private, regarding it as a highly personal matter reserved for one's own absorption. I am not sure this was the correct response. I was once more receptive to displaying my emotions, but over time, with all the suffering and horrors I had witnessed, I had also become progressively reluctant to reveal my true nature, until I even feared to do so.

As I thus contemplated, I looked up and noticed that Neoptolemus was approaching our tent. My heart sank. *Oh, no*, I was thinking. I should have gone with Cassandra. My legs were frozen in place, preventing me from darting away. That would have been a ridiculous reaction at this stage, demonstrating the revulsion I had of him, which I tried to suppress. So I simply waited for him to arrive.

"There you are, Polyxena," Neoptolemus greeted me, smiling in an obvious attempt to be nice. "I've missed seeing you."

"Why?" I tersely replied. "We're not lovers."

"Perhaps not yet," he said, smirking. "But that will change soon enough. Since you're going to be mine, you might as well adjust to it."

"Don't count on that, Neoptolemus. After what you've done, it's unlikely you'll ever get any affection from me."

"You know, you could treat your conquerors with a little more respect," he said, raising his voice. "It's very foolish of you to offend the man who holds your future in his hands. I'll thank you to keep that in mind."

"You can threaten me all you like. It won't change anything."

"Damn you, Polyxena! I came here wanting to be friendly, and you thwart me with your obstinacy. Get a grip on your situation, wretched woman. I can have you flogged here and now."

I was pushing him and knew it. No doubt he could carry out his threat, and this served no useful purpose for me. A more conciliatory overture was beneficial for me, as he inferred, but my nature rebelled against this, against my better judgment, and I was reluctant to apply the effort despite the potential harm I faced.

"You wouldn't dare," I exclaimed rashly.

He glowered, and I saw him clench his fist in readiness to strike me, but he checked his mounting rage, keeping himself under control. For the moment, I was safe.

"What will it take," he asked, breathing heavily, "to get some kindness out of you? That's all I ask, a bit of kindness. I don't deserve this hostility out of you."

"Yes, you do," I snapped back at him. "You've proven yourself to be a cruel man. Am I just supposed to forget that?"

He turned red, demonstrating to me that he had a conscience and was embarrassed, if not repentant, over his conduct. In seeing this, I was momentarily touched by his revealed contriteness, to the degree that I actually considered softening my harsh stand against him, and I questioned my obtuseness over the issue.

"I'm sorry about what I did," he almost moped. "You're right; it was cruel. I wish it had never happened, but it's done, and I can't do anything about it now."

"What do you want from me, Neoptolemus?" I asked.

"Some respect. Recognition that I acted cruelly as a result of war," he entreated. "I'm not by nature the coldhearted beast you accuse me of being."

"I haven't accused you of anything."

"Indeed you have," he angrily asserted. "Your look of scorn makes your accusation patently evident. I see the hostility in your eyes. Don't try to deny it. You hate me, don't you?"

How was I to respond to that? Yes, I loathed him, but was it prudent to openly admit to this aversion when he held my future safety in abeyance? The smart approach was to placate him with falsehoods. Perhaps if I, for temporary's sake, appeased him with allusions suggestive of my potential interest in him, I could forestall his wrath, thereby improving my standing with him.

"I hate what you did," I said. "I need time to recover from my dismay."

Instantly, he flashed his teeth in a broad grin, his eyes lit up, and he transformed himself into a self-assured person, brimming with confidence in his conviction that I indeed favored him.

"I knew it," he blurted out in his smugness. "Deep down you *are* attracted to me. Don't try to deny it."

His conclusion very much alarmed me. I had no idea I was imparting such an impression with him, and certainly that was far from my purpose. He took my answer to its most extreme level, drawing an inference from it that had no basis in fact and seeing a ray of hope in whatever expectations he had of me that did not exist. I was compelled to correct his misinterpretation.

"That's not what I said," I emphasized as strongly as I could without actually yelling at him.

"You implied it," he quickly replied, undismayed, his confidence intact. "I don't need to hear you saying it. Your meaning is clear. You said that eventually you would again see me in a positive light, that you hated what I had done, not me as a person."

Was that what I said? He had me doubting my own words in his erroneous assessment. If indeed he was under this mistaken illusion, I had a problem. My best recourse was honesty, so I would not raise any unrealistic presumptions in him, even if this meant bursting his bubble at present.

"Don't misjudge me," I cautioned him sternly. "Whatever I imply is not subject to speculation. I will be precise in my meaning of what I tell you."

I expected him to come right out and ask me if I loved him, but he avoided doing so, preferring the obscurity afforded in doubt to the certainty of knowing I did not, finding the ambiguity easier to cope with.

"As you say," he remarked. "I'll be coming here every day to see you. Be here. I don't want to have to look for you."

He saw himself as my master and acted the part, and I was certainly in no position to dispute that assumption. As his captive, I was indeed nothing more than a slave to him. His promise to visit me daily did not settle well with me. I found my conversations with him straining, not flowing easily for me, especially not when he applied his own meanings to the things I told him. I wished I had never met him.

"Where else would I be?" I answered sarcastically. "It's not like I have a range to roam about in."

"Just see that you are," he declared and turned around and walked off, smirking all the while. His presence, more than any factor in my circumstance, existed to remind me of my prisoner status, and he did his best to promote this feeling in me. I was highly agitated over this, distressed in my anxiety over not being able to find an escape from my predicament. I needed no reminders of my servitude obligations to my conquerors, the situation was well understood, yet Neoptolemus had to emphasize the point to me, for no other purpose than to push his overlordship on me. I was not meant to be a submissive, compliant, servant to do a man's bidding, neither as a princess nor as a captive. I thought of myself as being a free spirit. Who is delusional now?

My reality mitigated against my deeply felt sentiments. There was no avoiding the reach of Neoptolemus, try as I might to convince myself otherwise, and my contrary wishes amounted only to foolishness. He owned me; that was the actuality facing me. I may, for the moment, feel better in my denials of this, but the truth would prevail itself upon me in the end, and it behooved me to accept, rather than fight, my condition. Preoccupied with such thoughts, I worked myself into a state of utter depression when I decided to return to the tent and take my place beside Mother. Life was not worth living.

My present melancholy did little to improve the morale of the others in the tent, for they readily sensed my troubled nature in the introspective quietness I exhibited. Mother, used to my habits, abided my indulgence at first but gradually became herself troubled over it and sought to relieve me of my despondency.

"What's wrong, dear?" she asked me. "You look so sad."

"What's to be happy about?" Andromache interjected. "Polyxena is reacting properly to our plight."

"No, this is not like her," Mother said. "She's always been good at adjusting to things. Something's wrong here."

"It's Neoptolemus, isn't it?" Cassandra said.

"Yes," I finally answered, then paused. In that hesitation I evoked an undivided attention out of the group as everyone eagerly awaited my further explanation. "I can't cope with this," I went on. "He thinks I love him. Nothing I can say will distract him from this notion. And the truth is, I hate him. He means to see me every day, threatening me if I do not. I want to run away from him, hide from him, anything to keep from seeing him, but there's no escaping him. What can I do?"

Temporarily, I silenced them, each of them reflecting on my situation and seemingly very absorbed in their deliberation, but I did not solicit the sympathy I expected, their attitude being that I should consider myself fortunate rather than complain about it. They did not directly say this, but I could detect it in the way they looked at each other as if minimizing my concerns.

"He has already claimed you, Polyxena," Mother then said. "Why fight it? What's the use in torturing yourself over possibilities not available anymore?" Andromache and Thalia nodded in agreement with this. Cassandra merely looked on.

"You're luckier than we are," Andromache then added. "If this man loves you, he will be kinder disposed toward you and treat you better than we can expect from whomever selects us. You should be thankful for that."

Had I grossly overblown my problem? Certainly, they had me believing that. My obstinacy was apparently unwarranted, and I was unappreciative over what was a fortuitous circumstance for me; that is what they suggested. The only obstacle remaining for me was that I had to convince myself of this truth.

Cassandra viewed my predicament with deeper regard, looking sympathetically at me and demurring in giving me extra counsel, saying nothing that supported the opinions of Mother and Andromache, but neither did she back me. She had already informed me of her position, that I should submit to Neoptolemus or at least act the part of being his lover, and she felt no necessity to expound on this. By not speaking, she succeeded remarkably in reminding me of the precautions she gave me. So in a sense, her message was the same as that of the others. It appeared I was the only one who was out of touch with the realities of my condition. I did not readily accept this realization, and all I can say about having spoken of my problem was that my depression was not alleviated. I felt no improvement to my downcast spirit and slipped under the sheets on my cot, seeking my afternoon nap. So much for confiding my feelings in others.

I was more cheery the next morning, the sun's warmth penetrating my body as well as my temperament, the beauty of a glorious sunrise, even if displaying the charred remains of Troy, still a wonderful sight to behold despite our current hardships. It represented a constancy for me, much sought after in our unstable environment. It was eternal, and I savored it to the fullest, rising early to walk from my tent and greet it, enjoying the brightness unfolding upon our compound and the surrounding shore. Helios had a special place in my heart. He excelled in bringing pleasures that the other gods did not, the sheer delight in seeing his journey from day to day. Was any other god as benign to us?

Later that morning, after I had completed some chores I had been assigned, I stood outside our tent, absorbing the sun's healing powers, when I spotted two Greek lords coming my way, lords by the capes they wore, reaching down their backsides. As they neared, I recognized them as Odysseus and Agamemnon, no doubt visiting us to examine their future prizes, the women of Troy. I opened the flap of our tent, leaning my head inside, and alerted everyone inside of their approach and then waited for them to make their arrival, thinking it improper to walk away after they had already seen me. Soon they stood before me.

"Polyxena, if I remember right," Agamemnon greeted me.

I nodded my assent, smiling at the great king. He smiled back, eyes aglow, and then looked at Odysseus.

"I still think I should take her for myself," he said to him. "She's too lovely to hand over to that crass youth."

"She is," Odysseus replied, "but a promise is a promise, Lord. And she's quite young. My guess is she lacks the skills in bed that you're used to."

"There's something to be said for the naïveté of the young, a freshness, allowing for more discretionary procedures. And who can resist the touch of their soft, beautiful flesh?"

"In the dark, they're all alike, lord," answered Odysseus, unimpressed.

"Not in the day, Odysseus. Visual pleasures are as gratifying as tactile ones, and I prefer the sight of lovely young bodies, glistening in sweat and smelling of it. You can have the Trojan queen, Hecuba. Enjoy her in your darkness." Agamemnon roared in laughter, then glanced at me again. "You're amused by this, aren't you?" he said.

In all honesty, I suppose I was, until the king mentioned Mother and the more serious aspects of our disposition came to the forefront again, depriving me of the lightheartedness required in appreciation of his comments. Still, I think I blushed when he focused his attention back on me. I could feel my face burning. My response was my usual smiling.

"She's embarrassed," Agamemnon said, still laughing. "Well, I didn't come here for her, as much as I might like that. It's Cassandra I want to see. She's in there, isn't she?"

"Yes, lord," I answered.

"Hah! She can speak," he bellowed. "Never mind fetching her. I'll see for myself. You stay here and keep Odysseus company while I visit Cassandra." With that, he entered the tent.

They had a way of flaunting their supremacy over us, ordering us to do this and that, as if a perfectly natural arrangement for them, reminding us they were our masters. This was the prerogative of conquerors, of course. I had to get used to that if I was going to survive.

I felt a tenseness in being by myself with Odysseus. He was instrumental in the killing of Astyanax, being its instigator, as he proposed putting an end to Priam's lineage, although I was not certain about it. I have also heard the decision was forced on him by Agamemnon. Whatever the case was, he was more coldhearted than I first believed. You would never think it looking at him, for his eyes expressed an insight and warmth that belied his true nature. As my uneasiness mounted, he appeared to take note of this and decided, to my relief, it was up to him to initiate our conversing.

"You are the woman Achilles loved," he said. "He spoke to us about you."

"I also loved him," I said.

"Yes, he was convinced of that. But he allowed his love for you to lure him to his death, very careless of him. A man of his strength and talent, brought down by an even greater force: the power of love."

Again, I found myself victimized by the actions of Paris and Deiphobus. To the Greeks, I was responsible for their hero's death. My fear was that nothing I could say in my defense would sway them from their convictions.

"I already told Neoptolemus I had no part in his death," I said. "My brothers contrived the scheme without my knowledge. I was torn with grief when I found out."

Odysseus looked into my eyes as if probing into them to ascertain my sincerity. I could not tell what he thought, but a chill came over me, leaving me with a distinct feeling that he questioned it.

"So you say," he then said. "Neoptolemus said nothing to us about that."

He did not believe me, confirming my deepest fears were well-founded. I was indeed seen as the cause of Achilles's death to the Greeks, stigmatized by this, and might come to suffer for it. You have cursed me, Aphrodite. Forgive me my derogatory aspersions. You orchestrated that Achilles and I should love each other, and now this love posed a major obstacle to me, held against me for consequences I had nothing to do with or ever wanted.

"Where does that leave me?" I asked, more to myself than Odysseus, awakening to the gravity of my situation. "No one will believe me. My only comfort is that I know the truth, that I loved Achilles and he loved me."

"No need to worry yourself sick over it," Odysseus replied, casual in his dismissal of my fears. "Agamemnon has already agreed that you be given to Neoptolemus. Your future rests in his hands. Adjust to this."

"I understand. Thank you for your kind words. When will this happen?"

"Whenever he chooses, but my guess is in two, perhaps three weeks, by the time we're ready to sail. Agamemnon needs to complete his business with your former allies. He wants to secure treaties with them, maybe levy tributes on them. The price they must pay for having opposed us."

"I don't think that will do him much good," I said, happy at having the subject changed.

"He will fail?"

"They won't pay any tributes or accept any treaty conditions your king imposes on them. Whatever promises they make now will be hastily discarded."

"And your reason for believing this?"

"They saw how long it took you to take Troy, that you've depleted much of your force in the process. Their thinking is that your victory was acquired at great costs to you, and this will deter you from ever again embarking on another such venture. My guess is, the minute you leave these shores, they will disavow all the promises they made."

Odysseus glanced curiously at me, the intensity of his concentration quite evident in his gaze. The revelation I gave him may have even impressed him. I think he privately agreed with my assessment but refrained from openly declaring this, for he gave no indication that he disputed what I told him.

"An interesting observation," he remarked. "You seem to be well-informed on the subject."

"Father discussed it with me. He kept me updated on what was happening."

"Apparently he had a lofty opinion of you."

"He wanted to know what I thought about things. I think he valued my judgment, or at least he seemed interested in my opinions."

"How old are you?"

"Eighteen, Lord."

"For being eighteen, and a woman, you are very competent," he said, following up his compliment with a perceptive gaze. "We know it was you who talked the Amazon queen into coming to Priam's assistance, a notable accomplishment, because that's how you met Achilles. Priam may have valued your judgment, but let me caution you, Polyxena, among us, the opinion of women is of no importance. Nor is it favored. As men, we look to ourselves for advice and guidance. Women have no place in such affairs. While you have impressed me with your intelligence, I do not recommend you demonstrate this to others who will not appreciate seeing these qualities in a woman."

"Neither did the Trojans," I was quick to point out when he reminded of the patriarchal order regulating both our societies. "My father was the exception."

Odysseus smiled, appreciating my response, and I think he held me in higher esteem as a result of our speaking than before, but I had to be careful that I was not drawing any false conclusions, easily done when in the presence of a man renowned for his cunning.

"Good," he said. "We understand each other."

By this time, Agamemnon had emerged from the tent, without Cassandra, which surprised me. I was sure he would take her with him. The king looked at me, apparently sensing what I was contemplating.

"I leave her to your mother," he said, "for a few more days, until my cravings get the best of me."

"Thank you, lord," I replied. "Mother is frail and presently in need of our company."

"Oh, stop it! You sound just like your sister. I'm a fool for granting her my concession. You Trojan women are so demanding."

"I'm sorry, lord."

"I bet you are. I'm doing this for my benefit, not hers. I don't want to hear any endless whining coming out of her, destroying my tranquility. I can bear the arrows and spears of my enemies easier than the nagging and complaints of a disgruntled woman."

Odysseus and I glanced at each other, a faint smile coming to both of us. I could envision myself better suited to be claimed by him rather than the hotheaded Neoptolemus and wished such would be the case. I could only speculate on what he thought of me, but overall, I had the feeling that I left a favorable impression on him, although he did not actually express this, and that he was essentially tight-lipped over his thinking. But I was not sure. The trouble with my exchanges with him was that I was left with uncertainty, in a fluctuated state between wanting to believe things about him and then doubting if I correctly perceived these.

"Come, lord," Odysseus said. "Let's get back to our work. There's a lot to do."

"Of course," Agamemnon answered. "Women should not distract us from that. Yet they do. Life is complicated enough without their incessant preoccupying my mind. Inform your sister I shall soon return for her. She's not going to talk me out of my intentions the next time."

"I shall, lord."

"Why is it that I, as king, am allowing myself to be manipulated by others?" I heard him say as he walked off with Odysseus. "Why should Neoptolemus have Polyxena when I desire her myself? I blame you for that, Odysseus." They were an interesting pair, I thought as I saw them stroll away, speaking to each other as equals rather than as king to vassal. I surmised this was because Odysseus was not intimated by rank or status, another feature that elevated him in my eyes.

Whatever Cassandra had said to Agememnon, I had to congratulate her for insisting that her position be met. It could not have been easy to stand up to the mighty king, and that she succeeded in doing so spoke well for her. She could be amazingly headstrong if the situation demanded it. My respect and admiration for her was significantly enhanced over what had to have been an extraordinary performance on her part. I was eager to learn what she did and hurried into the tent to see her. I found her huddled with Andromache and Mother, consoling themselves. Apparently, it had been more of an ordeal for her than I imagined.

"How did you do it?" I asked Cassandra. "I was sure Agamemnon would take you with him."

"I only postponed it," she said, her studied look diminishing my ardor. "I promised him to be the obedient and submissive woman he desires but only if I could remain with Mother as long as possible. He did not like it but ultimately conceded to my wishes."

"That's it?"

"It was far from easy, Polyxena," Andromache interjected. "They argued over it for the longest time. The king was not keen on listening to a woman. You should have seen her. She stood her ground. Great Agamemnon backed down ."

I was remiss in hinting that I may have been disappointed this was all there was to it, because that assuredly was not my true feeling. In fact, I was extremely proud of Cassandra, recognizing the courage required to pull it off. I could not have done it. I glanced lovingly at her, my respect for her apparent. She glanced back and nodded, indicating to me she apprehended the high regard in which I beheld her.

"Too bad I missed it," I said. "Agamemnon requested that I stay with Odysseus."

"And you complied," Andromache said.

"Yes, I complied," I reacted, somewhat peeved that my own actions should be considered less than appropriate. "I did not see myself as having a choice."

"Of course, you didn't. I didn't mean to suggest that. My point was to make you realize how courageously Cassandra behaved."

"I never questioned it, Andromache," I snapped back, flustered by her insinuation that my conduct was somehow inferior to Cassandra's. "But realize also, the risks Cassandra took were not hers alone. We could all have been jeopardized by it. Agamemnon is not a person to trifle with. His rage could easily be vented against us all."

The strain of our confined habitation was starting to reveal itself. I was perhaps more affected by this than the others, unable as I was to escape from it with my previous habit of riding Zephyrus, and I became careless in my statements, thoughtlessly blurting them out without concern over how damaging they might be. Andromache's face turned red, receiving my words as a reprimand, which was not my intent, for her neglect in comprehending the full consequences that Cassandra's actions entailed. Worse, I had unwittingly minimized my sister's boldness by alluding that she might have endangered the rest of us by her singular confrontation with Agamemnon. Cassandra, of course, understood this clearly enough and was herself embarrassed by what she probably now considered her selfishness. None of this response was what I wanted or even meant to imply.

"Forgive me," I said, apologizing for my rash outburst. "My words were unkind. I did not mean to undermine what Cassandra did."

"She fought to care for your mother," Andromache exclaimed, suggesting that I failed in that connection.

"I know," I answered, regretting my words. "I am remiss in not appreciating that."

Mother remained quiet throughout our discussion, unwilling to choose any preference in a confrontation involving her; that was my conclusion anyway. She shifted her glances from Cassandra and Andromache to me as we spoke, essentially a blank gaze that was devoid of expression and gave little indication as to what she was actually thinking. My guess was that she favored Cassandra who, after all, defended her actions as being on Mother's behalf. Who could view this in an unfavorable light? Cassandra had obviously endeared herself to Mother, while my behavior, I have to be honest about it, manifested itself in tendencies to get away from her and seek my solace elsewhere. But I did not do this to inflict any pain upon her or with any malicious intent; rather, I saw no other means available for me, my nature being that of enduring my afflictions in solitude.

All three looked at me, a sorrowful expression on their faces, not improving my standing with them one bit. Was I suddenly cast as the villain in this drama because I had dared to question the wisdom of Cassandra's behavior? I admired her for her obvious courage, yet my own words negated what I felt and twisted my meanings into a more controversial context. Frustrated and disapproving of my conduct, I went to my cot and fell into it, saying nothing more.

CHAPTER XXIII

MY DEPRESSION WAS GETTING WORSE. I was sinking into an abyss of horrible dejection, where I saw no solutions to the melancholy making its claim on me and enveloping me with increasing despair. My despondency was enhanced by my rebellion against the confinement that was becoming ever more oppressive for me. At times, I just wanted to scream and run away from it all, but where could I go? The unproductive and idle days were dragging ahead at an excruciatingly slow pace, adding irritation to the hopelessness already possessing me. I was not in a good frame of mind, and although I tried my best to keep these feelings from impinging on others, I did not think I was succeeding at this. I was desperately longing for a change, any change, to my present circumstances, anything that would take me away from here, from the people I knew. I needed something different.

True to his word, and adding to my woes, Neoptolemus made the frequent visit he had threatened me with. I say threatened because I did not look forward to these, even if they did provide temporary relief to my boredom. They never turned out to my satisfaction, and the resultant strain often made me more miserable. Try as I might, I could not shake him from an unwarranted belief that I was enamored with him, and this compounded my problem. He flat-out refused to accept what I told him, even when I was being totally honest about it. On one particular day, all the frustrations our encounters imposed on me came to a head, causing me to commit one of the biggest blunders of my life. It all began simple enough, very similar to the four previous days he had visited me. I was standing outside our tent when I spotted him coming. My immediate impulse was to enter the tent, as I similarly felt on the other days and failed to follow through with, but that would have evoked an angry reaction out of him, and I wanted to avoid that.

"Good to see you, Polyxena," he said upon arriving. "You look surprisingly well today."

"Really?" I answered. "I don't feel that way."

"You're turning into a worrywart. Needlessly I say. We'll soon be leaving. I'm looking forward to our time together."

This meant a permanent separation from Mother, Cassandra, and Andromache, as well as Thalia. With its impending reality nearing, the thought of losing the people closest to me was a bit unnerving just the same. I blanched on hearing him.

"What's wrong?" Neoptolemus said after noting my distress. "I thought you wanted to get out of here."

"I did, but now I'm not sure."

"There's nothing left to keep you here anymore. Look at it." He extended his outstretched arm to the city. "Troy is in ruins. You have no place else to go."

What was certain to me was that I would not get any sympathy from Neoptolemus, not even any understanding. What would he know about the pain of losing a loved one? For all I knew, he had never loved anyone, that is, before his presumed love for me. He never really knew his father and, in fact, lived in envy of him and may have even despised him because of this. His coldhearted disposition had no room for tenderness, for feeling an attachment to a place and people. He could never know of the sorrow gripping me over missing Mother.

"You have nothing to say?" he next said, agitated over my deliberation, which precluded me from immediately responding to him. "I know what's bothering you. You don't want to be with me. That's it, isn't it?"

Indeed it was, but how would I affirm it with tact? "To be truthful," I said, "I'm nervous about it."

"Why?" he snarled, his irritation mounting.

"I'm afraid of you."

"What on earth for?" he reacted, seeming genuinely surprised. "I've never touched you, never forced myself on you, kept my distance from you even when I desired otherwise, allowed you to be with your mother. If anything, I've been too lenient on you. I should have taken you from the start. I had that prerogative, you know."

"Don't flatter yourself with your kindheartedness," I angrily responded. "Just what did you expect? There is an evil side to you. You've shown me the cruelty you're capable of. I saw you kill my father, an old man carrying no weapon, and Adromache's baby, utterly defenseless."

"Stop endlessly shoving that down my throat! It's over."

"I'll never forget that."

"I strongly urge that you do. As of this moment, never mention my misdeeds to me again. I am willing to forgive your complicity in my father's death, why can't you do the same?"

He had completely dismissed from his mind what I had told him about his father's death, as if I had never spoken to him about it at all, and I was furious over that. My words meant nothing to him.

"You didn't listen to anything I said about Achilles," I rebuked him.

"Oh, I heard you. But I didn't believe it."

"You admit this to me? What does this portent for our relationship? Am I to be distrusted whenever I say something you don't want to hear?"

"That's not what I meant!" he now yelled, unable to keep his fiery temperament in check.

"Maybe not, but I see no promise in our future together, too many obstacles stand in our way. Why can't you concede we're not meant for each other and allow someone else to have me?"

"What?" he shouted, outraged over my suggestion. "You can't mean that."

"Yes, I do," I hastily replied, losing sight of the disparagement my declaration implied. "We have nothing in common with each other that I can see. Our relationship has no chance of working out."

His reaction was one of stunned disbelief, my assertion incomprehensible to him, and he responded accordingly, both confused and agitated.

"I thought we loved each other," he said, glowering at me.

His unfounded conclusion offended me. I had, to my knowledge, never once alluded to any action that promoted or hinted at his erroneous perception, and I felt compelled to dispel the notion possessing him, even at the cost of alienating him.

"Have I ever told you I loved you?" I said. "No! I have not! You're making an invalid presumption, building something up in your mind that does not exist."

"It's not true. As much as I love you, for you not to be affected by that, not to feel the same way about me, it can't be."

"I'm sorry," I replied, genuinely feeling sad for him. I realized I still had it within my power to reverse my stance, thereby giving a protective element to my insecure future, but for some inexplicable reason, I resisted this. I was now utterly at his mercy, my disposition subject to his whim, or more precisely, to the emotionalism in which he would react to my disclosure. To my astonishment, he was still in denial, not accepting my words or believing them false.

"You must love me exactly as much as I love you," he groaned, sounding more as if he was entreating me to see things his way, voicing a desperate hope, one running counter to the expectations I had shattered for him. "You don't feel the intense longing I feel for you? A desire to be with me?"

"I don't," I truthfully answered, daring to say what might possibly be detrimental to me. "I wish I could tell you otherwise."

"Spare me your sentiments," he shouted out. "You're lying. You loved my father, so you can damn well also love me."

"You are not Achilles."

"By the gods! I will not stand for this! All my life I have been told this and have tried my best to live up to his image. I have fought as courageously as he did, facing enemy warriors as boldly as he and slaying nearly as many. And what do I hear from you? I am not Achilles, you say. No, I'm not, but I am as good as he and will not be deprecated by you."

"Emulating your father does not make you the same man."

"Am I to endure this? Tell me what attracted you to him, why you cannot give me that affection. He is dead. I will not live in envy of a dead man."

"Aphrodite generated our mutual interest in each other. I can't give any other explanation than that. He and I adhered to her wishes and found ourselves in love. We responded to what she had arranged for us."

"That tells me nothing. If this is all Aphrodite's doing, as you believe, then I ought to be rewarded with your love if I were to make sacrifices to her and properly propitiate her. Do you expect that to happen?"

"I don't know."

"I get the impression you intentionally want nothing to do with me. If that is so, you will sorely regret it."

"Why do you always resort to threats when things are not to your liking? That's no way to endear anyone to you."

"Then you're saying it's not a lost cause for me. Given the time, you may yet fall in love with me. You can learn to love me."

That possibility existed, although I placed little faith in such a transition occurring for me. Nothing in his character and appearance had any appeal for me, heavily mitigating against this. And I feared him. Even if I could surmount these trepidations, and I had no confidence that I was able to, the anxieties would always be there, preventing me from warming up to him and keeping a barrier between us. The prospect of having a loving relationship was not promising. At best, I would abide him, masking an endearment not present. At worst, my situation would become intolerable under the strain my pretense imposed on me.

"Possibly," I said. "I can't tell at this stage."

"Don't be so damn inconclusive about it. You sound as though your eventual affection for me poses a major chore for you. I'm a despicable dog you reject out of hand but might warm up to if you see fit, a filthy swine who can only be seen and approved of at the worst possible compromise to oneself."

"You said that, not me."

"That's what you think," he declared, furious over his own conclusion.

I said nothing and, in my quietness, inadvertently unleashed a torrent of rage in him that had me trembling in its fury. He lashed at me in anger, shouting out profanities, and startling me with his rancor.

"Miserable wretch! Trojan bitch! Whore!" he cursed, repeating himself in his defamation of me until, at last, he regained his senses to threaten me more. "Since you see me as such a lowlife, too disgusting to be around, I am acting accordingly. I don't want to disappoint the expectancy you have of me. I'm not giving you the satisfaction you seek in anyone else's company. If I cannot have your love, nobody's going to have it."

He then turned about and stormed off, his vituperations filling the air, leaving me paralyzed in my consternation, to say nothing of my dread of him. He affirmed what I most feared in him: his uncontrolled vehemence toward anything opposing his expectations or notions. But I was not guiltless in the reaction I elicited from him. I had provoked him—I knew it—and should have exercised better judgment. This greatly upset me. I attempted to reconstruct our conversation to learn at what point I went too far but was unable to find my answer. One thing I learned though: never again to deny him the possibility of an amiable relationship arising between us. The anxiety I was now feeling was not worth it. I had to make amends and was resolved to do that next time I saw him, whenever that might be.

I staggered back into the tent, still reeling under the verbal onslaught I was exposed to, so that I might find some solace in lying there. Everyone was looking at me, apparently having heard the argument that arose between Neoptolemus and me. Theirs was not a look of empathy, but rather of disdain, evidently out of a conviction that I was jeopardizing their well-being as well as mine, and I was discomfited by the stares they gave me. But I was not going to let it disturb me further; I had had enough bad encounters for one day.

Cassandra, in particular, was perturbed, her hard glares cutting to my inner core. I knew at once that I had committed a grave mistake.

"What is the matter with you?" she said as I was about to sit down on my cot. "I told you to reciprocate the love he has for you. You did the opposite!"

"I didn't know it would end the way it did," I replied truthfully.

"Can't you see the damage you've done? Neoptolemus is your new master; he controls your future. In spite of everything I warned you about, you did not listen to me. I fear for you now."

Cassandra's worried comportment did not help matters. I recognized I had erred, but she aggravated the anxieties possessing me to such a degree that I actually became chilled when I contemplated my blunder. Hearing her almost made me believe there was no way out for me, that my mistake was irreversible and precluded any opportunity to atone for my offense, whatever that may have been. I was jolted by her insinuation, my awareness that I may suddenly be in a dire situation.

"You're scaring me, Cassandra," I said. "Please don't. I have enough to worry about as it is."

"Pay attention to me," she emphasized. "The next time you see him, swoon over him, make it appear you love him. Do what you have to, but convince him of your sincerity, even if you pretend."

"I'm not good at playing those games. You know that."

"Stop resisting what I say!" Cassandra harshly rebuked me, a look of utter terror in her eyes. "You are in serious trouble. I'm telling you how to avert the danger I see facing you. Promise me you will do this."

She had me in near panic, her horror-struck countenance unnerving me completely, and I was unable to shake the fear she had instilled in me. Her penetrating eyes, expressing the dread obsessing her, were extremely unsettling, leaving me bereft of any sound reasoning that might have prevailed upon my senses under more normal circumstances. I nodded my consent, left speechless in my apprehensiveness to say anything.

"Good," Cassandra said. "Put on your best show. It's critical."

What had I done? I admit that I may have given Neoptolemus the provocation that caused my alienation to him, but I was very much at a loss over how I managed this, unclear of the word choices, the phrases I used to bring this about. I unwittingly allowed my discomfort in his presence to rob me of sound judgment and lost my self-control. His vehement reaction came as a profound shock to me, astonishing me with the acerbity and suddenness in which he concluded our discussion. What could I do now? I needed to see him and apologize to him for my unseemly conduct, if such it was, and make the necessary overtures to him that Cassandra thought crucial. I was willing to do this, but had no opportunity at present, another setback for me, depriving me of the tranquility I now most needed.

I was mollified in some measure, however miniscule, by my sister's intimation that I still had a small chance of redeeming myself. Her cautionary advice suggested I would have another meeting with Neoptolemus by which to accede to his wishes. If I had a clearer understanding of how I ran afoul of him in our earlier conversation, I could make the adjustments that were in my best interest; however, I remained bewildered over where I had gone astray, and this left me to my own interpretations as to its assessment, not necessarily correct. I have to initiate the advances demonstrating my feigned adoration the next time I see him, that much I knew. I was reasonably confident that he could not stay away from me for long, and the opportunity to avail myself on his good graces favored me. Still, this was not going to be a relaxing time for me, and I had difficulty finding any peacefulness during the rest of the day.

Mother and I, despite my occasional need to get away from our proximity, actually became considerably closer to each other than at any previous time I can recollect. I suppose my attitude toward her had changed. I was seeing her more in a tragic light than before, recognizing the painful outcome life's experience had imparted on her, particularly in the loss of all her sons, except for Helenus, and I haven't heard of him since Troy fell. Agonizing over these heartbreaking events at first, she then developed a stoic detachment from her sorrows and settled into a calm acceptance of all that fortune would thrust upon her, and in this, she bore her difficulties with great dignity, endearing her to me. No woman had ever carried such a burden, and that she did so without going mad speaks well for her. She merited my respect, and I came to love her for all that she had endured. I was moved to make things as comfortable for her as I could, as were Cassandra and Andromache, no longer regarding these tasks as a duty but a privilege.

She responded to my tenderness in her own special way, with her eyes emitting a cheerful aura and a loving smile that warmed my heart, and she retained the quality that made her care more for me and those around her than herself. Though we were grown women, she saw us as children in need of her maternal guidance. Once, I might have thought this belittling to me, but now, I saw the well-meaning purpose behind it and appreciated her efforts and the sincerity in which she declared her intent. We sat in each other's company more frequently now, consoling ourselves and giving us the encouragement necessary for enduring our adversity. We knew we faced separation, and this awareness bore heavily upon us.

"The Greeks will be sailing soon," Mother said to me. "Our time together is short. We may never see each other again."

"In less than a week from what I've heard," I replied.

"Dear Polyxena, I shall miss you so. With everything that's happened to me, this will be the worst for me."

"Do you mean that, Mother? I have not been the most obedient of your daughters. At times, I felt as though I was a disappointment for you."

Tears trickled down Mother's face, and yet she smiled through her muffled crying, a sight that touched me so deeply that I could scarcely keep from weeping myself.

"You were," she said, "but I loved you for it. You, among all my daughters, had a very distinctive personality, unique in almost every respect, challenging for me, but in a truly wonderful way. Your rebellious nature was, for the most part, tempered by a benign spirit. I never saw any maliciousness in it. And I know you loved Priam, and he so loved you, perhaps even more than Hector. I did not understand why then, but now I do."

Hearing Father mentioned was all I could take. The floodgates to my eyes gushed forth my tears. I hugged Mother tightly, clinging to her as if a mere child, and together, we wept. The sight of us in our commiseration must have affected Andromache and Cassandra as badly as it did me, for soon, they were also sobbing alongside us, even Thalia joined the chorus, and it seemed the longest time before we finally regained our composure and managed to go about our daily business. But I was overcome with a sense of relief, mixed with both sadness and joy, and strongly felt as if I had been purged of my inhibitions toward my mother, a good feeling.

Later that morning, I went outside to see if Neoptolemus would make his usual visit. He normally came around this time, but after our last parting, I fully expected him to stay away, at least for a while, until he recovered from the blow I dealt him. I hoped I was wrong, for I needed to speak to him, to alleviate the tenseness hounding me, and to set things straight between us. I had no desire for any hostility ruling our relationship, preferring friendliness to enmity, to the extent possible when such powerful emotions as love are involved. He did not come at his usual time, accentuating my anxieties. Resigned to the conclusion that no redemption was in the offing for me this day, I reluctantly turned about, preparing to enter the tent again for protection from the glaring sun, when I spotted him coming from behind the tent most distant from ours. My heartbeat accelerated. I was searching for the words I might use to resolve our differences, without any coming to me. *Let this be a good meeting*, I entreated the gods.

He was slow in arriving, revealing his own uncertainty in the shuffling approach, and I waited on him, thinking what this might portent. My mouth dried in the tension dominating me. When at last he stood before me, we peered into each other's eyes at length, not saying a word, as if trying to ascertain the thoughts preoccupying us. His expression, strange to say, was one of regret rather than the frustrated anger so prevalent before.

"I'm sorry about yesterday," I spoke first.

"Are you?" he asked, having difficulty looking at me, his eyes shifting to the ground or to either side of him.

"I am. I didn't mean to suggest that I could not find an accommodation with you, that there was no chance for any relationship arising between us."

"Why tell me this now?" he groaned, nearly in tears. "When it's too late."

"Too late?" I tensed up.

"You forced me into doing something I didn't want to do. Why couldn't you be respectful to me?"

"What do you mean?"

He broke out crying, angry at himself, his face contorted in anguish.

"Did you think I was joking when I said that if I can't have you, nobody will? I meant it. I came here to inform you of my actions— against you. I was so angry at you, I wanted to hurt you. I'm so ashamed."

Frightened, I sensed that the gravest consequences faced me. His contrite reaction to my apologetic words enhanced my trepidation to even greater levels, making my nervousness nearly intolerable for me.

"Tell me," I demanded, not really wanting to know, but deeming it necessary to relieve my stress. "What did you do?"

"I fabricated a story about Achilles and you, and they believed me. Damn this world! I won't be able to take it back."

I had a distinct feeling that the story he concocted spelled a disaster. Everything in his demeanor—the dread in which regarded his inability to recant it, the torment he was suffering on its account— were indications that I had been put in a position from which there was no retreat. But how could this be? How was it possible that mere words could have such momentous ramifications that they cannot be taken back? I had to know what he said.

"What was your story?" I asked.

He was reluctant to tell me, red-faced and distressed, hesitating for what seemed the longest time, but finally spoke.

"I told Agamemnon and Odysseus and the others that the ghost of Achilles came to me as I walked past the borrow where his ashes rest and beckoned that his love here—you—be united with him in death before we set sail."

I gasped and knew I was doomed.

"By your death, we not only appease Achilles, but Poseidon as well, for it's customary to make a sacrifice to assure us favorable winds for our return journey. Everyone agreed to this necessity. Yes, it's now seen as necessary. Oh, Polyxena," he broke down completely, weeping uncontrollably. "What have I done?"

I was too petrified to answer him, the shock of his story implanting itself, horrifying me. No escape existed for me, the uncompromising nature of the account sealing my fate. That it should come to this, being undone by a man whose love I spurned. That was the truth of it: my rejecting the love of Neoptolemus was my downfall. I was a dead woman: Neoptolemus had seen to that.

"I loved you," he moaned, using the past tense as if I had already departed. "Why did you have to offend me so?"

"My honesty has victimized me," I finally answered him, determined not to have him see me crying. "I was never good at being deceitful, even when my safety was at risk. It is one of my weaknesses."

"Forgive me, Polyxena."

"Never!" I shouted at him, my repressed anger surfacing to prevail over my distress. He had rashly acted upon a presumed guilt on my part that I had rejected his love. What love? Not once did I allude to possessing a love for him. If he believed this, it was due to his own estimation of a situation that was not rooted in reality. His fantasizing led him to his absurd conclusions, and I was to pay the full price for it. The more I reflected over this, the angrier I became.

"My love for you robbed me of sound judgment," he lamented. "Say you forgive me so I can find solace in what I've done."

"I curse the day I ever met you!" I continued yelling at him. "I was warned to stay away from you, but I tempted fate. It was the biggest mistake of my life."

"You're justified in being angry with me. Understand it wasn't me, but for love's sake, I acted the way I did."

"For love's sake?" I screamed at him. "What twisted notion of love is this—that you would consign the object of your love to cruel death? What am I supposed to be—grateful?"

"This is not what I wanted. Had you not misled me into believing that our love had no chance of succeeding, I would never have done this. You have yourself to blame."

"Get away from me!" I could no longer abide his presence, made all the more intolerable for me with his unmanly, cowardly sniveling. "I never want to see you again!"

He slunk away, disgraceful in his obsequious acquiescence. I would have preferred his irrational tirades to this subservient conduct. He made a pitiable spectacle of himself, but I loathed him to the extreme now and, in my impassioned state, saw nothing redeeming in his regretful posturing.

Stunned, still not believing it, I staggered back toward my cot, the ashen faces of my mother and sister and also Andromache telling me they had been shaken over our heated exchange. I was resolved not to shed any tears over what the fates had decreed for me, but I knew my eyes were glazed over and negated my attempts at composure.

"Oh, Mother," I moaned when I saw her sitting on her cot, slumping down beside her. "I am heartsick to tell you this." I broke down despite all my efforts to remain calm, horribly guilt ridden that I should bring such unhappiness to Mother in these trying times. I wanted so desperately to spare her any further suffering. "They're going to kill me."

Perhaps they did not hear all that was said, for I could see their shocked expressions, the horror of my words registering with startling swiftness in their minds, leaving them reeling in its wake.

"Surely you're wrong," Mother replied, her voice trembling. "Say it's not so."

"I'm afraid it is," I said.

"But why? How...?"

"I am to be sacrificed to Poseidon, to ensure them a smooth sail home. It's a custom of theirs. Whenever they undertake a major sea crossing, they make an offering to the sea god so he is propitiated into granting them a safe passage."

"This is true," Cassandra said. "I was told Agamemnon actually sacrificed his daughter, Iphigeneia, to bring his ships to Troy. For being great seafarers, the Greeks take no chances on their voyages, doing what they must to secure protection from the gods."

"His own daughter?" I muttered, even under my strain thinking this incredible. "What manner of men are these Greeks?"

"Not that different from our Trojans," Cassandra answered. "Fearing the wrath of the gods if they are slighted or ignored."

While intrigued momentarily by this diversion in our conversing, the issue at hand was too grave to be sidestepped and again prevailed over us, especially Mother who was so distraught that I was unable to calm her.

"Why you?" she asked, softly weeping.

I was reluctant to inform her, wishing not to add to her pain, but realized the truth would be revealed to her sooner or later anyway.

"There's more to it," I told her. "I foolishly offended Neoptolemus, and he retaliated against me by conjuring up a wild story about me, saying that Achilles's ghost demanded my death. He said I have myself to blame for this, and I now believe he is correct. Cassandra repeatedly warned me about him, but I chose to ignore her advice. Yes, I made the choices leading to this. I could have avoided it all, had I been more careful."

"That's only partly true, Polyxena," Cassandra said. "Let me remind you that your first encounter with him was quite by accident, fated to happen, not foreseen by you. You did not choose it."

"Indirectly, I did, Cassandra. I could have ridden away when I saw him coming, but I waited until he learned of me."

"You did not know who he was."

I gave Cassandra a comprehending gaze, nodding my concurrence. So it was truly fated to happen. In a strange sort of way, I took comfort in that, perhaps because it absolved me of the culpability I railed against myself all this time. If it was indeed my destiny to have my fatal encounter with him, then this was a matter in the hands of the gods, nothing could have averted it. It was all preordained. Achilles once asked me, can we deny our destiny? He was convinced we could not and acted accordingly, accepting that he was going to die at Troy. Can I do any less? Silently, I thanked Cassandra for the enlightenment she gave me, a revelation greatly alleviating my torment.

"My dear daughter," Mother sobbed, clinging tightly to me. "What shall I do without you? You have been a source of such joy to me."

Joy? Surely that was an overestimation. Maybe during these past few days, but certainly that was questionable in my earlier experiences with her, but she was an older woman now and needed her assurances, and I was not about to diminish what comforted her. I was relieved that my concern for her still held prominence in my thinking, despite all the other concerns that might have distracted from this, so I saw a value in her perceptions, as it provided solace for me as well as her.

"Our separation is inevitable, Mother," I said. "The Greeks will send us on our different paths. My fate will not alter this."

We hugged. She kissed me on my forehead, understanding me, even if burdensome to her, and muffled her weeping as best as she could. I delicately passed her into Andromache's hands when I was overcome with an urge to release myself from her despondency, which oppressed me in that it accentuated my depression. I embraced Cassandra in turn, still grateful for her helpful words to me.

"Thank you, Sister," I said. "You have awakened me to understanding my misfortune."

"Have courage, Polyxena," teary-eyed Cassandra said. "Accept what the fates have decreed for you. Let the Greeks know the mettle Trojan women are made of."

She pleased me with those words, instilling in me a resolve to bravely embrace the end in store for me. I was not going to depart this world bemoaning my destiny, whimpering like a child, giving the Greeks the pleasure of seeing me stripped of my dignity, cowardly in my exhortations for mercy. Once again, Cassandra gave me the strength of will to undergo the ordeal awaiting me. I was truly indebted to her.

I lay awake in my cot late into the night, reflecting over the circumstances that brought me to this point, trying to ascertain how these came about and make sense out of what was so incomprehensible to me. Despite my inclination toward recognizing that my fate had been preordained for me, there remained a side of me that rebelled against its acceptance and strove to seek answers other than I presumed. I was searching for clarifications to my skepticism, to discover the reasons why things happened as they did.

Ultimately, the responsibility for the fate befalling me is mine. I made the choices that were to result in the consequences unfolding for me. To say I was manipulated by the wiles of devious-minded gods is misleading. No one forced me into taking my rides on Zephyrus, which were to lead to my first meeting Neoptolemus, nor to make my follow up visits with him. These were actions I took upon myself, motivated in large measure by my curiosity in getting to know him better, despite the frequent unfavorable view in which I perceived him. True, Father wanted me to continue my contacts with him to learn about what the Greeks planned, but he imposed no demand on me to do so. It was voluntary on my part, largely due to vanity. I thought it exciting to perform as a spy, or as I envisioned the task. These were matters of my choosing, and for better or worse, the results that ensued can only be attributed to what I was instrumental in creating. But is that the correct explanation?

How do I explain Neoptolemus's reaction to me? I have no recollection of ever leading him on to draw the conclusions about my loving him as he did. Was this the proverbial unrequited love the poets so often lament over? If so, is this not your handiwork, Oh Goddess? From the very beginning, I saw no attraction in him and was even conscious of carefully avoiding his ever acquiring that notion, saying nothing that might engender such a false impression. Somehow, I failed in this, although I am unable to determine when that might have occurred. These are the mysteries in life that offer no adequate explanations. Were I to relive the same days, I would still not know what I did wrong or what I would do differently. Yet it is this, more than any other single factor, that is the direct cause of my impending death. You are a cruel goddess, Aphrodite. More than any other of the deities, you involve yourself in the lives of mortals, bringing about our demise through the pain and suffering you afflict us with. Greater misfortune has been caused by your interference than all other conspiracies combined.

There are trade-offs to everything we do. We are left to ponder over what might have occurred had we embarked upon a different course, often regretting the actions we have taken and dissatisfied with the conditions of our selected path. There is a paradox in this: if we are happy in our circumstance, we do not question what we have done, but if not, then we deplore the direction we chose, thinking we could have done better. It is the end result that determines the correctness of our actions, and yet the venture must be initiated before this is known to us. How different things would be had I never been sent to the Amazons. My life would probably bear no resemblance to what it has been this past year, and I might even be happier for it. Most assuredly, the reasons calling for my death would not have existed for me. I would never have met Achilles, which, in turn, would have precluded my ever knowing his son, Neoptolemus. So the question for me is whether, with full knowledge of my impending doom, I regret the path I have taken?

I have no clear answer to that. A life-changing decision I made during that time was when I refused to go with Antiope. She begged me to come with her, and I deeply wanted to, loving her more than anyone I had ever met until then, but my loyalty to my servants and to Troy stood in the way, perhaps beclouding my judgment. Lovely Antiope, so dear to me, sweet in my memories. Now that I am thinking of her, I realize how much I long for and miss her. I have no doubt we could have had a good life together in Themiscyra. The only time in my life that I ever felt truly free were the days I spent with her, hunting with her, riding on my noble Zephyrus—I so loved that horse. Adding to the futility of my decision was that I had been assumed dead by my family members, the very reason I had denied her pleadings for me, so I could see them again. It would never have made a difference. I literally came back from the dead to them. Staying in Themiscyra would have assured me greater happiness than returning to Troy.

But had I done so, I would never have met Achilles. My most vivid and most endearing memory is of him, the love that arose between us, the night we brought our love to fruition beside the campfire, the single most treasured event of my life, nothing else coming even remotely close in comparison. He aroused sensations in me that I had never experienced and can scarcely define, no description giving adequate justification to the intensity of the feelings that enveloped me. A thousand subsequent lovemaking sessions could not equal the one I had with him. His strength and beauty, his awesome masculinity intoxicated me, gratifying my deepest cravings, sending my passions soaring. I loved Achilles and was so enthralled in knowing he loved me. What value can anyone put on having had such an intensely rewarding encounter? Were I even to advance to an old age, I would never again relive such an ecstatic moment.

Was it all worth it? Can I appropriately maintain that the best experiences of my life have transpired for me and that nothing in my future can equal or surpass the rewards already achieved? If true, then I have lived a full life, as satisfying as can be expected, an awareness not only pleasurable for me, as far as that was possible, but also enlightening. It meant that I had accomplished in my time what many do not achieve during their entire lives, a realization very comforting for me in my duress.

With such thoughts, I convinced myself that my life has been a rewarding adventure for me, especially this past year. Despite all the heartache and pain, the horror of losing the things I cherished and loved, the suffering I saw and endured, and the fate I, in great measure, brought upon myself, I would not exchange my life's experiences for anything. As I so reflected, I drew courage from it, the strength that comes from the conviction of knowing that even if my life was destined to be short, I had truly lived it. My time in this world was well spent, and I should have no regrets.

Chapter XXIV

I AM NOW IN MY PRESENT setting, where I began my deliberations, searching for the meaning behind the events that have been thrust upon me, revealing my thoughts to you, Divine Aphrodite, needing to learn what purpose my life has served so that I might find my peace. And I am still bereft of the serenity I feel must result from knowing this. No answer has come to me. Disclose your secret to me, and grant me the contentment I seek.

The Greeks sail into days, and the time is at hand in which I must ensure a secure voyage for them. Preparations are being made in front of the tumulus where the ashes of Achilles and his best friend, Patroclus, were encased. A wooden platform, I was told, standing about a man's height has been erected on the barrow's western side, which faces the sea. Upon this elevated structure, so everyone will have a full view of the proceedings, I am to be sacrificed, an offering to the sea god, Poseidon, whom the Greeks more fear than revere. But above that, I am to placate the restless spirit of great Achilles, crying out for my company so that it could find some happiness in the afterlife. What an incredulous story Neoptolemus has concocted. In serving this dual purpose, my death is both necessary and highly anticipated. Although meant to be a solemn occasion, it has all the trappings of a grand spectacle to me. I am certain priests and seers, advisors and commanders, kings and lords, and masses of soldiers will look upon me, judging me as I face death. It is early morning. I presently wait upon the guards to come for me and once more lose myself in my thoughts.

As expected, Neoptolemus did not have the courage to see me again after our last sordid meeting, no doubt due to his inability to cope with having been instrumental in destroying the one love of his life, as I believe he regarded me. Had he come, I would have avoided seeing him. It still seems so inconceivable to me, all my associations with him, that it should come to such a conclusion. He blames me for directing him into taking his fateful steps. Can this be true? I am no longer able to piece together all the exchanges I had with him, and a thorough scrutiny of my alleged culpability in the affair now eludes me. Perhaps I did contribute to bringing about my downfall. I knew all along that he loved me. I should have denounced this love from the start but do not remember if I did.

Poor Neoptolemus. Like Oenone, he embarked upon a course that offered no chance for reversal of the measures taken. And unlike me, he will have to live with that. How easy can that be for someone who has caused the death of a person loved? He is the one who ought to be pitied, not me. But if I did indeed forgive him, he would consider himself totally exonerated of any complicity in my death. I cannot give him the peace of mind such an absolution would entail. I may be selfish in my attitude toward this, but at this juncture, my feeling is that I should hold him accountable for his heedlessness and let him suffer accordingly for it. It serves him right.

My depression clings oppressively about me. I am unable to shake it off, but I now believe I am actually well served by my deplorable state. In my gloomy outlook, I have developed a strange longing for having my misery put to an abrupt end. I would even go so far as to say that I have a death wish. As these feelings preoccupied me even before Neoptolemus consigned me to my fate, I cannot attribute the downward spiral I find myself in to his maneuverings. Instead, my own disposition accounts for it. I derive no pleasures from anything I saw, heard, or did, seeing a sadness in everything, not the kind of sadness that makes one cry but, rather, that projects a sense of hopelessness, depriving one of all encouragement, seeing the world as an uncompromising, cold, unfeeling, alien place, a place where one does not belong. This is my present world, and I increasingly look to death as a my only escape from it.

By now, our dispositions have been determined for us, and we learned that Andromache had been awarded to Neoptolemus by Agamemnon as compensation for his loss of me. Unbelievable.

"How am I to live with that cruel man," Andromache mopes as we sat in our cluster in the tent, "after what he did to my infant son?"

"Such is our lot," Mother says. "Women are nothing more than trophies of war. Men rule over us. We are but chattel to them."

"I'll kill myself first. I won't be a slave to that beast."

"Yes, you will," Cassandra says to Andromache. "We all will, because we are women. Only Polyxena is spared from the degradation the rest of us will have to endure."

I think it ironic that Cassandra should suggest I am more fortunate than the rest of them, but in a manner of speaking, she is right. My worries will soon be over, while theirs will just begin. This implies, of course, that their new masters will be cruel and oppressive tyrants, which is by no means known to them and could be utterly wrong. Yet it is better for me to believe such will be the case, making my misfortune—or should I say fortune?—more palatable for me.

"At least I won't leave these shores," I say. "Troy shall remain my home."

I detect their disagreement What home? they are thinking. Troy is but a heap of ashes and stone, no more place to desire. The truth is that they know they are better off leaving here and, in spite of what they were saying, not one of them would trade places with me. I am the outcast among them, confirming to me that I live in a world I no longer belong in. In speaking about their potential futures, they negate mine, having already accepted I have no more role in their lives. This is the natural thing for them to do, for they at least have a future, and I should not disparage them for it. My preference now is to have it over with as soon as possible. I want no more part of this world.

"You shall rest with Hector, my beloved husband," Andromache says.

"And Priam, your father," Mother adds. "And my other sons. I am not granted my request to die here. I am to go with Odysseus. My only consolation is that he has agreed to take Thalia with us."

I am wrong. Mother would exchange places with me.

"And you, Cassandra?" I ask. "Is it certain that Agamemnon will take you?"

"Yes, to my great misfortune," Cassandra answers, a wild look in her eyes. She really despises the man, more than I initially thought.

"I don't think he'll treat you badly," I say, sharing my impression of him. "He seems to be more bark than bite to me."

"Not him," Cassandra replies, "but Clytemnestra, his wife."

"You know this?"

Cassandra leans toward me, whispering in my ear.

"I shall soon follow you in death. Clytemnestra and her lover will kill me, and also Agamemnon."

She astonishes me with the clarity in which she predicts her end and mystifies me why she does not fight against this, instead accepting it as if a natural outcome for her.

"If you see this," I whisper back, "aren't you going to warn Agamemnon?"

"Why would I do that?"

"To prevent him from returning to Mycenae, protecting yourself by his going elsewhere."

"I have no intention of stopping his murder, even if I die likewise. He shall pay for having waged war on Troy. It's a fitting retribution." she hisses out her antipathy for him.

I know Cassandra means it. She bears a greater hostility for the Greeks than anyone else, and it is in her nature to seek retaliation against them. No leniency or conciliation exists for my sister. She is bent on revenge. And if her own life is forfeit in the process of meting out such vengeance, she will have found that price worth it. She impresses me with the sheer determination in which she sees her cause, not as much as flinching to avert the harm it presents to her. My intention is to face death with dignity. Cassandra's stance will be one of defiance. I can easily envision her spitting into her executioner's face before he carries out his foul deed.

Still believing I have the time, not expecting the guards until midmorning, I decide to dress myself up as well as I can. Strange that this would be a concern in my circumstance, but if I am going to be center of attraction, I would look the part. If the Greeks are right in that I will indeed meet Achilles in the afterlife—I lack their assurance of this, but hope it is true—I want him to see me at my best. Thalia, deeply saddened but trying to cheer me up, helps me in my preening, sponging my body and arranging my hair back into a ponytail. She gives me a freshly cleaned white chiton, and I must admit, when she holds a small mirror before me, I look as beautiful as I ever have. She has done her work expertly.

"Are you pleased?" she asks me, on the verge of tears.

"Very much so, Thalia," I answer, smiling at her. "I want to thank you for your devoted service to me. I've been remiss in expressing my gratitude, but you've been a great help to me this past year, especially when we were with the Amazons."

Thalia starts weeping, my words deeply touching her. I give her a loving hug, and that makes matters worse, causing her to burst out in open sobbing, unable to keep her feelings in restraint.

"You must help me one more time," I say to her. "Do not cry like that. It makes things more difficult for me. It will weaken my resolve, rob me of the courage I now am most in need of."

She backs away, nodding her assent through her flowing tears, looking so forlorn in her grief. I am moved to great pity at seeing her so distressed but refrain from allowing this to shake my determination to keep my emotions in control. I am going to embrace my end courageously. No one will see me whimpering or begging for lenience. I will do as Cassandra so aptly phrased it, show them what mettle Trojan women are made of.

"They're coming," Cassandra suddenly announces to us, looking out of the tent, bringing me back to the present.

"Take good care of Mother, Thalia," I tell her, releasing her from my grip and addressing the others, "I'm ready for them. How do I look?"

My question must have struck them as odd indeed. They look at each other, searching for my meaning over why that should be consequential for me at such a time, as if I thought I was going on a courtship. But I pose a favorable image for them. I can see it in their eyes. They are marveling at my appearance, indicating that I please them. I hug everyone in turn, saying my farewell, and stand in readiness when the soldiers come, a small guard unit of five men, led by Odysseus.

Odysseus pauses as he glances at me, scanning me from head to toe with his eyes, seemingly surprised at how I present myself to them. He appears dazzled by what he sees.

"It's time," he then says. "As for the rest of you, gather up your belongings and come with us. This tent will be taken down. You'll be spending your remaining day or so here with your new masters."

Odysseus next directs that I move along, and I leave the tent, with the guards on both sides of me and he in front of me, proceeding toward the tumulus that had been erected for Achilles, a distance away. Trailing us, at a considerable interval, are the rest of the women quartered with me. My thoughts drift from me as our procession heads forward, searching out for distractions in an attempt to circumvent my reality, seeking an escape from what is happening to me.

I think of the people who have meant the most to me, who touched me with their kindness or love, leaving their tender imprint in my heart. Penthesileia is in my thoughts at the moment. In many ways my mentor, she endeared herself to me with her tolerance of my faults and her willingness to accept me as I am. She loved me. My days with her and her Amazons were the happiest of my life. Her involving me with the planning of campaigns and important discussions, soliciting my opinions on matters of great significance, always treating me with respect and consideration, and appreciating the femininity she saw in me; surely this bespoke of the love she bore me. She was, I think, the person I most admire in life. Were I to choose who I would single out as having had the most favored influence over me, she is foremost deserving of that credit. I loved Penthesileia, as much as I loved Antiope.

Antiope. How can I give words to the special relationship we had? She was so loving to me. Beautiful beyond description, her exquisitely sculptured body so wonderful to behold, so alluring to me, enticing me into an intimacy with her I never thought possible, so cherished for me. We saw our mutual frailties and readily dismissed these as unimportant, recognizing that only our love truly mattered. And we made the most of it, relishing the pleasure and contentment we found in ourselves. The tears she shed when learning of Penthesileia's death, when she pleaded that I come with her, her lovely face revealing her torment, is a vision of her as clear as if had occurred but yesterday. I must shift my thoughts from her or else I will break down in tears, nullifying my resolve at courage.

Lycus comes to my mind now, how he died in my arms. That charming, endearing old man who imparted his knowledge of tactics and strategies on me as if I had been one of his generals. I shall never forget the look of pain and then gratification as I held his head in my arms and saw the sparkle from his eyes diminish and go out. He was good to me and trusted me, and I am grateful to him for that.

Why is my time with the Amazons the most memorable for me in my contemplations? I think that eventful episode in my life had the deepest affect on me, leaving me with my most vivid memories, both pleasant and painful. Even in recollecting this under my present strain, it stands out as having been a unique happenstance for me. More than anything else, it represents a time when I truly felt I was free, released from the patriarchal domination dictating my life in Troy, the prerequisites of protocol, the impositions of courtly etiquette, all the pressures exerted by the mandates in place to keep us in our subservient position. Living with the Amazons was a touch of independence for me, an exemption to the life that constricted me and defined my attitudes and behavior. It was a life that had a special kind of appeal to me, working its subtle indoctrination upon me so I now long for it and preoccupy myself with it to rid myself of my present trepidations.

I am here again, in the field massed with standing soldiers clad in their armor in an erect posture, walking through the aisleway created between the ranks toward the platform in front of me. I have been so absorbed in my reflections that I was not even aware of having arrived at this point. Everyone is looking at me, some with sad faces, perhaps those are the Greeks I had met in my frequent rides from Troy. There is a hushed silence among them. Nobody is saying a word. There are so many of them, as if the entire enemy force has been called upon to witness my execution. It's so silly for me to say this, but I am glad I took the time to dress well for the occasion. Does that make any sense at all? Odysseus remains in front of me, leading me onward, and we are near the tumulus of Achilles. I see Neoptolemus standing atop the wooden stage in his white tunic and golden-laced sandals, with a blue cape extending down his backside, looking quite noble for all that.

Below the platform, I see Helen standing beside her one-time husband, Menelaus. Her face is very pale, and her eyes are glazed over. She appears most distraught, finding it awkward to look at me. Her down-turned lips render her a horribly saddened countenance, and I think she is overcome with remorse. This is the first time I have seen her since the night Troy was taken. I had been told that Menelaus would not let her visit us while we were in our tent, considering such a gesture unworthy of a Spartan queen. Yes, Helen was again royalty, her husband readily accepting her back into the fold, despite their years of separation, as if this interval had never occurred. I knew all along she would suffer the least among us, if losing the one great love in her life is discounted. I'm not sure that can be done. The loss of Paris will forever haunt her, and she will never fully recover from it, of that I am certain. So I feel compassion for her. Like the rest of us, she has a heavy burden to carry. In exchanging protracted glances with her, I sense that an understanding still exists between us. She remains my friend in spite of all that has happened.

I am now at the bottom of the platform, where the steps are emplaced to lead me to its stage, and who is waiting for me there? None other than my brother, Helenus. Treacherous Helenus. Traitor to Troy. I glare at him, making the hostility I bear known to him. He is ashamed and red faced, scarcely able to look me in the eyes, averting my cold stares by turning his head to the side. I am permitted my pause to hear him and perhaps speak to him.

"I'm sorry it has to end like this for you, Polyxena," he tells me.

"Why should you be?" I answer. "Mine is only one of many deaths you caused. You have no more brothers, and Father was cruelly slain by Neoptolemus. Why pretend now that my death is regretful to you?"

"You don't believe me, but it's true. I tried my best to dispute the story Neoptolemus told them, saying it was false and motivated by nothing more than vindictiveness on his part. But he was most persuasive, pleading for his father's sake. The fact that Achilles's love for you was known to them gave credence to his arrogation."

"He told me you are his good friend. I doubt you tried very hard to deny his story; that would have alienated you from him, and traitor that you are, you could not have abided that."

"I had no idea he would resort to such an extreme proposal. What did you do to turn him so against you?"

"Ask him," I raise my voice. "You brought the monster to our shores." Helenus recoils at my rebuke, startled.

My anger for Neoptolemus is still with me. I thought I had gotten over it and was able to view his behavior in a more sympathetic light, but evidently, that is not the case. That I called him a monster reveals my innermost regard for him, and this will assist me in maintaining my decorum when the time comes. I will cling to this contempt I bear to bolster my resolve if I find it faltering. As for Helenus, he is beyond redemption and does not merit sympathy or forgiveness from me. Even the sorrowful expression on his face cannot be considered as sincere. He has disgraced himself in my eyes and remains the most dishonorable of all my brothers.

A guard prods me to ascend the steps, telling me I have talked long enough with Helenus. Odysseus stops him from badgering me, but the soldier has succeeded in hastening my pace. I climb up the stairs as I see Agamemnon standing directly below me, in front of the mound. I cannot make out his exact disposition, but he appears most somber, almost as if displeased.

I reach the top of the platform and look at Neoptolemus who is trying to avert his glances from me, but he now gazes at me and appears awestruck, a stunned demeanor marking his initial perception of me. His face turns pale and a glaze comes to his eyes. A sorrowful expression predominates him, and I think he deeply regrets what he has done. He should. I hope that, for the rest of his life, he will be tormented by the actions committed on this day. What does it matter? I shall not be there to ever see it, and I will not spend my last moments of life caring what he thinks. One thing is certain, he will not see me pleading or crying in my defense. I shall meet my end calmly and with courage. I am now assured I can accomplish this.

Odysseus binds my hands behind my back, using the waist cord of my chiton for that purpose. For an instant, he had me near panic, thinking I would be undressed for everyone to gawk at. That would have undermined my efforts at serenity completely.

"Must I be tied up?" I ask him. It is a humiliation for me, portraying me as unwillingly accepting my fate.

"Poseidon must see you as an offering," Odysseus answers, "in all your vulnerabilities, as helpless, if not afraid. Get on your knees, Polyxena."

I drop down, resting my body on my knees, never very comfortable for me. Neoptolemus, knife in hand, now stands directly behind me, Odysseus on my side. I look over the throng standing grim faced and in eerie silence before me, stretching to the shore. I see Mother in tears below me, Andromache clings to her, also crying. Cassandra, next to them, does not weep. She looks at me in a concentrated stare and nods at me. She instills her own determination at defiance in me, filling me with a resolution to remain steadfast in my dignity. I nod back my approval.

Neoptolemus speaks now, but I do not hear what he is saying. I ride on Zephyrus through the Dardanian Gates and around the northern walls of Troy. The wind rushes by me, spreading out my hair and fluttering my clothes as I approach the seashore west of the city. I feel the exhilaration so familiar to me whenever under the power of that noble mount, my kindred spirit, as I gallop toward the campgrounds of the Myrmidons, and when I arrive there, I stop. I see Achilles step out from his tent handsome as can be, smiling widely, eyes sparkling, coming to me. He stands below me, lifts his hand to me, and helps me descent Zephyrus by grasping my waist with his strong hands. We embrace and kiss, the sweetness of my lips meeting his, enrapturing me, filling me with utmost joy. I melt in his arms. Oh, Aphrodite. You have blessed me. No time in my life has been more pleasurable, more rewarding, more fulfilling than that which I spent with Achilles, now again to be with me. I thank you, Divine Goddess. You have given me my answer. Let it be forever said that I, Polyxena, loved and was loved by Achilles. Through our love, and for love's sake, I have achieved immortality. Like the many heroes who fought and died at Troy, my name will be remembered.

Afterword

My primary source of reference for writing this novel was the *Meridian Handbook of Classical Mythology* by Edward Tripp. The other books referred to in my acknowledgments served only to provide additional information on characters used to complete the principle ones already chosen from Tripp's book. I make no apologies for the liberties taken, as much of the stories about many mythological personages are themselves inconsistent and even illogical. A case in point: Helenus, according to the myth, prescribed four conditions to the Greeks that had to be met before Troy was to fall, the fourth condition being that Philoctetes, who was at Lemnos recovering from a snakebite, be sent to Troy's shores, but he is the man who shot the fatal arrow that killed Paris. Since Helenus did not advise the Greeks until after the death of Paris, when he lost his claim to the widow Helen to Deiphobus and was captured by them, his fourth condition makes no sense. Mythology makes no attempt at explaining such discrepancies, nor is it important. It is, after all, based on legendary accounts of events and figures and requires no accuracy, historical or otherwise. Yet the mythology surrounding the Trojan War is surprisingly coherent and allowed this story to be pieced together just by reading what is written about each individual character.

Polyxena is not mentioned in Homer's *Iliad*, arising out of ensuing legends, and she appears to be a creation of later classical writers when there was a movement afoot to romanticize the stories surrounding Troy's fall. She is featured in the plays *The Trojan Women*, and *Hecuba* by Euripides, and written about by Hyginus, the Roman mythographer, in his anthology, *Fabulae*, and is in Virgil's *The Aeneid* (Book III) and Ovid's *Metamorphoses* (Book XIII) among other sources. Variations exist on stories about her, but it is her love for Achilles and his love for her that are the particulars associated with them. It is generally conceded that Neoptolemus killed her, but probably not for the reason presented in this novel. Very little is actually said about her, except to give justification to her being sacrificed, demanded by the ghost of Achilles, and that she met her death gracefully. Yet it is sad—as much of mythology is—and I strove to make it even more so by linking her death to her having rejected Neoptolemus's love, thus bringing it upon herself, although unwittingly.

I took liberties in how I presented Penthesileia's entrance into the Trojan War. The myth suggests that she actually came to Troy, but I thought this could just as easily have implied she fought on Troy's behalf elsewhere. The war involved major battles away from Troy among its allied cities and kingdoms, and I thought I would draw attention to this with the Amazons conducting their own campaign by threatening the Greeks along their northern flank. This also afforded a more plausible vehicle by which Polyxena should meet Achilles. By spending days with him as he escorted her back to Troy, it kept them in closer, continuous contact, in which a romance could blossom between them. This seems more credible to me than the love-at-first-sight explanation through a lull in the fighting (even if Aphrodite wills it).

Neoptolemus is often called by his original name, Pyrrhus (red haired), particularly in classical Latin literature, which, in turn, led William Shakespeare to apply that designation in his plays *Troilus and Cressida* and *Hamlet*, dramas in which he is alluded to, though not an actual character. In the myths, he is not named Neoptolemus (literally, young soldier) until Odysseus fetches him to fight in Troy, following the counsel of Helenus. I chose to keep his name intact throughout the book for clarity's sake.

Age can be a thorny issue when dealing with mythological figures, especially as they relate to each other, and nowhere does it become more problematic than with Neoptolemus and Achilles. Achilles was sent to the island of Scyrus by his mother, Thetis, to prevent him from fighting at Troy, as she preferred he lead a long life to dying young in battle. While there, he had an affair with the king's daughter, Deidameia, who then gave birth to a son she named Pyrrhus after Achilles had already departed for Troy. This means that Neoptolemus would only have been around ten years old when he was fetched by Odysseus to join the war effort. It cannot be imagined that a prepubescent Neoptolemus could have slain the warriors he is credited with. I rationalized that the buildup for the war could have lasted years, rather than months, with constructing the ships and all, absorbing Achilles's time after leaving Scyros, but even this creates a dilemma. Achilles's heroic stature rests in his having preferred the fame of an early death to the obscurity ensuing out of old age. He must die while young. By making Neoptolemus fifteen years old, which I thought would make his infatuation with Polyxena more believable, I was probably pushing this requirement, making Achilles, as Polyxena surmises, about thirty years old. Of course, I could have made Polyxena younger, but that might have made the romance between her and Achilles less credible. You can go on and on like this without finding a correct solution. It is best to accept the ages as written and not stress over whether it makes a lot of sense.

I describe the Greeks in the present-day term. In Homer's *Iliad*, they are called Achaeans or Danaans or Argives. This familiar designation lumps them together more neatly and is clear enough, connoting the same.

References are unclear about the number of daughters and sons born to Hecuba. Nineteen total is usually the accepted number, although Priam is credited with having sired as many as fifty sons if his mistresses and concubines are included. And of these nineteen, the references I used named only five daughters. That would mean the other fourteen were sons, although I could not find all their names in any book.

To the more interesting question: why did I, being of male gender, decide to write this novel in the first person. Primarily it was due to how I structured my novel. She appeals directly to the Goddess Aphrodite, and because she renders her thoughts rather than speaks, she can continue doing so up to the moment of her death. The reader is Aphrodite. It should be noted that at no time did I ever conceive myself as being her. Rather I saw myself as a recipient of all she had to impart -her attitudes, conjectures, and beliefs- much as a psychologist recording verbatim the words of his patient. I carefully avoided comprehensive descriptions of the love sequences, preferring to use broadly based sensations common to us all, short of adjectives that lead to distinctions, so that the gender difference did not detract from her character. I felt that, if I did not get too detailed and kept her emotions on a less inclusive level, I could pull it off. I am hoping I succeeded.

CPSIA information can be obtained
at www.ICGtesting.com
Printed in the USA
BVHW031106020819
554877BV00034BA/17/P

9 781951 020927